Six Stories

Stefan Zweig was born in 1881 in Vienna to a wealthy Austrian-Jewish family. Recognition as a writer came early; by the age of forty he had already won literary fame. In 1934, with Nazism entrenched, Zweig left Austria for England, and he became a British citizen in 1940. In 1941 he and his second wife went to Brazil, where they committed suicide the following year. Zweig's best-known works of fiction are *Beware of Pity* (1939) and *Chess* (1942), but among his other outstanding achievements were his many historical biographies, which were characteristically based on psychological interpretations of his subjects.

Jonathan Katz is a Fellow of Brasenose College, Oxford, and the University's Public Orator. He is the translator of Stefan Zweig's *Beware of Pity* (originally published in this translation as *Impatience of the Heart*) as well as works by Goethe, Theodor Storm and Joseph Roth.

T0333100

STEFAN ZWEIG

Six Stories

Translated by Jonathan Katz

PENGUIN BOOKS

PENGUIN CLASSICS

UK | USA | Canada | Ireland | Australia
India | New Zealand | South Africa

Penguin Books is part of the Penguin Random House group of companies
whose addresses can be found at global.penguinrandomhouse.com.

This collection first published in Penguin Classics 2024
004

Translation copyright © Jonathan Katz, 2024

The moral rights of the author and translator have been asserted

Set in 11.25/14 pt Dante MT Std
Typeset by Jouve (UK), Milton Keynes
Printed and bound in Great Britain by Clays Ltd, Elcograf S.p.A.

The authorized representative in the EEA is Penguin Random House Ireland,
Morrison Chambers, 32 Nassau Street, Dublin D02 YH68

A CIP catalogue record for this book is available from the British Library

ISBN: 978-0-141-19282-6

www.greenpenguin.co.uk

MIX
Paper | Supporting
responsible forestry
FSC® C018179
www.fsc.org

Penguin Random House is committed to a
sustainable future for our business, our readers
and our planet. This book is made from Forest
Stewardship Council® certified paper.

Contents

Translator's Foreword vii

*The Invisible Collection: An Episode from the German
  Inflation (1924)* 3
Episode on Lake Geneva (1918) 20
Leporella (1925) 30
Buchmendel (1929) 60
The Buried Candelabrum (1937) 92
Burning Secret (1911) 206

Contents

Translator's Foreword

In the years following the end of the First World War Stefan Zweig, already a widely known writer of biographies and literary criticism as well as poetry, drama and prose fiction, turned his attention with renewed confidence to the short story, or *Novelle*, a form perhaps most famously illustrated in his later *Chess* (*Schachnovelle*), also known in English translation as *The Royal Game*. Zweig's earlier attempts in this genre had met with some success, but one especially – *Burning Secret* (*Brennendes Geheimnis*) – first published in 1911, had been printed separately and continued to sell in large print runs to considerable acclaim throughout the succeeding years and decades. As a portrayal of the anxieties and insecurities of childhood and early adolescence (doubtless partly autobiographical) and of the ambiguous relations of child to adult, and as one of Zweig's several penetrating attempts to explore the psychology of feminine desire, this story has enjoyed great appeal among those generally sympathetic to the author's strengths.

Already prominent in *Burning Secret* are the acute psychological insights which the *Novelle* form above all allowed Zweig to explore, and which may be seen similarly at play in the most vivid sections of the only full-scale novel he completed to his satisfaction, the 1939 *Impatience of the Heart* (*Ungeduld des Herzens*), also known in English versions as *Beware of Pity*. In that novel, sharply developed character sketches and studies of individual human complexities form almost self-sufficient episodes of note-worthy narrative power and economy, if often complicated by an extravagance of vocabulary and prose style that has divided Zweig's readers despite his – at times – otherwise enormous popularity. In his 1972 biography of Zweig, Donald Prater compared the best of the short stories with those of Somerset Maugham; like those, he wrote, Zweig's *Novellen*, though not written in Maugham's 'flat, spare style, and lacking his realism', are 'convincing in their depiction of the dark passions lying just beneath the surface of our daily life'.[1]

The first four stories in this selection, first published separately at various times over those ten years, were brought together in 1929 in a single volume entitled *Little Chronicle* (*Kleine Chronik*.[2] Much social comment, indeed, one might say a contemporary 'chronicled' portrait of some of society's fault-lines, is presented in this collection, including the author's hatred of war and its consequences, the tragedies of economic decline and the German Inflation period, and the unthinking brutality in the treatment of 'have-nots' in those turbulent post-war times. For Zweig's contemporary readers, in bringing together such personal and societal traumas the title of the collection may also have intentionally, or ironically, called to mind the type of news digest found in newspapers such as the influential Vienna *Neue Freie Presse*, for which Zweig himself was for a time a correspondent in Switzerland, and in which, almost from its earliest numbers, a regular miscellaneous *Kleine Chronik* column summarized social, political, cultural and institutional events of the preceding few days.[3]

The Invisible Collection (*Die unsichtbare Sammlung*), is a 'frame story' in which the main action is related to the first-person narrator by a fellow passenger on a train journey. The story first appeared in the *Neue Freie Presse*, on 31 May 1925.[4] The explanatory subtitle, *An Episode from the German Inflation*, was in the original publication , perhaps suggesting that the tale could stand as merely one minor example of the economic devastation wrought in this period on countless individual victims of no great importance in the general scheme of things. The period itself was remembered, and later vividly described in more general terms, by Zweig in *The World of Yesterday*, the memoir written in his last years of exile and finally delivered to his Stockholm publisher shortly before his suicide in 1942.[5] But we may also see a personal connection with Zweig's own, at the time admittedly much more comfortable, position as a highly successful collector of manuscripts, prints and autographs. The personal interest allowed some exactitude of detail concerning the elderly blind man's treasured, though now non-existent, collection, as well as some level of empathy with the irony of the principal character's passionate, and ultimately tragic, devotion to his imagined possessions.

It has been observed that, for all their narrative and emotional power, Zweig's depictions of this and other sorry victims of circumstances in the ethnic, economic and class hierarchies of the times betray some detachment, and even condescension.[6] On the other hand we also find in these stories a forensically focused approach, not only to the outer characteristics and habits of such persons, but also to their feelings and motivations; if there is on some level a failure on the author's part to identify fully with his characters, still he shows no lack of compassion or depth of feeling. It remains true that such moral judgements as the stories contain are made, or suggested, more through objective observation than sentimentality, and in this way Zweig seems easily capable of casting blame where it belongs.

So it is with the maidservant Crescenz in the third story, *Leporella*, starting her life as an impoverished and unprepossessing orphan, and after a supposed change of fortune employed, exploited and ultimately abandoned by a feckless minor aristocrat. The character of the woman evinces in readers an uncomfortable mixture of revulsion and sympathy, while the moral message is presented as an almost inevitable result of the callous self-centredness and unthinking agency of the Baron who brings about her downfall. 'No fierce moral indignation here, only the sadness of plain statement of fact,' says the Zweig biographer Elizabeth Allday, who at the same time notes the author's call to consider well the plight of the 'outcast' in this and in other stories.[7] *Leporella* was written between 1924 and 1925, but did not appear until 1928 in the second part of a two-volume collection, *Present-day German Storytellers (Deutsche Erzähler der Gegenwart)*.[8]

Another outcast figure is the wartime peasant deserter Boris, rescued in 1918 from Lake Geneva, though to no ultimately good purpose, in the second story. *Episode on Lake Geneva* first appeared in July 1919 under the title *Episode vom Genfer See* in the Vienna periodical *Modern World (Moderne Welt)*. Several times republished in Leipzig and Vienna between 1921 and 1928 as *The Runaway (Der Flüchtling)*, or under its original title, the story was eventually included in *Kleine Chronik* as *Episode am Genfer See*, and again after that in further collected editions printed in Vienna, Leipzig and Zürich. The theme of the despairing exile was possibly suggested to the author by an account he had heard in Switzerland of a perilous journey across the lake, and a possible link has also been found between this story, especially in its touching on Russian themes, and Zweig's reading of Tolstoy's 1857 short story *Lucerne: From the Recollections of Prince Nekhliudof*. Set in the final year of the war, and thus carrying a direct and contemporary pacifist message, the *Episode* has been among the most translated of all Zweig's stories. The hopelessness, and eventual suicide, of the runaway are clearly placed in the context of the 'neutrality', political and human, with which he is met at the Swiss lakeside despite the initial expressions of sympathy shown by some of the onlookers.

The shameful indifference of the comfortably secure, particularly when in crowds, towards the disadvantaged rouses Tolstoy's burning outrage in his *Lucerne*, while Zweig's observations are quieter and more depressingly resigned. The moral message of the *Episode* is bleak, once again conveyed in stark objective terms in the final words of the story. It is a 'summarizing' technique seen also in the closing paragraphs of yet another 'outsider' tale, that of the uprooted Galician Jewish bibliophile Jacob Mendel in *Buchmendel*. This best-known among Zweig's treatments of Jewish themes, published in three parts in three separate numbers of the *Neue Freie Presse* at the beginning of November 1929, and then included in *Kleine Chronik* in the same year, is at once a touching account of an extraordinary personality and at the same time an essay on the strange peculiarities of memory, both that of the first-person narrator and that of Mendel himself. It is only through an immense initial effort of recall that the narrator manages to recapture his earlier encounters with the uniquely impressive book dealer's feats of memory and erudition.

As in *The Invisible Collection*, in *Buchmendel* Zweig can depict the subject of his major character's obsessive passion with the insight of his own more privileged, but perhaps relatively superficial, personal expertise. Mendel has, through force of circumstances, transferred the all-absorbing, intense devotion of his early Talmudic training to the world of more secular scholarship and bibliography. But in the process he has not become any more worldly, or any more able to protect himself from the brutal realities of life, once he loses contact with those who have tolerated him and given him respect and refuge. Here, though, a more positive human note, even perhaps some limited optimism, tempers the narrator's sadness on hearing the tragedy of Mendel's downfall, for the account of Mendel's more recent life and misfortunes has to be given by an unlikely second narrator, the former 'toilet-lady' Frau Sporschil. Naive and uneducated as she is, but gifted with unprejudiced compassion towards one who has earned her instinctive respect and affection, hers becomes the unpretentious voice of humanity and understanding which inspires the narrator's closing moral reasoning.[9]

The longer story, or short novel, *The Buried Candelabrum* (*Der begrabener Leuchter*), termed by Zweig himself a Jewish 'legend', was written in exile from Austria. It was completed in Ostend, where Zweig was able to take advice on both style and content from his friend Joseph Roth,[10] and first published in 1936 (as were further printings of the *Episode on Lake Geneva*, *Buchmendel* and *The Invisible Collection*) in a collection called *Kaleidoskop* by Zweig's Vienna publisher Herbert Reichner. The following year it was reissued separately as a single volume. The language is deliberately archaic and rhetorical, the subject matter historical and rabbinical, but also clear is the author's emotional engagement with the oppression and sufferings of the Jewish diaspora, in which he was now of course compelled to regard himself a fellow participant.[11] In the touching dialogue between Rabbi Eliezer and the young Benjamin, as they wander in hope of rescuing their sacred Menorah from the barbarian plunderers, the child asks the Elder why the Jewish people have been uniquely chosen for such a fate. The little boy's question, says the Rabbi, is simply the oldest that their people's hearts have asked since time immemorial: 'why has God so treated us, among all the nations, with such harshness, despite our serving Him as no other people ever served Him? Why us? Why hurl us beneath the feet of others, to be trodden upon? Were we not the first to know Him, to praise Him in the unfathomable mystery of His being? Why destroy what we build, shatter our hopes, deny us any lasting rest in our wanderings and rouse nation after nation against us in ever renewed hatred?'

The Rabbi can inform Benjamin expertly enough about Jewish history and custom and lore, but here can do no more than acknowledge, and endorse, the child's question. 'Everything that man has', he says, 'is given to him but on loan, and his moments of happiness are fleeting as the wind.' Benjamin is destined to find his own purpose in life, and to explain himself and his mission to his people and to posterity, but in all likelihood their suffering will continue: 'perhaps precisely this is the meaning of our unending wanderings in exile, that what is sacred becomes all the more so the further [the] distance, and that our hearts are simply made more humble at times of great need.'

Like the biographer Elizabeth Allday, but a few years after her book appeared, I first became interested in Stefan Zweig and his writings while I was India in 1979, having previously heard his name in England without properly appreciating the impact he had once made on readers throughout the world, and indeed was still making in many countries outside the English-speaking world.[12] I remember with much gratitude and affection my introduction to *Beware of Pity*. My father-in-law Shri N.G. Katti, a Sanskrit scholar as well as a science teacher, had taught himself German in order to read this and other books in their original language. I also came to know that many other Indian readers of the English translations shared his love of both Zweig's and Somerset Maugham's work, and were used to drawing comparisons with some of the best of India's own leading writers of fiction, especially in the short story form, in many of their own rich vernacular traditions.

Jonathan Katz
July 2023

Notes

1. Donald Prater, *European of Yesterday: a Biography of Stefan Zweig* (Oxford: Oxford University Press, 1972), p. 135, fn2.

2. Stefan Zweig, *Kleine Chronik* (Leipzig: Insel Verlag, 1929). The best bibliographical notes, and brief but lucid commentary on content and reception of the stories, are available in German in the excellent *Stefan-Zweig-Handbuch* edited by Arturo Larcati et al. (Berlin: Walter de Gruyter, 2018).

3. The first issue of this originally liberal newspaper was printed on 1 September 1864. Publication continued through the interwar years, and even after the *Anschluss*, until 1939. The *Kleine Chronik* column first appeared in the issue of 27 February 1865, apparently replacing or absorbing the previous regular information notices of Viennese social and economic events.

4. The contents page of *Kleine Chronik* gives the year 1924, meaning no doubt the year in which Zweig wrote the story.

5. The memoir (*Die Welt von Gestern*), in the words of its most recent English translator, Anthea Bell, was 'a quintessentially humane document and a record of European culture in the late nineteenth and early twentieth centuries, [and] stands as a sane, civilized counterblast to the horror of war as [Zweig] already knew it, and as a well-informed and sometimes quirkily individual account of the cultural life of his time.' (*The World of Yesterday*, London: Pushkin Press, 2009, p. 11). The social consequences of the German Inflation period are described in the chapter 'Out into the world again', pp. 336ff.

6. See, for example, David Turner, 'The Human Ideal in Stefan Zweig's *Novelle*: Some Complications and Limitations', in *The World of Yesterday's Humanist Today*, ed. Marion Sonnenfeld (Albany, NY: State University of New York Press, 1983), pp. 157–67.

7. Elizabeth Allday, *Stefan Zweig: A Critical Biography* (London: W. H. Allen, 1972).

8. *Deutscher Erzähler der Gegenwart* (Berlin: Wegweiser, 1928).

9. See the introduction by Ritchie Robertson to his translation of the story in *The German–Jewish Dialogue: An Anthology of Literary Texts, 1749–1993* (Oxford: Oxford University Press, 1999), pp. 233–4.

10. A moving account of this phase of the two authors' often tortured friendship may be read in Volker Weidermann's *Summer Before the Dark*, translated by Carol Brown Janeway (London: Pushkin Press, 2016).

11. See Prater, *European of Yesterday*, p. 259.

12. Zweig's importance and current legacy are examined in a valuable collection of critical scholarly articles under the title *Stefan Zweig and World Literature: Twenty-First-Century Perspectives*, ed. Birger Vanwesenbeeck and Mark Gelber (Rochester, NY: Camden House, 2015).

Six Stories

The Invisible Collection: An Episode from the German Inflation

At the second station beyond Dresden an elderly gentleman entered our compartment. He greeted everyone courteously, and then nodded in my direction as if acknowledging a close acquaintance. For a moment I could not recall who this man was. Then, with a gentle smile, he gave me his name, and of course I recognized him immediately; this was one of Berlin's most renowned art and book dealers. In peacetime I had often visited his premises to inspect, or indeed purchase, autographs and books. So on this occasion we chatted for a little while, if somewhat inconsequentially; then suddenly he began to explain what had brought him to these parts, and where he had just been:

'I have to tell you – you see, this is just about the strangest experience I have been through in all my thirty-seven years in the business. You won't need me to explain how things have been in this line of work since the value of money pretty well evaporated overnight. All of a sudden, our friends of the newly rich class seem to have discovered a passion for old Madonnas, not to mention incunabula, paintings, engravings and what have you. You simply can't conjure up enough of these things to satisfy them; in fact, you really have to be on your guard, or they'll completely clean out your premises. Give them half a chance and they'll have the cufflinks off your shirt and the lamp from your desk. Really, it's getting tougher and tougher finding any merchandise at all to sell – you'll pardon me for using such a vulgar word for things you and I truly value and revere – but these types of client I'm talking about have accustomed even me to regarding, say, a wonderful early Venetian printed book rather in the same light as an overcoat costing so-and-so many dollars, or seeing an original Guercino drawing as just another embodiment of a few hundred francs. There's no defence against the unremitting persistence of these purchase-mad people. Anyway, it happened once again recently; I was completely emptied out overnight, and to be honest I was on the point of pulling down the shutters, so ashamed was I to see our old family business – we're now in our third generation – with nothing in stock but bits of worthless trash that a little while ago wouldn't even have burdened a local street-trader's cart.

'Well, that was the predicament I was in, and it made me go back to our old ledgers, hoping to track down one or two former clients from whom I might extract a few duplicates, if they had any. That kind of customer list is something of a graveyard at the best of times, and all the more so these days. Not much in the way of gleanings; the majority of our former clients had long since been forced to auction off whatever they had, or else they'd died. Those still in the land of the living didn't exactly promise much. But then, to my surprise, I stumbled on a whole bundle of letters from a person who was very likely our oldest client of all. This man had completely escaped my memory, simply because, since 1914 and the outbreak of the war, he had never once come back to us with any order or even inquiry. The correspondence we did have with him – and I am not exaggerating here – went back close on sixty years. He had made purchases from both my father and my grandfather, but as far as I could remember he hadn't once darkened our doors in all of my own thirty-seven years in the trade. From all I could see I surmised that he must have been a fairly unusual, old-fashioned eccentric type, one of those now almost extinct bookworm individuals out of a Biedermeier painting, specimens that very occasionally survived here and there, in minute numbers, in smaller provincial towns until shortly before our time. He wrote in a neat calligraphic hand, with the due amounts underlined in red ink, and the figures each time repeated in words to avoid any risk of error. This, and the fact that he used only torn-out flyleaves and old envelopes for these communications, pointed to the niggardliness and obsessive frugality of a hopelessly provincial character. The signing of these peculiar documents included not only his name but also the full formal title: 'Councillor for Forestry and Economy, Retired; Lieutenant, Retired; Iron Cross, First Class'. As a veteran hero of the 1870s, I deduced, if indeed still alive, he couldn't have been a day under eighty years of age. Still, for all this oddity and absurd thriftiness, he showed a quite singular astuteness when it came to collecting old prints, and on top of it exceptionally fine taste and connoisseurship. So, as I slowly assembled the orders he had made over the best part of sixty years, the earliest of which still referred to the now obsolete old silver groschen, it gradually dawned on me that, at the time when a single taler could buy you a whole sheaf of the finest German woodcuts, this little provincial gentleman must have been quietly putting together a whole stash of engravings that would more than hold its own next to the most vaunted of the collections amassed by the new rich class. What this man had acquired from us alone in the course of half a century, paying each time only a small sum – a few marks and pfennigs – represented an astonishing worth today; and apart from this, it was a reasonable assumption that he had picked more things up just as advantageously at auctions, and no doubt also from other dealers. True enough, no orders had been received from him since 1914. But I was too familiar with what's been going in this business to have missed any news of such a hoard being auctioned or sold off privately; either this curious gentleman was still with us, or the collection itself was now in the hands of his heirs.

'My interest thus roused, the very next day – by which I mean yesterday evening – I set off right away for one of the most unlikely provincial towns in Saxony. As I made my way from the little station down the main street, it seemed to me scarcely possible that here of all places, among these very ordinary small-town houses with their correspondingly petit-bourgeois contents, there could be living an owner of the most glorious Rembrandt engravings, and Dürers and Mantegnas, in unimpeachable, complete sets. Imagine my astonishment at discovering from the post office, when I inquired there whether there was a certain Forestry and Economic Councillor of this name in town, that the elderly gentleman was indeed still alive. By late morning I was on my way to see him; I'll confess my heart was somewhat aflutter!

'I found the dwelling with no difficulty. It was on the second floor of one of those cheaply constructed residential buildings no doubt knocked together by some journeyman speculator half a century ago. The downstairs floor was occupied by a worthy local master tailor. On the upper floor I saw to the left the name plate of a post office official, and yes, there on the right was the name of my Forestry and Economic Councillor. I knocked, a little apprehensively, and an elderly, white-haired lady with a neat little black lace cap came to the door. I handed her my card and inquired whether the Councillor might be at home. Clearly taken aback, she looked with discernible suspicion first at me, and then at the card. In an old building in this little backwater of a town a visit from the outside world was apparently a genuine event. Nevertheless, she asked me courteously to wait, took my card, and went back into the front room. I heard her whisper quietly, and then suddenly a booming male voice broke through: "Ah, Herr R., from Berlin – from the famous antiquarian dealers! But of course, of course, show him in! It will be such a pleasure!" And the little old lady came scurrying back to invite me into their worthy little parlour.

'I took off my coat and followed her in. It was a modest room; in the middle, standing quite upright, was an elderly but still sturdy gentleman with a bushy moustache, wearing a semi-military style corded jacket. He extended both hands warmly towards me, but despite this unmistakable gesture of joyous, spontaneous greeting there was a peculiar stiffness in his bearing; he didn't come even a single step towards me. Slightly disconcerted, I had to make the approach myself in order to take his hand. But just as I was about to do so I noticed, from the way he held his hands motionless straight out in front of him, that rather than meeting my hand he was actually waiting for the contact. That was when I realized: the man was blind.

'From my earliest days I have always felt uncomfortable when confronted by a blind person; I've never managed to fend off a certain shame and embarrassment at sensing that this person was fully alive and at the same time knowing that his sense of me was different from mine of him. And so this time too I had to overcome my initial alarm at the sight of those inert, glassy eyes staring into the void beneath the bristling white brows. But their owner soon put me out of my misery; the moment my hand met his he shook it vigorously, loudly repeating his words of welcome with the utmost affability: "A special visitor indeed!" he exclaimed with a broad smile, "a miracle, no less, one of the greats from Berlin ending up here in our little backwater . . . but caution's the word when you have one of the top antiquarians on your trail! As we say in my part of the world, guard your doors and pockets when the gypsies are about! Yes, I suspect I do know what made you track me down . . . business is at a low ebb these days in our poor, run-down Germany – no buyers any more, so the great dealers' thoughts turn once more to their old customers, and they're wanting to gather in their flocks . . . But

I'm afraid with me you're out of luck, sir – we poor old pensioners are happy enough if we have a crust of bread to put on the table. Today's insane prices in your line of business have left us far behind . . . people like us are *hors de combat* once and for all!"

'I was quick to explain that he had misunderstood me, that I had not come with any thought of selling him anything; I just happened to be passing through the neighbourhood and hadn't wanted to lose an opportunity to pay my respects to a customer of so many years, who also happened to be one of the country's truly great collectors. The last words were hardly out of my mouth when a strange transformation appeared in the old man's face. He still stood, stiffly upright, in the middle of the room, but now his expression suddenly brightened, betokening a sense of the deepest pride; he turned to where he supposed his wife to be, as if to say, "You hear that?" Then, turning back to me, in a voice brimming with joy – not a trace of that military brusqueness that he had adopted just now, but a gentle, indeed tender tone:

' "That really is so kind of you . . . but I cannot allow you to have come here in vain. No, you must see something you won't meet with every day, even in your splendid Berlin . . . a few pieces the like of which you won't find in Vienna, let alone that godforsaken Paris. Yes, in sixty years of collecting you come across all kinds of things that certainly don't turn up on the average street stall. Louise, let me have the key to the cupboard."

'At this point something unexpected happened. The old lady, who had been standing next to him and listening politely to our conversation with a friendly smile on her face, suddenly raised both hands towards me, apparently pleading, and at the same time shaking her head assertively to signal something I couldn't immediately understand. Only then did she go up to her husband and lay both hands gently on his shoulder: "But, Herwarth," she chided him, "you haven't asked the gentleman whether he has time now to view the collection – it's nearly midday already, and after you've

8

eaten you have to take your hour's rest, remember that's what the doctor expressly ordered. Wouldn't it be better to show the gentleman all your treasures after lunch, and then we can have coffee together? And Annemarie will be here then too, and she knows everything much better than I do, and will be able help you."

'And then once again, just as she finished speaking, she made the same urgently pleading gesture, of course without his noticing anything. This time I understood her. She obviously wanted me to decline the offer of a viewing there and then, so I quickly made up a prior lunch appointment, saying it would be a pleasure, an honour, to see his collection later; I could not do so before three o'clock, but would very happily return after that hour.

'The man turned round again, displaying the kind of pique one expects of a child deprived of his favourite toy. "Ah yes, of course," he muttered, "these Berlin experts, they never have time for anything. But on this occasion you will have to *find* the time, sir; we are not just talking of a few odd pieces – there are twenty-seven portfolios, each one for a different old master, and there isn't one that isn't full. Very well, three o'clock – but please be punctual, or we'll never get through it all!"

'Again, he stretched out his hand in front of him. "Be warned, sir, you may be delighted by what you see; on the other hand you may be vexed! If the latter, your envy will double my pleasure! That's the way among us collectors, isn't it – we want everything for ourselves, nothing for the others!" This was followed by another mighty handshake.

'His wife went to the door with me. Throughout the whole meeting I had noticed a distinct unease about her, a sign of anxiety and embarrassment. But just at the door she stuttered some words, keeping her voice low: "Do you think . . . might my daughter . . . well, could she come to see you before you return to us? It would be better . . . better for various reasons . . . I suppose you'll be taking lunch at the hotel?"

9

' "Yes, that's right, and I would be delighted – it will be a pleasure," I replied.

'And, good as the old lady's word, one hour later, when I had just finished my meal in the dining room of the little hotel on the market place, in came a woman past her first youth, plainly dressed and with a diffident expression in her eyes. I went over to her, introduced myself and declared I was ready to go back with her at once to see the collection. But this was met with a sudden blushing, and that same bewildered embarrassment that I had seen in her mother, and she asked whether she could have a few words with me before we set off. She was clearly in difficulty; each time she braced herself to say something, that volatile flush reappeared all the way up to her forehead, and her fingers played restlessly with her dress. At last she began, hesitantly, constantly struggling to find the words: "My mother sent me to see you . . . she told me everything, and . . . well, we want to ask a big favour of you . . . you see, we would like to explain to you before you see Father . . . Father will of course be wanting to show you his collection, and it's the collection . . . you see . . . it's no longer quite complete . . . there are quite a few things missing from it . . . actually, I'm sorry to say it's a rather large number . . ."

'She had to catch her breath again, and then looked at me and said hastily: "I must be honest with you. You know what times we're living in, you'll be the first to understand . . . After the war broke out, Father went completely blind. His eyesight had been up and down even before that, but it was the mental strain in the end that robbed him of it completely. You see, despite his seventy-six years of age he was absolutely intent on joining the forces going to France, and when the army failed to advance the way it had in 1870, he became terribly upset; his eyes deteriorated with alarming speed from then on. Otherwise he is still in fine fettle. Just a little while ago he was still walking for hours on end and, believe it or not, even going out on his beloved hunting expeditions. But now his walks are a thing of the past. Now his sole remaining pleasure is his collection; he looks at it every day . . . I mean, of course, he doesn't actually *see* it – he can't see anything any more – but he takes out all the folders every afternoon so that he can at least touch and *feel* the contents, one piece after another, always in the same order he has known them in for decades. He has no other interests these days; I have to read him all the auction reports from the newspaper, and the higher the prices he hears, the happier he is . . . because . . . well, this is the awful part of it, Father doesn't understand anything any more about prices, or about these times . . . he has no idea that we've lost everything and couldn't survive now even a couple of days a month on his pension . . . added to which, my sister's husband died in action and left her with four small children . . . but Father knows nothing about all our material difficulties. To begin with, we saved, that is, we saved more than before, but that didn't help at all. Then we started to sell – of course we weren't going to touch his beloved collection . . . I mean we sold the small amount of jewellery we had, but heaven help us, how much was that? Every pfennig Father had to spare over the last sixty years went on his prints. And then the day came when there was nothing left . . . and what could we do? Then . . . then . . . well, Mother and I sold one of them. Father would never have allowed it; he hasn't the least idea how bad things are, how hard it is to root out the odd scrap of food on the black market, and he doesn't know either that we lost the war, and Alsace and Lorraine with it. These are things we always avoid reading to him from the newspaper, just to preserve his peace of mind.

' "It was a really valuable piece, the one we sold, a Rembrandt etching. The dealer offered many thousands of marks for it, and the hope was that that would see us through for years. But you know how money just melts away . . . we had deposited all of what we didn't need immediately in the bank, and in two months it was gone. So we had to sell another print, and then another, and the dealer always sent the money so late that it had already lost its value when we got it. Then we tried the auctions, but there too we were cheated despite the prices being in the millions – by the time the millions reached us they were nothing but waste paper. That's how all the gems in the collection gradually disappeared, right down to a few remaining good pieces – merely in order for us to eke out the most meagre existence; and Father has no inkling of any of this.

' "You can see now why my mother was so alarmed when you came today . . . because when he opens the folders for you, the secret will be out. The point is, we have filled the old mounts – and he knows every single one of them by the feel alone – with reprints or leaves of the same size and type to replace the ones we sold, so that he won't notice anything when he touches them. But just so long as he can feel them and count them for you (he knows their exact order perfectly well by heart) he'll experience the same pleasure he had before, when he could see them himself. There's no one else in this little town of ours that Father would consider worthy to be shown his treasures, and I really think he loves every one of the folios with such a passion that it would break his heart if he suspected that everything had disappeared long ago. You are the first person in all these years, ever since the director of the Dresden Prints Department passed away, that he has wanted to show his portfolios to. So this is why I beg you . . ."

'Suddenly the middle-aged lady raised her hand to her eyes, and I could see the tears welling there.

' ". . . we are begging you . . . please don't destroy his happiness . . . and don't make *us* unhappy . . . don't take away this last illusion he has! Help us keep him in the belief that all the leaves he describes to you are still there in front of him . . . it would kill him if he had the slightest suspicion. Yes, perhaps we have wronged him in a way, but what else could we do? One has to live, and human lives, four orphaned children like my sister's, are surely more important than printed sheets of paper? Up till now we have done nothing in all of this to ruin his contentment; he delights in leafing through all the folders for three hours every afternoon, talking to each and every print as if to a personal friend. And today . . . well, today could be his happiest day of all, the one he's been longing for for years, because he can show the things he loves most in the world to a genuine connoisseur. Sir, I beg you most earnestly, do not shatter his pleasure!"

'Nothing I have just told you can express the emotional effect of what she said to me. God knows, as a dealer these days you see a good many of these shamefully ruined people, outrageously cheated and ravaged by the Inflation, people who've seen their most precious ancestral heirlooms extorted from them for no more than a bread roll – but here I was now, faced with an extraordinary stroke of fate, and one that struck me with particular vehemence. As you can imagine, I promised to do my best, and to say nothing.

'We went back together – on the way, to add to my already considerable sense of outrage, I learned about the ridiculously paltry payments with which these two poor, innocent women had been hoodwinked, and this merely strengthened my resolve; I would do my utmost to help them. We went up the stairs, and we'd hardly opened the door before we heard the old man's voice calling merrily to us from the inner room: "Come in! Come in!" With that heightened sensitivity of the blind, he must have taken in our footsteps on the staircase.

' "Herwarth was quite unable to sleep today, he was so impatient to show you his treasures," said the old lady with a smile. A single glance from her daughter was enough to reassure her that I was already on their side. Spread out on the table lay the stack of portfolios, and as soon as the blind man felt my hand he seized my arm without any further greeting and forced me down into the chair.

' "So, here we are, we'd better get going at once – there's a lot to see, and you Berlin gentry are always pressed for time! Now, this first folder is all Master Dürer. And I think you will soon see that it is pretty well complete – and each exemplar finer than the last! Well, anyway, judge for yourself, just look at this" – he opened the portfolio and revealed the first leaf – *The Great Horse of 1505!*

'And then, showing the kind of tender fastidiousness with which one might otherwise touch something precious and fragile, he removed from the portfolio, with his fingertips cautiously avoiding any unnecessary contact with the surface of the paper, a mount containing a blank, yellowed sheet, and held up this worthless scrap of paper in front of him, wholly inspired. He gazed at it for several minutes, of course without seeing anything, but he was evidently ecstatic as he held the blank leaf at arm's length before his eyes, his face as if by magic displaying the concentrated expression of a fully sighted admirer. And into his eyes, staring with their deadened pupils – was this merely a reflection of the paper, or was it rather some mysterious inner glow? – there came, all at once, a gleam of recognition, a brightness mirroring what he contemplated.

' "So," he said proudly, "have you ever seen a finer copy? See how sharply, how clearly every detail comes out – I have compared it with the Dresden copy, but that one was quite flat and dull next to mine. And, what's more, there's the provenance! Look here," and he turned the sheet round and pointed with his fingernail at certain places on the reverse side, also blank, with such exactness that I found myself peering carefully at the plain paper to see if the annotations really were there after all – "there you have the stamp of the Nagler collection, and here are Remy and Esdaile; I'll warrant they never suspected, these distinguished predecessors of mine, that their prize piece would one day end up in this humble little room."

'I felt a cold shudder down my back as I watched the old man in his ignorance so eagerly extolling the beauty of an entirely blank sheet, and it gave me an eerie feeling to be contemplating it along with him as his finger picked out, with absolute precision, to the millimetre, all the previous owners' invisible marks that he imagined were still there in front of him. My throat tightened at the ghastly sight, and I was lost for words; but when, in my perplexity, I looked up at the two women, I saw once again the imploringly raised hands of his wife trembling with anxiety. So I took hold of myself, and resumed my chosen role.

'"Unbelievable!" I finally managed to stammer. "A superb exemplar!" And immediately his whole face beamed with pride. "But that's nothing yet," he boasted, "wait till you've seen my *Melancholia* or my illuminated *Passion*; you're unlikely to see such quality in any other copy. There, just look at this." And again his fingers gently passed over an imagined image. "The freshness of it, the crisp line, the warmth of tone! Enough to stop them in their tracks, our Berlin friends and all their expert dealers and museum specialists!"

'And on it went, this rush of triumphant commentary, for a good two hours. I have no words to describe to you how uncanny it was being with him and going through these hundred – or more likely two hundred – blank pages, or at the most execrable reprints, which in the memory of this tragic, innocent figure were so surpassingly real that he could appreciate, and describe in unerring detail, every one of them in their correct order; the invisible collection, which must have been long ago scattered far and wide, was for this blind, tragically deceived man as present and real as ever, and the passion in his viewing of its images was so overwhelming that I was on the verge of believing in them myself. Only once was the somnambulism of his certainty disturbed by a danger – momentary, but alarming enough – of his waking and realizing the truth: he had again been praising the sharp definition, this time of his Rembrandt *Antiope* print (a proof copy, which must indeed have been of inestimable value), and as he did so his nervously perceptive finger had just lovingly traced over a particular remembered line on the print, but without his heightened sense of touch encountering the familiar depression in the substituted paper. Immediately a shadow seemed to come over his face, and his voice faltered. "This *is* the *Antiope*, isn't it?" he murmured, slightly bewildered, whereupon I immediately leaped into action, took the sheet in its mount out of his hands, and enthusiastically described the now missing print, which was fortunately also familiar to me, in as much detail as I could recall.

'At this there was a visible relaxing of tension in the blind man's face; and the more I enthused, the more brightly shone, in this gnarled, wasted figure, a jovial cordiality, an honest and upright human sincerity. He turned triumphantly towards his wife and daughter: "Here for once is someone who really knows a thing or two!" he exulted. "Here at long last is someone whose word you can believe when he tells you what my prints are worth. You have always doubted, always scolded me because I put all the money into my collection: it's true, I admit it, over these sixty years no beer, wine, tobacco, travelling, theatre, books, only constant saving, and more saving, for these prints. But you'll see one day, when I'm no longer here – and then you'll be rich, richer than anyone in town, rich as the richest in Dresden, and then finally you'll thank me for my foolishness. But as long as I live, not a single leaf leaves this house – they'll have to carry me out first, and only then my collection."

'As he spoke, his hand tenderly stroked the long-ago ravaged portfolios as if they were living beings – it was awful, yet at the same time deeply moving, to watch; never once, in all the years of the War, had I seen so perfect an expression of pure joy on a German face. Next to him stood his wife and daughter, mysteriously resembling the women portrayed in that old German master's etching: they have come to the Sepulchre, and are standing before the opened, empty tomb; their faces express fear and awe, but also an ecstatic happiness. Just as there, in the picture, one sees the radiance of the disciples in their heavenly perception of their Saviour, so these two poor, ordinary, humble women, worn and ageing, seemed themselves illumined by the old man's childlike, blissful joy; they were half laughing, half in tears, a sight more touching than any I had ever known. But the old man simply could not have enough of my praise; he went on repeatedly stacking and turning the leaves, thirstily absorbing my every word. It was, I fear, a relief to me when the deceiving portfolios were finally pushed aside and, with great reluctance, he had to leave the table free for coffee. But what was my guilty feeling in breathing a sigh of relief, next to the burgeoning, tumultuous happiness, the immense high spirits of this man, who seemed suddenly thirty years younger! He regaled me with a thousand anecdotes about his various purchases and lucky finds, all the while fumbling at the folders and rejecting all offers of help as he did so, trying again to bring out one more prize piece, and then another; such was his elation, he might have been drunk on wine. When, however, I finally said I must take my leave, he was quite taken aback; he became petulant as a self-willed child, and stamped obstinately, saying I couldn't go, I'd hardly seen half of what there was. And the two women were sorely pressed to get him to see, in his stubborn annoyance, that he could not detain me any longer, because I had a train to catch.

'When he did at last give up his desperate opposition and submit, and I was about to go, his voice became quite mellow. He took both my hands, and his fingers fondly explored them, and all their joints, with all the expressive sensitivity of the blind, as if the fingers themselves wanted to know more about me and show the kind of affection that mere words cannot convey. "Your visit has given me very, very great pleasure," he began, and I shall never forget the emotion that welled beneath his words. "You have done me such a service – finally, finally, after so long, I have been able to look through my beloved prints again in the company of a true connoisseur. But you shall see, sir, that your visit to this blind old fellow was not made in vain. I can promise you here and now, and my wife is our witness, that I intend to add a codicil to my will, appointing your distinguished and trusted house, and no other, to auction my collection. You shall have the honour" – here he laid his hand lovingly on the pillaged portfolios – "of administering this unknown treasure right up to the day when it is to be dispersed to the wider world! I only ask you to promise me one thing – that you will compile a fine catalogue: that shall be my gravestone, and I could wish for no better."

'I looked at his wife and daughter, who were clasping each other tightly; an occasional tremble went from one to the other, as if the two formed one single body, its tremors uniting the emotions of both. I myself felt the imposing moment of it, as this touchingly unaware man entrusted to me, as a costly treasure, his invisible, long-vanished collection. Deeply stirred, I made him the promise that I knew I would never be able to fulfil; and once again a gleam appeared in his inert eyes, and I sensed a deep inner urge to touch me bodily, so clear was the tenderness and the affectionate pressing of his fingers, which held mine in gratitude and solemn commitment.

'The women accompanied me to the door. They dared not speak; his acute hearing would have caught every word. But how radiantly they looked at me, so warm in their tears, brimming with thankfulness! In utter bewilderment I groped my way down the stairs. I was, to tell the truth, ashamed; like the fairy-tale angel, I had entered an impoverished household and given a blind man the power of sight for a bare hour simply by colluding shamelessly in a white lie. But, if I am more truthful, I had turned up there more as a sleazy huckster intending to trick someone out of a few valuable pieces. Nevertheless, I took far more with me when I left: I had once again been privileged to see a pure and lively passion at a dull, cheerless time, a kind of spiritually illumined ecstasy devoted wholly to art, a kind that our people nowadays have long since unlearned. And I experienced – I have no other way to put it – a feeling of reverence, however ashamed I still felt, without really knowing why.

'I was already outside on the street when I caught the sound of a window opening above, and I heard my name called: sure enough, the old man had been determined to follow me, with his sightless eyes, in the direction he assumed I was taking. He leaned out so far that the two women had to take the precaution of supporting him; waving his handkerchief, he cried out: "Have a good journey!" and it was a fresh and eager voice, more like that of a young lad. I shall never forget the sight of him: the joyful face of a white-haired old gentleman up there at the window, poised high above all the grumpy, troubled, busy people on the street, gently raised up out of our wretched everyday world on a white cloud of benevolent delusion. And I could not help thinking again of that old saying – was it not Goethe's? – "Collectors are happy men." '

Episode on Lake Geneva

Close to a bank of Lake Geneva not far from the little Swiss town of Villeneuve, one summer's evening in the year 1918 a fisherman who had rowed out into the lake became aware of a strange object out in the middle of the water. Coming closer, he recognized a primitive craft constructed of loosely lashed timbers, and a naked man clumsily attempting to paddle it forward using a plank as an oar. The astonished fisherman steered up to it, helped the exhausted man into his own boat, covered his naked body with netting, for want of anything better, and then tried to speak to this shivering creature that crouched down fearfully in a corner. But the latter answered in a strange foreign language, of which not a single word resembled anything in his own. The helpful fisherman soon abandoned any further efforts; he gathered in his nets, and with hastening strokes of his oars rowed back to the bank.

As the contours of the shore gradually cleared in the early-morning light, the naked man's face also began to show more distinctly. A childlike smile emerged from the tangle of beard surrounding his broad mouth; one hand was raised and pointing, and repeatedly – it sounded half like a question, half like a statement – the man stammered a single word that sounded something like 'Rossiya', and the closer the boat came to the shore the more elated became his voice. At last the boat scraped up onto the beach; the fisherman's womenfolk, who were waiting there for the catch, screamed and ran off in all directions, just like those handmaidens of Nausicaa so long ago, at the sight of the naked man in the fishing net. Only slowly at first, enticed by the strange news they heard, various men from the village began to assemble, and presently, with due ceremony, the worthy local bailiff came to join them, eager in pursuit of his duty. The gentleman's instructions and considerable wartime experience were enough to inform him immediately that this must be a deserter who had swum over from the French side of the lake, and he was already bracing himself to conduct an official interrogation. This formal process was, however, quickly robbed of any dignity, let alone utility, by the fact that the naked man, who in the meantime had received jacket and denim trousers by courtesy of some of the villagers, was unable to respond to any question except by repeating over and over, and more and more nervously and diffidently, the question Rossiya? Rossiya?

Somewhat annoyed by this lack of progress, the official ordered the stranger, by means of gestures he could not misinterpret, to follow him; whereupon amidst the jeers of the local youth, who had by now woken from their sleep and appeared on the scene, the man, dripping wet, legs half exposed, his jacket and trousers fluttering about him, was conducted to the municipal office and there placed in custody. He made no resistance and uttered not a word; but now his bright eyes had darkened in disillusion, and his high shoulders were drawn in as if in fear of a beating.

Meanwhile, news of the human catch had spread to the nearby hotels and, happy at the prospect of a pleasant diversion to relieve the normal daily monotony, several ladies and gentleman came over for a viewing of the wild man. One lady brought him some sweetmeats, which he left untouched like a mistrustful monkey in the zoo; a gentleman took his photograph. Everyone chattered away merrily around him, until at last the manager of a big hotel, who had lived abroad for some time and had acquired a number of languages, directed at the already terrified captive first some words in German, and then some Italian, English and finally Russian. Barely had he uttered the first word of Russian when the frightened man suddenly came to life, and a wide smile appeared and split his good-natured face from one ear to the other. Feeling immediately at ease and more confident, he started to tell his whole story. It was very long and very convoluted, and our fortuitously found interpreter clearly could not grasp every narrative detail, but here are the essentials of what had happened to this man:

He had been fighting in Russia, when one day he and a thousand others were packed into trains and transported far away, then loaded onto ships and taken even further, through lands so hot, as he put it, that your very bones were baked soft under your skin. At length they were disembarked somewhere or other, and then again packed into trains and taken to a place where all of a sudden they had to storm a hill, but he couldn't say anything more about that, because right at the start of the assault he had taken a bullet in the leg. The crowd listening to this had their questions, and his answers, translated for them by the hotel manager; they quickly realized that the fugitive had been fighting with those Russian divisions in France that had been sent halfway round the world, through Siberia and Vladivostok and all the way to the French front. They felt a certain pity for him, but at the same time their curiosity was roused: how had he been able to attempt this extraordinary escape? With a half smile that was part good-natured and part sly, the Russian replied frankly: as soon as he had sufficiently recovered, he had asked the hospital workers in which direction Russia lay, and they had shown him which way it was. He had retained a rough idea of this by following the position of the sun and the stars, and so had secretly absconded, walking by night and throughout the day hiding from patrols in haystacks. For ten days he had lived on bread that he begged and on fruit, until he finally got to this lake. His account now became more vague; apparently, coming as he originally had from the region of Lake Baikal, when he saw the undulating shape of the land in the evening light on the far side, he had assumed that this must be Russia. Anyway he had stolen two wooden boards from a hut; lying down on them on his belly and using an old plank as an oar, he had made his way far out into the lake, and that was where the fisherman had found him. The anxious question with which he ended his muddled account, namely whether he could be home by tomorrow, was no sooner translated than greeted for its naivety by loud laughter, but this soon gave way to sympathy, and each of the bystanders handed over a few coins or banknotes to the poor fellow as he looked around in abject bewilderment.

Meanwhile a more senior police officer had shown up from Montreux in answer to a telephone call and had taken some pains to compose an official written record of the incident. In addition to the fact that the temporary interpreter had proved less than adequate, the stranger's lack of education, to an extent almost incomprehensible to Westerners, soon became obvious; his knowledge even of himself hardly went beyond his first name, which was Boris, and he was able to give only a highly confused set of impressions of his native village, to the effect that its inhabitants were serfs of the Prince Meshchersky – 'serfs' was his word for them, although that system of bondage had in fact been abolished long ago – and that he lived with his wife and three children fifty versts away from the great lake.

Now began deliberations as to what should happen to him, and in the meantime he stood looking blankly, shoulders hunched, as people argued all around him. Some were of the opinion that he should be delivered up to the Russian legation in Bern; others feared this would mean his being sent back to France. The police officer went through the whole difficult question of whether the man ought to be treated as a deserter or a foreigner with no papers; the local District Council Clerk categorically denied any obligation on their part to feed and accommodate this stranger. Then there was a Frenchman, who heatedly declared there was no need to make such an issue over this wretched runaway, he should be either set to work or sent straight back; to which two women objected that he was hardly to blame for his own misfortune, and it was criminal to turn people away and dispatch them to a foreign country. What had started as a chance event was now threatening to turn into a political dispute, when suddenly an elderly gentleman, a Dane, intervened and stated in a resolute tone that he would himself pay for this man's upkeep for a week; that should be long enough for the authorities to reach an agreement with the embassy. This unexpected solution satisfied both official and private sides.

As the discussion became increasingly animated, the fugitive had gradually, apprehensively, raised his eyes; his gaze was now fixed intently on the lips of the hotel manager, for amidst all the confusion he knew this was the only person who could explain his fate to him. He clearly had some limited sense of the turbulence his presence had provoked, and when the verbal sparring subsided, and silence ensued, he instinctively, pleadingly, raised both his hands towards the manager, like a pious woman before a sacred image. No one could fail to be moved by the power of this gesture, and the manager went up to him, warmly reassuring him that he had nothing to fear; he could stay here safely out of harm's way, and for the time being a place would be found for him in the hotel. The Russian was about to kiss his hand, but the manager quickly withdrew it and stepped back. He pointed to the neighbouring house, a small village inn where the man would be given food and lodging, and again said a few heartening words to comfort him. Finally, with a friendly wave, he turned back up the street towards his hotel.

Without moving, the fugitive stared after him; as this one person who understood his language gradually receded from sight, his face, having just now brightened, once again clouded over; with longing eyes he followed the manager as he walked away up to the hotel above the lake, without so much as a glance at the others there, who smiled in bemusement at his strange bearing. When one of them kindly touched his arm and pointed towards the inn, his shoulders seemed to droop; he bowed his head, and made his way to the door. The bar was opened for him. He slumped down at a table, where the maid brought him a glass of brandy as a welcome, and there he sat motionless, with a dazed look, for the whole of the rest of the morning. The village children kept peering in through the window, laughing and calling out to him, but he didn't even raise his head. People coming in looked at him curiously, but he stayed put with his eyes fixed on the table, his back hunched, timid and shy. When a crush of customers arrived for the midday meal and filled the room with laughter, their words buzzed round him in their hundreds, words he did not understand; horribly aware of being the outsider, he sat deaf and mute amidst these general high spirits, and his trembling hands could hardly so much as lift the spoon from his soup. Suddenly a big tear ran down his cheek and fell on the table. He looked round nervously; the others had seen it, and all of a sudden fell silent. He felt ashamed, and his heavy, shaggy head sank lower and lower down towards the black tabletop.

It was getting on for evening before he moved. Guests came and went, but he was unaware of them, and they hardly noticed him now. He sat in the shadow of the oven, much as if part of the shadow himself, his hands laid heavily on the table. The people all forgot that he was there, and no one noticed when he rose to his feet and, plodding along silently like an animal, made his way up to the hotel. One hour, two hours, he stood there at the entrance, submissively holding his cap in his hand, not disturbing anyone with so much as a glance, until finally the strange sight of this figure, standing rigid and dark as a tree trunk before the glittering front of the hotel and seemingly rooted to the ground, was noticed by one of the young hotel errand boys, who then called the manager. At the sound of his own language, a slight glimmer returned to the gloom of the fugitive's face.

'What can I do for you, Boris?' asked the manager good-naturedly.

'Begging you pardon,' returned the Russian, 'I was wanting to know if . . . If I could go home.'

'But of course, Boris, of course you can go home,' the manager smiled.

'Tomorrow?'

The manager looked more serious. The smile was gone, so imploring had the question sounded.

'No, Boris . . . not tomorrow, not yet, not till the war is over.'

'When, then? When will the war be over?'

'Only God knows that, Boris. We mortals can't yet say.'

'And before it ends? Can't I go before that?'

'No, Boris.'

'Is it so far away?'

'Yes.'

'Many days still?'

'Many days, Boris.'

'Well, I think I'll go anyway, sir. I'm strong, and I don't get tired.'

'But you can't, Boris. There's a border between here and there.'

'Border?' He stared blankly. He'd not heard the word before. Then he spoke again, with that remarkable persistence he'd shown: 'Then I'll swim over it.'

The manager suppressed a smile. But he felt the pain himself and explained gently, 'No, Boris, you can't do that. A border – that means it's a foreign country. The people won't let you through.'

'But I'm not doing them any harm! I threw away my rifle. Why shouldn't they let me go back to my wife, if I beg them in Christ's name?'

The manager was feeling more and more dispirited. A bitter feeling rose up in him, and he answered, 'No, they will not let you through, Boris. People aren't interested in Christ's word these days.'

'But what am I supposed to do, sir? I can't stay here! The people don't understand me here, and I don't understand them.'

'You'll learn soon enough, Boris.'

'No, sir,' the Russian's head sank low, 'I can't learn anything – all I can do is work on the land, nothing else. What can I do here? I want to go home! Show me the way, please!'

'There's no way right now, Boris.'

'But sir, they can't stop me going back to my wife and children! I'm not a soldier any more.'

'Yes, they can, Boris.'

'What about the Tsar?' he asked suddenly, trembling in anticipation and reverence.

'There isn't a Tsar any more, Boris. The people got rid of him, deposed him.'

'No Tsar any more?' He stared dumbly at the manager, as the final spark went out in his eyes. Then, quite wearily, 'So I can't go home?'

'Not yet, Boris. You'll have to wait a while.'

'Long?'

'I can't say.'

The face grew more and more gloomy in the dark. 'I've

already waited so long! I can't wait any longer. Show me the way. I'm going to try.'

'There *is* no way, Boris. They'll arrest you at the border. Stay here with us. We'll find work for you.'

'The people don't understand me here, and I don't understand them,' he repeated obstinately. 'I can't live here! Help me, sir!'

'I just can't, Boris.'

'Help me, sir, for the Lord's sake. Help me, I can't bear this any more!'

'I can't, Boris. Nobody can help anyone at the moment.'

They stood facing each other in silence. Boris twisted his cap in his hand. 'Then why did they take me away from my home? They said I had to defend Russia and the Tsar. But Russia is far away, and then the Tsar, you say they . . . what was it you said they did?'

'Deposed him.'

'Deposed.' He repeated the word, without knowing what it meant. 'What am I to do now, sir? I *have* to get home! My children are crying for me. How can I live here? Help me, sir, help me!'

'I can't, Boris.'

'And nobody can help me?'

'No, not at the moment.'

The Russian bowed his head even lower, then said abruptly, in a flat tone, 'Thank you, sir,' and turned to go.

Slowly at first, he walked back along the path. The manager kept him in view for some while, surprised that he did not head for the inn but carried on down the steps to the lake. He sighed deeply and returned to his duties in the hotel.

As chance would have it, it was the same fisherman who came upon the naked body of the drowned man the next morning. He had carefully left the trousers and cap and jacket they had given him at the lakeside and entered the water just as he had come out of it. A report was made of the event, and as the name of the stranger was not known, a simple wooden cross was set over his grave, one of those little crosses that mark the final resting places of the nameless, places with which our great continent is now covered from one end to the other.

Leporella

Her real name was Crescentia Anna Aloisia Finkenhuber; she was thirty-nine years old, born out of wedlock in a small mountain village in the Ziller valley. Under the heading 'special characteristics' in her domestic service record there was merely a horizontal dash, indicating 'none'. If any official had been really forced to offer some depiction of her character, the briefest glance at that heading in her booklet would unquestionably have invited the observation: 'resembles a mountain horse, toughened, bony and scraggy'. There was, to be sure, something unmistakably equine in her expression – the heavy lower lip, the long, coarse oval of her tanned face, a dull, eyelashless stare, and, above all, that hair – thick, felt-like and greasy as it drooped down over her brow. What was more, her gait showed something of the stubborn, mulish nature of an Alpine nag stolidly hauling the same old wooden baskets, with the same jolting tread, come winter, come summer, up and down stony mountain tracks. When freed from the halter of her own employment, Crescenz was in the habit of dozing off, her bony hands loosely folded together, elbows akimbo, rather the way beasts of burden stand in the stall, her senses seemingly shut down. Everything about her was hard, wooden, cumbersome. Her thinking was laborious, her understanding slow. If she ever had a new thought, it would enter only sluggishly into her inner consciousness, as if having to pass through a thick sieve. But once she had actually absorbed something new, she hung onto it with grim and possessive tenacity. She never read anything, not even newspapers or the prayer book; she found writing irksome, and the awkwardly formed letters in her kitchen notebook were strikingly reminiscent of her own clumsy, albeit always sharply angular, figure, which lacked any detectable sign of the feminine. All the harshness of her bones, her brow, her hips and hands was amply matched in her voice, which despite its thick, guttural Tyrolean tenor always sounded somewhat rusted – hardly surprising, considering how Crescenz never wasted unnecessary words on anyone. Nor had anybody ever seen her laugh; in this respect too she was just like an animal, for lack of language is one thing, but it is surely an even more cruel deficiency that God's simpler creatures lack the gift of laughter, that joyously free, expressive outburst of feelings.

Being an illegitimate child, Crescenz was reared at the expense of the local community, and then hired out to service, first as a maid at the age of twelve, and later as a cleaner in a travellers' hostelry, from which service, having attracted some attention for the dogged, manic perseverance in her work, she advanced to a cook's position in a well-respected tourist inn. There she would rise at five every morning, work, sweep, clean, polish, manage the fire, brush, tidy up, cook, knead, churn, strain, wash up and do the laundry, far into the night. She never took any leave, and never set foot outside, except to go to church. The meagre circle of light from the kitchen range served as the sun for her; the innumerable logs it consumed in the course of a year were her woodland.

The menfolk around the place left her in peace, whether because a quarter of a century of this grim, robotic toil had purged every element of womanhood from her, or because she coldly and dourly fended off any possible approach. The one and only diversion she found was in cash, which she assiduously hoarded with the hamsterish instinct of the rural labouring class, ensuring that in old age she would not have to be choking on the bitter fare of the community poorhouse.

Indeed, it was purely for the sake of money that this lumpish creature had first forsaken her Tyrolean stable at the age of thirty-seven. An employment agent happened to have spent a summer break there and, seeing her slaving away madly day and night in kitchen and parlour, lured her, with the enticement of doubling her wages, to Vienna. Throughout the journey Crescenz exchanged not a single word with anyone. Eschewing the other passengers' kindly offers to lift her one piece of luggage, which contained all of her possessions, up into the rack, she kept the heavy wicker basket resting firmly across her already aching knees, her dull peasant's mind allowing her no idea of the big city other than the likelihood of theft and deceit. During her first days in Vienna she needed to be accompanied to market; she feared the city traffic as a cow fears the automobile in the country. But, as soon as she could manage those four streets, she no longer needed anyone; off she trotted with her basket, without raising her eyes, from front door to market stall and back home again, where she returned to the sweeping, fire-lighting and clearing up around the new range, just as she had done at the old one; she noticed no difference at all. At nine o'clock, as if still in the village routine, she retired to bed and slept like an animal, mouth open, until the alarm clock rang in the morning. Nobody, perhaps not even she herself, knew whether she was happy here; she approached no one, and responded to instructions with a wooden 'yes, very well' or, if she felt differently, with a grumpy shrug of the shoulders. She took no notice either of the neighbours or of the other domestics. As for the sneering looks she had from her more easy-going fellows in service, they slid like water from the leathery carapace of her indifference. Only once, when a young girl mockingly mimicked her Tyrolean patois and wouldn't let up ribbing her for not responding, she suddenly grabbed a piece of burning wood out of the range and lunged with it at the appalled and screaming creature. From that day she, and her temper, were carefully avoided, and no one ever dared poke fun at her again.

Every Sunday morning, though, Crescenz set off for church in her wide-fitting pleated skirt and flat rustic bonnet. On one single occasion – it was the first day's leave she had taken since coming to Vienna – she tried going for a walk. She didn't want to use the tram, and over the whole cautious route she plied through the perplexing network of streets, she saw nothing but one stone wall after another. She got no further than the Danube Canal, and there she stared at the fast-flowing stream as if she recognized something familiar. Then she turned round and trudged back the same way she had come, sticking close to the houses while anxiously avoiding the road itself. This one and only exploratory walk was presumably a disappointment to her, for it was the last time she left the house; from then on she spent her Sundays just sitting by the window, either busying herself with needlework or with her hands quite empty. And so the capital brought no real change to the long ingrained treadmill of her days, except that at the end of each month it was now no longer two, but four, blue banknotes she took in her gnarled, weathered and bruised hands. She would always subject these banknotes to long and distrustful examination, ritually unfolding them, and finally smoothing them flat, almost tenderly, before laying the new ones together with the others in the yellow carved wooden box she had brought with her from the village. This crude, unprepossessing little treasure chest was the entirety of her secret, the very meaning of her life. At night the key to it lay beneath her pillow. Where she hid it during the day, no one there ever discovered.

Of such a character was this peculiar 'human being', as she may be named even if it was precisely the human element that was only obscurely and weakly observable in her manner. On the other hand, perhaps only a being precisely so blinkered and withdrawn in her senses could endure service in a household which was itself peculiar in the extreme, namely that of the young Baron von F—. As a rule the servants there were unable to tolerate the fractious atmosphere any longer than the minimum contractual time from their appointment to their handing in their notice. The angry, indeed hysterical, shouting issued from the mistress of the house. Already of a certain age, this daughter of a fabulously wealthy Essen industrialist had met our considerably younger Baron (whose title by the way was questionable, and his financial circumstances no less so) at a spa, and with precipitous haste had married the handsome young beau, model of aristocratic charm that he was. The honeymoon once over, however, the newly-wed soon had to admit that her parents, for whom sound financial standing and competence were paramount, had been justified in their opposition to this over-hasty marriage. It soon became clear that her husband, whose earnestness had quickly slackened, quite apart from his numerous and hitherto unmentioned debts, was somewhat more devoted to his continuing bachelor gallivanting than to his marital duties.

Though not exactly inconsiderate, given that he was at heart as genial as the next frivolous young fellow, this dashing cavalier *manqué* was easy-going to a fault, and profligate in his general attitude; he had no time for accounting, and no concern for capital and interest, all of which he considered a mark of small-minded plebeian penny-pinching. No, for him the easy life; whereas what *she* wanted was the safe, orderly domesticity of the Rhineland bourgeoisie, which irritated him no end. And when, despite her wealth, he had to haggle with her over any paltry sum, and when to cap it all his book-keeping spouse went so far as to deny him his crowning desire, namely a racing stable, he found little reason to trouble himself any more in any marital relations with this broad-necked, heavily built North German woman, whose loud and overbearing voice fell unpleasantly on the ear. He put her on ice, as the saying goes, and although there was no actual harshness on his part, he nonetheless kept her quite decidedly at arm's length. If she took issue with him, he would listen with courtesy and an air of sympathy, but the moment the sermon was over he would blow away her impassioned admonishments along with his cigarette smoke and go his own sweet way without the slightest inhibition. This unruffled, almost bureaucratic courtesy was a bitterer pill for the frustrated wife to bear than any actual defiance, and as she was utterly powerless in the face of her husband's refined, never abrasive but always devastating politeness, her pent-up wrath now turned violently in a new direction: she fulminated against the other staff and discharged her essentially justifiable, but here quite inappropriately applied, indignation with full force on the innocent. The consequences were inevitable: in the space of two years she had to change maids all of sixteen times, once indeed following a genuine violent fracas, which it had taken a sizeable settlement to resolve.

Crescenz alone remained unshaken amidst this raging tumult, steadfast as a cab-horse in the rain. She declined to take sides, was unfazed by any of the changes and seemed not even to notice the constant introduction into her service quarters of new strangers, along with all the new names, hair-colours, odours and personal manners. She herself talked to none of them and took in her stride the noisy slamming of doors, the disrupted midday meals, the wild hysterical outbursts. With complete indifference she went busily from kitchen to market, market back to kitchen, quite unconcerned with what was happening outside her own private sphere. Hard and impassive as a flail, she beat her way through day after day, and in such manner two years in the city flowed by uneventfully, bringing little widening of her inner world, except that the stack of blue banknotes she kept in her box gained an inch in height, and when she wetted her finger and counted the notes one by one at the end of the year, they had almost reached the magic figure of one thousand.

Still, Fortune's drill is diamond-tipped, and Fate, in all its insidious cunning, knows perfectly well how to intrude from unforeseen places and wreak complete havoc on even the rockiest nature. With Crescenz, external factors came into play in no less banal a guise than her own character. After a lapse of ten years it had so pleased the State once again to order a census, to which purpose every residential building was sent a form of the utmost complexity, to be accurately filled in with the residents' particulars. Not trusting the impenetrable and only phonetically correct scribble of the domestic staff, the Baron chose to fill out the forms himself, and to this end he had summoned Crescenz, like the others, to his room. When he asked for her name, age and place of birth it transpired that he, being an ardent huntsman and a friend of the landlord of that locality, had not infrequently shot chamois in that same Alpine corner, and that a guide from her native village had accompanied him for all of two weeks. And when it turned out that this same guide was, astonishingly, none other than an uncle of Crescenz, and furthermore the Baron was at that moment in genial spirits, the fortuitous discovery gave rise to a lengthier conversation, and with it yet another surprising revelation: the Baron had in the course of that visit supped at the very inn where Crescenz was in service, and had partaken of her excellent venison roast. This was all of little consequence, but still the coincidence was indeed remarkable, and for Crescenz, who was now for the first time meeting anyone here who knew anything of her homeland, it was frankly miraculous. There she stood before him, her face blushing with interest, bowing awkwardly, flattered when he started joking with her, imitating her Tyrolean dialect, asking her if she could yodel, and other such childish sillinesses. Finally, amused at his own drollery, he administered a familiar, rustic-style slap on her hard hindquarters and dismissed her with a laugh: 'Off with you, good Cenzi, and here's two crowns extra, just for being from the Zillertal!'

To be sure, this was in itself hardly a great passion-stirring moment. Nevertheless, the effect of the five-minute conversation on the fishlike, subterranean emotions of this stolid creature was something like that of a stone thrown into a bog: ripples forming, first slowly and gradually, which then rolled sluggishly outwards to reach the edge of her consciousness. For the first time in years, this obstinate, taciturn woman had conducted a real conversation with a fellow human being, and it seemed to her a supernatural stroke of providence that this person, the first to speak to her, this individual right here amidst the stony city jungle not only knew of her mountain home but had actually tasted one of her own venison roasts! And to cap it all there was that familiar slap on the behind, which in peasant language betokens a kind of laconic wooing of any female. While Crescenz would never have dared presume that this suave, distinguished gentleman had in fact intended such an approach, the physical familiarity did somehow startle, and waken, her sleeping senses.

And so began, from this chance opening, a stirring, a turbulence in layer after layer of the depths of her inner being, and out of this, at first clumsily but then more and more distinctly, there emerged a new feeling, rather like that sudden recognition with which a dog, at some unexpected moment, comes to acknowledge his master amidst all the other two-legged forms that surround him; from that moment on he runs after him, greets with barking or wagging tail this authority that Fate has set over him, and in willing submissiveness obediently follows his tracks step by step. This was exactly the way that Crescenz's restricted circle, thus far defined only by the five familiar concepts of money, market, kitchen, range and bed, now admitted a forceful new element which demanded space and assertively thrust aside everything else she had known. And with that rustic's avarice that will never relinquish its grip of anything once gained, she thoroughly absorbed this new element into her dull senses, and into their confused instinctive world. It did take some time for the change to reveal itself, and the first signs were barely noticeable; there appeared, for example, a special new zeal in the care she took in cleaning the Baron's clothes and shoes, while those of his wife continued to be left to the chambermaid. Or she would now often be seen in and around the corridor, keenly hastening to relieve the Baron of his hat and stick the moment the key sounded in the front door. She attended to the cooking with twice her former care, and went so far as to find her way laboriously back to the principal market hall, just to procure venison for a roast. And there were also some signs of extra attention in the way she dressed.

It took a week or two for these first green shoots of new sensibility to issue from her inner world. Many further weeks were needed before the first impetus was enhanced by a second, initially vague, notion, which by and by acquired colour and shape. This second feeling was in fact merely a complement to the first; namely a hatred, initially ill-defined but gradually laid vividly bare, of the Baron's wife – this woman who was able to live and sleep and speak with the Baron without feeling anything like Crescenz's reverential devotion to the man. Whether she, now being instinctively more observant, had witnessed one of those painful scenes in which her idolized master had been shamefully humiliated by his petulant wife, or whether it was that the Baroness's rigid and disdainful North German reserve was made doubly apparent by comparison with her husband's jovial affability, Crescenz, for whatever reason, all at once began to confront her unsuspecting mistress with a degree of defiance, a prickly animosity communicated through innumerable little barbed remarks and spitefulnesses. The Baroness now had to ring at least twice before Crescenz would respond, which she then did with calculated slowness and all too clear reluctance, her raised shoulders invariably expressing resistance from the outset. Orders and instructions were now received by her with taciturn glumness, and the Baroness never quite knew whether she had made herself understood; but if she then repeated herself, just to be sure, her request was met with a resentful nod of the head or scornful 'Yea, heard yer first time'. Or immediately before a theatre evening, the Baroness might be rushing round in a state of anxiety because an important key had gone missing, and then half an hour later the same key would unexpectedly be found hiding in a corner. Telephone calls and messages for the Baroness she made a regular habit of forgetting; when questioned, she just flung back at her a blunt 'Jus' forgot!' without the faintest hint of remorse. She never looked her in the eye, perhaps fearing she would not be able to contain her hatred.

Meanwhile, household disagreements led to increasingly unpleasant scenes between the Baron and his wife. No doubt Crescenz's unconsciously provoking sourness also played its part in the irritability of the Baroness, who grew more and more highly strung as the weeks went by. Already unsettled in her nerves as a result of an excessively prolonged maidenhood, and then additionally embittered by her husband's indifference, the tormented woman was steadily losing her mind. Bromide and veronal proved ineffectual remedies for her fretfulness; her overstretched nervous restraint erupted all the more violently in her exchanges, and she broke down in tears and hysterical outbursts, though without receiving the least sympathy from anyone, or even any semblance of good-natured support. In the end the doctor who was called advised a stay of two months in a sanatorium, a suggestion that was welcomed by her otherwise quite unconcerned husband with such sudden solicitude that she, her suspicions newly roused, at first resisted. But eventually the trip was agreed on, and her own personal maid chosen to go with her; Crescenz was to remain in the spacious dwelling alone to serve the master.

This news, that his Lordship was to be entrusted to her care alone, acted like a sudden stimulant on Crescenz's impassive senses. As if some force had wildly shaken up her every strength and energy in a magic vessel, there now surfaced from the depths of her being a hidden sediment of passion, the colour of which imbued every aspect of her behaviour. That languid clumsiness all at once departed from her stiff, frozen limbs; the electrifying news seemed to have suddenly liberated the joints of her body, to have lightened and quickened her pace. No sooner had the time come to prepare for the journey than she was running from room to room, up and down the stairs, going out of her way to pack all the suitcases and personally haul them out to the car. And when the Baron returned from the station late in the evening, handed his coat and stick to Crescenz, who rushed eagerly to receive him, and let out, with a sigh of relief, the words 'Departure happily accomplished!' something remarkable happened: all of a sudden there appeared around Crescenz's tightened lips – otherwise, like any animal, she never laughed – an intense stretching and twitching. The mouth went crooked and widened horizontally, and suddenly a grin shone forth in the middle of her idiotically brightened face, showing such animal-like unrestrained openness that the Baron, in surprise and embarrassment at the sight, felt ashamed of his improper familiarity and without saying anything retired to his own room.

This transient moment of discomfort was, however, soon over. Within the next few days the two of them, master and handmaid, were soon united in breathing, and savouring, the same beneficial air of freedom. The wife's absence had, as it were, relieved the atmosphere of its overhanging cloud; the husband, so liberated and now happily disburdened of that constant need to give an account of himself, came home late the very first evening, and the silently attentive Crescenz offered him a most welcome contrast to the excessively discursive reception he would have from his wife. Crescenz, for her part, flung herself with passionate new enthusiasm into her daily duties, rose specially early, cleaned and scrubbed till everything sparkled, polished every door handle like one possessed, conjured up particularly mouth-watering dishes; and to his surprise the Baron noted at the first midday meal that, all for him alone, the prize service and cutlery had been brought out which normally left the silver cabinet only on special occasions. Though generally unobservant, he could not help sensing the scrupulous, almost tender-hearted care this extraordinary creature was taking, and, being essentially tender-hearted himself, he was not slow to express his appreciation. He praised the meals she made, imparted a few friendly words here and there, and when the next morning, which was his name-day, he found a cake beautifully prepared and topped in sugar with his initials and coat of arms, he smiled playfully at her: 'You'll be spoiling me yet, Cenzi! And what am I going to do when – God forbid! – my wife comes back?'

Now this kind of tactless indiscretion on the part of a master before his servant, a familiarity verging on the cynical, might perhaps raise eyebrows in some other lands, but among the older Austrian aristocracy it was really nothing very unusual. It was a casualness just as typical of the gentry's behaviour, both in and out of the saddle, as it was of any great disdain of the rabble. Just as sometimes archdukes, confined for a time in some minor Galician outpost, would have the sergeant bring over a common hussy from the brothel in the evening, later to hand her back half-naked to the same procurer, unconcerned by the thought that all the local riffraff would be licking their lips over the juicy story next day, so a high-born nobleman would as soon sit together with his coachman or groom as with a businessman or university professor. But this apparently classless familiarity, as easily received as dispensed, was in truth the precise opposite of what it seemed to be. It was always known to be entirely one-sided, and it ended the moment his Lordship rose from table. And since the minor gentry were ever obliged to ape the manners of the real grandees, the Baron felt no inhibition whatsoever in expressing himself so disrespectfully about his wife in front of a lumpish Tyrolean peasant woman, so confident was he of her silence, and of course quite heedless of the keen interest with which this gauche country maid lapped up his belittling language.

He did nevertheless exercise a certain restraint for a few days, before abandoning all caution. But then, assured by various signs of Crescenz's discretion, he began to settle himself comfortably back into a bachelor existence in his own dwelling. Without further explanation he summoned Crescenz, on his fourth day as a grass widower, and calmly asked her to lay on a cold supper for two in the evening and then take herself off to bed; he would look after everything else. Crescenz received the order and said nothing. Not the slightest eye movement gave any indication whether the true meaning of his words had sunk beneath that low forehead of hers. But her master very quickly came to see, to his surprise and amusement, how well she had understood what he had really had in mind. Coming in late that evening from the theatre in the company of a young singing student, not only did he find the table choicely laid and adorned with flowers, but the second bed in his bedroom had been invitingly, if somewhat blatantly, made up, with his wife's silk dressing gown and slippers lying ready. The liberated husband could not but smile at the lengths this curious creature had gone to, and therewith the last trace of inhibition departed in the face of this confidante's helpfulness. Next morning he rang for her to come and help with the charming intruder's dressing, and that finally put the seal on the silent understanding between the two of them.

It was also in the course of these days that Crescenz acquired her new name. Our lively little opera student, who was just then working on the part of Donna Elvira, and took to jokingly elevating her affectionate friend to the role of Don Giovanni, had once said to him with a laugh, 'Come on, call your Leporella!' This name amused him, precisely because it so grotesquely parodied the scrawny Tyrolean, and from then on he never called her anything else. The first time she heard the name, Crescenz looked up in bewilderment, but after that, beguiled by the sheer music of it, and having no idea what it meant, she positively relished her rechristening, taking it as a mark of ennoblement. Every time the boyish Baron called her so, she would part her thin lips and expose her yellow equine teeth, and in servility, like a tail-wagging dog, hurry along to her gracious Lordship to receive his latest command.

The name was indeed meant in jest, but with unintended acuity the budding opera diva had adorned the quirky Crescenz with a verbal barb that suited her uncannily well; like Da Ponte's depiction of the Don's colluding companion in crime, this ossified old maid took a peculiarly appreciative pride in her master's adventures. Was it merely the satisfaction of finding the ardently hated baroness's bed every morning in disarray and defiled by now one young body, now another, or might there have been in her a touch of secretly felt conspiracy with her master's profligate self-indulgence? At any rate this rigid, inflexible spinster displayed a positively passionate commitment to assisting the Baron in his various exploits. Though in her own body, overburdened and rendered sexless by decades of domestic toil, she had long ago ceased to feel any cravings, as a procuress she was gratifyingly rewarded by discreetly seeing, after only a few days, another female visitor into the bedroom, and a third one shortly after that. The role of

43

accomplice was as good a tonic for her dormant instincts as was the tingling perfume of that erotic atmosphere. Crescenz truly lived up to her new name, and like the resourceful Leporello himself she was ever lively, alert and at the ready. Surprising new qualities surfaced, as if engendered by the flowing heat of her burning complicity: little ruses of every kind, mischievous words and deeds, not to mention inquisitive eavesdropping, prying and spying and gleeful jollity. She would listen behind doors, peer through keyholes, poke about in rooms and beds, fly up and down stairs in a weirdly excited state the moment she sniffed the arrival of any new prey, and little by little this vigilant curiosity, this nosy interest of hers, brought forth from the wooden husk of her former apathy something like a truly living person. To the astonishment of all the neighbours Crescenz became suddenly approachable, chatting with the maids, cracking crude jokes with the postman and starting to indulge in tittle-tattle with the women in the market. And once in the evening, when the lights in the yard had been put out, the servant girls overheard from the room opposite a strange humming that came from the normally silent window: in a rough, half-muted, rasping voice Crescenz was actually singing one of those Alpine songs of the dairy-women out on the pastures in the evening. The faltering sounds of the monotonous melody stumbled clumsily from her unpractised lips; but for all that, it was a strangely arresting thing to hear, for Crescenz was now for the first time since her childhood trying to sing again, and there was something stirring, moving, in those hesitant notes that now came painfully out into the light from the darkness of her long buried years.

This remarkable change that came over his devoted servant was noticed least of all by its unconscious begetter, the Baron. After all, do we ever normally turn back to face our own shadow? Yes, we sense it faithfully and silently following in our wake, sometimes hurrying before us like a desire of which we are still unaware, but how rarely do we trouble to observe its parodying of us, or recognize ourselves in that distorted shape? The Baron sensed nothing in Crescenz other than that she was always there ready to serve him, completely silent, dependable and devoted to the point of utter self-denial. And it was this very discretion, this natural distance she kept in any private situation, that he found to be of particular benefit. On occasions he would casually praise her a little, the way one pats a dog, or now and again even share a joke with her, or condescend to give her ear a little pinch, or slip her a banknote or a theatre ticket – things of no great moment for him, nonchalantly taken from his waistcoat pocket; she, though, would store them away reverentially in her treasure chest. Gradually he became used to thinking aloud in her presence and even trusting her with more complicated tasks – and the greater his signs of confidence in her, the more thankfully and assiduously did she extend her efforts. There gradually appeared in her a strangely probing, sniffing, ferreting instinct for searching out, and indeed anticipating, his every wish; it was as if her whole life, with all its own desires and strivings, had left her own body and entered his. She saw everything through his eyes, listened out for signs of what was in his mind, and driven by an almost wanton enthusiasm enjoyed with him all of his pleasures and his conquests. She beamed every time a new female crossed the threshold, showed her disappointment, as if frustrated in her hopes, if he came back in the evening without such tender company. Her previously dulled mental processes were now as nimble and impetuously active as only her hands had been before, and a wakeful glint shone in her eyes. A human had been awakened within the haggard, wearied beast of burden – a human being closed, to be sure, and withdrawn, but at the same time cunning and dangerous, calculating before decisively acting, restless and scheming.

So it was that once, when the Baron arrived home earlier than usual, he stopped in surprise in the corridor: had he not heard a strange giggling and laughing from behind that kitchen door, though she was otherwise invariably silent? And now here she was, Leporella, in the half-open doorway, rubbing her hands on her apron, looking cheeky but at the same time bashful. 'Begging yer pardon, m'lord,' she said, with her eyes skirting the floor, 'but I got the – confectioner's daughter here . . . pretty little thing in all . . . she'd be ever so pleased to make yer acquaintance, sir.' The Baron looked up, surprised, not quite knowing whether he should be angered at such barefaced forwardness or amused at her obligingly playing the procuress. Finally his masculine curiosity prevailed: 'Very well, let her take a quick look at me if that's what she wants!'

The girl, a blonde, fresh-faced slip of a sixteen-year-old whom Leporella had gradually cajoled with coaxing and flattering, now came out with blushes and embarrassed giggles, and as the maid nudged her out through the door she did a clumsy turn in front of this elegant personage whom she had, it was true, often watched with half-childlike admiration from the confectionery-shop window opposite. Her prettiness did strike the Baron, and he proposed she join him for tea in his room. Unsure whether she should accept, she turned round to ask Crescenz, but the latter had already disappeared into the kitchen with conspicuous haste, so that the girl, thus lured into the adventure, could do nothing but accept the Baron's dangerous invitation, blushing and thrilled with curiosity.

Nature, however, does not make leaps: even if, under the influence of a twisted, misconceived passion, Crescenz's dulled and hardened essence had managed to give birth to some level of genuine mental activity, still her blinkered, newly learned thinking could not stretch beyond the next stage, being as yet more akin to the short-term instincts of an animal. Completely immured in her fixation with serving, in every way, the master she loved with canine loyalty, she quite forgot the absent wife. So much the more dreadful was her awakening: it fell on her like thunder from a clear sky when one morning the Baron, short-tempered and irascible, entered with a letter in his hand and gave notice that she should get everything in the house in order, since his wife was returning from the sanatorium the next day. Crescenz stood there, pale in the face, mouth wide open in shock: the news had pierced her like a knife. She simply stared and stared, as if she hadn't understood. And so greatly, so alarmingly did this bolt from the blue disfigure her face that the Baron felt he had to calm her at least a little and say something cheerful. 'I get the feeling, Cenzi, you're not exactly overjoyed either. But there's nothing to be done about it.'

Now something was already really beginning to stir in her stony expression, something working its way from deep down, as if from her very entrails: a forceful spasm, which was gradually returning a deep red to those cheeks just now blanched. Something now very slowly rose to the surface, over strong pumping heartbeats: her throat quivered with the strength of the effort. And then at last it came out, muffled, between gritted teeth. 'Migh' be . . . migh' be . . . som'at could be done.'

The words had escaped her with the harshness of a lethal gunshot. And so malignant, so darkly resolute was the expression on her contorted face after this violent unburdening, that the Baron involuntarily started back in amazement. But already Crescenz had turned away again and begun to scour a copper vessel with such convulsive fervour that she might have wanted to break her own fingers in the act.

The return of the wife brought stormy weather back into the household, slamming the doors, raging through the rooms and sweeping away that comfortably genial atmosphere in a cold blast. Whether it was that local gossip or anonymous tale-telling letters had reached the deceived woman's ears and informed her of how shamefully her husband had abused his domestic prerogatives, or whether it was his irritable, and all too manifest, ill humour on her return that vexed her, at all events her two months in the sanatorium appeared to have done little for her severely frayed nerves, for fits of tears sometimes spilled over into threats and hysterical scenes. Marital relations were becoming more unbearable by the day. For several weeks the Baron manfully braved the onslaught of her rebukes with the good grace he had consistently maintained up till now, responding evasively and consolingly whenever she threatened him with divorce or letters to her parents. But this very indifference of his, cool and loveless as it was, drove the friendless woman, surrounded thus by hidden hostility, ever deeper into her increasingly fraught agitation.

Crescenz had well and truly armoured herself in her former silence. But this silence had now become aggressive and hostile. When her mistress returned she remained obstinately in the kitchen, and on being finally called out she avoided welcoming her back home. She stood there, sulkily stiff-shouldered, like a block of wood, and any question put to her she answered so gracelessly that the impatient Baroness soon turned away from her. Into her unsuspecting mistress's back, however, Crescenz shot a single glance containing all of her pent-up loathing. Her hungry emotions felt unjustly robbed by this homecoming, now that she was plucked from the joys of service she had loved so passionately and cast back to the kitchen and its range, no longer to enjoy the intimacy of that nickname, Leporella. For the Baron was cautiously wary of revealing, in front of his wife, any fondness for Crescenz. At times, though, exhausted by the hateful scenes, and in need of any kind of consolation and unburdening of himself, he would creep into the kitchen to find her, and flop down on one of the hard wooden chairs, if only to groan: 'I can't take much more of this!'

These moments, in which her idolized master sought refuge in her company from his overwhelming tension, were blessed above everything Leporella ever knew. Not that she ever ventured an answer, or even a word of consolation. Sunk in herself and her own silence, she just sat there, from time to time looking up at him, her deity now turned victim, with understanding eyes, sympathetic and deeply pained. And her wordless compassion did soothe him, but no sooner had he left the kitchen than that angered knitting of the brow would creep back, and her heavy hands would vent her fury, beating it out on a defenceless cut of meat or scouring and rubbing away at dishes and cutlery.

Eventually the stifling gloom following the Baroness's homecoming was shattered and discharged with tempestuous force. One unsavoury domestic scene had ended with the Baron completely losing his patience, abandoning his customary schoolboy posture of submissive indifference and loudly slamming the door behind him. 'I've had enough of this now,' he yelled, with a rage that rattled the windows at the far end of the house. And, still red in the face, with anger unabated, he strode out into the kitchen and found Crescenz, who was quivering like a tightly drawn bow. 'Pack my trunk this moment and get my gun out – I'm going for a week's hunting. The devil himself wouldn't tolerate another minute in this hell. We have to put an end to this.'

Crescenz looked at him, bright-eyed. Here he was, master once more. 'Righ' enough, sir! There 'as to be an end t'it!' And, twitching with zeal, she hurried from room to room getting everything together from cupboards and tables, and every nerve in that coarse-built frame of hers twitched with eager tension. She herself took the trunk and gun out to the car, but while he fumbled for words to thank her for her help and attention his eyes turned from her in alarm. For over her tightened lips the malice was visibly spreading once again, in that smile that never failed to disquiet him; he could not help thinking of an animal tensed and poised in ambush, waiting to spring, when he saw her lying in wait like this. But then she simply bowed again meekly and whispered huskily, with almost offensive familiarity, 'Wishin' sir a safe journey, jus' leave things to me.'

Three days later, the Baron was called back from the hunt by an urgent telegram. His cousin was waiting for him at the station, and a single glance was enough to tell him, being already uneasy, that something distressing must have occurred; the cousin fidgeted nervously as he looked at him. After a few courteous preliminary words, the Baron learned the truth: his wife had been found dead in her bed that morning, the whole room filled with coal gas. Sadly, a careless accident had to be excluded, his cousin told him; since it was now May, the gas oven had been long unused, and the poor Baroness's taking of veronal in the evening indicated suicidal intent. Furthermore, the household cook, Crescenz, stated that she had remained alone at home that evening and had heard her unhappy mistress enter the antechamber during the night, apparently in order to turn on the gas at the meter, which had been carefully switched off. On the basis of this information the police doctor who had been summoned had ruled out any possibility of an accident, and recorded a case of suicide.

The Baron began to tremble. At his cousin's mention of Crescenz's testimony, he suddenly felt the blood run cold in his hands. A hideous, repellent thought welled up in his mind like a nausea, but he suppressed this seething, painful sensation with all the force he could muster and submissively allowed his cousin to take him back to the house. The body had already been removed, and in the reception room his relatives were waiting with gloomily hostile faces; their condolences had the coldness of a knife blade. With a distinct accusatory tone, they felt compelled to mention how it had, regrettably, been no longer possible to keep the 'scandal' under wraps, since the maid had rushed out onto the steps that morning screaming stridently, 'Me lady mistress 'as gone and topped 'erself!' They had, they said, arranged for a discreet burial, because – again the cold knife point went straight for him – unfortunately the incident was preceded by all kinds of unwelcome gossip that had roused an unpleasant level of general interest. The forlorn Baron listened in bewilderment, raised his eyes involuntarily for one moment in the direction of the closed door to the bedroom, then timidly looked away again; he wanted to think something through and then exorcise it, a troubling idea that would not be kept down, but all this spiteful talk was perplexing him. For another half hour the relatives stood around chatting in their mourning black, then finally taking their leave one after the other. He remained there alone in the empty, half-darkened room, trembling as if under a severe blow, head throbbing, exhaustion in every joint of his body.

There was a knock at the door. 'Come in,' he said, startled. And from behind him came hesitant footsteps, a hard, insidious, shuffling tread that he knew so well. Overcome with a sudden dread, he felt as if his back and neck were screwed tight in place and an ice-cold tremor rippled over his skin, all the way from his forehead to his knees. He wanted to turn round, but his muscles refused. There he stood in the middle of the room, silent, trembling, hands rigidly down at his sides, all too conscious of the cowardly image this guilty, complicit posture projected. But try as he might, his limbs would not obey him. And in the driest, most impassive, matter-of-fact tone, the voice behind him said, 'Jus' want'ed to ask, if Sir was ta'ing dinner a' home or not.' The Baron's body shook more and more violently, and now that icy chill had travelled as far as his breast. Three times he strove in vain to speak, before he could finally force out the words: 'No, I won't eat anything now.' The steps shuffled out again, and he hadn't the courage to turn around. Then suddenly the stiffness relaxed; a shudder went through and through him, a retching nausea, or cramp. All at once he sprang back towards the door and rapidly turned the key to prevent that footstep, that hateful tread that followed and haunted him, from coming in to accost him again. Then he flung himself into his chair, so as to quash a thought that he had no wish to entertain but kept creeping up into his head, cold and slimy as a snail. And this uncontrollable thought, which it so appalled him to face, filled every corner of his mind, inescapable, clammy and repulsive, and kept a hold of him throughout the whole sleepless night and the hours beyond, still persisting as he stood silently in black at the head of the coffin during the funeral.

The day after the burial the Baron hurriedly left town. Every face he encountered was now too unbearable; amidst their sympathy, these people – or was it just his imagination? – had a strangely watching, tormentingly inquisitorial look. And even inanimate objects were now speaking malicious and accusing words. Every piece of furniture in the house, but especially in the bedroom, where the sweetish smell of gas seemed to linger around every article, repelled him even if he merely happened to unlatch a door. But the really intolerable nightmare, even of his waking hours, was the cool, unmoved indifference on the part of his former confidante, who acted as she went round the now empty house as if nothing whatsoever had happened. Ever since that moment at the station when the cousin had brought up her name, the Baron shivered at any prospect of meeting her. At the sound of her steps approaching he would immediately fall prey to a nervous unease; he could no longer bear the thought, let alone the sight, of that careless, shuffling gait, or the self-contained, taciturn coldness. He was thoroughly repulsed by the mere thought of her, of her grating voice and greasy hair, her stolid, animal-like and merciless insensitivity;

indeed, there was an element of his anger directed at himself, for lacking the strength to sever forcefully, once and for all, this bond that so throttled him. So he could see only one way out – by flight. He packed his trunks secretly without saying a word to her; all he left was a perfunctory note, to the effect that he had gone to stay with friends in Carinthia.

The Baron stayed away for the whole summer. Called back urgently just once to Vienna to deal with the deceased's estate, he chose to arrive discreetly, stay in a hotel and leave that ominous presence that awaited him at home none the wiser. Crescenz learned nothing of his return, because she spoke to no one. Left at a loose end, she sat gloomily, owl-like, in the kitchen all day, hardly moving, went to church twice a week – up till now it had been only once – and received her instructions, and money for settling the accounts, through the Baron's solicitor, but from the Baron himself she heard nothing. He neither wrote nor sent any word. There she sat in silence, and waited. Her face grew harder, more drawn, her movements wooden once more, and thus she waited, and waited, for weeks on end in an uncanny state of torpor.

But when autumn came, matters of urgency no longer allowed the Baron to extend his absence, and he was forced to return home. He stopped and hesitated on the threshold. His two months with close friends had made him almost forget much of it – but now that he was to be physically confronted by his nightmare, by this person who could well be his partner in crime, he felt just that same old oppressive, almost crushing paroxysm. With every step he took as he ascended the steps more and more slowly, the invisible hand rose to clasp and grip his neck. In the end it was only through a sudden, violent mustering of all of his willpower that he could command his rigid fingers to turn the key in the door.

Taken by surprise, Crescenz rushed from the kitchen the moment she heard the click of the key in the lock. She saw him, stood for a moment pale in the face, then bent down, as if to duck from view, so as to take up the bag he had put down. No word of greeting came to her lips, and he too said nothing. Silently she carried the bag into his room; he followed in silence, and waited, looking out of the window without speaking, until she had left the room. Then quickly he turned the key.

That was their first encounter after close on three months.

Crescenz waited. And the Baron waited too. Would it pass, this ghastly seizure of horror that he had experienced on seeing her? It did not. Even before he saw her, the very sound of her footsteps outside in the passage was enough to provoke a fluttering of discomfort. He couldn't touch his breakfast, he disappeared from the house hastily every morning without addressing a word to her, and stayed out late into the night simply to avoid her presence. The two or three instructions he had to communicate to her were given without looking at her. It suffocated him even to breathe in the same room as this ghoul.

Meanwhile Crescenz sat in silence the whole day on her kitchen stool. She stopped cooking for herself. Any food sickened her, and she avoided all human contact. She just sat and waited, demure-eyed, for the first whistle from her master, like a dog that had been beaten and knew it had done something bad. Her slow wits could not comprehend what precisely had happened; all she knew was that her lord and master was shunning her, not needing her any more, and this alone smote her to the core.

On the third day after the Baron returned there was a ring at the door. A calm, grey-haired, clean-shaven gentleman stood there with a suitcase in his hand. Crescenz was on the point of dismissing him, but the intruder insisted that he was the new servant, whom the master of the house had requested to come at ten o'clock, and she should kindly announce his arrival. Crescenz turned deathly pale and stood for a long moment with fingers stiffly outstretched in the air. Then her hand fell like a mortally wounded bird and with a cursory 'Find yer own way then' she slammed the front door, turned on her heels and went back to the kitchen.

The new servant stayed. From that day on the master no longer needed to address a word to Crescenz, and all communication was made through the calm, elderly new valet. Crescenz learned nothing of what was happening in the household, and it all washed coldly over her like a wave over a stone.

These oppressive conditions persisted for two weeks, wearing her down like some illness. Her face grew pinched and drawn; her hair suddenly started greying around the temples. Her movements were completely lifeless. Almost the whole time she sat rooted to her stool like a block of wood, without uttering a sound and staring blankly at the empty window; but at those moments when she did work, she did so with a savage zealousness resembling an outbreak of rage.

After these two weeks, one day the new servant made his way to his master's room, and the Baron could tell, from the restrained and discreet way in which he waited, that the man had something particular to communicate to him. The servant had already had occasion to complain about the surliness of the 'Tyrolean bumpkin', as he scornfully called Crescenz, and to suggest handing her her notice. Feeling somewhat embarrassed, the Baron gave the appearance of ignoring the suggestion for the time being. However, whereas on that occasion the servant had simply bowed and withdrawn, this time he took the bull by the horns and, adopting a strange, almost diffident expression, finally managed to stammer out the message that if his Lordship might kindly not judge him wholly ridiculous, he . . . he could . . . well, no, he could not put it any other way . . . he found her actually *frightening*. This brooding, malevolent creature was impossible to live with, and the Baron must be unaware what a dangerous person he had under his roof.

The Baron could not help starting at this word of warning. What was the man getting at? What did he really mean to say? To be sure, he did now tone down his message – he couldn't point to anything specific, he merely had the feeling that this person was a kind of mad wild animal, and she might easily harm somebody. Yesterday, when he had turned round to give her some instruction, to his surprise he had suddenly caught a look in her eye – of course, a look is just a look, and you can't say too much about that, but this one had been such as to make him feel she was about to spring at his neck. From that moment he had gone in fear of her, yes, he was even fearful of touching the food she prepared. 'The Herr Baron cannot know', he said in conclusion, 'how dangerous an individual this is. She never speaks, she never says anything, but it's my opinion she's capable of murder.' Startled by the word, the Baron shot a sharp glance at the complainant. Had he heard something specific? Had some suspicions come to his ears? The Baron, feeling his fingers begin to tremble, quickly put aside his cigar so that his hands would not be seen shaking in agitation. But the face of the elderly man was completely ingenuous – no, he surely knew nothing. The Baron hesitated. Then suddenly he pulled himself resolutely together, his mind made up. 'Just wait a little. And if you have any further hostility from her I'll simply dismiss her from service.'

The servant bowed, and the Baron, thus relieved, sank back. Whenever his thoughts returned to that secretive, insidious creature, his day darkened. Best, he considered, for it to happen while he was away, at Christmas perhaps – the very thought of this longed-for freedom lifted his mood. Yes, that's the best option, he reassured himself – Christmas, when I'm not here.

But just the next day, he had hardly sat down in his room after eating when there was a knock at the door. Looking up

unconcernedly from his newspaper, he murmured, 'Come in!'
And in shuffled those grating, hated footsteps, the constant bane
of his dreams. The Baron started; like a skull, pallid and bleached
white, the fleshless face quivered above her now emaciated black
figure. The sight of her provoked in him a hint of pity despite
the horror, as the fearful steps of this utterly broken woman
paused humbly at the edge of the carpet. And in order to hide
his confusion he took pains to appear unsuspecting. 'So, Crescenz, what is it?' he asked. But the question did not sound jovial
and friendly, as intended, but came out rather as a peevish rebuff.

Crescenz did not move but simply stared down at the carpet.
Finally she managed to force out the words, like someone pushing an obstacle out of the way with a foot: 'Yer servant, 'e says
to me, he says Sir's gonna sack me.'

Acutely embarrassed, the Baron got to his feet. The speed of
it had taken him by surprise, and he began fumbling with his
words – no, it hadn't been meant quite that way, she should
really try to be on better terms with the other staff, and other
such random thoughts that happened to fall from his lips.

But Crescenz stood stock still, shoulders hunched, her gaze
fixedly piercing the carpet. With embittered doggedness she
kept her head down, bull-like, allowing all his conciliatory offer-
ings to float over her, awaiting just one word which never came.
And when he finally fell silent, exhausted and somewhat
repulsed by the contemptible role he was having to play of
cajoling and appeasing a servant, there she remained, stubborn
and mute. Then she did manage some clumsy words: 'Jus'
wanted ter know, was it 'is Lordship as told Anton ter sack me?'

She forced it out, harshly, unwillingly, violently. And it struck
the Baron like an extra blow, already overwrought as he was.
Was this a threat? Was she challenging him? All of a sudden he
lost all his cowardice, and with it every ounce of pity. All the
hatred and revulsion that had been dammed up within him for

weeks on end now combined in a flash with his longing to see the end of it. In a sudden and complete change of tone he switched to that cool objectivity that he had learned to use so well in the ministry, and casually informed her that yes, indeed, she had heard aright, he had in fact given the man a free hand in managing all matters pertaining to the household. For his own part he wished her well and would endeavour to have the dismissal revoked, but if she further persisted in her poor relations with the servant, well, then he would have no option but to dispense with her services.

And firmly gathering all of his resolve, resolutely determined not to flinch in the face of any subtle hints or insinuations, he accompanied these last words with a direct glance at this woman who, in his estimation, might be threatening him, and looked her straight in the face.

But the look on Crescenz's face, as she raised her eyes from the floor, was merely that of a wounded animal that has just seen the pack of hounds breaking out of the bushes in front of it. 'Thankin' you, sir,' she managed to say almost inaudibly, 'I'll be on me way . . . and won't be troublin yer Lordship any more.' Whereupon slowly, without turning, she shuffled out of the room, shoulders now sinking, her steps stiff and wooden.

In the evening, when the Baron returned from the opera and picked up the mail from his desk, he noticed something strange and square-shaped lying there. Turning up the light, he saw that it was a carved wooden box of rustic design. It was not locked: what lay inside, neatly arranged, were all the little things that Crescenz had ever received from him, those few cards that came from the hunt, two theatre tickets, a silver ring, the complete stack of her banknotes, and in among these things he found a snapshot that had been taken twenty years earlier in the Tyrol, and in it her eyes, clearly startled by the flash, stared with that same wounded, afflicted expression that they had had when she took her leave of him a few hours earlier.

Somewhat bemused, the Baron pushed the box to one side and went out to ask the servant what these belongings of Crescenz could be doing on his desk. The servant immediately offered to call his adversary and require her to explain herself. But Crescenz was not to be found in the kitchen, or in any other part of the house. It was only the next day, when they heard the police report that a woman about forty years old had committed suicide by jumping from the Danube Canal bridge, that the two of them no longer needed to ask where Leporella had fled.

Buchmendel

Back again in Vienna, returning from a visit to one of the outer districts, I was caught under a sudden unexpected cloudburst; people had to take refuge from the fierce downpour and run for safety into doorways and shelters, and I too quickly looked round for somewhere to take cover. Fortunately you'll find a coffee house on just about every street corner in Vienna; I hurried over to the one I saw right opposite, my hat dripping and my shoulders already drenched. I went in, and the place turned out to be one of those typical old-style suburban cafés, completely lacking any of the new-fangled trappings found in your German-style inner-city music venues. It was traditional bourgeois Viennese, filled with the kind of ordinary local people who are more interested in the newspapers than the pastries. It was already evening, and by now the air in the place, no doubt sticky enough at the best of times, appeared heavily marbled with blue smoke rings, and yet all seemed clean enough, what with the obviously new mock-velvet sofas and the shining new aluminium cash-register. In my haste I hadn't taken in the name, which I could have seen outside, but why should I have taken any interest in this anyway? Now I was sitting in the warmth, peering impatiently through the smoke-tinted blue of the windows and wondering how long it would take for this irritating shower to be so kind as to allow me to manage a few more kilometres.

So there I sat with nothing else to occupy me, and before long I succumbed to that languid inertia which the interior of every Viennese café stealthily emits with narcotic effect on its customers. In this state of mental vacuity I glanced around at the others present, one by one. The artificial light, combined with the smoky haze in the room, cast an unhealthy grey shadow around all their eyes. I looked at the young woman sitting at the till, and how she mechanically put out the sugar and spoons for each coffee cup to be distributed by the waiter, and half-consciously and without much interest I read the completely uninspiring advertisements on the walls. I was, in fact, almost beginning to enjoy this mindless diversion when suddenly, and in a curious way, I was awakened from my torpor by an ill-defined inner stirring, rather like the first stage of a mild toothache when you can't yet say for certain whether it is on the right or the left, or in the upper or lower jaw; I merely felt a vague tension, an indeterminate sense of unease. You see, all of a sudden – I couldn't have said how – it dawned on me that I must have been in this place once before, years earlier, and that some distant memory connected me with these walls, chairs, tables, this same smoke-filled room.

But the more I racked my mind trying to recover the memory, the more mischievously and annoyingly it eluded me, like a jellyfish glimmering dimly in the nethermost regions of my consciousness and just too far away for me to grab hold of it. In vain I examined each and every item of furnishing; yes, there were some things I didn't recognize at all, for instance the cash-register with its bright ringing sound as it finished its sums, and the imitation rosewood wall-covering; these must have been more recent fittings. But all the same, I knew for certain I had been here twenty years ago or more, and there was some definite trace, however hidden, of my former self remaining here like a long overgrown old nail buried in a tree trunk. I strained every sense within me to probe both the room and my own consciousness, but I simply could not for the life of me get there and recapture that lost memory buried deep at the back of my mind.

It was vexing, the way it always is when you are compelled by some failing to face the shortcomings and imperfections of your mental powers. But I refused to give up hope. All it needed, I was sure, was some tiny mnemonic hook. My memory works in a curious way, at once both good and bad; on the one hand it can be contrary and stubborn, but then again it can be unbelievably faithful. It swallows up the really important matters, whether events or faces, be they things I have read or those I have personally experienced; it completely buries them in its dark recesses, giving nothing up from this underworld unless forced to do so, and certainly not by any simple exertion of will. But the minutest little jog, a picture postcard for example, or a few lines written on an envelope, a scorched sheet of newspaper or the like, would be enough to haul up what I'd forgotten, like a fish at the end of the line; up it would leap again, completely fresh and alive, from the dark surface of the water. And then I would recall every detail of a person I'd met, his mouth, the gap showing between his teeth on the left side when he laughs, not to mention the brittle sound of the laugh itself, and the accompanying twitch of his moustache, and how a quite new face appears as a result – all of this I see at once before me, with absolute clarity, and I will remember for years to come every word that person addressed to me. But if I am to see and feel past events in this way, I will always need something to spark my senses, some small assistance from actual reality.

And so on this occasion I closed my eyes in order to concentrate harder and shape, and eventually grasp, that mysterious little hook that I so badly needed. But still nothing came. Nothing whatsoever! Lost for good! And I so deeply resented the wretched, quirky memory machine I had between my temples that I could have struck my own forehead with my fists, the way people sometimes take it out on a faulty slot machine that fails to deliver what they've paid for. No, I could sit here no longer like this, so infuriated was I by my failure of recollection; in sheer annoyance I got to my feet, intending to take some air. But then, strangely enough, the moment I took my first steps across the room, I experienced the first flickering glimmer. On the right, next to the till, I remembered, there must be a way through to another room, windowless and with only artificial lighting. Yes, I was right: there it was; the wallpaper was different now, but unmistakably the proportions were as I remembered, a rectangular space, the precise contours being rather blurred in my mind but still those of that back room, the games room.

Instinctively I looked around for particular features, and as I did so my nerves tingled in joyful anticipation of soon knowing all. Two billiard tables lay idle, like stagnant mud pools covered in green algae, and in the corners were small tables, at one of which two councillors, or perhaps professors, were playing chess. In another corner, just next to the iron stove, where you went through to get to the telephone, there was another small square table. It was seeing this that suddenly brought it all back to me. Yes, of course! This was Mendel's place! Jacob Mendel, 'Buchmendel', Mendel the book man, *his* place; I was back here again twenty years on, here in his headquarters, so to speak, the Café Gluck on the upper Alserstrasse. Jacob Mendel! How could I have forgotten him for such an unconscionably long time, that most singular of characters, a legend of a man, a Wonder of the World in a class of his own, a name to conjure with in university society and in a small, rarefied circle – how could I have let him fade from my memory, that sorcerer of the book world who used to sit right over there every single day from dawn to dusk, a veritable icon of erudition, the fame of the Café Gluck personified?

It took me no longer than this one brief moment of reflection, of turning my vision back in on myself, for my rekindled memory to present to me the most vivid possible image of his inimitable figure. I saw him at once in perfect clarity, just as he had been, sitting at the square table, its discoloured grey marble top constantly heaped with piles of books and papers. There he was, steadfast and imperturbable, his bespectacled eyes hypnotically glued to some book, murmuring and humming as he read, his head and its poorly polished flecked pate swaying gently to and fro, as it had first learned to do at the cheder, his Jewish junior school back in the East. At this table – never at any other – he would pore over his books and his catalogues, much as he would have been taught to read his Talmud at school, singing in a low voice, swaying all the while like a dark-clad rocking cradle. Yes, a cradle indeed, for just as this rhythmical, hypnotic rocking enables a small child to fall asleep and escape the world, so in the belief of those pious brethren the soul can move more easily into the grace of mental absorption if the otherwise idle body is kept swaying back and forth. And, truth to tell, Jacob Mendel saw and heard nothing at all of what was happening all around him. Right next to him there was the rowdy babble of the billiard players, while markers ran around, the telephone rang, someone would come to scrub the floor, and someone else might be getting the stove lit. Mendel noticed none of this. Once I remember a live coal falling out, and you could already smell it smouldering and burning its way through the parquet floor before one of the guests noticed the infernal stench and, realizing the danger, rushed over to put it out. Did Jacob Mendel, sitting almost on top of the fire, have any inkling of what was going on? Not a bit of it, though he was already succumbing to the fumes. No, he read the way others prayed, or the way gamblers play at cards, or drunks stare vacantly into space. He read with a kind of absorption so moving for me that, ever since then, other people's reading has seemed profane in comparison. In this little Galician bookdealer, Jacob Mendel, I had as a young man, for the first time in my life, encountered the mysteriousness of absolute concentration – something shared by the artist and the scholar, by the truly wise and the completely mad, that tragic combination of joy and affliction that comes with total obsession.

I was taken to see this man by a senior colleague from the university. At the time I was researching the Paracelsian physician and magnetizer Franz Mesmer, a figure little known even today, and I have to say I was having only limited success. The available relevant sources proved inadequate, and the librarian, whom I, the innocent novice reader, had asked for guidance, had churlishly informed me that such bibliographical work was for me to pursue, not for him. That was when I first heard the name Mendel from my colleague. 'We'll go together and see Mendel,' he promised. 'He knows everything; he'll get hold of anything you need. He'll produce the most recondite book from the most forgotten German bookseller. You won't find a better brain anywhere in Vienna, and what's more he's a real one-off, the lone survivor of a dying breed, a bibliosaur!'

And so off we went together to the Café Gluck, and sure enough, there he sat, Book-Mendel himself: the spectacles, the untrimmed beard and black garb, rocking this way and that as he read, like a bush swaying darkly in the wind. We went up to him, and he didn't notice us. He just sat reading, with his upper body swaying pagoda-like over the table while behind him his threadbare black gaberdine coat hung from a hook, pockets bulging with journals and slips of paper. To announce our presence, my friend gave a forthright cough. Even then Mendel noticed nothing; his spectacles remained fixedly close to his book. After a little while my friend knocked hard on the table, as loudly as you might hammer on a front door. The sound was enough to make Mendel look up and instinctively push his ungainly steel-rimmed spectacles up onto his forehead; under his shaggy, ash-grey brows we saw the two extraordinary eyes peering at us, small, black, alert eyes, as agile in their movement as a snake's tongue. My friend introduced me, and I explained what I was looking for, starting – this was a ploy expressly recommended by my friend – with a show of strong irritation over the librarian who had been unwilling to help me. Mendel leaned back and studiously cleared his throat. 'Unwilling, was he? Unable is more like it, I'd say! The man's a dunce, a worn- out, grey-haired old ass! I've known him, God help me, a good twenty years, and in that time he's learned nothing. People like him – all they're good for is pocketing their wages! Tell those Herr Doktors they'd be better off heaving bricks around rather than sitting over their books.'

With this emphatic unburdening of his heart the ice was broken; now at last he good-naturedly motioned to me to sit down at the marble-topped table strewn with notes and memoranda, this altar, as it were, of bibliophiles' revelations, hitherto quite unknown to me. I hastily told him what I wanted, namely other works from Mesmer's time about magnetism, as well as any later books or tracts arguing for and against Mesmer himself. No sooner had I finished than Mendel closed his left eye tightly for a moment, as if taking aim before shooting. But this gesture of concentrated attentiveness lasted no more than a second, and then out it came all at once, with complete fluency, as if he were reading from an invisible catalogue – a list of at least two or three dozen books, each with details of place, year of publication, and an approximate idea of price. I was dumbfounded. Although I had had some preparation, this was quite unexpected. My amazement, though, seemed to please him, for he immediately went on to play the most wondrous extensions and variations on the theme of my inquiry upon the keyboard of his expert bibliographical memory. Might I also wish to know something about the somnambulists, and the first trials of hypnosis, and perhaps Gassner and his exorcisms, or Christian Science, or maybe Madame Blavatsky? Once again, out came a stream of names, titles, descriptions, and I now finally realized what a unique marvel of memory I had come upon in the person of Jacob Mendel, a veritable encyclopedia, a walking universal catalogue. Utterly stunned, I gazed at this bibliographical phenomenon that had wound up here in the unprepossessing, not to say somewhat scruffy, guise of a little Galician book dealer; he had reeled off some eighty names at speed, hardly even having to think about it. Still, deep down he was obviously quite pleased at having played his trump card; he now wiped his glasses with a cloth that had presumably once been white. To disguise my astonishment a little, I asked tentatively which of these books he could obtain for me, should the need arise.

'Well, we'll see what we can do,' he grunted. 'Come back tomorrow. Your Mendel will come up with something for you between now and then, and what hasn't shown up we can look for somewhere else. A bit of *nous* will get you a long way.'

I thanked him courteously, but in the very act of trying to be polite I stumbled into a moment of immense stupidity by suggesting to him that I might note down the titles of the books I wished to have. As I was speaking I felt the warning elbow in my side; it was my friend, but too late. Mendel had already shot a glance at me – and what a glance! – both triumphant and offended, disdainful and superior, a truly regal look such as Shakespeare's Macbeth might have given when Macduff invites the invincible hero to throw in the towel without fighting. But then again he laughed for a moment, his outsized Adam's apple rippling curiously up and down; clearly he'd had some difficulty swallowing back a particularly blunt reply. Of course any imaginable bluntness on good, honest Buchmendel's part would have been entirely justified. Only a stranger, a know-nothing – an *amhorez*, as he would have put it in Yiddish – could have been foolish enough to make such an offensive suggestion as writing down a book title for Mendel of all people, as one might for a novice bookshop junior or library clerk, as if that incomparable, adamantine bibliophile's brain had ever needed any such crude assistance. Only later did I see how insulting my supposedly courteous offer must have been to the unique genius of this man; for Jacob Mendel, this small, hunched Galician Jew, completely enfolded in the tangle of his own beard, was indeed a Titan of the memory. Behind the chalky, grimy forehead, and what looked like its coating of grey moss, there stood in invisible lettering on the pages of his mind, as if stamped in steel type, every name and detail that had ever appeared on the title page of a printed book. You only had to mention a book once, whether printed yesterday or two hundred years ago, and he would immediately tell you, with unerring accuracy, its place of publication, the name of the publisher, and both its new and second-hand price, and he also remembered with faultless precision the cover design, the illustrations and any related facsimiles. He saw every work, whether he had held it in his own hands or merely seen it once at a distance in a bookseller's window or library, with the same clarity of vision as that of the creative artist who sees both the images of his own inner realm and those as yet invisible ones of others' worlds. He could recall the sale of a book two years earlier in Vienna for four crowns when he saw the same book offered in a Regensburg dealer's catalogue for six marks, and in addition he would know who the purchaser was. No, Jacob Mendel never forgot a title or a number; he knew every plant, every minute living organism, every stone in the ever-oscillating, protean bookseller's universe. His knowledge in every subject exceeded that of the specialists; he had mastered the contents of library collections better than the librarians, knew by heart the stocks of most firms better than their owners, despite all their notes and card indexes, and all the while the only resource he had to call on was the magic of memory, this incomparable mental recall, of which no adequate account could be given except by looking at a hundred different instances of its working. Of course, this faculty of his could only have been schooled and honed to a level of such demonic infallibility through what is the eternal secret of any perfect accomplishment, namely concentration. Beyond the books themselves, this remarkable man knew nothing of the world; for him, phenomena only acquired true reality once they had been cast in type, once they had been brought together in a book and thereby, in a way, sterilized. But even then he did not read these books for what they conveyed, that is for their intellectual and narrative content. His passion was roused only by the name and the price, by the physical appearance and a first title page. Ultimately it was thus unproductive and uncreative, essentially just a list of a hundred thousand names and titles stamped on a mammal's brain tissue instead of the pages of a book catalogue, but this specifically antiquarian memory of Jacob Mendel was nevertheless, in its unique perfection, a phenomenon comparable with Napoleon's memory for facial characteristics, or Mezzofanti's for languages, or one might think of Lasker for chess openings or Busoni in music. Had it been professionally engaged in a public forum, say in a university seminar, that brain could have instructed, and indeed astounded, thousands, or hundreds of thousands, of students and scholars, and could have brought great benefit to the learned world, an incomparable gain for those public treasure houses we call libraries. But such a higher world was to this diminutive, uneducated Galician book-pedlar, who had mastered little outside his Talmud learning, permanently closed, and so these fabulous abilities of his could make their mark only as an esoteric kind of knowledge on offer at the back-room marble-topped table in the Café Gluck. One day, though, come the great psychologist who has the patience and perseverance to do what has not been attempted, or at any rate achieved, up till now, that is to chart and classify all the types and subtypes and varieties of that wonderful faculty we call memory, in the way that Buffon managed to order and group the divisions of the animal kingdom, then he will find that he has to give some thought to Jacob Mendel, supreme expert in prices and titles, nameless master in the field of antiquarian book lore.

As for his business, it is true that especially among the ignorant Jacob Mendel passed for nothing more than a small-time book trader. On Sundays the same regular advertisement appeared each week in the *Neue Freie Presse* and the *Neues Wiener Tagblatt*: 'Old books for sale, best prices paid, come now to Mendel, Obere Alserstrasse', followed by a telephone number, which was in fact the number of the Café Gluck. He would forage around in the storehouses, and once a week cart his booty back to his head-quarters, helped by an elderly assistant with a Kaiser-style beard; from there he would take it all on elsewhere, because he lacked the necessary official permit for keeping a regular bookshop and had to remain a small-time trader. It was an occupation with small returns. Students sold him their textbooks, and these would pass periodically through his hands from one academic year to the next. Otherwise he would find and procure any works that were required, with a small mark-up. You could take his advice without having to pay much at all; in any case money meant little, if anything, in his realm. He was never seen in anything other than that shabby old gabardine. Morning, afternoon and evening he took a glass of milk and two bread rolls, and at midday they brought over something small for him from the restaurant. He didn't smoke or play cards; it could even be said that he didn't really live; it was just the two eyes behind his thick glasses that truly lived, keeping this enigmatic being's brain constantly fed with words, titles and names. And that soft, fertile brain tissue greedily sucked in the nourishment, as does a meadow the innu-merable raindrops that fall on it. Mendel had no interest in people, and of all human passions he perhaps knew only the one that is most human of all, namely vanity. If someone came to him wanting information, having tried all other avenues to the point of exhaustion, and if he was instantly able to answer the query, that was enough to satisfy Mendel, indeed to please him, in addition, perhaps, to the fact that in Vienna and elsewhere there were a few dozen who respected, and needed, his expertise. In every one of those vast sprawling conurbations that we call cities, with their millions of inhabitants, you can find, scattered in a very few places, a small number of facets that reflect one and the same universe in miniature, invisible to the majority and valued only by the connoisseur who recognizes and shares his brethren's passions. These booklovers all knew Jacob Mendel. Just as those who needed advice about music scores would go to Eusebius Mandyczewski at the Gesellschaft der Musikfreunde and find that friendly figure sitting there in his grey cap surrounded by his files and scores, ready with a smile on his face to solve the most intractable problems, and just as today anyone seeking information on the Altwiener Theater would automatically go straight to the omniscient 'Father' Glossy, so with just the same trusting certainty the few surviving stalwart Viennese bibliophiles of those days, the moment they found they had a particularly hard nut to crack, would make a pilgrimage to the Café Gluck to find Jacob Mendel.

To watch Mendel at work in such consultations was for me, young as I was and curious about everything, a particular kind of pleasure. He would normally turn his nose up at any run-of-the-mill book presented to him, merely snapping the cover shut and muttering, 'Two crowns', but if what came before him was a rarity, or even perhaps a unique exemplar, he would sit up respectfully and put a sheet of paper under it; on such occasions you could immediately see that he was ashamed of his dirty, ink-stained fingers and blackened nails. Then he would start tenderly, carefully, turning the pages one by one, and showing enormous reverence as he did so. At these moments no one would think of disturbing him, any more than one would intrude on a true religious believer at prayer. And, to be quite honest, there was indeed something redolent of the religious ceremonial in his way of examining, touching, smelling and appraising, if you saw the ritual manner in which he followed these stages through. His crooked back moved this way and that while he muttered and grunted away, scratched his head and emitted a strange series of primal sounds, such as a protracted, almost fearful 'Ah!' and 'Oh!' of rapturous admiration, and then again a rapid, startled 'Oi' or 'Oi vey!' if it turned out that a page was missing or had fallen victim to bookworm. At length he would weigh the volume respectfully in his hands, and sniff at the rectangular surface, taking in its scent with his eyes half closed, every bit as rapt as a sentimental young girl smelling a rose. It goes without saying that in the course of this complex procedure the owner of the item had to be very patient. But once the examination was complete, Mendel very willingly, indeed very enthusiastically, imparted the required information, with the bonus every time of wide-ranging anecdotes and dramatic accounts of prices fetched by other copies of the work in question. At these moments he seemed to brighten, to become younger and livelier. There was only one thing that could seriously embitter him, and that was to be offered money by some novice in return for an appraisement. That would make him recoil, clearly offended, like an expert gallery curator who has just given an opinion and had a tip pressed into his hand by an American tourist passing through. The point was that having a precious book in his hand meant the same to Mendel as would for others a first meeting with an attractive young woman. These occasions were his Platonic nights of love. He was in thrall to books, never to money.

Distinguished collectors, among them the founder of the Princeton University library, accordingly tried, but in vain, to hire him as a consultant and buyer. Mendel always declined. The Café Gluck was the only conceivable place for him. Thirty-three years earlier he had arrived in Vienna from the East, a hunched young man with a soft, black beard still downy on his cheeks and ringlets hanging by his temples; he was to study here for the rabbinate, but before long he had forsaken the severe One and Only Jehovah and transferred his devotion to the resplendent thousandfold pantheon of books. That was when he had first stumbled upon the Café Gluck, which gradually became his place of work, his headquarters, his post office – in short, his entire world. Like a lone astronomer watching the myriad stars every night through the tiny round lens of his telescope, observing their mysterious journeys and the transformations in their bewildering complexity, and how they would disappear and then come back to life, so would Jacob Mendel peer out through his glasses from his square table into the world of books, into that other universe, that world above our mundane existence, eternally revolving, ever regenerating.

It was clear that he was highly respected in the Café Gluck; we for our part felt that the café owed its reputation more to its invisible professor's chair, as we might have said, than to its eponymous musical patron, the composer of *Alceste* and *Iphigénie*, Christoph Willibald Gluck. Mendel was as integral a part of the furnishings as the old cherry-wood counter or the two crudely patched billiard tables or the copper coffee pot, and his table was granted the protection of a sanctuary, largely because his numerous customers and inquirers were always strongly, if cordially, encouraged by the management to place an order, and in this way the greater financial beneficiary of Mendel's expertise was the large leather money pouch worn about his waist by head waiter Deubler. In return, admittedly, Mendel did enjoy a number of privileges. The telephone was at his disposal, he had his mail collected, and all his orders were taken care of. The nice old lady who looked after the toilet brushed his coat for him and took his washing to the laundry once a week. For him, and for no one else, the midday meal could be brought over from the nearby restaurant, and every morning the proprietor, Herr Standhartner, would come in person to his table to welcome him (though it must be said that more often than not Mendel was already buried in his books and quite oblivious of this greeting). He would enter the café punctually at half past seven in the morning and didn't leave until the lights were put out. He never spoke to the other guests or read a newspaper, and any changes in the place passed him by. When Herr Standhartner once asked him courteously whether he now found reading easier under the new electric light than by the pale and irregular glow of the old gas lamps, he just stared in bemusement at the glass bulb; this novel development, despite the several days of noise and hammering that had gone into the installation, had wholly escaped his attention. Only through the two circles of his spectacles, only through these sparkling, imbibing glass lenses, were the countless thousands of tiny black organisms of the letters filtered into his brain; anything else that happened around him simply passed over his head like so much meaningless ambient noise. The truth was that he had spent over thirty years, all the waking hours of his life, here at this square table and nowhere else, reading, comparing, calculating, in a continuous unbroken dream interrupted only by real sleep.

I was therefore overcome by a kind of deep misgiving when I saw that same marble-topped table, at which Jacob Mendel's oracular utterances had been delivered, lying gloomily empty here in the same room, bare as a tombstone. Only now that I had grown older did I appreciate how much is lost along with such a person when he departs this life, first of all because the value of anything truly unique grows greater by the day in this world of ours, a world which is becoming irremediably uniform. But in addition to that, the younger and inexperienced man I had been had, out of some deep, intuitive feeling, become greatly attached to Jacob Mendel. In him I had for the first time in my life gained an inkling of one great mystery, namely that anything that is truly special and exceptional in this life is, as I have said, attained only through intense inner concentration, in fact by an almost unearthly monomania close to madness. Moreover I had come to understand that a pure life of the intellect, a total abstraction in a single idea, can after all still be realized in our day and age, a no less profound immersion than that of the Indian *yogi* or the medieval monk in his cell; indeed, I saw that it could be found under an electric light near the telephone in a local café, and as a young man I had seen this exemplified more truly in a completely obscure little bookdealer than in any of the poets and writers of our times. And yet I had managed to forget all of this – admittedly in the war years, and at a time when I was similarly immersed in my own work. But now, thinking of him as I stood before that empty table, I felt a kind of shame, as well as a revived curiosity.

Where was he now, and what had happened to him? I called the waiter and asked. No, he replied, unfortunately he did not know the person; no one of this name had frequented the café in his time. Perhaps the head waiter would have more information. The head waiter, preceded by his pot belly, lumbered over to me, hesitated, and thought for a moment; no, he too knew no Herr Mendel. But could I be thinking of Herr Mandl, the Herr Mandl from the haberdashery shop in the Floriangasse? Hearing this brought a bitter taste to my mouth, a taste of the transitory: what is the point of living, if the wind dogs our feet and blows away any last trace of us the moment we leave? For thirty or even forty years a man had breathed, read, pondered, spoken in the small space of this room, while it took only three or four years to pass before 'there arose a new king over Egypt, which knew not Joseph'. And so the Café Gluck knew not Mendel any more, Jacob

Mendel, Buchmendel, Mendel of the Book! I was close to anger when I asked the head waiter if I could speak with Herr Standhartner, or if there was some other old employee still working there. Oh, Herr Standhartner, good heavens! Herr Stadhartner had sold the business long ago. He'd passed away, and the old head waiter, he was now living at his little place near Krems on the Danube. No, there was no one else here from those days. But wait . . . yes! There was one, Frau Sporschil was still here, the toilet lady, or 'chocolate lady' as she was sometimes more vulgarly known; though she surely wouldn't remember individual customers. But my immediate thought was: no one forgets a Jacob Mendel. I asked if she would come and see me.

And come she did, Frau Sporschil, white-haired, dishevelled, her dropsical feet taking the necessary steps out from her little realm out at the back, hastily wiping her reddened hands on an old cloth. She must have been just now sweeping her dingy little quarters, or cleaning windows. I could tell at once from her diffident manner that she was feeling uncomfortable being called so suddenly to the more respectable front room and standing under its big electric light bulbs. At first she looked up at me, cowering distrustfully and eyeing me cautiously as if wondering what I could be wanting with her – probably nothing good. But the moment I asked after Jacob Mendel she stared at me with her eyes actually filling with tears and her shoulders heaving.

'My God, poor Herr Mendel, and there's still someone thinking of him now! Yes, of course, poor Herr Mendel!' She was almost weeping, so moved was she, as old people so often are when reminded of their younger days and some long-forgotten acquaintance. I asked if he were still alive.

'Heavens, no, poor Herr Mendel – it must be five or six years since he passed away, no, even seven. Such a nice man, a good man he was. And when I think just how long it was I knew him, it was all of twenty-five years and more, he was already here when I first came. A crying shame it was, the way they let him die.' As she spoke she became more and more animated. She asked if I was a relation of his; no one else had ever shown any interest or asked about him. Didn't I know, then, what had happened to him?

No, I assured her, I didn't know anything; could she please tell me the whole story? The good woman now became shy and embarrassed, repeatedly wiping her damp hands on the towel. I could understand why; she felt awkward, the toilet lady with her grimy apron and tousled white hair, to be standing there in the middle of the café, and she kept looking anxiously to right and left to see if one of the waiters might be listening. I suggested we go into the back room, to Mendel's old table, where she could tell me everything she knew. She nodded appreciatively, thankful for my understanding, and led the way, the old lady already a little unsteady as she walked, with me following. I noticed the puzzled look in the eyes of the two waiters, who sensed some connection between us; a few of the other guests also seemed surprised at this odd pairing of individuals. We went over and sat down at the marble-topped table, and there she gave me her account – later supplemented with some further details by another source – of the demise of Jacob Mendel, Buchmendel.

Well then, she told me, he had continued to come to the café after the war broke out, arriving at half past seven every morning, day in, day out. He sat right here at this table, just as before, and studied all day long. And they'd all had the feeling, and often spoken about it to each other, that he didn't have the faintest idea there was a war going on. She assumed I remembered how he never looked at any of the newspapers, and never talked to anybody else. But even when the newspaper vendors were raising hell with their shouting about the latest extra editions, and all the other people were running up to buy them, he never even got up from the table, and never listened. He didn't notice that the waiter Franz was missing – he'd actually been killed at Gorlice – and had no idea that Herr Standhartner's son had been taken prisoner at Przemysl; he never said a word about how the quality of the bread was worsening by the day, and never complained that instead of milk he was being given some ghastly kind of fig coffee. Only on one occasion did he appear surprised that so few students were coming to the Café Gluck these days. 'Dear me, the poor man, his only love, his only interest in this world was his books.'

But then one day the disaster struck. At eleven o'clock that morning an ordinary policeman turned up with a member of the secret police; the latter revealed the badge in his buttonhole and asked whether a certain Jacob Mendel frequented the place. They both went straight over to Mendel's table. Mendel, in his innocence, still thought that they wanted to sell some books, or had some question for him. But they told him there and then that he had to go with them, and then they took him away. It had been a real scandal for the café, said Frau Sporschil, and all the guests had gathered around poor Herr Mendel as he stood there between the two officers with his glasses pushed up under his hair, looking first at one and then the other and not understanding at all what they could be wanting with him. She herself had told the policeman on the spot that this must be some mistake; a man like Herr Mendel couldn't hurt a fly. At that the secret police officer had screamed at her not to meddle in official business, and then the two had led Mendel away. It was a long time before he was seen again, a good two years. To this day Frau Sporschil didn't know what they had wanted from him. 'But I swear to God, Herr Mendel can't have done anything wrong. They made a mistake, I'll lay my life on that. It was a crime against that poor, innocent man, a crime!'

And she was right, the good, kindly Frau Sporschil. Our friend Jacob Mendel really had done nothing wrong; all that he was guilty of (and I only learned all the details later) was a crass, if rather touching, act of stupidity, in itself quite improbably idiotic in those insane days, and explicable only if one considers the man's total absorption and uniquely unworldly character. One day, apparently, a postcard had been intercepted and had found its way into the office of the military censors, whose duties involved overseeing all correspondence with other countries. The postcard was written and signed by a certain Jacob Mendel, and duly franked for sending abroad, but – and this was the unbelievable thing – the country it was intended for happened to be an enemy state. The missive was addressed to a Jean Labourdaire, Bookdealer, Paris, Quai de Grenelle, and in it one Jacob Mendel complained of not having received the eight most recent issues of the monthly journal *Bulletin bibliographique de la France*, despite his advance payment of the annual subscription. The lower-ranking official employed in the censorship department, in peacetime a secondary school teacher by profession specializing in Romance languages, now having changed into the blue uniform of the reserves, was taken aback to be handed such a document. No doubt some idiotic kind of joke, he thought. Every week two thousand letters must have crossed his desk, which he had to comb through meticulously in search of any suspicious communications or expressions suggesting espionage; but nothing had ever come his way as absurd as this, that someone in Austria should casually write to an address in France, that is to say feel completely comfortable in posting a card to a country at war with his own, as if the borders between the two had not been sealed with barbed wire since 1914, and as if every god-given day the nations of France, Germany, Austria and Russia were not violently reducing each other's male populations by several thousands. His immediate reaction was therefore to put the postcard away in his desk drawer as a mere curiosity, without thinking to refer the absurdity any higher up. A few weeks later, however, another card appeared before him, also written by Jacob Mendel, this time to a bookseller by the name of John Aldridge, Holborn Square, London, requesting that he find for him the most recent numbers of the *Antiquarian*; again, the signature was that of this curious individual Jacob Mendel, and with endearing naivety the full address was added. At this point our uniformed schoolmaster friend began to feel slightly uncomfortable in his official capacity. Was there some secret encoded meaning beneath this doltish joke? Well, anyway, he got up and clicked his heels and deposited both cards on the Major's desk. The latter first shrugged: how odd! Then he alerted the police and told them to investigate whether this fellow Jacob Mendel actually existed. Within an hour Jacob Mendel was arrested and led before the Major, still bewildered and uncomprehending. The Major laid the mysterious postcards out in front of him. Did he admit that he was the sender? Roused by the severe tone of the question, but more so at having been rudely interrupted while consulting an important catalogue, Mendel's response was sharp, almost rude: of course he had written the cards. Did one not have the right to claim what one had paid for in advance? The Major swivelled round in his seat to talk to the Lieutenant at the desk beside his. They exchanged knowing looks: here's a complete idiot! The Major thought for a little while whether he should just give this simpleton a sharp dressing down and throw him out on his ear, or rather treat the matter more seriously. Whenever this kind of doubt or dilemma arises, the natural first step chosen by almost any office will be to file a report. Writing a report is always a good idea; even if it leads nowhere, it'll do no harm – at most, there'll be just another page or two of verbiage to add to the millions already in existence.

Alas, in the present case harm *was* done, and to a poor, innocent person; for the third question, and its answer, brought something fateful to light. The first demand was for his name: Jacob, *recte* Jainkeff, Mendel. Second question, occupation: pedlar (he had no bookdealer's licence, only a permit for street-trading). The third brought the catastrophe. Place of birth? Jacob Mendel named a small town near Petrikau. The Major raised his eyebrows. Petrikau, that was in Russian Poland, wasn't it? Near the border? Suspicious, this, very suspicious! The Major's tone hardened. When did you acquire Austrian citizenship? Mendel's glasses stared at him in bemusement, not quite understanding the question. 'Answer me, out with it!' shouted the Major. 'Do you have papers? Where are they?' Mendel replied that he had no papers apart from his pedlar's permit. The Major's brow furrowed more sternly. Mendel should explain, once and for all: what was his nationality? What had been his father's? Austrian or Russian? In complete calm again, Mendel replied: Russian, of course. And he himself? Oh, well, he answered, he had slipped over the Russian border thirty-three years ago, and had been living in Vienna ever since. The Major was becoming more and more exercised. So when, then, had he acquired Austrian citizenship? 'Why should I?' Mendel replied. He had never bothered with such things. So he was still a Russian citizen? And Mendel, who had been bored by this tedious line of questioning from the outset, answered unconcernedly, 'Yes, you could say so.'

The Major threw himself back so firmly that his chair gave out a groan. So it had come to this! In Vienna, the Austrian capital, while a war was raging, at the end of the year 1915, after Tarnów and the great offensive, here was a Russian walking around free and unimpeded, writing letters to France and England, and meanwhile the police took no interest whatsoever. And those halfwits in the newspapers were writing how surprised they were that Conrad von Hötzendorf didn't go straight to Warsaw, and the people on the general staff were astonished that spies were passing information to Russia on every troop movement.

The Lieutenant had also got up now and was standing at his desk. The conversation quickly changed into an interrogation. Why had Mendel not immediately presented himself to the authorities as a foreigner? Mendel, still unaware of what was really at stake, replied in his sing-song Jewish intonation: 'Why would I suddenly have to go and do that?' The Major took this retort, a returned question, as a challenge, and in a more threatening tone asked, 'Did you not see the public notices?' No, said Mendel. And he hadn't read a single newspaper either? No.

The two officers stared at Jacob Mendel, who was now beginning to sweat apprehensively, as if a visitor from another planet had suddenly landed in front of them. The telephone rang, typewriters rattled away, orderlies ran around, and Jacob Mendel was transferred to a cell in the garrison, to be sent on from there to a camp with the next batch of prisoners. When ordered to follow the two escorting soldiers, he stared in incomprehension. But not knowing what they wanted from him, he was still not very greatly alarmed. After all, what harm could the man with the gold on his collar and the grating voice have in mind for him? In his higher world of books, there were no wars, no misunderstandings; in that world there was only eternal knowledge, and the search for more of it, knowledge of words and figures, names and titles. He therefore trotted off compliantly down the stairs between the two soldiers. Only when they were at the police station, and he was ordered to empty his pockets and surrender all his books and his briefcase, which contained hundreds of important notes and addresses of customers, did he begin to flail around in a rage, so that they had to restrain him. But as they did so his glasses fell from his forehead onto the floor, and this magical telescope that showed him the sublime world of the mind was shattered into countless pieces. Two days later he was transported, in his thin summer coat, to a concentration camp for Russian prisoners of war at Komorn.

There is no surviving testimony to the mental horrors Jacob Mendel must have suffered during those two years in a prison camp without books – his beloved books – and without money, among all his resigned, coarse, largely illiterate fellow prisoners in this vast human dungheap. We have no witness to what he had to endure when separated from his unique higher realm, deprived of its ethereal element like an eagle with clipped wings. But little by little the world, emerging sober again from its insanity, has come to know that, of all the barbarities and criminal infringements of that war, none was more senseless, more gratuitous, and thereby morally more indefensible than the rounding-up and internment behind barbed wire of wholly innocent civilians for the most part too old for military service, who had for many years made a foreign country their home and, out of a trusting faith in the basic rules of hospitality which are to be found honoured in even the remotest regions on earth, had failed to take the opportunity to flee in good time. This crime against civilization was committed with equally callous negligence in France, Germany and England, indeed on the soil of every part of this Europe of ours when it descended into such folly. And perhaps Jacob Mendel would himself, like countless other innocents thus inhumanly herded together, have fallen wretched victim to madness or dysentery, or starvation or nervous collapse, if a coincidence – and a peculiarly Austrian one – had not brought him, in the nick of time, back to his real world.

Many a time after he disappeared, letters from distinguished customers arrived addressed to him at the Café Gluck. Among the correspondents were, for instance, Count Schönberg, former governor of Styria, a fanatical collector of works on heraldry, and Siegenfeld, who had been Dean of the Theological Faculty, now working on a commentary on St Augustine, and the octogenarian retired Admiral Edler von Pisek, who was engaged in revising his memoirs; all of these were loyal customers who had frequently written to Jacob Mendel at the café. Of the letters a few were redirected to our missing person at the prison camp. And there they fell into the hands of the officer in charge, who as it happened was a good-hearted man and was astonished at the eminence of the acquaintances of this grimy little half-blind Jewish inmate who, having had his spectacles broken, and lacking the money to buy new ones, now sat hunched up in a corner like a mole, grey, eyeless and mute. Surely there must anyway be something special about a man who has friends of that caste! So he allowed Mendel to reply to the letters and ask his patrons to speak up for him. And they did not fail him. With the zealous solidarity always found among true collectors, His Excellency and the Dean brought their best connections into play, and their combined assurances secured the return of Mendel to Vienna in 1917 after his confinement of more than two years, albeit on the condition that he report every day to the police. Nonetheless he was able to return to the free world of his old and tiny narrow attic room, could once again go to view his beloved book displays, and, best of all, could now be back in his 'headquarters'.

Mendel's return to the Café Gluck from a hellish underworld was described for me, from her own observation, by the excellent Frau Sporschil. 'One day – Jesus, Mary and Joseph, I can't believe my own eyes! – the door, it's pushed open, you know, the way it always was with him, just a little bit, and in he hobbles, poor old Herr Mendel! He's got a worn-out old army cloak on, mended all over the place, and something on his head that could once have been a hat he'd probably got out of a rubbish tip. There's no collar on his shirt, and he looked like death, pasty face, grey hair and all, and pitiful thin. Anyhow, in he comes, straight in, just like nothing had happened, says nothing, asks nothing, goes straight over to that table and takes off his coat, not like he used to do, you know, quick and easy, but quite a struggle it was. He hasn't got no books with him this time, he just sits down without a word, and all he does is stare into space with his eyes all empty and worn out. It was only bit by bit, 'cause we gave him all the letters and stuff that had come for him from Germany, that he started reading again. But he was never the same man after that.'

No, he was never again the same, no longer the *miraculum mundi*, the wondrous universal catalogue of books. Everyone who saw him at that time had the same sad story to tell: something seemed irretrievably lost in his otherwise languorous eyes, which now looked asleep whenever he read. Yes, something had been destroyed once and for all; the lightning-fast, ghastly red comet of bloodshed must have crashed into the distant, peaceful star of his world of books. His eyes, for decades accustomed to looking at the gentle, silent printed letters with their graceful, insect-like serifs, must have beheld unutterable horrors in that barbed-wire human enclosure. The lids now heavily overshadowed those once so alert pupils sparkling with irony. Once so lively, now sleepy and red-rimmed, those same eyes languished behind his poorly mended glasses laboriously tied together with thin string. And still more tragic, within that marvellous edifice of his memory some pillar must have collapsed and thrown the entire structure into disorder, for so delicate a thing is the human brain, this mechanism formed of the most subtle of substances, a fine-tuned precision instrument designed to organize all of our knowledge, that the merest blocked capillary, a damaged nerve, a fatigued cell or even so much as a displaced molecule, can finally arrest the entire wonderful harmony of a mind. And in Mendel's memory, that unique keyboard of knowledge, the keys were now sticking after he returned to the café. Every so often someone would come for information, but all he could do was stare with a look of exhaustion, not quite understanding what they were asking; he couldn't hear properly, and anyway would then forget what had been said to him. Mendel was no longer Mendel, just as the world was no longer the world. He no longer swayed back and forward as he used to, wholly engrossed in his reading; now, most of the time, he sat rigidly still, his glasses only mechanically turned towards the book, and nobody could tell whether he was really reading or was simply lost in a world of his own. More than once, according to Frau Sporschil, his head fell heavily onto the book in front of him and he would fall asleep in broad daylight. Sometimes he just went on staring for hours into the pungent light of the acetylene lamp that they had put on his table during those days when the coal ran short. No, this was no longer the celebrated Buchmendel, wonder of the world, but a useless, wearily breathing assemblage of clothes and beard, purposelessly seated on what was once the throne of the Pythian oracle. No longer was he the glory of the Café Gluck, but a source of shame, an unclean, evil-smelling, repellent sight, an embarrassment, an unnecessary parasite.

At least that was the way the new owner of the café, Florian Gurtner, thought of him. Gurtner, a native of Retz, had in the year of scarcity, 1919, enriched himself by doing deals in flour and butter, and more recently had inveigled the upright and trusting Herr Standhartner into selling him the Café Gluck for a paltry eighty thousand crowns, in fast depreciating paper currency. He then pitched in with his sturdy rustic hands and quickly renovated the time-honoured coffee house décor of the place with expensive-looking furnishings, cleverly buying new armchairs at the right moment for worthless money, and installing a marble entrance porch; what's more, he was already in negotiations to take over the neighbouring *lokal* which he could turn into a dance hall as an extension to the Gluck. This hasty programme of improvements was, you can imagine, hardly assisted by the presence of a Galician parasite who remained the sole occupant of one of the tables every single day from morning till evening while consuming no more than two cups of coffee and five bread rolls. To be sure, Standhartner had specially mentioned his old guest in positive terms to Gurtner, and had tried to explain how eminent and important a man this Jacob Mendel was; when they came to discuss the inventory attending upon the sale, he had included Mendel as a lien, as it were, in the contract. However, Florian Gurtner had, alongside the plush furniture and spanking new aluminium cash register, also brought in the solid business instincts typical of those entrepreneurial times and was merely waiting for an excuse to rid himself of this last troublesome remnant of suburban unsightliness from his elegant new establishment.

A good opportunity soon presented itself. Things were not going well for Jacob Mendel; the last of his saved banknotes had been shredded in the paper mill of the Inflation, and his customers had all faded away. A return to small-time book-peddling, climbing stairs, hawking one's wares and scraping a pittance together, all of this was now beyond the strength of the exhausted man. He was in a wretched state, as was obvious from a hundred little indications. Only rarely now did he have food brought over from the restaurant, and he was taking longer and longer to pay the small amounts required for his coffee and bread rolls; once he was a good three weeks overdue. Already at that stage the head waiter was minded to turn him out on the street, had not good Frau Sporschil taken pity and promised to settle the debt herself.

But next month came the real misfortune. Several times by now the new head waiter had noticed a discrepancy when they came to do the tally for the bread and cakes. More rolls regularly turned out to be missing than had been ordered and paid for. His immediate suspicions naturally fell on Mendel; more than once his feeble old jobbing assistant had come to complain about not being paid for half a year or more and hadn't been able to get anything at all out of him. The head waiter was particularly vigilant as a result, and only two days later, lying in ambush behind the fire screen, he managed to catch Mendel in the act, stealthily leaving his table, slipping into the front room and quickly relieving the bread basket of two rolls, which he then greedily wolfed down. When settling the account that evening, Mendel claimed he hadn't eaten any rolls at all that day. The missing items were now explained. The waiter reported the matter forthwith to Herr

Gurtner, and Herr Gurtner, happy to have been handed the long-awaited pretext, bawled mercilessly at Mendel in front of all the customers, accusing him of the theft and making much of his own restraint in not calling the police there and then. But in no uncertain terms he ordered him off the premises immediately, and for good. Jacob Mendel just shivered in fear, said nothing, got up from his chair and stumbled out.

A 'crying shame' was how Frau Sporschil described this departure. 'I'll never forget it, how he stood there with his glasses pushed up on his forehead. White as a sheet he was. Didn't even take the time to put his coat on, though it was January, and you know, that really cold one too. And he left his book lying on the table, he was so frightened. I only saw it there after he'd got up and I wanted to go and give it back to him, but he'd already hobbled to the door; I didn't really feel like following him out into the street, because there was Herr Gurtner standing in the doorway shouting after him, and all the people stopped and gathered round. Yes, a crying shame, I'm telling you, and I felt ashamed myself, ashamed to the core. Nothing like that would ever have happened with old Herr Standhartner; just think of it, chasing a man out for nothing more than a few rolls! Herr Standhartner would've had him eating there for free for the rest of his life. It's these people these days, they've got no heart, turfing a man out when he's been sitting there every day for thirty years – a shame, that's what I call it, and if you ask me I wouldn't want to have to answer for it to the good Lord.'

She had grown quite agitated, the good woman, and with the passionate loquacity that comes with old age she kept repeating what she'd said about the shame of it all, and how Herr Standhartner would never have stood for anything like this, and so on. In the end I did finally manage to ask her what had become of our Buchmendel, and whether she had ever seen him again. At this she pulled herself together again, but then went on even more excitedly:

'Every day when I went past his table, believe you me, it really got to me. I kept thinking, where is he now, poor Herr Mendel, and if only I'd known where he lived, I'd have been there in a flash and brought him something hot to eat, 'cause where else would he get the money from to keep warm and feed himself? And he didn't have no family anywhere as far as I know, not a soul. Anyway in the end, when I heard nothing of him for ever so long, I felt it must be all over and I'd never see him again. And I did wonder about whether to get a mass said for him, because he was a good man, and after all we'd known each other for more than twenty-five years, hadn't we?

'And then one morning in February, about half past seven, I was just cleaning the brass bits on the windows and all of a sudden – you could have knocked me down with a feather – all of a sudden the door opens, and in comes our Herr Mendel. You remember how he always used to sidle in, looking a bit lost? Well, this time it was different. The first thing I notice is he's, you know, swaying this way and that, and his eyes all glazed and, my God, the way he looks, he's nothing but beard and bone! I can see right away how it is, and I say to myself, he's got no idea what's going on, he's like in a daydream, like sleepwalking in broad daylight, he's forgotten everything, all that about the bread rolls and Herr Gurtner and the horrid way they chucked him out – no idea of anything. Thank God Herr Gurtner hasn't come in yet, and the head waiter's just gone for his coffee. So I pitch in myself, and I tell Herr Mendel not to hang around or he'll get himself thrown out again by that horrible chap' (at this point she looked round nervously and immediately corrected herself) 'I mean, by Herr Gurtner. So I call out to him, "Herr Mendel!" He stares at me. Then, at that moment, I can't tell you, it was awful, suddenly everything must have come back to him, 'cause he winces something terrible and starts shaking all over, you know, not just his hands and fingers but his whole body trembling, you can see it, all the way up to his shoulders, and then he quickly stumbles back towards the door and falls down in a heap. We telephoned for the ambulance and they took him away, all in a fever he was. In the evening he died. Pneumonia it was, very bad, the doctor said, and he also said he wouldn't really have known what he was doing when he came back to us. He wasn't really in control of himself, just like somebody sleep-walking. I mean, stands to reason, when someone's been sitting at a table for thirty-six years, that's going to be like home to him, isn't it?'

We went on talking about him for quite a while, being as we were the last two people on this earth to have known this extraordinary person, I to whom as a young man he had, despite the minute compass of his existence, given my first glimpse of a life wholly defined by the mind, and she, the poor, worn-out old toilet lady who had probably never read a book but felt a strong tie to this companion in her lowly, impoverished world, having for twenty-five years brushed his overcoat for him and sewn on his buttons. Different though we were, there was still a wonderful understanding between us as we sat together at Mendel's old, now abandoned, table in company with the shadows and memories we conjured up together. For memories can always provide a bond, and doubly so when those are loving memories.

Suddenly, as we were chatting, Frau Sporschil remembered something: 'Mercy me, I'm becoming so forgetful! The book! I still have that book that he left on the table. After all, where could I go to get it back to him? And afterwards, when no one came back for it, well, then I thought to myself it might be all right to keep it, as a memory. You don't think that was wrong of me, do you?'

She quickly brought it out of her little hide-away at the back, and I was at pains to suppress a gentle smile, for precisely at the most poignant moments there is a mischievous tendency for a comical and sometimes ironic element to intervene. What she produced was, of all things, the second volume of Hayn's

Bibliotheca Germanorum erotica et curiosa, a work well enough known to any collector as a classic compendium of 'gallant' literature. So this scabrous inventory was the final legacy – *habent sua fata libelli* – of the deceased magician to these unknowing, worn-out reddened and chapped hands that I dare say had never held any book other than the prayer book. Yes, I had difficulty squeezing my lips and preventing a smile forcing its way out onto my face, and this slight hesitation on my part seemed to unsettle the worthy Frau Sporschil. Was it then after all something valuable, or did I think it was all right for her to keep it?

I shook her hand most warmly. 'Please do keep it, and don't worry at all. Our old friend Mendel would be only too delighted that at least one person, out of the thousands that owe their thanks to him for their books, still remembers him.'

And then I left, feeling more than a little shame before this fine elderly woman who, in a simple and yet most human way, had remained so true to a now departed soul. Unlettered she may have been, but she had at least kept a book as a way of remembering him better, while I, the educated one, had forgotten Buchmendel and not thought of him for years; and I, if anyone, should have known that the only true reason for producing books in the first place is to bind us to our fellow human beings beyond our final breath, and thereby defend ourselves against those implacable adversaries of the life of every one of us – transience and oblivion.

The Buried Candelabrum

It was the third afternoon hour on a bright June day in the year
455. In the Roman Circus Maximus a combat between two gigantic Heruli and a sounder of Hyrcanian wild boar had just ended
bloodily when a certain unrest began to spread among the many
thousands of spectators. At first only those close by had noticed
how a messenger, covered in dust and clearly having just dismounted after a furious ride, entered the imperial stand. The
stand, separated from the common people, was adorned with
decorative carpets and sculptures; seated there was Maximus
Caesar, surrounded by his court officials. Hardly had the messenger delivered his news to the Emperor before the latter,
contravening all accepted custom, rose to his feet with the games
still in full swing, followed with an urgency no less striking by all
the assembled courtiers, and soon all the senators and other dignitaries had also deserted their allotted seats. So precipitate an
interruption could have been caused only by some serious event.
Notwithstanding the sharp fanfares immediately announcing
another animal combat, and despite the opening of the grille and
the resounding roar of a black-maned Numidian lion entering
the stadium to face the gladiator's short swords, a darkening and
irrepressible wave of unease had now broken out, topped by a
pale foam of inquiring and fearful faces, and was now passing
rapidly from row to row. Already now people were leaping up
and pointing to the emptied seats of the more distinguished

orders, noisily questioning each other, calling out and whistling; and in no time a wild rumour was raging – no one knew where it had started – that the Vandals, those deeply feared pirates of the Mediterranean, had arrived in the harbour with a mighty fleet and were already making their way towards the unprepared city. 'The Vandals!' The word was uttered, and passed from mouth to mouth, first in a faint whisper, but then suddenly grew to a strident outcry. 'The Barbarians!' yelled a hundred, a thousand voices thundering over the rounded stone terraces of the Circus, and now in one huge mass the people were rushing in crazed panic towards the exit, as if swept forward by a hurricane. All order was gone; the guards and sentries fled their posts and ran with all the others; people were leaping over the stone rows, fighting their way through the mêlée with fists and swords, trampling over screaming women and children, and at the outlets surging funnels were forming of confused, shrieking masses. Within a few minutes the mighty structure of the Circus was completely emptied of the eighty thousand spectators it had only a little while ago confined in dark, roaring throngs. The vast, silent marble tiers of its great oval lay void under the summer sun, resembling an abandoned quarry. All that remained in the arena below – the combatants themselves had long since taken to their heels along with the crowds – was the now forgotten lion, shaking its black mane and roaring its challenge into the sudden emptiness.

And it was indeed the Vandals. Messenger upon messenger now came rushing in with tidings ever more grave. With a fleet of a hundred ships and galleys, the invaders had arrived, an agile, rapidly mobile horde; white-cloaked Berber and Numidian horsemen, with their speedy long-necked steeds, were already advancing apace ahead of the main force of native Germanic warriors, and by tomorrow, or at most the day after that, these bands of brigands would have reached the city gates, where no defences were ready to meet them. The Romans' mercenaries

were campaigning far away outside Ravenna, and the city's forti-
fied defensive walls had lain in ruins ever since Alaric overran the
city. Defence, indeed, was anyway far from anyone's mind; the
rich and influential among the citizens hastily prepared their
mules and loaded their carts, in order to leave and save both
themselves and whatever part of their possessions they could.

It was, however, already too late. The people were not minded
to watch their overlords oppress them in times of plenty and
then simply slink away like cowards when their luck was up. And
so when Maximus, their Emperor, attempted to abscond from
the palace with his retinue, he was showered first with curses
and then with stones; finally the embittered populace fell on this
craven quitter, slaughtering its wretched Caesar on the road
with clubs and axes. To be sure, the gates were later shut and
barred, as they were every evening, but this only served to lock
the people's very fears in with them. Forebodings of a dreadful
end hung heavily, like some pestilential miasma, over the silent
gloom of their houses, and a suffocating shroud of darkness fell
over the forsaken capital, crippled as it was by terror and dismay.
Meanwhile the ever-indifferent stars shone high overhead, easy
and untroubled, and on the azure vault of the sky the moon
hung its silver crescent, just as it had on all other nights. Rome
lay sleepless, quaking in fear, and awaited the Barbarians as does
a condemned man, his head ready on the block, the now ineluct-
able blow of the axe already hovering above him.

Meanwhile slowly, surely, methodically, the triumphant Vandals were advancing along the empty road from port to city. The
blond, long-haired Germanic warriors marched century by century in disciplined order at a well-trained military pace, while
ahead of them, restlessly, the auxiliaries of the desert, the Numidians, some dark-skinned and some pitch-black, wheeled and
repeatedly turned, stirrupless, their beautiful thoroughbreds.
Midway along the line rode Genseric, King of the Vandals.

Contentedly free at heart, he smiled down from the saddle at his
marching column. This experienced old veteran had long known,
through his scouts, that he need not fear any very serious resistance; this time what awaited them was an easy campaign, rather
than any decisive battle engagement. And in truth, not a single
enemy soldier showed his face. It was only at the Porta Portuensis, where the finely paved harbour road meets the interior of
Rome, that the King had his first encounter; for there Pope Leo
came to meet him in all his Papal regalia, with the full complement of clergy in attendance. This was the same august Pontiff
who had, a few years earlier, so gloriously moved the dreaded
Attila to spare the city of Rome, and at whose earnest request the
heathen Hun had acquiesced with incomprehensible humility.
On this occasion Genseric, too, dismounted at once on seeing the
majestic old grey-beard and courteously limped forward to meet
him, his right leg being lame. But the king forbore to kiss the ring
on the pontifical hand, nor would he piously bow the knee before
him, for he, as an Arian, regarded the Pope as a heretic, a mere
usurper in the true Christian realm. And as for the Pope's earnest
entreaty, delivered in a prepared Latin speech, that he might deign
to spare the Holy City, he received the request with cold indifference. No, he replied through his interpreter, there need be no fear
of any bestial behaviour on his part; warrior that he was, he was
also a Christian, and he would not put Rome to the torch, nor
destroy her in any other way, even though this same avaricious,
aggressive Rome had razed other cities to the ground in their
thousands. He would, in his magnanimity, spare both the property of the church and the lives of the womenfolk; he would
claim no more than the rights of the stronger, the conqueror, and
plundering would be done *sine ferro et igne*. But – these words
were added threateningly, while his equerry helped him back into
the stirrup – he strongly advised his Holiness to open the city
gates without further delay.

Genseric's demand was acted upon. Not a single spear was brandished, not a sword unsheathed. Within an hour the whole of Rome was at the mercy of the Vandals. But this victorious invading force was not merely some unruly horde bursting over the defenceless city. The men marched in, along the Via Triumphalis, in closed ranks well disciplined by Genseric's masterful iron hand, these tall, sturdy, flaxen-blond fighters, staring only momentarily in curiosity at the thousands upon thousands of white-eyed statues, whose silent lips appeared to be promising handsome plunder. On passing through the gate, Genseric himself made straight for the Palatinum, the abandoned imperial residence. But he neither acknowledged the rehearsed obeisances of the senators who waited fearfully in line for him, nor allowed any banquet to be prepared. For the gifts with which the richer citizenry hoped to mollify him he spared hardly a glance; on the contrary, this seasoned soldier at once applied himself, bent over a map, to drawing up a plan for the swiftest and most exhaustive appraisal of the city and its resources. Each district was put under the command of a century, and each of the subordinate commanders was made responsible for the behaviour of his own men. For what now followed was no wild and anarchical looting but a well-planned, methodical stripping of all that was to be found. First, on Genseric's order, the gates were closed and placed under guard, lest so much as a single bracelet or coin anywhere in this vast city should escape him. Next, his soldiers seized all the boats, carts and pack-animals and pressed thousands of the slaves into service, for the purpose of dispatching, with all possible haste, every single piece of treasure that Rome possessed, to be taken to the pirates' hide-out on the African coast. And now the plundering began without delay, systematically, coolly, dispassionately. Over the next thirteen days the living city was subjected to a calm, skilled evisceration, rather as a slaughtered animal is dismembered by a butcher; and every last item was torn away from its still gently quivering body.

The separate detachments each went from house to house, from temple to temple, led by one of the Vandal nobles and accompanied by a secretary; and from each house and temple they brought out any item that was at once valuable and removable – the gold and silver vessels, clasps and brooches, coinage, jewellery, amber necklaces from Nordland, Transylvanian furs, malachite from Pontus, Persian forged swords. They got the workmen to remove the mosaics neatly from the temple walls and lift the porphyry slabs from the peristyles. Everything was done according to plan, everything with expert precision. To avoid damage, winches were used to bring down the bronze teams of horses from the triumphal arches, and slaves were made to strip the gilded tiles one by one from the roof of the temple of Jupiter Capitolinus after the building had been relieved of its contents. Only the bronze columns, too massive to be removed and loaded in the urgency of the moment, Genseric ordered to be hammered to pieces or sawn up for their metal. Houses and whole streets, one after the other, were painstakingly cleaned out, and no sooner had the invaders completely emptied the dwellings of the living than they turned their attention to breaking open the tumuli, the abodes of the dead. From the stone sarcophagi they tore the jewelled combs out of the decaying hair of deceased princesses, and the gold bracelets from now fleshless skeletons; precious metal mirrors and signet rings were snatched from the corpses, and even the obol, placed in the mouth of the dead to pay the infernal ferryman for safe passage to the next world, fell prey to these rapacious hands.

All this booty was gathered together and piled up in separate heaps at a preordained place. There lay the gold-winged Nike next to a bejewelled chest containing the mortal remains of a female saint, and beside them a high-born lady's gaming dice. Bars of silver were stacked alongside purple garments, precious glass and base metal. Every piece was duly recorded by the scribe in his angular northern hand on a long parchment sheet, so as to lend the theft at least some semblance of probity. Genseric himself, together with his retinue, limped here and there through this tumult of activity, touching articles with his staff, examining all the jewels, smiling approval all round. He looked on with satisfaction as cart upon cart, boat upon boat was stacked high before leaving the city. But no house burned, no blood was spilled. In calm and regular order, as when in a mine the empty and the fully loaded trucks go up and down, for thirteen days the Vandals' conveyances went back and forth between harbour and town. Each of them departed full, each returned empty, and the mules and oxen were soon gasping under their burdens; never before in living memory had so much booty been transported in thirteen days as was now seen in this wholesale sacking by the Vandals.

For all of these thirteen days no human voice was heard throughout this city of a thousand dwellings, for everyone spoke in a whisper. No one laughed. Musical instruments fell silent in the houses, and in the churches the singing ceased. The only discernible sounds were of the hammers removing anything more persistent from its moorings, the crash of falling masonry, the creaking of overloaded wagons and the deep lowing from exhausted beasts of burden repeatedly tormented under scourge and whip. Occasionally a dog howled, its food forgotten by its owner in his own fearful hour of need, and sometimes a trumpet sounded through the gloom from over the ramparts to signal a change of guard. Within the houses people held their breath. The city, this capital and conqueror of the world, lay devastated, and when in the evenings the wind blew along the empty streets the sound was like the feeble groaning of a wounded man who feels the last of his lifeblood flowing from his veins.

On that thirteenth evening of the great plundering, the Jews of the Roman community sat together in the house of Moses

Abtalion on the left bank of the Tiber, where the yellowish river bends sluggishly like an overfed snake. Moses Abtalion was not one of the most distinguished among his own people, nor was he a scholar of scriptures or the Talmud, but simply an industrious workman no longer in the bloom of youth; still, they had chosen his house for their meeting because his ground-floor workshop afforded more room than the other narrow, constricted spaces in which they lived. On every one of these thirteen days, their faces worn and ashen, they had sat together in their white funeral shrouds, and in their dark, shuttered shops among the suspended rolls of material, the whitened cloths and capacious vats, they had prayed in a state of dogged, well-nigh stupefied obduracy. Thus far they had suffered no ill at the hands of the Vandals. On two or three occasions barbarian troops, accompanied by noblemen and scribes, had made their way through the low, narrow streets of the Jewish sector, where dampness from frequent inundations lingered like a fungus in the floorstones of the houses and still dripped and ran coldly down their encrusted walls. A single contemptuous glance on the part of the experienced robbers was enough to persuade them that they would find nothing to loot in this squalid quarter. No gleaming marbled peristyles here, no brilliant gilded triclinia, no bronze urns or statues hidden away. And so the plunderers showed no interest and moved on, presenting no risk of ransacking or pillage.

Nevertheless, the Jews of Rome were heavy at heart, and they huddled together in fear and foreboding. For any misfortune that struck the cities and lands where they had settled – this certain knowledge they carried with them from generation to generation – sooner or later would invariably spell disaster for them above all. When times were good, the gentiles forgot them, paid them no attention. Then the nobles adorned themselves lavishly and indulged in fine building and flamboyant spectacle, while the common people satisfied their coarser cravings with hunting, gambling and games. But always, when luck turned against them, they blamed the Jews. It was ill for the Jews if the country was defeated by enemies, ill for them if a city was plundered, ill indeed if plague or illness came upon the land. Any evil in this world, the Jews knew well, would without fail eventually come to torment them, and this too they had long ago come to know – that there was no possible rebelling against this their fate, for they were ever and everywhere few and weak and powerless. They had no weapon but prayer.

Thus the Jews prayed every evening, and late into the night, through all of these dark and menacing days of rapine. For what other recourse had the righteous man in an unrighteous and barbarous world, where again and again it was force that decided all? What other recourse than to turn away from this world, to God? And so it had been, age after age. Now it was from the south they came, now from the east or west, now the fair, now the dark, strangers, foreigners and robbers all; scarcely had one pack of plunderers conquered before another came and fell upon them in their turn. Everywhere on earth the godless were at war, and there was no peace for the righteous. Thus had Jerusalem been taken, thus Babylon and Alexandria, and now it was the turn of Rome. Where rest was sought, unrest was found; they longed for peace, yet war oppressed them. No man could escape his destiny; nowhere but in prayer could refuge, calm and comfort be found in this ravaged, forsaken world. For wondrous indeed is prayer, that beguiles one's fears with the greatest of promises, calms the soul's torment by singing litanies, and in its wafting murmurs raises the heart's heavy burdens to God. And so it is good to pray in the hour of need, yet better still to pray in company, for all that weighs heavily is made light when borne by many, and all that is good is better in the eyes of God when done by us together.

Here, then, together sat the Jews of Rome, and together they prayed. Their pious murmurs flowed gently and steadily from beneath their beards, in concert with the rippling play of the Tiber as its waters ceaselessly chafed the planked riverside below their windows and washed the banks in its smooth, endless course. Not one of the men looked at any other, and yet their weak old shoulders swayed uniformly in rhythm while they prayed and chanted the words of those same psalms that they, and their fathers and grandfathers before them, had chanted hundreds and thousands of times in the past. Their lips hardly even knew that they spoke, their minds hardly perceived what they sensed; the quavering, plaintive tones rang forth as if from an obscure, dreamlike trance.

Suddenly they started, and a shock abruptly raised their bowed backs; the knocker had been powerfully struck on the door outside. The Jews had always felt an instinctive alarm at any unforeseen occurrence. What good could ever be expected of a knock on the door late at night? The murmur of prayer ceased at once, as if sheared through with a blade, and as all fell silent the sound came more clearly from the lapping of the river flowing relentlessly by. They listened, their throats tensed in apprehension. Another loud knock, and a fist impatiently hammered at the outer door. 'I shall go,' said Abtalion, as if talking to himself, and he shuffled out. The wax candle, which was melted and stuck on the wooden table, inclined its flame timorously and flickered before the sharp draught of air from the opened door, and likewise the hearts of all these men trembled and recoiled in fear.

Only on recognizing the new arrival did the terrified brethren catch their breath again. It was Hyrcanus ben Hillel, overseer of the Imperial Mint, pride of his community by virtue of being the only Jew permitted entry to the imperial palace. To him had been granted by the court the special privilege of residing beyond the Trastevere, and he was allowed to wear coloured garments, a mark of distinction; now, however, his cloak was torn, his face soiled.

Sensing he had come with a message, they all crowded around

him, impatient to hear him at once, already fearing some baleful news suggested by the agitation they saw in him. Hyrcanus drew a deep breath. All could see that the words would not come easily from him. Finally he spoke, with a groan of sorrow:

'It is all over. They have it. They have found it.'

'Found what? Found whom?' they all cried as one.

'The candelabrum, the Menorah! I had hidden it under the refuse in the kitchen when the barbarians came. I deliberately left the other sacred implements in the treasury – the table with the showbread, the silver trumpets, Aaron's rod, the altar of incense – too many of the servants knew about our treasures, and I could not hide everything. Only one precious object I wanted to rescue from the temple, Moses' candelabrum, the candelabrum from the house of Solomon, the Menorah. They looted all the other treasures, stripped the chamber bare and they were searching no further; I was feeling such relief in my heart that we had saved at least this one of our sacred symbols. But one of the slaves, a curse be upon him, spied on me as I hid it and betrayed me to these robbers, hoping to purchase his freedom. He told them the place where it was buried, and they dug it out. Now everything is stolen that once stood in the Holy of Holies, in the house of Solomon – table, vessels, priestly headplates and now the Menorah. Tonight, as we speak, tonight the Vandals are carrying the Menorah off to their ships.'

For a moment they all fell silent. Then loud lamentation broke forth from all their blanched faces, cry upon cry:

'The candelabrum . . . woe to us, and woe upon woe . . . our Menorah, God's lamp . . . alas for us, alas . . . the lamp from the table of our Lord . . . our Menorah!'

The Jews swayed and stumbled against each other like drunkards, beating their breasts with clenched fists, holding their hips and wailing as if burning with pain, the dignified elders now frenzied with grief as if suddenly blinded.

'Silence!' came a sudden commanding order, and all obeyed at once. The voice was that of the eldest and wisest among them, the great scriptural scholar Rabbi Eliezer, known to them as Kab ve Nake, the 'pure and clear'. His age was close on eighty years; his face rested beneath a beard of snowy white, his forehead lined by the ploughshare of relentless pondering; but the eyes beneath those bushy brows were as ever bright as stars, and kindly they were too. He raised his hand, and it was slender, ridged and yellowed like the parchment on which he had written; waving it before him he appeared to slice the air, as if to quell the outcry like a noxious cloud and make clear the space for level-headed words.

'Silence!' he called again. 'Children alone cry out in fear; grown men apply thought. Be seated, all of you, and let us take counsel. The mind is more active when the body rests.'

Abashed, the men returned to their stools and benches. Rabbi Eliezer then spoke softly, privately, as if somehow counselling none but himself:

'To be sure, misfortune has struck, a great misfortune, I own. Long ago, these our sacred possessions were taken from us, and none of us save Hyrcanus ben Hillel could go to see them in the Emperor's treasury. Nonetheless we knew that they had been held safe from the days of Titus on, that they were still there, that they lay near to us. The Roman strangers seemed more benign to us when we considered that our holy implements, which had wandered for thousands of years, which had been in Jerusalem and Babylon and had always returned home to us, were then resting, robbed though they were, in the same city wherein we dwelt. True, we had no holy table on which to place our bread, but still, whenever we broke bread we could have that table in our minds; we could not put lamps on the sacred stand, but still, when we lit a lamp we bethought ourselves of our Menorah, which lay orphaned in the stranger's house.

These things were not in our possession, but still we knew that they were secure and guarded. Now once more that wandering must start afresh, and our candelabrum must go, not to our ancestral home as we had foreseen, but taken perforce away from us, and who can imagine where it is bound? But let us not lament. Lamentation alone is of no avail. Let us now consider well where we stand.'

The men took in his words, bowing their heads, and said nothing. The hand of the old scholar moved up and down, up and down as he stroked his beard and continued, still as if addressing his own thoughts:

'The candelabrum is of purest gold; so often have I asked myself – why did God require so costly a dispensation from us. Why did he demand of Moses that our lamp should have such weight, with its seven cups and its hammered patterns of buds and blossoms? Often I questioned whether this very costliness had not created danger for it, for always from riches comes evil, and what is costly attracts robbers. But then I came to my senses and realized how idle are our thoughts; what God commands has a purpose beyond our knowledge and understanding. Yes, now I do understand: it is precisely *because* these our holy things were so precious that they have been preserved through the ages. Had they been mere common, unembellished metal, the robbers would heedlessly have broken them up and melted them for swords or chains. But no, they kept safe these costly things precisely *for* their costliness, having no idea of their sacredness. That is why one robber plunders them from another, and not one of them dares destroy them, and each of their wanderings brings them at last back to God.

'Let us now consider well. The barbarians – what do they know of our holy possession? All they see in our Menorah is that it is of gold. If we could simply appeal to their greed, we would give them twice, three times its value in gold and perhaps we might ransom it from them. We cannot fight, we Jews; our strength is in sacrifice alone. We must send word to all our scattered people in every land, asking them to help us, so we may together set our Menorah free. This year we must give twice, thrice our normal offering to the Temple, we must spare the very clothes off our backs, the ring from every finger. We must buy back our holy candelabrum, even if it costs us seven times its weight in gold.'

A sigh went up, and he broke off. Hyrcanus ben Hillel sadly raised his eyes.

'It is in vain. I have tried once already,' he said calmly. 'It was my first thought too. I approached their valuers and counting clerks, but they were rude and sharp with me. I even insisted on seeing Genseric – I offered him a king's ransom. He sat there shuffling his feet and hardly deigned to listen. I was going out of my mind; I just forced him to hear what I was saying, then boasted of its having been in Solomon's Temple, no less, and taken away from Jerusalem, stolen, by Titus as the most precious token of his triumph. That was when the barbarian began to see what he'd secured; he laughed insolently: "I have no need of your gold – I've piled up so much here, I could plaster my stables with it and hammer jewels into the horses' hooves. But if this really was Solomon's candelabrum, then it's not for sale. And if Titus had it carried before him in his triumph in Rome, then it shall be carried before me likewise in my triumph over Rome! So it served your God? Then it shall now serve the true God. Away with you!" And with that he dismissed me.'

'You should not have left!'

'You think I just went on my way? I threw myself at his feet, clasped his knees. But his heart was yet harder than the iron of his shoes. He kicked me out like a stone, and his minions beat me with their sticks and drove me away; I was lucky to come out alive.'

Only now did they understand why Hyrcanus' clothing was torn and notice the smears of blood on his forehead. There they sat, so silent and motionless that the clattering of the carts could be heard from afar working through the night, and now too the distinctive dull echo of the Vandal trumpets went from one end of the town to the other. Then all was silent, and one thought was in every mind: the great plunder was ended, the Menorah lost!

Rabbi Eliezer raised his eyes wearily. 'It is this night they take it hence?'

'This night. They are to carry it to the ships in a cart along the Via Portuensis; indeed, as we speak it may be on its way. Those trumpet blasts just now were calling the rearguard together. Tomorrow morning, it will be loaded onto the ship.'

The Rabbi's head sank ever lower over the table, and it was as if he fell asleep while listening. Like one half-absent, he seemed unaware of the anguished attention the others paid him. Then suddenly he looked up and said calmly:

'This night, you say? Good, then we must go too.'

All were astounded. But the old man repeated his words, with firm composure:

'We must go too. It is our duty. Remember the scriptures and what they demand of us. When the Ark itself went forth, we set out with it, and only when it was at rest could we rest ourselves. When the very emblems of God are journeying, we must journey with them.'

'But how can we travel over the sea? We have no ships.'

'At least, then, we shall go as far as the sea; it is but one night's journey.'

Now Hyrcanus rose to his feet: 'As always, Rabbi Eliezer counsels us aright. We must go too. It is but a part of our eternal wandering. When the Ark and the Menorah move, the people move with them – yes, the whole congregation.'

At that moment from the corner came a timid, tentative voice. It was the badly crippled carpenter Simche.

'But what,' he wailed, 'what if they seize us? They have already dragged hundreds into slavery. They'll beat us, kill us. They'll sell our children, and we'll have gained nothing, achieved nothing!'

'Silence!' countered another voice. 'Swallow your fear! If one of us is taken, so be it, he's taken. If one dies, he dies for the sacred lamp. All must go – all of us *shall* go.'

'Yes, all, all,' they cried together, a confused clamour of voices.

But with a sign the Rabbi commanded silence. Once again his eyes closed, as was his habit when needing to ponder. Then came his word:

'Simche is right. Do not vilify him as a coward, a weakling. He is right; it is not for all to risk their lives and lay us all point-lessly at the mercy of these robbers in the night. Nothing is more sacred than life itself: it is not God's will that even one should perish to no avail. No, Simche is right; they would seize our young, enslave them in their city. No, our strong young men and our boys must not go out with us into the night. But it is different with us. We are old, and an old man is useless to others, and to himself above all. We cannot row their galleys for them, we who barely have the strength to shovel the soil for our own graves. Death itself, when it takes us, can take little more from us. Ours is the duty – it is for us to follow our precious pos-session. Those of us alone, therefore, who have passed their seventieth year shall come together now and prepare to go.'

Out from the throng stepped the old grey-bearded men. Ten they were, and when Rabbi Eliezer, the Pure One, himself came up among them, they were eleven. Here are the Fathers, the wellspring of our people, thought the younger Jews, and there they stood in all their solemnity, the last remnants of an era now past. The Rabbi once more turned from them to join the rest of the crowd:

'We shall go, we the old, the grey-beards. Do not trouble yourselves, you others, over our fate. And one thing yet: we must take with us one child, one boy, who shall be witness for us to the next generation, and to the next after that. Our final day is not far off, our light is half extinguished, and soon our voice will be quelled. But forthwith one should live, and for many a year, who hath seen with living eyes the Menorah of our Lord's table, so that this certainty may live on from line to line, from one generation to another, this conviction that our holiest object is not for ever lost to us but will survive to wander further on its unending journey. A child, as yet unreasoning and uncomprehending, must go with us to bear testimony for us hereafter.'

All were silent. Every one of them, his heart full of foreboding, thought of a son of his own, and what it would be to send this child out into the night and its danger. But, just as soon, Abtalion the master dyer had risen to his feet.

'I shall go now and bring Benjamin, my grandson. Seven years he has lived, as many as are the arms of the lamp, and in this I see a sign. Prepare yourselves meanwhile for the way ahead; for sustenance bring whatever you may find in my dwelling, and I will bring the boy.'

The elders sat down around the table, and the younger men brought them wine and food. But before the breaking of bread the Rabbi intoned that prayer that for all time their forefathers had recited three times each day. And three times now the thin, broken voices of these old men repeated the same yearning prayer: 'Merciful one, grant in thy loving kindness that thy glory may return to Zion, and to Jerusalem the service of sacrifice.'

★

The prayer was spoken three times, and the elders prepared themselves to go. With calm deliberation, as if performing a sacred ritual, they shed their robes and tied them in a bundle together with their shawls and leather prayer thongs. Meanwhile the younger brethren fetched bread and fruit for the journey, and strong sticks to support them as they walked. Then each of the elders wrote on a parchment sheet what should become of his possessions should he not return, and the others signed as witnesses.

Meanwhile Abtalion the dyer had ascended the stairs. He had first removed his shoes, but the decaying wooden steps groaned under his solid weight. Cautiously he pushed open the door into the chamber in which, being poor, all of them had to sleep – householder's wife, daughter-in-law, daughters and grandchildren. Through the cracks of the fastened skylights came an uncertain misty glimmer of the moon's rays, dank and pale. Abtalion tiptoed, but for all his caution he saw that his wife and daughter-in-law had woken, and their startled eyes stared up at him attentively from their beds.

'What is it?' asked a voice in alarm.

Without stopping, Abtalion felt his way over to where he knew his little grandson Benjamin lay in the left-hand corner of the room. There, gently, he leaned over the child's lowly bedding. The boy, fast asleep, had his fists angrily clenched above his breast; wild and fervent must have been his dreaming. Abtalion tenderly stroked the boy's tousled hair, trying to wake him. At first the child did not stir but seemed momentarily calmed, sensing something of the grandfather's caress through the dark mantle of sleep, for his fists unclenched themselves, his tightened lips opened a little, and he smiled unconsciously and placidly stretched his arms. Abtalion felt an aching pain at having to rouse this innocent child from his now gentler dreams but, steeling himself, he held the boy and shook him more firmly. The child woke suddenly and looked around with hunted eyes. A child he was, of no more than seven, but a Jewish child in foreign parts, one already well accustomed to startled awakenings at unforeseen events. Just so would his father spring up in alarm when an unexpected knock came at the door, and so would they all, no less the old and the wise, dread the reading of a new edict out in the streets, or chill in their hearts when an emperor died and another succeeded. For anything new meant danger and evil for the Jewish quarter of the Trastevere, where this young life was lived. Benjamin had not yet learned his Hebrew letters, but one thing he did know – to fear everything and everyone on earth.

As the boy's bewildered eyes stared up at him, Abtalion hastily placed his hand over his mouth to stop him crying out in terror. As soon as he recognized his grandfather, he relaxed and became calm again. Abtalion bent down and whispered close to him:

'Take your clothes and your shoes and follow me. But quietly now, so no one hears.'

Benjamin rose immediately, sensing a secret plan and proud that his grandfather was making him party to it. Without a questioning word or even a glance, he felt round for his clothing and footwear.

They were just tiptoeing towards the door when the mother raised herself from her pillow and asked, tearfully and anxiously:

'Where are you taking the child?'

'Be silent!' he answered brusquely. 'You, a woman, are not to question!'

He closed the door behind him. All of the women in the room must now have awoken; from behind the thin wood came a confusion of voices and sobs, and as the eleven elders, and the child among them, left the house and started on their way, the whole street was aware of their perilous mission, as if the fearful message had somehow seeped through the walls. From every dwelling came groans of despair. But the old men neither raised their eyes nor looked around. Quietly, unflinchingly, forth they went. It was close on midnight.

To their astonishment the city gate stood open and unmanned; no one was there to question or stay their night-time journey. That trumpet-call that they had heard had summoned together the last of the Vandals, and for their part the Romans, fearfully crouching behind closed doors, dared not yet believe that their trials were over. Thus the street that led to the harbour remained quite empty – no carts or wagons, not even the shadow of a man; nothing but milestones gleaming white in pale moonlight. The nocturnal pilgrims passed unhindered through the open gate.

'We are too late,' pronounced Hyrcanus ben Hillel. 'The freight wagons must be far ahead of us; perhaps they were already on the way before the trumpet sounded. We must hurry.'

All quickened their pace. At the head went Abtalion, hefty stick in hand, with Rabbi Eliezer to his right. In between the old men of seventy and eighty tripped the tiny feet of the seven-year-old, timid and still a little sleepy. Behind them, in rows three abreast, came the remaining elders, their bundles in their left hands and staves in their right, heads lowered, as if following an invisible coffin. All around them hung the oppressive haze of the Campanian dusk, with not even the faintest breeze to abate the thick, swampy vapour that floated clammily over the fields and cast forth the stench of putrid soil. The sky was close and suffocating, and out from it a green and sickly moon flickered feebly. It felt eerie on such a sultry night to be heading into the unknown, passing the rounded burial mounds that lay motionless like dead animals along the way, and all the ransacked houses, whose open windows stared blankly, like the eyes of the blind, towards the spectacle of these aged pilgrims. So far, though, there appeared to be no danger; the deserted road still slumbered, its surface whitened in the mist like a frozen river. There was no visible sign that the plunderers had passed this way, until suddenly a single burning villa appeared over to their left. Its roof ridge had already collapsed and tumbled inside, but the smouldering glow remained, reddening the rising coils of smoke, and each of the eleven elders had the same thought as they contemplated the scene: it was as if they saw before them the pillar of cloud and fire that attended the holy Tabernacle when their forefathers had followed behind the Ark, just as they themselves now followed on in pursuit of their precious Menorah.

Between the two old men, grandfather Abtalion and Rabbi Eliezer, the young boy plied his footsteps, panting to keep up and striving hard not to slow their progress. He kept silent, just like the others, but in his breast the fear was immeasurable, his little heart beating mightily against his ribs with each pace he took. Gripped by fear, a wild and wordless fear, he knew not why these old men had taken him from his bed at night. Where were they were leading him? Never before in his young life had he been out under an open night sky and the vast heavens beyond. All he had known of night was from looking out in their familiar little lane in the Jewish quarter; there the night was no more than a narrow sliver of black. There, to be sure, one needed feel no fear, for the sounds that filled the night were familiar ones; as sleep came upon him, he would hear the men's voices at prayer, the coughing of the sick, the movement of feet, the yowls of alley cats and neighing of horses, and close by on his right and left were his mother and sister to protect him as he lay, never alone, enveloped in the warmth of their breathing. But here it was different; here, the night was a vast, threatening emptiness. Never had he felt so small, a tiny child beneath this cavernous, limitless dome. If the men had not been there watching over him he would have been in tears, or would have tried to hide somewhere, anywhere, from this silent enormity that pressed down upon him. Happily, though, his little heart had room not only for fear but also a glowing pride, a pride that the elders – those same elders before whom even his mother would not venture to speak, before whom the youngsters quaked – these venerable wise men had chosen none other than him, the smallest of all, to go with them. He could not know why they had taken him, or where they would go but, child that he still was, he sensed without any doubt that something momentous must be happening to bring them out on this night-time quest. And so with his whole being he longed to show himself worthy of their choice, constantly straining his little legs to lengthen his steps into a manly stride, and mustering all his courage to temper the timid beat of his heart. But the way was long; he was soon tired out, and fear overcame him as he saw their shadows suddenly lengthening and then disappearing before him in the gloomy moonlight, and the only sound was that of their echoing tread on the flattened stone road. And now, without warning, a bat suddenly shrilled and darted obliquely through the blackness and touched his forehead, and the child cried out in terror and seized his grandfather's hand:

'Grandfather! Grandfather! Where are we going?'

Not even turning his head, the old man growled back angrily: 'Silence! Keep going! You are not to question!'

The boy felt cowed, as if from a blow, ashamed that he had failed to check his fear. 'I should not have asked!' he chided himself.

But Rabbi Eliezer, the 'pure and clear', looked severely over the tearful child's head at Abtalion:

'Have more sense yourself! How could the child not ask us? How could he not wonder at our tearing him from his sleep, taking him out into the strangeness of night? Why, I ask, should he not know the reason for our setting out on this venture? Has he not, by his very blood, a share in our destiny? Will he not for long hereafter bear our troubles, longer for sure than we ourselves? Our eyes will be long closed in death, while he lives on to bear witness to another generation, he the last to have seen in Rome the Lamp of our Lord's Table. How can you want to keep him in ignorance, this boy whom we have chosen not only to know, but in future to tell others, of this night?'

Ashamed, Abtalion had no answer. Rabbi Eliezer leaned down tenderly to the boy and stroked his hair to reassure him.

'Ask, child, be brave and ask whatever you wish, and I will answer you. Much worse to remain in ignorance than to ask; he alone who asks much can learn much, and he alone who understands can attain righteousness.'

The boy's heart swelled with pride that this wise elder, so universally revered, should speak to him so genuinely. He could have kissed the Rabbi's hands in gratitude, but his shyness defeated him and his lips trembled without uttering a sound. Rabbi Eliezer, though, who had lived his long life in books, also knew well enough how to read the heart's thoughts in the depth of silence. He sensed the boy's pulsing impatience to know what lay in store for him, and where their journey was to take them. Tenderly, the old man drew the little hand closer to him, and it lay light and tremulous as a butterfly in the cool of his own.

'I will tell you where we are going, and I will keep nothing from you. There is no wrong in what we are doing, and though others may not know of this quest of ours, God looks down on us and knows our thoughts; He knows, as we ourselves, what is once begun, but none but He knows how it ends.'

While Rabbi Eliezer spoke to the child, neither he nor the others relaxed their pace; indeed, those behind them quickened their steps so as to draw level with the two of them and share in the old man's words to the innocent young boy.

'An ancient path is this which we now tread, my child, one

trodden long ago by our fathers and our forefathers. For we have ever, over endless ages, been a nation of wanderers, and so we have become again, and who knows, perhaps such is our fate, to remain so for ever more. Not like other peoples do we have earth beneath us to call our own, land wherein we may sow and reap our own crops. Only on wandering feet do we pass ever over others' lands, and our graves are dug in the soil of strangers. But scattered as we are, and cast like weeds between the furrows from one end of this world to another, nevertheless we remain one people, sole and undivided among the nations, united by our God and by our faith in Him. It is an invisible tie that binds us, an invisible power that holds and preserves us as one, and that invisible power is none other than our God. I know, child, that this is hard for you to grasp, for your senses perceive only what is before your eyes, and can seize and hold only the bodily real, such as earth and wood and stone and metal. That is why other peoples have fashioned even their gods from substances – from wood and stone and worked metal. But we, we alone, place our faith in that which cannot be seen; we seek a meaning which is beyond our senses. All of our pain, all our troubles, have arisen from that compulsion that makes us forsake what is tangible and drives us for ever to seek what may not be seen. But stronger is he who entrusts himself to the invisible than he who depends only on the tangible, for the tangible soon passes, while the invisible endures for ever. And in the end the spirit is stronger than force. That is the reason, the only reason, why we have survived the passage of time from age to age, and by oath have bound ourselves to the timeless; only because we kept faith with the Invisible One has that same Invisible One kept faith with us. Yes, I know that it will be hard for you, a young boy, to understand what I have said – indeed often, in moments of need, we ourselves have failed to see how God, and that righteousness wherein we have put our trust, forbear to reveal themselves in this world of ours. But even though you may not now understand me, my child, do not be perplexed, but hear me further.'

'I hear you,' replied the boy, at once shy and inspired.

'In just this belief in the invisible, our fathers and forefathers went forward through the world, and to convince themselves that they alone believed in this unseeable God, who never reveals Himself and whom no graven image can ever encompass, they made for themselves a sign. For our human understanding is narrow, and it cannot grasp the infinite; only, once in a while, a shadow of the divine descends into our life and casts a faint trace of it into our life here on earth. But in order that our hearts be ever mindful of our duty to serve the invisible, which is justice and eternity and mercy, we fashioned for ourselves implements for service, tools that demanded of us constant watchfulness, namely a great lamp, which we call the Menorah, whose candles burned unendingly, and an altar, on which the showbread was ever present and continually renewed. No, these things, which we know as sacred, were not representations of the divine being – please understand this – such as the gentiles have made in their sacrilegious error; they were rather testimony to our eternally watchful faith, and wherever our wanderings took us, there they went with us. Contained in a chest, which we call the Ark, they were guarded by us in a tent we name the tabernacle, and this our ancestors, themselves homeless just as we now are, carried everywhere with them on their shoulders. When the tabernacle rested, together with its sacred contents, then we too could rest, and when it continued along its way, then we too continued our journey. Resting and moving, by day or by night, for thousands of years we the Jewish people would cluster around this Holiness, and as long as we keep alive this sense of its sacredness, just so long we remain one people, no matter what strangers surround us.

'But now listen. The sacred objects there safeguarded were an altar, on which were laid the showbread and the nourishing fruits brought forth from the earth, and there also vessels, from which the smoke of incense rose up to God, and further there were placed the Tables of the Law, in which God had made his covenant with us. But most visible and striking of all these things was a great lamp, whose light unceasingly brightened the altar in its Holy of Holies. For God loves the light that he brought into being, and it was in gratitude, for the light that he imparted to our eyes and to our senses, that we made this lampstand. Beaten from the purest gold, it was artfully fashioned; from the broad stem its lamp-cups were raised high on its seven branches, the whole decorated and embossed with wreaths and flowers in bloom. When the seven lamps were lit on their seven pommels, the lights shone forth from out of its golden flower and our hearts were blessed as we looked upon them. And every time that light broke forth on the sabbath day our souls truly became temples of devotion. So it is that not a single thing on earth can match, as a symbol, the form of this lamp, and wherever a Jew is to be found who still puts his faith in the holiness of our God, in every house, in every land under any of the four winds, there also will be found just such a Menorah, raising its seven arms in prayer.

'Why seven?' asked the boy, tentatively.

'Ask, my child, yes, ask, for by asking you shall learn. Special and hallowed is seven above all our numbers. In seven days God created the world and mankind, and what can be more wonderful than that we are here in this world, that we sense it and love it and discern its Creator? By virtue of the light that He made, God taught our senses to see and our hearts to know. That is why the sacred lamp, with its seven arms, itself reveres the light, both the outer light and that which is within. Yes, also an inner light has been vouchsafed to us by God, through the holy scriptures; just as we see the light of the outer world by looking, so that inner light comes to us through our understanding. As is the flame to the senses, so is scripture to the soul; in the holy scriptures, all is written, be it the deeds of God and those of our forefathers, be it the true measure of every action, of what we may and may not do, and the creativity of the spirit and the prescriptions of the Law. In two ways do we behold the world through the grace of God's light, first from outside us by our senses and second within us by the soul; and thanks to His revelation we can even grasp something of God's own nature. Do you understand me, child?'

'No,' sighed the boy diffidently.

'Then there is just one thing you must keep in your mind; the rest you will come to understand later. Remember this one thing, of all that I am telling you: the most sacred of all the symbols that went with us on our wanderings, and the only ones to survive with us from the earliest days of our existence, were the holy writings and the lamp, the Torah and the Menorah.'

'The Torah and the Menorah,' repeated the boy reverently, and clenched his hands so as to fix the words more firmly in his memory.

'Now listen further. There came a time, long ago, when we tired of our wandering. For man desires land, just as land calls for man. And when after many long, homeless years we came into that land that Moses promised we would have, we claimed it as our own by right. There we ploughed and sowed, trained vines and tamed animals, made fruitful fields and fenced and hedged them, rejoicing in our hearts that we were not to be for ever merely despised exiles, a bane to the strangers among whom we found ourselves. Indeed, we believed our wanderings were now at an end for all time, and rashly dared to say that ours was this land, as if land could ever really belong to any man, to whom in truth nothing is granted but on loan. We men are for ever forgetting that having does not mean holding, and to possess is not to keep for one's own. Where we feel ground beneath our feet, there we may build our house, and vainly hope to fix and settle our roots in the soil, as trees do. Yes, in such wise did we first build houses and cities; and as each of us had a home to call his own, it could only be right for us, in giving thanks to Him, our God and Protector, to make a home for Him too in our midst, a dwelling exalted and holy above all dwellings, a House of God. And it came to pass, in those blessed years of peace and rest in our own land, that a king came to rule over us, one rich and wise who was named Solomon . . .'

'Praise be to His name!' interjected Abtalion quietly.

'Praise be to His name!' repeated the other elders as they strode on.

'. . . who built a house on Mount Moriah, that place where once our forefather Jacob saw in his sleep a ladder leading up to heaven, and on waking said, 'This is a holy place, and holy shall it be to all peoples on earth.' There Solomon built our House of God, our Temple, and most gloriously was it crafted of stone and cedar wood and of fine worked metal. And when they, our ancestors, looked up and beheld its walls, their hearts were strengthened in the belief that God would dwell always among us and grant us peace for ever more. As we ourselves rested in our homes, so did the tabernacle rest secure in its holy place, and in the tabernacle rested also the Ark which we had carried with us through all those long years. Day and night the Menorah cast up its seven flames before the altar, and all that we held sacred lay safe within the Lord's holiest sanctuary, and for all that He was, and will ever remain, invisible to our eyes, yet God rested at peace in the land of our forefathers, in the Temple of Jerusalem.'

'May mine eyes look once more upon it,' murmured the elders as they walked, as if in communal prayer.

'Hear me further, my child. Everything that man has is given to him but on loan, and his moments of happiness are fleeting as the wind. That peace we enjoyed was not to last as we had thought; for from the east there came a savage people who burst in upon our city just as the robbers you have seen burst in upon the city of these our recent hosts. Whatever could be seized, they seized, and what could be carried they took away, and what could be destroyed, that they destroyed. That alone which was invisible, on that they could not lay their hands – the Word and the very presence of God. But the Menorah, our holy lamp stand, they tore from the Lord's table and carried off, not because it was holy – that was beyond the comprehension of these sons of Satan – but because it was of gold, and robbers are always lusting for gold. And along with our people themselves they took lamp and altar and all the vessels, dragging all into captivity, to Babylon . . .'

'Babylon?' interrupted the boy timidly.

'Ask, my child, ask freely, and may it please God always to give you an answer. Babylon – so was that city called, a great and mighty city, great as this Rome you know, and so far was it from our homeland that we did not recognize the very pattern of the stars above. If you are to imagine how far those sacred possessions of ours then travelled, just consider that it is but three hours we have now been walking, yet already our bodies are weary and aching, but that Babylon was three thousand hours away, and more! That should tell you how far away our Menorah was taken by those robbers. But mark this too: God thinks nothing of any distance. When He saw that His word was still held sacred by us even in our banishment – and per- haps precisely this is the meaning of our unending wanderings in exile, that what is sacred becomes all the more so the further such distance, and that our hearts are simply made more humble at times of great need – yes, when God saw that we had stood the test, He then roused the heart of a king of that nation that was so foreign to us. The king recognized the wrong he had inflicted upon us and allowed our forefathers to return to the promised land, and gave back to them the lamp and the other treasured pieces from the tabernacle. So was it that our forefathers came back home from Chaldea to Jerusalem, enduring deserts, mountains and the thickest undergrowth. From the ends of the earth they returned, not in mind alone but truly in body, to the place where we have always been and shall always be in our thoughts. Once again, we built our Temple on the Mount of Moriah, and once again the seven-flamed light of the Menorah shone out in its true home before God's altar, and together with it our hearts glowed in joy. But mark this well, that you may fully see the meaning of this journey on which we now find ourselves: not one thing made by mankind is so holy, so ancient, so widely travelled through time and place from land to land, as this our seven-armed lamp, for it is the costliest of all pledges we have ever had in token of our people's oneness and purity. And at any time when our fortunes darken, then always the light of our Menorah is put out and seen no more.'

Rabbi Eliezer here broke off; his voice seemed spent. The boy looked up, and his eyes themselves were gleaming like little flames, eager to listen and concerned that the account might now be at an end. The old man smiled to see the child's impatience and stroked his hair to calm him:

'How your eyes burn with inner fire, my boy! But fear not, our destiny is never at an end, and even if I were to continue the story for years on end you would still not know the thousandth part of the long path we are bound by fate to tread. Listen further, for I see you listen well and eagerly. Hear how it was, and what happened, when we returned to our homeland. Once more we thought that our Temple was now firmly founded for all time. But soon there came enemies again, from over the sea; from this very land they made their way where now we dwell as strangers, and they brought with them a future emperor, a warrior governor, named Titus . . .'

'Cursed be his name!' murmured the elders as they walked.

'. . . and he breached our walls, and razed our Temple to the ground. His insolent, evil feet entered the Holy of Holies and he tore the sacred lamp from the altar. Solomon's glorious veneration of God he vengefully plundered, and took our leader back to Rome in chains, where he paraded our sacred possessions in triumph. There the foolish people vaunted and rejoiced in his victory, as if their forces had conquered God and dragged him back in chains among their captives. And so proud was the impious villain of his outrage, and so pleasing to him our humiliation, that in his conceit he had a mighty arch built as a monument, whereon images of his plundering of God's property were engraved and enshrined in marble.'

Benjamin's attentive eyes looked up again. 'Do you mean that arch with all those carved stone pictures of people? The one in the great square, that huge arched gate that Father told me about and said I mustn't ever go through?'

'That one, my boy. Pass by that triumphal gateway without ever looking at it, for it is a reminder of our people's most painful day. No Jew may pass through that arch, which shows in images how they jeered at the things we will always hold sacred. Every time, you must think of . . .'

The old man stopped short. Hyrcanus ben Hillel had suddenly leaped forward from behind them and quickly placed his hand over his lips. All were taken aback by such audacity, but Hyrcanus now silently pointed to the road ahead. There they could just make out in the uncertain, misted glow of the moonlight a dark shape creeping slowly, worm-like, along the white road, and now, as the elders stood still and held their breath, the silence was broken by the creaking sound of heavily loaded wagons. Their column was but dimly discernible as it gradually moved forward, but from above it there came glimmers of brightness, as from the spear-like stems of crops in the morning dew, and these must be the lances of the Numidian rearguard watching over the carts of plundered goods.

Those sharp-eyed auxiliaries must already have caught sight of the party following behind, for immediately they had turned their horses and were now heading straight for them with weapons at the ready and letting out shrill cries. Upright in their stirrups, their white burnouses fluttering around them, they charged as if on winged steeds, and the eleven elders involuntarily huddled together and shielded the child in their midst. Shouting loudly, the Numidians instantly charged down in a single onslaught, and when they were almost directly upon the terrified old men, to examine who these unknown followers might be, they sharply stayed their horses, making them rear up suddenly. The now fading moon gave uncertain light, but they soon saw that these were no warriors following them to fight over the booty, but merely a few frail grey-beards making their way harmlessly through the night, each carrying a little bundle and stick in hand, no strange sight to them, who in their native Numidia often encountered pilgrims on their way from one sacred spot to another. They smiled trustingly at the elders, and white teeth glistened from their fierce, dark faces. Then came an abrupt, shrill whistle from one of the band, and they wheeled their horses again and were off, swift as a flock of birds in flight, back to their booty, while the old men were left motionless with the passing shock they had suffered, hardly daring to believe that they had been so spared from harm.

Rabbi Eliezer, the pure and clear, was the first to recover himself. Gently he patted the boy's cheek.

'A brave lad you are!' he said, bending down to him. 'I held your hand, and I never once felt it tremble. Would you like to hear more from me now? You still don't know where we are going and why we are wide awake at this hour.'

'Yes, please go on,' the boy pleaded.

'I was telling you, you remember, how Titus – a curse be upon him – carried off our holy possessions to Rome and in his vanity had them paraded all through the city. But after that shameful day the emperors of Rome stored away our Menorah, with the other things from Solomon's Temple, in a house they graced with the name 'Temple of Peace', an absurd name to choose, as if peace could ever come about or dwell for long in this strife-ridden world of ours. God, however, would never allow to remain in an alien temple those things which had once adorned His own Temple in Zion. So very soon he sent a fire, and that fire utterly destroyed the building and all that it housed, save that our sacred lamp was rescued from the devouring flames, and so it was once again made clear that no fire, no distance, no thieving hand of man could have any power over it. It was a sign, a warning from God that those robbers must return the sacred implements to their sacred home, wherein they would be revered not for the value of their gold but for their sanctity alone. But do fools ever understand such a sign? Does the stubborn heart of man ever bow in submission to good sense and reason?'

Rabbi Eliezer sighed at these words, and then continued:

'So they took those things and stored them away once again, this time in another house of the Emperor, and because they remained there under lock and key for long years and decades, the Romans came to believe that all this was now their own property and would remain so for ever. Yet behind any robber there will always be another close on his heels, and what the one has once forcibly taken will sooner or later fall prey to that second robber. Rome fell upon Jerusalem, and in its turn Rome fell prey to Carthage. The Romans robbed us, but soon came their turn to be robbed, and just as our holy sites were desecrated, so have theirs now suffered their own defilement. But our own property, our Menorah, our own sacred symbol, has gone with the other plunder, and those wagons ahead of us there in the darkness are carrying away what is precious to us beyond all other things. Tomorrow it will be loaded onto a ship to be taken away to a foreign land, far out of reach to our longing eyes. Never again will it shed its light for us, old as we now are. And so, just as the body of one beloved is conducted to the grave by those who have loved him, and in this way they show that love by sharing his final journey, so do we now accompany our beloved Menorah on its journey into exile. It is our holiest possession that we are losing. Do you now understand the mourning of this our sorrowful quest?'

Benjamin's head was lowered in silence as he walked on, apparently pondering what he had heard.

'But always remember this, my boy: it is as a witness that we have brought you with us, so that in days to come, when we ourselves are in our graves, you may testify that we stayed true to that which we hold sacred, and you will teach others to do likewise. You may strengthen their faith in our belief, that this our Menorah will yet one day return from its wanderings in the darkness, will again one day with its seven flames gloriously brighten the altar of the Lord. We woke you so that your heart would awaken within you, that hereafter you may tell of this night to those who succeed us. Remember well, and comfort others with the telling, that you have seen with your own eyes the great lamp that wandered and survived through thousands of years, as did our people themselves survive in their wanderings among strangers. And firm as a rock is my faith that it will never perish, as long as we ourselves continue to live.'

The boy remained silent. Rabbi Eliezer, the pure and clear, sensing some resistance in that silence, leaned down. 'Have you understood me, Benjamin?' he asked.

Still the child would not yield. 'No,' he countered, 'I don't understand. If . . . if, as you say, it is so precious to us, so holy, this Menorah, why do we let them take it from us?'

The old man sighed. 'You are right to ask, Benjamin. How indeed do we allow this? Why do we not stand up to them? But one day sooner or later you will come to know that in this world what passes for right sides with the stronger, and not with the truly righteous. Always it is violence that forces its will on mankind; the good and the just have no such power. To endure injustice, that is all we have learned from God, and not to impose our right through strength of hand.'

Rabbi Eliezer spoke these words with bowed head as they walked on. Then suddenly, abruptly, the boy let go of his hand and halted. The question from the child to the old man was direct, almost imperious:

'But what about God? Why does God allow this robbery? Why doesn't He help us? Didn't you say that He is the just, the almighty one? Why does God side with the robbers and not with the just?'

All were appalled at the words, and stood in horror as if their hearts were suddenly stilled. The boy's fractious question had cut through the emptiness of night like a trumpet blast, a small child declaring war on God. Ashamed of this child of his own blood, Abtalion angrily chided his grandson:

'This was blasphemy – be silent!'

But Rabbi Eliezer interjected:

'No, rather be silent yourself. Why reproach this guiltless child? His innocent heart has asked no more than we ask ourselves every hour of every day, yes, you and I and every one of us, even the wisest of us, as long as we have existed. This child's is simply the oldest question our people's hearts have asked: why has God so treated us, among all the nations, with such harshness, despite our serving Him as no other people ever served Him?

Why us? Why hurl us beneath the feet of others, to be trodden upon? Were we not the first to know Him, to praise Him in the unfathomable mystery of His being? Why destroy what we build, shatter our hopes, deny us any lasting rest in our wanderings and rouse nation after nation against us in ever renewed hatred? Why test us so mercilessly, always us and only us, whom first he chose for himself and first initiated in his mystery? No, let me not lie to a child. If his honest questioning be blasphemy, then I am myself a blasphemer, every day of my life. See, all of you, I confess it openly; I too am restive and endlessly upbraid our God. Day after day, I too, at eighty years of age, ask the same question which this guileless child has asked: why does God force on us, and us alone, such affliction? How can he countenance the denial of our rights, and even assist those who rob from us? Though for shame I may beat my breast a thousand times, yet I cannot suppress this feverish questioning. No Jew would I be, no human at all, were I not thus daily tortured by these thoughts, which death alone will silence.'

A shudder went through the elders. Here was their Rabbi, the pure and clear, more impassioned than they had ever seen him, his indictment of God welling from some most private corner of his being. Could this be their fellow elder, his whole body trembling with pained emotion, averting his glance in shame from the child who now gazed up at him with questioning and wondering eyes. But Rabbi Eliezer quickly contained himself and, bending down, again spoke soothingly to the boy:

'Forgive me, Benjamin, for addressing them, and another who is above all of us, instead of giving you an answer. You have asked me, in the simplicity of your heart, why God allows us, and Himself, to suffer such iniquity. And my answer, the most honest I can give, shows my own simplicity: I do not know. We do not know what God plans, and we cannot know His thoughts. But whenever I reproach Him, being deluded in my pain and in the endless sufferings of all of us, I try to take comfort in telling myself that there must be some sense, some reason, in the pain He allots us, and perhaps every one of us has been paying for some wrong. Who can say who committed that wrong? Was it perhaps Solomon the Wise, who was not so wise when he built the temple in Jerusalem, as if God were a human being desiring a single place to reside amidst but one single nation? Was it perhaps a sin to make God's house so splendid an edifice? Did gold count for more than piety, marble more than our inner strength? Perhaps we Jews went against God's will in ever wanting to be a nation like others, wanting to have a land, a home of our own, and wanting to be able to call the Temple 'ours', to call God 'ours' in the way we might say 'my hand' or 'my hair'. It may have been for this reason that He razed the Temple, and had us cast out from our homeland, so that we would not merely fix our eyes and our hearts on what is manifest to all, but in our belief remain true to Him, the unreachable and invisible. Is this perhaps the true way for us, the very way along which we are never to cease our wanderings, though looking ever sadly back, gazing yearningly forward and always longing for that rest which is never to be found. For there will only ever be one way of holiness, that on which man cannot know whither he is bound, and yet persists in his journey, just as we now stride forward into darkness and danger this night, not knowing where it will bring us.'

The boy was listening eagerly, but the Rabbi's words were almost at an end:

'Now, though, ask no more, my boy. Your questioning goes beyond what I can answer. Wait, and be patient. God Himself may one day answer you, from within your own heart.'

The old man fell silent, and the other elders were silent too. There they stood in stillness on the path, enveloped by the silence of the night, and it seemed to them that they stood alone in the utterly timeless darkness of the world.

Suddenly one of them shuddered and raised a hand. Visibly gripped by fear, he motioned to the others to listen. And indeed a sound was clearly to be heard coming through that quietness, faint at first as if someone lightly stroked the strings of a lyre, a dark, swelling tone that soon grew stronger, as of the wind or the sea emerging from the gloom. In no time a powerful squall, brief and sudden, burst through the sultry air, flinging up the branches of the trees along the road, as if in their terror they had a will to suspend themselves in the emptiness above, and the bushes quivered. The old men, deeply stirred by what had been said of their destiny and of the presence of God, quaked in expectation; might they now perhaps hear His answer, for was it not written that His presence might be felt in the gusting of the storm, his voice heard even through the gentle rustling of the wind? Each of them lowered his head and listened intently; instinctively linking hands, that they might protect one another before the enormity that faced them, each felt the throbbing pulse, a tiny, urgent hammering, in the hand that he clasped.

But nothing came. The great turbulence of the wind dropped as quickly as it had risen, and presently the grass stirred no more. It was nothing. No voice to be heard, not a sound to appease the fearful stillness. As one after another they raised their eyes again from the ground, over to the east they beheld the first glimmer of daylight rising, a gentle opal, above the darkness. It had been nothing more than the rush of wind that is always felt before the break of day; nothing more than that wondrous daily arrival on earth, morning in the wake of night. As they stood there, still disquieted, the distant ruddiness of dawn gathered strength, and the contours of the land gradually emerged from the haze. Now it was clear; the night was over, the night of their quest.

"'Tis dawn,' murmured Abtalion, his voice restrained, almost disconsolate. 'Let us pray.'

The eleven old men drew close together, Benjamin remaining a little apart; too young to share in their prayers, he looked on, his heart swelling. The elders brought forth their shawls from the bundles they carried and laid them over their heads and shoulders. They tied the thongs of their phylacteries around their foreheads and left arms, nearest the heart. Then they turned towards the east, for there was Jerusalem, and gave thanks to God the Creator of all, and praised Him in the Eighteen Blessings. Softly they intoned and sang, their bodies swaying to the rhythm of the sacred words. Some words were beyond the child's understanding, but he saw the fervour of the elders' bodily movement as they sang, just as he had seen the stirring of the bushes beneath that divine wind before dawn. After their solemn 'Amen' they all bowed their heads, then folded their prayer shawls and made ready to be on their way once more. Old men they were, yet they looked now even older in the slowly wakening light of day, the lines on their foreheads now deeper and sharper, darker the shadows about their eyes and mouths. They might have just risen from their own deathbeds, so tired and spent they looked beside the young boy they now led on along their path's final, most painful stage.

Bright and already sweltering was that Italian morning, as the eleven elders and the young child arrived at the harbour of Portus, where the Tiber disgorges its yellowed, listless waters into the sea. Few of the Vandals' ships remained in the roadsteads; one after another they departed, ensigns streaming victoriously on the masts, bulkheads heavy with booty. Presently there was but one still lying at anchor by the quay, greedily ingesting the last of the looted Roman goods now being unloaded from groaning carts. Wagon after wagon rolled obediently forward for emptying, burden after heavy burden borne up over the wooden planks on the slaves' brown shoulders, or raised high on their heads. Chests and coffers there were, brimming with gold, and round amphoras of wine, but however much they hastened, they could not meet the impatient orders of the ship's captain, and the whips of their overseers were driving the slaves on, faster and faster. Now the last of the wagons was at the side of the ship, the one which the elders and Benjamin had followed through the long night, for in this one rested the Temple's sacred lamp. The wagon's freight was still concealed beneath straw and cloths, but the elders, their eyes fixed on the overloaded cart, trembled before the imminent unveiling. Now was the moment of truth, now or never must the miracle occur.

The child's eyes were all the while directed elsewhere. It was at the sea that he gazed, as one bewitched, for never before had he seen this wonder. Here it was, an endless blue mirror, brilliant in its arched vista that stretched to that distant sharp line where its water met the sky. The enormity of it seemed even greater than the dome of night in which he had, also for the first time, seen the vast canopy of stars spread out high above him. Transfixed, he watched the playful waves chasing, tumbling each other, one leapfrogging over the next, then instantly breaking into foam with a little high-spirited chuckle, continually then retreating and again reforming. He sensed the exuberance in this blissful sport, something he had never dared dream of in the drab, gloomy alley where his people laboured in their poverty. Impulsively he stretched out his child's breast, yearning for growth and strength, to drink in such air, such life, to invigorate his timid Jewish blood to the depth of his being. How irresistible it was for the enchanted child to stride forward to very water's edge, to stretch his little arms, to take and savour at least one probing breath of this infinity; his spirits raised beyond all he had ever known, at the prospect of such wondrous beauty he felt himself blessed as never before in his life. Ah, how free, how untrammelled was everything here! Here the gulls circled and darted down and up again like white arrows, here the lovely ships' sails billowed sleek and silky in the wind. And suddenly, as Benjamin closed his eyes and threw back his young head to quaff more avidly the cool, salty air, there occurred to him those first imposing words he had been taught: 'In the beginning God created the heaven and the earth.' And now for the first time the name of God, which hitherto he had heard so often on the lips of his elders, was filled with meaning and substance.

A cry startled the boy. The eleven elders had let forth a loud shriek, all as one, and immediately he ran back to them. The coverings had just been torn from the last wagon, and as the Berber slaves bent to heave out a silver statue of the goddess Juno, weighing several hundredweight, one of them kicked aside the Menorah, which lay in his way; the precious lampstand fell clumsily from the wagon, rolling to the ground. A single cry of horror went out from the old men as they witnessed their most sacred emblem, which Moses himself had looked upon, which Aaron had blessed, which had stood on the Lord's Table in Solomon's Temple, now pitifully befouled in dung from the team of oxen and defiled by dust and filth. The black slaves looked up in astonishment at the sudden outcry, not understanding what had caused such consternation among these ridiculous old men who now gripped each other's trembling arms in shared terror; surely no harm had been done to them? But the overseer's whip was already in play over the naked backs of the slaves, and subserviently they returned to their labour and sank their arms into the straw, now bringing out a stele of lustrous porphyry, and immediately after it yet another mighty statue. This they tied with ropes at throat and foot and hauled over the gangplank onto the ship, like a corpse of one they might have slaughtered. With quickening speed the wagon was yielding the last of its contents. All that remained was the lamp, eternal symbol, lying unheeded at the foot of the cart, half hidden by one wheel. The elders, still clasping one another's arms, trembled in one united hope: might the plunderers in their haste somehow fail to notice this treasure? Could they perhaps overlook it? At this final fateful moment, could a miracle occur, and the Menorah be saved?

But at that moment one of the slaves noticed the lamp below the wagon; he bent down and picked it up, heaving it onto his shoulders. Lifted up on high, it glowed brilliantly in the sun; it was as if its splendour intensified the brightness of the day. Here for the first time in their lives the elders looked upon the lost sanctity of their people, but alas, in the very moment when at last they could set their eyes on their most beloved sacred emblem, it was now leaving them for a strange and distant land! With both hands the broad-shouldered black slave supported the great weight of the lamp on his back, balancing it carefully as he hurried over the swaying planks of the gangway. Five steps, then another four, and then the holy treasure would be gone for ever. As if propelled by some unknown power, the eleven old men pressed forward, still holding each other fast, on to the steps of the gangway, their eyes half blinded by tears, mouths muttering wildly, indistinctly. They stumbled forward like drunks, ready to lend their longing eyes and eager lips, to touch with one final pious kiss the most sacred object they knew. One alone, Rabbi Eliezer, remained clear in his mind amidst the pain he suffered. With irrepressible force he gripped Benjamin's hand so painfully tight that the child almost cried out.

'Look upon this! Look on! You will be the last of us to see our holy possession. You will be the witness of how they took it, robbed it, from us!'

Though not fully comprehending the words he heard, the child sensed deep within himself the elders' suffering; here for sure a great injustice was being done. An anger, that burning anger that children know, coursed through him, and without knowing what he was doing, this small child, a mere seven years old, freed himself from the others and rushed upon the slave, who had just now stepped onto the gangplank, labouring unsteadily beneath the weight he carried. No! Never would this stranger be permitted to take away their sacred Menorah! The boy hurled himself wildly upon the mighty figure of the Berber, attempting to wrest his booty from him.

The slave, heavily laden, tottered under this sudden unexpected attack. Here was a mere child hanging from his arm, but as he struggled to keep his balance on the swaying boards the slave lost his footing, stepped off to one side, and tumbled off beneath his heavy load, dragging the boy with him and instantly losing hold of the lamp. Bearing down with his whole weight he struck out at the right arm of the child, who still clung to him. Benjamin, feeling the crushing pain through every limb of his body, let out a piercing howl, but the cry was not to be heard above the commotion all around, for all were now shouting at the same time – the elders scandalized at the horror of seeing their Menorah rolling in filth and dung, and the Vandals yelling out in anger from the ships. The overseer immediately leaped forward and started driving the elders back with his whip. Meanwhile the slave, who had risen to his feet in fury, kicked the groaning child out of his, heaved the Menorah back onto his shoulders and quickly fled with it over the gangplank and onto the ship.

The eleven elders paid no attention to the child. None of them noticed him as he lay crumpled and groaning on the ground, for their eyes were elsewhere. They saw nothing but the Menorah, which was now passing up the steps on the slave's back, its seven cups looking heavenward like a sacrificial offering to God. In horror they watched their treasure casually passed from the hands of one stranger to another and finally tossed away onto a heap to join the rest of the plunder. Now the whistle sounded, a chain noisily raised the anchor, and far out of sight below deck, where the galley slaves sat tethered at their benches, forty oars began to sweep back and forth to the drumbeat of command. The ship lurched forward, foam churning white behind the keel, a swishing sound accompanying its onward glide as the hulk rose and fell, like a body breathing, in the waves. Sails full blown, the galley had left its anchorage and was now steering towards the vastness of the open sea.

The elders stared after the ship as it faded from sight. Again, they held each other tight, trembling together, their bodies forming a single chain of pain and trepidation. All had inwardly nursed the hope, without confiding it to each other, that even now at this late moment a miracle might occur. And yet the galley had now been ushered forth across the waters on a gentle, following breeze filling its sails, and the smaller its outline grew in the distance, the more the hopes in their hearts melted and vanished in the great ocean of their grief. Now the ship was a mere small glimmer resembling a distant gull on the wing, and presently the elders' eyes, clouded with tears, saw nothing but the blue emptiness of the sea. Away with all hope! Yet again the sacred lamp, ever unresting, had departed from them into the wilderness.

Only now did they turn their eyes from the sea and remember their young lad who still lay, groaning with the pain of his shattered arm, where he had been struck down by slave and lamp. Now they lifted his small, bloodied form and laid him on a plank litter. It shamed them deeply to think that this child, for all his tender years, had done what none of them had dared do. Well might Abtalion fear the wrath of the women when he brought back his grandson, in this crippled state, to his mother and daughter. But a comforting word was at hand from Rabbi Eliezer, the pure and clear:

'Do not sorrow, and do not lament the boy's suffering. For remember what is written: God laid low that man who laid his hand on the Ark to steady it, for it is against God's will that human hands should touch what is sacred. This child he spared, with no more than an injured arm. Perhaps there is a blessing in this very pain, perhaps even a calling.

Tenderly he stooped down over the moaning boy: 'Nay, do not resent your pain, Benjamin, but accept it, and welcome it. Pain itself is a part of your heritage, for through suffering alone do our people survive, and only through need do we find our creative power. A great thing has befallen you, for you have touched what is truly sacred and yet suffered no more than a bodily injury, rather than losing your life. Perhaps through this very pain you are marked out, and there is some meaning hidden in your destiny.'

The boy looked up at him, strengthened in his faith. The pride the Rabbi's words had given him eclipsed the pain he had felt from his broken arm, and not one more groan was heard from him as they brought him back to his home.

Many a troubled year followed in the Roman Empire after that night of sacking by the Vandals, and in the span of one human life more happened than would be commonly seen through seven whole generations. Emperors followed one another in relentless succession; after Avilius came Maiorannus, Libius Severus and Anthemius, murdering or expelling their rivals, and once again Germanic forces broke in on the city and plundered as before. And again there came a new line of emperors, again only within the lifetime of a single generation, deposing, replacing each other, till finally came the last of all the emperors at Rome, Licerius and Julius Nepos and Romulus Augustulus. Then did Odoacer and Theodoric, hardened warriors from the north, seize power. Redoubtable Gothic rulers they were, who thought their rule so tempered and toughened by might and discipline as to endure for ever, but their day too passed within one generation, and again came invaders on the move from the north to establish themselves in Italy, while beyond the sea to the east there rose a second Rome in Byzantium. It was as if, ever since that dreadful night of the Vandals when the holy Menorah departed through the Porta Portuensis, there could be no more peace, no rest in that thousand-year-old city on the Tiber.

Those eleven elders who had followed the sacred lamp on its last journey of exile had long since departed this world; indeed, their children after them were long buried, and their grandchildren were by now themselves grown old. But one still lived, and that was Benjamin, Abtalion's grandson, witness to the events of that dreadful night. The little child became a young lad, and in due course passed through adulthood into old age. Predeceased by seven of his sons, one of his grandchildren was struck dead when during the reign of Theodoric a mob torched the synagogue. But Benjamin himself lived on, his arm permanently crippled. Just as in the forest, when a storm has brought down trees to right and left, one alone, the mightiest of all, still stands towering, so did this ancient elder outlive the years, and witness the passing of emperors and the fall of kingdoms. Him alone did death pass by in reverence, and his name stood high and almost holy among the Jews throughout the lands. Benjamin 'Marnefesh' they called him on account of his stricken arm, for the meaning of this name is 'He whom God hath sorely tested'. None other did they honour as they honoured him. He was the last, alone of those who had looked with their own eyes upon the holy lamp of Moses, the candelabrum from Solomon's Temple, the Menorah which lay, now orphaned of its sevenfold light, buried in the darkness of the Vandals' treasury. When merchants came to Rome from Livorno or Genoa or Salerno, from Mainz or Trier, or from the Levantine lands, before all else they made their way to his house to see before them the man who had himself seen the sacred emblems of Moses and Solomon. And there they would pay him reverential homage, as if he himself were a sacred image, and in fear and awe would look at his crippled arm, and with their fingers touch the hand that once had touched the Lord's Menorah. The tale was known to every one of them, for in those days the spoken word travelled as quickly as does the written word today, but still unendingly they urged Benjamin Marnefesh to tell them what he had seen and done that night, and again and again he would repeat the story of his journey with the eleven elders. And every time he patiently recalled the departure of the Menorah a lustre seemed to go forth from his luxuriant white beard when he came to the words vouchsafed to him by Rabbi Eliezer, the pure and clear, who had left this world so long ago. No cause was there for despair, he told them; as the Rabbi had said, the wandering of the holy lamp was not yet complete, and it would one day return to Jerusalem to see an end to its dishonour, and the people would again gather around their treasured emblem now thus restored to them. So comforted, the pilgrims would leave him, and his name would be woven into their prayers, that he might yet be long with them on this earth, he the consoler, the last and only living witness of their holy Menorah.

And so it was that Benjamin, the sorely tested, the child of that night of ancient memory, reached the age of seventy, and of eighty, and eighty-five, and at last of eighty-seven years. The weight of time could now be seen on his bending shoulders, his eyes had lost their sharpness, and sometimes he was wearied before the evening drew nigh. But none of the Roman Jews would willingly believe that death could touch him, so powerfully did his very living attest the reality of that great past event. It seemed unthinkable that those human eyes which had looked upon the Lord's lamp should finally cease to see, without having witnessed the return of that same Menorah; his continuing presence on earth was to them a cherished sign of God's good will. No feast day could be celebrated without him, and his name must be marked at every service. When he walked among them, their eldest ones bowed piously before him, and each of them would utter a blessing where he trod, and wherever they came together in sorrow or joy, there the highest place at their table was made ready for him.

Thus did the Jews of Rome revere Benjamin Marnefesh, on this occasion as always, as the oldest and worthiest of their congregation. In due accordance with custom, they assembled at the cemetery on the saddest day of the calendar, Tisha B'Av, the ninth day of the month of Av, the day of the Destruction of the Temple. This was the day of dismal memory, on which their forefathers had been made homeless, cast out and scattered like salt over all the lands of the earth. No longer were they to sit together in their house of prayer, for that house had just been defiled and razed by the rabble. Instead, they felt it incumbent on them to be near to their dead on this day of great sorrow; outside the city walls, where their forefathers had been buried in the soil of strangers, they came together, and together bewailed their own homeless exile. Among the tombs they sat, some of them on headstones already shattered. Knowing that here they were close to their fathers, whose heirs they were in suffering too, they read the names and the eulogies of their forebears. Above some of the names symbols were carved into the stone, two crossed hands standing for the priesthood of one of them, a washing jug of a Levite, a lion of Judah, a star of David. On one of the upright stones was depicted the seven-branched Menorah, indicating that he who lay here in eternal rest had once been a sage, a very light to lighten Israel. Facing this tomb, his eyes turned keenly on it, sat Benjamin Marnefesh among his fellows, his head strewn, like theirs, with ash and his clothing torn; their heads were bowed, one and all, like willow trees bent forward over the darkened waters of their affliction.

It was late afternoon. The sun was already sinking behind

the pines and cypresses, and the Jews crouched like so many ancient tree stumps; gaily coloured moths flitted around them, and dragonflies with rainbow-hued wings alighted airily on the men's bowed shoulders, and in the thick grass beetles ran playfully over their shoes. The golden foliage, fanned in the breeze, wafted scents of herbs as the velvet calm of evening drew on, but the Jews could not raise their eyes nor lift their spirits. Unceasingly immersed in ever-renewed grief, unceasingly they recalled the oppression of their people in collective lamentation. Neither eating nor drinking, they could pay no heed to the beauty of that receding day; all they could do was intone together their chants of woe for the destruction of the Temple and the fall of Jerusalem. And though every painful syllable they cried was long seared into the memory of every one of them, still these faithful souls recited again and again their hallowed words, ever renewing the acuteness of their sorrow, the more painfully to tear their tortured hearts. Grief was indeed all they wished to feel in this their darkest of days, for only by themselves sharing in the sense of abandonment and oppression could they bethink themselves of the oppression and agony of their deceased ancestors. And so they would recount to one another all of the tragic history of the Jewish people through every age. And just as here in Rome, so on this day and at this hour in every town and every congregation throughout the world did Jews sit close to the ground near the graves, with ash on their heads and their clothing torn, and thus did they speak and intone the same lamentation, that of Jeremiah when he spoke of how the daughters of Zion were fallen, and had become a mockery among the nations. And those who spoke, and those who listened, knew that just this grief, this sorrow of exile and abandonment, was the one force uniting them through all the lands on earth.

While they sat and murmured their laments, and assailed their hearts in the pain of remembrance, they did not notice the sun growing more golden, or the pines' and cypresses' darkened trunks now starting to redden, as if from some lustrous inner light. It escaped them that the ninth day of Av, the day of the great mourning, was slowly nearing its end, and the hour had come for the last prayer of the day. But now, from beyond, there came a creaking sound from the rusty gate of the cemetery. On hearing it, and knowing for sure that someone had entered, they still did not rise. The newcomer stood in silence and waited until the prayer had been said. Only then did the first elder of the community look at the new arrival and greet him: 'A blessing on you. Peace be with you, brother Jew.'

'Blest be these who tarry here,' answered the stranger. And again the elder spoke:

'From where have you come, and which is your community?'

'The community that was mine, that is no more; I have fled here from Carthage by ship. Great things have come to pass. The Emperor Justinian has sent an army from Byzantium to face the Vandals; Belisarius, his general, has stormed Carthage, stronghold of those pirates. The king of the Vandals is held captive, his kingdom brought down. Everything that the robbers have taken over these many years has been taken as booty back to Byzantium. The war is over.'

The Jews looked on indifferently, hardly reacting and not even rising. What was Byzantium to them, or for that matter Carthage? Amalek, the Edomites, they had seen it all before! What was new? Were not these heathen folk constantly waging purposeless wars, now one side winning, now the other, but never a victory for the righteous? What was any of this to them? Carthage, Rome, Byzantium – what could these mean for them, for whom one city alone counted – Jerusalem?

Only Benjamin Marnefesh, the sorely tested, now looked up alertly:

'And what of the Menorah?'

'It is whole and undamaged, but seized as booty by Belisarius. They say he is taking it to Byzantium, with all the rest of the plunder.'

Now the others were startled, for they well understood Benjamin's question. Once more the sacred lamp was to be wandering on its way to a new unknown land of strangers. The news came to them like a flaming torch tossed into the dark edifice built of their grieving. Leaping to their feet, they pressed forward over the graves and surrounded the stranger, sobbing and weeping:

'Ah, woe! To Byzantium! . . . Over the sea again! . . . Again into heathen lands! . . . Yet again they are taking it away in triumph, just as did Titus, cursed be his name! . . . Again and again, from foreign land to foreign land, but never to Jerusalem . . . Woe, ah woe to us!'

A red-hot iron had been pressed onto an old wound. The darkest fears and anxieties were awakened in every one of them; if the Lord's sacred treasure were to wander, then they themselves must wander too, once more to strange and foreign lands, yet again forced to seek a home where none might be found. Thus had it always been, ever since the destruction of the Temple, and again and again had their lives been shattered too. Pains old and new met in dread confusion. They wept all as one, sobbed and wailed, and the little birds that had sat serenely on the ancient stones now took flight in fear of the tumult that seethed around them.

Only one, the aged Benjamin, remained seated quietly on the mossy stone, and said nothing while the others clamoured and wept. Involuntarily he had clasped his hands; he sat like one dreaming, and smiled gently to himself before the tombstone on which was depicted, engraved, the Menorah. All at once that weathered old face, nestling amidst the white hair and beard, had recaptured something of the small child that he had been, so many long years ago; gone were the wrinkles, the lips were softened, and it was as if the subtle smile now spread from his face over all his body, his bent frame seemingly communing inwardly with himself.

At length one of them again became aware of the old man's presence and felt ashamed at his own loss of restraint. Standing in reverence before Benjamin, he gently touched the arm of him who stood beside him. One by one they all fell silent, and soon all were gazing in breathless wonder at their elder, whose smile hung like a welcome white cloud over the dark despair they had felt. All was as hushed as the world of the dead beneath their feet, around whose tombs they stood.

Only the complete silence of the crowd made Benjamin aware that all were looking at him. Slowly, with difficulty, frail as he now was, he rose from the fractured stone on which he sat. Suddenly, as he stood before all of them he seemed possessed of a power they had never seen, his face ringed in the silvery white locks that cascaded from under his silk cap. Never had his people been so convinced as now that their Marnefesh, the sorely tested, had been sent for a purpose. But now Benjamin began to speak, and in his words they could sense the sanctity of a prayer:

'Now have I come to know why God has preserved me up to this hour. Repeatedly I have asked myself for what reason I still break the bread to no avail, and to what end death has thus far spared me, worn out with age and weary of life as I am, I who longed for nothing more than the calm and silence of life's end. Indeed I had lost all strength of spirit, so much suffering did I witness among our people, and my former trust had failed me. But now I see that there remains one task for me in this life. I have seen the beginning, and am now called to see the end.'

The others listened, awestruck, to his cryptic words. Presently one, the first among them, asked him tentatively: 'What do you mean to do?'

'I believe,' he answered, 'that God's purpose in preserving my life for so long, and with it the power of my sight, was that I might once again cast my eyes on the holy lamp. To Byzantium I am called, where perchance what the child failed to do may be achieved by an old man in his final days.'

All of them swayed and trembled in excitement and impatience. It defied belief that this fragile figure of an old man could win back their Menorah from the most powerful emperor on earth. And yet how enticing it was to trust in a miracle. One alone of them asked anxiously:

'But how will you ever survive so great a journey? Consider it – three weeks it will be, on treacherous wintry seas. I fear you will not be strong enough.'

'Strength will always be found when the task is sacred. Then too, when long ago those elders took me, a little child, along with them, they thought the journey would defeat me, yet I continued with them to the very end. But one need I do have, for my arm is crippled; there must be one to accompany and help me, one young and in the best of health, who shall himself bear witness to future generations, as I have done for yours.'

His eyes were turned searchingly on the circle around him, looking at the young men one by one, as if examining each of them, and each trembled before this testing glance that pierced him to the hushed depths of his heart. Each craved to be the one chosen for this mission, but not one of them dared step forward. All were waiting, their souls in fervour. But the old man lowered his head and murmured: 'No, I will not decide this. Let the choice not be mine. Let lots be cast. God may show me who is the right one among you.'

The men drew close together, plucked blades of grass from the abundant growth around the graves, broke them in different lengths and shared them round. The lot fell to Joachim Gamliel, twenty years of age, tall and strong, a smith by trade but unloved by the rest, for he was unlearned in the scriptures, an impetuous soul. There was blood on his hands, as he had fought and struck down a Syrian in Smyrna, then fled to Rome before he could be arrested. Indignantly, they wondered in their minds how the lot could favour this wild and fractious man instead of someone respectful and pious. But Benjamin Marnefesh looked only fleetingly at him when he came forward as the chosen one, and spoke briefly:

'Prepare yourself. Tomorrow we shall start.'

Over the whole day that followed that ninth of Av, those of the Roman congregation were busily occupied. Not a single one of the Jews attended that day to his normal business. All were collecting and bringing what money they had; the poor borrowed by pawning possessions, and the women gave up their clasps and precious stones. In all of them had grown a certainty that Benjamin Marnefesh was indeed chosen by God to free the Menorah from its latest captivity and dispose the Emperor Justinian, like Cyrus before him, to send their people home with their holy temple furnishing. Day and night they wrote to the communities of the East, to Smyrna and Crete and Salonica, to Tarsus, Nicea and Trebizond, requesting them to send emissaries to Byzantium, to gather funds so that the holy act of liberation might be brought to pass. They urged their brethren in Byzantium and Galata to make open every possible way to Benjamin, the sorely tested, as the man chosen by God for a supreme calling. At the same time the women prepared coats and cushions and provisions for the journey, that the lips of the pious should not touch anything impure on the seaward voyage. And although the Jews of Rome were forbidden to ride in wagons or on horseback, they secretly arranged for a cart to be brought outside the city gate, so that the old man should not be wearied even before starting his journey.

Great therefore was their admiration when Benjamin declined to board this conveyance. He would go on foot to

Portus, he asserted, just as, when still a weakling little child, he had made that other journey by night more than eighty years ago. To the others it seemed at first a bold, even wayward undertaking for a man so weakened by age willingly to set out for the sea on foot, but as they looked at him, to their astonishment, it was as if since the moment of his calling he had been utterly transformed, his every limb having absorbed in an instant a new power and a new warmth now flowing in his old man's blood. His voice, hitherto weak and dull, now rang with renewed strength and authority, almost wrathful in the way he repelled their concerns; and so, won over in respect for him, they assented to his demands.

Throughout the night the Jewish men of Rome accompanied Benjamin Marnefesh, the chosen one of their community, on the same path that once their ancestors had trodden while escorting the sacred Menorah. Without his knowing, they had in tow a litter, to carry the old man if his strength were to fail him. But Benjamin strode heartily on, indeed ahead of all. He spoke not a word as he went, and his thoughts dwelt solely on the distant past. At every milestone they passed, every turn in this road on which he had not set foot in all the years since that night of robbery and plunder, the more vivid and powerful grew the memory of that hour of his childhood. He recalled everything that had happened, heard in the balmy air the voices of men long dead, remembered every word that every one of them had spoken. Yes, there on the right had shone the pillar of fire from the house in flames, and here had stood the milestone at which the elders had lost all their courage when the Numidian horsemen had borne down upon them. He relived every question he had asked of the Rabbi, and every answer he had received. And as he came to the place where at dawn the elders had stood at prayer, he brought out his shawl and phylacteries, as all had done before him, and turning eastward he chanted the morning prayer of all his forefathers, and of the children and grandchildren who were to come after him, for so it ran, ingrained and cherished in their blood from generation to generation.

The others looked on in quiet amazement, for this was strange and incomprehensible. The season was closer to autumn than it had been on that occasion long ago; there was not the slightest hint in the sky of dawn yet breaking. How could any observant Jew mean to recite the morning prayer so long before the end of the night? Was this not against all common practice, an affront to custom and scriptural law? Nevertheless they clustered reverently around him as he prayed, for whatever their chosen one did, this could not be wrong.

His prayer now said, he folded his shawl and strode forth with renewed vigour; the observance itself had clearly refreshed him. And when at length they came to the harbour, and his gaze went far out over the sea, again within him the child came back to life, the little Benjamin, long forgotten, who once had looked out at this same wide stretch of waters, the same horizon. Eighty years ago it was, and here still was this sea, deep and unfathomable as the thoughts of God. Just as then, his eyes now brightened at the radiance of the sky; blessing each of those who had accompanied him, he said his final farewell and boarded the ship with Joachim. And just as, long ago, their forebears had once looked out, now these men's eyes watched with deeply stirred emotion as the galley moved away, and its sails swelled and billowed. They knew in their hearts that they would never again see the sorely tested one, and when at last the sail vanished from view, they felt themselves bereft and impoverished.

Firmly and steadily meanwhile the ship plied her way; the waves foamed and surged, and from the west dark clouds came into view. The crew looked on anxiously, fearing a storm and mortal danger, but though twice set back by heavy waves and adverse winds, the galley came safely through and, three days after Belisarius brought the plunder from the African coast to Byzantium, arrived intact.

Byzantium, after the fall of Rome as central power, became mistress of the empire and ruler of the whole world. That morning the city was swarming with people, for never in countless years had there been the promise of so glorious a spectacle as now, to delight a populace more devoted to games and festivals than to God and righteousness. Belisarius, conqueror of the Vandals, was to bring his victorious army, with all its captured booty, into the great Circus, there to parade before the Basileus, the Emperor, Lord of all Lands. People beyond number crowded streets adorned with bunting. One massive throng filled to bursting the almost infinitely long space of the Hippodrome right up to its rounded end, and the air was charged with the impatient expectation of an increasingly petulant, grumbling multitude, for they could not but notice that the imperial box, the cathisma, which lay hard by the giant oval of the stadium like an egg within its shell, remained wholly empty of spectators, for all its lavish columns and adornments. The Basileus himself was still to make his ceremonial entrance through the underground passage that linked this imposing structure with the imperial palace.

Finally came the strident trumpet fanfares to announce the great ceremonial moment. First of all to enter and form a brilliant backdrop in their red uniforms and flashing swords were the imperial guard, followed by the gorgeous rustling silk finery of the highest court dignitaries, and the priests and eunuchs; after them all appeared, beneath splendid canopies, two palanquins, one bearing Justinian, the 'Autokratos' Basileus, his head topped by a halo-like golden crown, and the other the Empress Theodora amidst the shimmer of her jewellery. As they came forward into the imperial enclosure, a sudden roar of jubilation burst forth from every crowded level of the stadium. Banished now was the memory that in that same grand space, only a few years earlier, another great multitude had risen up and rushed on that imperial box, occupied by the same Emperor, and that as punishment some thirty thousand had been slaughtered in that very place. Victory is always an efficient leveller of guilt, and the common mass are quick to forget. Intoxicated by pageantry and by their own zealous enthusiasm, these thousands of spectators shouted and howled in a clamour of adulation that reverberated and rocked the outer stone walling of the stadium. Here was an entire city, an entire world, quaking in approbation of the imperial couple, the son of Macedonian peasantry and his meretricious wife Theodora, who had, as older spectators still remembered, first danced here and exhibited her body naked before the public, and then sold that same commodity to all and sundry. But this too was largely forgotten, as commonly happens with any disgrace in the wake of victory, and with any atrocity when a triumph follows the victory.

But high up, poised in silence above the roaring mass of spectators who showered their thunderous venal applause, like so much waste water, over the returning victor, there stood another class of witnesses on the highest stone terraces, namely the still ranks of figures of stone, the hundreds upon hundreds of statues from Grecian lands. Torn from their temples, where nothing but peace had reigned, or dragged down from triumphal arches and columns, these images of the gods from Palmyra and Kos, from Corinth and Athens, now looked out, resplendent in the nakedness of their eternal white marble. Immune to transient emotions, wholly absorbed in the undying dream of their beauty, there they stood in mute indifference to the spectacle below, with not a thought to spare, let alone any respect, for earthly matters. Thus unmoved and unmoving, proudly they stared away over all these bloodstained human diversions, and out to the blue expanse of sea, whose purer effervescent waters stretched joyfully towards the Bosphorus.

Now another sharp burst of fanfares sounded from closer at hand, announcing the arrival of the great commander himself at the outer gates of the hippodrome. The portals were thrown open, and the noise of the crowd rose once again to a deafening roar of exultation. Now appeared the elite cohorts of Belisarius, the army that had established Byzantine dominance of the world, conquered all their foes and supplied them with the comforts of all the pleasures and games they could desire. Still more rasping and piercing were the cries that greeted the booty following behind the warriors, the seemingly limitless treasures of Carthage. First to be brought in were the triumphal carts once seized by the Vandals, and after them, borne on raised trestles, the jewel-bedecked thrones and altars of unfamiliar gods, and splendid statues doubtless fashioned by unknown craftsmen in the name of beauty. Then came chests filled to overflowing with gold, precious goblets and vases and silken garments. Everything that the robber bands had plundered for so long from all ends of the earth was now returning to the Emperor and his realm. At the sight of each costly wonder presented before them, the people whooped and cheered anew, fancying in their feverish credulity that all the riches and splendours on earth must be flowing back to him alone, to be his for evermore.

Amidst so dazzling a display of choice treasures, it was easy for the crowd not to notice that some of the objects brought in seemed of lesser, more meagre worth. There came, for instance, a small table with a gold overlay, two silver clarions and a seven-armed candelabrum. The response to these apparently undistinguished items was more muted, and no jubilant cries were to be heard. But high up among the throng of onlookers an old man uttered a groan, and with his left hand quickly seized Joachim's arm. After eighty years these elderly eyes were seeing what the small child had seen, the holy Menorah from the house of Solomon, the great lamp that his little hand had once clasped, an act that had caused the crippling of his arm for the rest of his life. Oh, blessed sight! This was that same eternal Menorah, in its invincibility ever passing through endless ages, and now a step further on its homeward journey! The old man sensed the grace of God in his seeing the treasured symbol once more, and it shook his whole being. No longer could he suppress his joy, and with utter abandon he cried out; 'Ours! Ours! Ours for all eternity!'

But none, not even those nearest him, heard this one man's cry, drowned as it was by a sudden joyous yelling from the whole vast assembled populace: Belisarius, the victor, had just entered the arena. Far behind the triumphal carriages, far behind the immeasurable quantities of booty, he walked forward in the same simple garb worn by his soldiers. But the people easily recognized their conquering hero, trumpeting his name, and his alone, at such volume that Justinian himself could only bite his lip in jealousy when his general bowed submissively before him.

The noise subsided, and the tension and the silence were quite as dramatic as the cheering a moment earlier. Gelimer, King of the Vandals, clad in royal purple as an object of derision, walked behind Belisarius, his vanquisher, and now stood before the Emperor. The slaves stripped him of his robe, and in defeat and humiliation he threw himself to the ground. For a moment not a single breath passed the lips of any one of the countless public. All were staring at the hand of the Basileus. What sign would he give? Would he grant mercy or not? And now they saw the sign of clemency; the vanquished would be spared his life, and the crowd thundered their rapturous assent.

One man alone among them had not looked on; Benjamin, his mind in turmoil, could gaze only upon the Menorah, now being carried slowly away across the arena. And as the sacred object disappeared with the procession, his senses darkened.

'Take me hence!' he said.

Joachim muttered quietly in displeasure. The brilliance of the extraordinary spectacle had greatly appealed to the young man, and he thirsted for more. But Benjamin's gnarled old hand clutched his arm and pressed hard. 'Take me hence! Take me hence!' And like a blind man groping and feeling his way, he held on firmly to Joachim's arm as they crossed the city, still every moment seeing nothing in his mind's eye but the Menorah, and, all the while impatient of the journey, he urged Joachim to deliver him without delay to the Jewish quarter. A sudden fear had gripped him, now that a momentous beginning and an end were at once in play, that his life might come prematurely to its end, and once again he might fail to rescue the sacred lamp.

In the synagogue at Pera meanwhile the congregation had been waiting for many hours for their illustrious guest. Just as in Rome, Jews were permitted to live only on one side of the river, so here in Byzantium their presence was not tolerated outside Pera, which lay on the far side of the Golden Horn. In Byzantium, as everywhere, living apart was their destiny, but therein lay also the secret of their survival through the ages.

Filled to overflowing, that small room was cramped and sweltering. In attendance were not only the Jews of Byzantium, but many others from far and wide, from Nicaea and Trebizond, Odessa and Smyrna, and the Thracian towns; emissaries had come from every community to witness the events and play their part. It was long since the news had gone out, and had spread to Jewish congregations on every shore of every sea, that

Belisarius had stormed the Vandals' stronghold and recaptured the eternal Menorah, along with all the other plundered treasures; no Jew anywhere throughout the empire could have failed to hear such tidings with the greatest elation. To be sure, this people was scattered, like chaff over the world's threshing floors, through many lands of many different tongues, but all that befell the symbol they held most sacred spoke directly to all of them alike, be it in sorrow or joy, and though often they might quarrel among themselves, and often their memories might fail them, their hearts would join together in brotherly oneness whenever danger appeared. Repeated persecutions and injustices merely forged afresh the iron bonds that held their downtrodden people fast together, in a unity that never flagged and never died. And the more harshly fate struck against any element among them, just so much the more strongly did their spirits incline to unity. So now too, the report that the Menorah, the temple lampstand, the illuminator of their people, had once more been liberated from its hidden imprisonment and was again on its wanderings, just as long ago it had been taken over lands and seas from Babylon and from Rome, was received by every Jew as if the Menorah's fortune were indeed his own. On the streets and in their houses they stood and debated eagerly, delving in the scriptures with their teachers and scholars to find the meaning of the Menorah's travels. Why, they wondered, had these started once again? Was this a matter for hope or for despair? Was there now to be an end to their persecution, or the beginning of new oppression? Were they soon yet again to be the driven out, the expelled, exiled wayfarers with no destination they knew, yet again untrusting wanderers like the Menorah itself? Or did the lamp's new-found redemption indicate also their own redemption, an emancipation and final homecoming, a final end to their exile and their sufferings? Their souls aflame with impatience, their envoys hurried from place to place to learn more of the Menorah's movements and fortunes. Great, therefore, was their dismay on hearing at length that this last surviving furnishing of the Great Temple was once more, as so long ago, to be paraded in profane triumph, now to be displayed before Justinian, the Emperor of Byzantium.

This was in itself profoundly stirring news, but wild excitement became a veritable frenzy when a communication from Rome informed all that Benjamin Marnefesh, the sorely tested one, who as a child had been the last on earth to see the lamp on the occasion of its robbery by the Vandals, was on his way to Byzantium. The first reaction was general astonishment. For years all Jews, however distant their communities, had known of the seven-year-old's divinely inspired deed in attempting to wrest the Menorah from the hands of the robbers, and how his arm had been crippled in the act. Mothers would recount to their children, and scholars to their disciples, the tale of Benjamin Marnefesh, who had felt the touch of God. His story had long since become the stuff of pious legend to compete with any to be found in the scriptures and to be learned therefrom. Of an evening one might often hear a telling of the tale by parents and revered elders, alongside the hallowed legends of good and evil, the deeds of Ruth and of Samson, of Haman and Esther. And now all of a sudden had come these tidings, marvellous and scarcely credible to their ears, of that same child, now a venerable old man, who not only still lived, but was making this journey over land and sea. He, the last witness of the Menorah, was on his way to see that precious object once more. Clearly this must be a sign from on high, for why else would God have preserved and spared a man beyond his normally allotted time on earth? No, he was called, and his calling was to bring the sacred candelabrum home, and therewith to deliver them likewise to their homeland. And the more they spoke thus with each other, the less did they doubt. The belief in a saviour to come, a redeemer, lay at all times deep in the blood of this exiled people, a seed that would always burgeon under the first slight warmth of hope, and that faith, now enkindled, burned bright, and that seed bore fruit in their hearts. Gentiles of the towns and villages where they lived observed with amazement the change that came overnight upon their Jewish neighbours. Normally timorous and cringing as they shuffled along, ever fearful of a taunt or a blow, now they walked with heads held high and an almost ecstatic spring in their steps. The miserly among them, who counted and saved every crumb, now bought rich apparel, while men who were previously tongue-tied now stood confidently and eloquently preaching hope in things to come, and women great with child now ventured out and made their way to the market to be the first to announce the news to the others, and children carried gaily coloured flags and garlands. Those most impressed by what they had heard even began to prepare themselves for the journey, rashly selling their belongings to purchase mules and carts and avoid the slightest delay when the call came to set off on their homeward journey to Jerusalem. Were they not themselves to be on the move when the Menorah was travelling the world, and was not the chosen envoy already on the way, he who as a little child had accompanied the lamp? When had there ever been any portent, any miracle to compare with this?

So it was that every community that came in time to hear of this great mission now chose one from among their number as an emissary, who would be in Byzantium to witness the arrival of the Menorah and duly take part in the deliberations. And all who were so dispatched exulted in their good fortune and blessed God's name. It seemed a marvel to them, in their restricted, subdued lives eked out in constant want and danger, that they of all people, insignificant small-time traders and humble workmen, should be permitted to play any part in so momentous an event, and to see with their own eyes the man whose life God had prolonged and destined for the deed of redemption. They bought or borrowed rich clothing as if they had been invited to a great banquet, they fasted and bathed and prayed constantly as the day of their departure approached, so that they could take up their mission in purity of body and soul, and when finally they set forth from their homes the communities of their villages or towns accompanied them for the first day of their journey. In every place they passed through on their way to Byzantium the pious would give them shelter and collected money for them for the recovery of the lamp. Proud and stately as ambassadors of a king, these lowly envoys of a poor and powerless people strode forth; meeting others on the way, they joined forces and went on together, excitedly discussing what would happen; and the more they spoke, the more intense was their excitement. And the more they thus roused one another's spirits, the more certain they became of their imminent witnessing of a miracle, and therewith the long-foretold turn in their people's fortunes.

There in the prayer house at Pera they now waited together, a heated, confused crowd, all talking, debating, questioning without end. And now came the boy whom they had sent out in their impatience for news; panting, he ran towards them waving a white cloth to show that their longed-for Benjamin Marnefesh had arrived from Byzantium in a boat and had now touched the shore. Those still seated leaped up, and those who just now had been talking so animatedly stood silent. One of the oldest of them collapsed in a faint and fell forward, unable to contain himself for emotion. But none, not even their leader, could find the courage to go out to meet their expected guest. Holding their breath, they stood and waited. And as the imposing figure of Benjamin, with his striking white beard and darkly scintillating eyes, approached the house supported on the arm of

Joachim and was brought in by the young lad, he gave the appearance of a true patriarch, the veritable lord and master of all that was miraculous. Now, finally, all of their suppressed enthusiasm broke loose. 'Blessed thy coming! Blessed be thy name!' they cried before him. In no time they had surrounded him, kissing the hem of his coat, and the tears ran on their withered cheeks. Pushing each other wildly, they thrust themselves forward, each wanting piously to touch with even with one finger the hallowed arm that had been broken in the child's moment of heroism. Their leader had to stand between them and Benjamin to protect him from being trampled underfoot in the fervour of the throng.

Benjamin himself, taken aback at such impetuous behaviour, wondered what they could want of him. What exactly were they hoping for? A sudden fear overcame him at the thought of the unbounded expectations they might lay upon his shoulders. Gently but urgently he demurred.

'Do not look at me in this way. You must not place such hopes in me as I never myself conceived. I can work no miracles. Let it suffice to hope, but patiently. It would be sinful to demand the certainty of a miracle.'

All lowered their heads, abashed that he had read their innermost thoughts, and ashamed of their unbridled impatience. Quietly they stepped aside, and their leader was now able to conduct Benjamin to the place they had prepared for him, carefully laid with cushions and clearly raised above the others. But once again Benjamin resisted:

'No, do not do this. I have no desire to sit above the rest of you; I am no more than any of you, and indeed I may be the lowliest in your midst. I am nothing but an aged man to whom God has left but little strength. I came only to observe, and to offer counsel, nothing more; you must not expect any miracles from me!'

Submitting to his wish, they allowed him to sit among them, the one patient soul amid their restlessness. Only now did their leader of the congregation rise to pronounce the greeting:

'Peace be with thee! Blessed thy coming and blessed thy going! Our hearts are gladdened to see thee!'

A solemn silence followed, and then the leader continued in a voice of calm restraint:

'We have letters from our brethren in Rome informing us of your coming, and we have done all that is within our power. Money we have collected, going from place to place and from household to household, that we might help bring about the redemption of the Menorah. We have got ready a gift to soften the Emperor's heart. The costliest of our possessions we have made ready to present to him, a stone from Solomon's Temple rescued by our forefathers when the Temple was destroyed. This we intend to offer to the Emperor. All his thoughts at this time are on building a great house of God, one more glorious than any known before, and for this he is bringing the greatest, the most revered riches from every land and every city. What we have done, we have done willingly and gladly. But it has alarmed us greatly to hear from our brethren what it is that they require of us, that we should secure an audience with the Emperor himself, that you might entreat him to return the sacred lamp. Greatly alarmed I say we are, for he who sits here upon the throne, Justinian, has no love for us. In his heart he cannot tolerate any who do not share and profess his faith in every detail, be they Christians of other kinds, or heathens, or Jews. And perhaps our sojourn in his lands may not last long, for soon he may drive us out. To this day he has not allowed even one of our number to appear before him. With shame in my heart I came here today to say this to you: what our Roman brethren request of us will never come to be; it is impossible for any Jew to be admitted to the presence of this Emperor.'

The elder fell silent, cowed and afeared. All bowed their heads in despondency. Where now the miracle? What change could be expected, if the emperor would not countenance the wish, nor even hear the words, of God's emissary? But again the elder spoke, and now his voice was more confident:

'Nevertheless comforting, indeed wonderful, it is to learn, as we have learned, again and again, that for God nothing is impossible. As I entered this house with heavy heart, there came to me one from our community, Zacharias the goldsmith, a pious and righteous man, and his message to me was that the will of our Roman brethren was yet fulfilled. While we spoke together and troubled ourselves to no purpose, this good man was quietly at work, and what had seemed impossible even to the wisest of us, that he has achieved by secret means. Speak, Zacharias, and tell us more.'

From far back in the room a hesitant figure rose to his feet, slight and hunched in form, shy and bashful at seeing that all were looking at him so inquisitively. He bowed his head to hide his blushing; unused to company in his quiet life and solitary place of work, he naturally feared to speak, and to be listened to. Several nervous coughs preceded his words, which came forth like those of a child:

'I deserve no praise, Rabbi,' he said in a low whisper. 'Not mine is the merit. It was God who eased the way for me. For thirty years the imperial treasurer has been well disposed towards me; for all of those years I have worked for him, day after day, and when a few years past the people rose up against the Emperor, and plundered and burned the houses of the courtiers, then for his safety I hid him for three days with his wife and child in my own dwelling, until the danger had passed. So I knew that he would grant me any wish, though I had never asked anything of him. But now, when I learned that Benjamin was coming, I approached him for the first time, and he went to the Emperor to inform him that a great but secret message would be sent to him from across the sea. And it was God's will that his words be heard, and the Emperor should see fit to give ear and act accordingly. Tomorrow, therefore, Benjamin and our leader are to be received at the palace, in the Emperor's audience room.'

Zacharias quietly and modestly sat down again. All around him the men fell silent in amazement. This was without doubt a miracle unheard of, that a Jew should be permitted access to the Emperor, the unapproachable monarch himself. In their hearts they trembled, and their widened eyes stared as awe and fear gave way to a sense of God's infinite grace. But Benjamin let forth a groan like one wounded:

'O God, my God! What burden is this that I must bear? My heart grows faint, and I do not speak the language of this place. How am I to stand before the Emperor, I of all people, and not another? It was only to bear witness that I was summoned, to set my eyes upon the Menorah, not to lay my hands on it, not to gain possession. Choose not me. Let another come forward to speak, for I am too old, too weak!'

His words were heard with alarm. A miracle had been granted them, and now the very one chosen for it was drawing back. But while they sat doubtfully pondering how they might overcome his hesitancy, Zacharias rose again slowly to his feet, and now his voice was stronger and more confident.

'No, you must go, and you alone. What I did cost me little effort, and yet it was for you and none other that I took it on myself. For I know for certain that if any of us can do so, you are the one who will bring the lamp to its place of peace.'

Benjamin stared at him. 'How can you know this?'

Zacharias repeated, calmly and resolutely: 'I know for certain, and have known for long. You, if any one of us, will bring the lamp to its place of peace.'

Shaken by the certainty of these words, Benjamin looked hard at their speaker, who returned his look with a smile of encouragement. Suddenly it occurred to Benjamin that he had looked into these eyes once before, and Zacharias too seemed to feel some such recognition, for his smile brightened and he spoke again, this time as if confiding in him alone, despite the presence of the others:

'You remember that night? And a man who went with you and the others? Hyrcanus ben Hillel?' And now Benjamin too smiled. 'How could I not remember him? Every word spoken, every shadow that fell on us, is still fresh in my mind.'

'I am his grandson. We are goldsmiths from of old. Whenever an emperor or a king has gold and precious stones and needs a jeweller or a valuer, it is one of our line he chooses. In Rome, it was given to Hyrcanus to guard the Menorah in its confinement. Ever since then, wheresoever we might be, we of this family have waited for the hour that might bring it to some other treasury and under our custody, for where there are treasures, there are we too to be found, as valuers and as artisans. My father's father said to my father, as I his son know from him, that after the night when your arm was injured, Rabbi Eliezer, the pure and clear, declared what you yourself in your innocence could not have known, that there must be a meaning in such a deed, some sense in the pain so suffered. If anyone, he said, then you, who were then that small child, would one day redeem the Menorah.'

A tremor went through them all. Benjamin lowered his eyes. Deeply moved, he spoke:

'No man was ever more good to me than was the Rabbi through that night. I hold his every word sacred. I have been faint-hearted, and I ask forgiveness. Once as a child I, this same I, was bolder. Time and old age have made me hesitant. But once again I implore you all, expect no miracle from me.

If it is your demand that I go to him who holds the sacred lamp, then let the attempt be mine, for, as it is said, woe unto him who declines a pious task. You see before you one who has no power of eloquence, but still might God impart to me the fitting words.'

Benjamin's voice had now become faint and timid, and his head hung low beneath the burden of his mission. He pleaded softly:

'Pardon me for leaving you now. I am an old man, tired by this day's happenings and my long journey. Please allow me to seek some rest.'

All deferred and made way for him to pass. Only one, only the irrepressible Joachim, could not restrain himself, and while conducting his wearied old companion to the place they had prepared for him he pressed him with questions:

'But what will you say to him, the Emperor, tomorrow?'

Benjamin would not look up, but answered in a murmur, as if to himself:

'I know not, nor wish to know, nor even think thereon. I have in myself no power at all. Everything must come to me as a gift, a gift from Him alone.'

For long hours still that night the Jews sat together in Pera. None could sleep, and they talked and deliberated without end, their eyes restlessly alive and watchful. Never had they felt themselves so close to the miraculous. What if the scattering of their people were now soon to end, and with it the cruelty of exile among the nations, the unending persecution and oppression, the constant terror of what might come the next hour or the next day? What if this old man who had sat among them in human form were in truth the promised one, one of those possessed of the power of words who had in former times appeared among them and proved able to move the hearts of kings to righteousness? Joy beyond imagining, grace unthinkable it would be, to bring their holy symbol home, to build the temple anew and live within its shadow. As if drunk and delirious they talked and talked of it the whole fevered night through, and their confidence grew ever more fervid. Forgotten now was the warning old Benjamin had given, that they should not expect any miracle from him; their observant reading of the scriptures had taught them unequivocally to trust in the certainty of God's miracles, and how else could they live, they the outcasts, victims of eternal persecution, if not in this ceaseless waiting for redemption to come? And the closer the night drew towards its end, the longer seemed to them their waiting, and they could scarcely restrain their hearts' impatience. Constantly glancing at the hourglass, chiding its sloth and tardiness, one of them would run to the window, or another out onto the street, in the hope of greeting at last the first light of dawn on the edge of the darkened sea and the first kindling of the day that might match the ardour of their hearts.

Their first elder was hard pressed to contain his congregation, otherwise so willingly submissive to him. All of them wanted to cross over to Byzantium with Benjamin, to stand in wait outside the palace while he was in conference with the Emperor and ruler of all the world; in this way they could feel themselves close to the miracle, and even participants, when it came. But the leader sternly reminded them how dangerous it could be for them to appear in a close and conspicuous group in front of the imperial palace, the people always being hostile, always a threat, to the Jews. Only through dire warnings could he persuade them to stay together in the prayer house at Pera and, unseen by the mob, pray to their unseen God while Benjamin was led before the emperor. And so they did pray and fast for that whole day, and so ardent was their praying that the yearning for home felt by every Jew in every land seemed to be contained in the heart of every one of them. Indeed, their minds were closed to any but this one thought: that he, their chosen one, must be able to fulfil the miracle, and thereby the curse of exile, by God's grace, could be taken from them.

It was nearing the appointed hour of midday when Benjamin, accompanied by the chief elder of the community, entered the great colonnaded square that lay before the imperial palace. Behind them was the sturdy young Joachim, and on his shoulders was borne a heavy load beneath a covering. Walking slowly and calmly, and serious in demeanour, the two elderly figures, clad in their simple dark robes, came to the Chalke, the brazen gateway forming the entrance to the sumptuous throne room of the Emperor of Byzantium. But still they were made to wait in the vestibule long beyond the appointed time; such was calculated custom at the Byzantine court, by which envoys and supplicants, being treated in this way, were encouraged to appreciate the exceptional indulgence vouchsafed them in seeing the face of the world's most exalted potentate. For an hour, then a second hour, and a third, the old men were cold-heartedly left on their feet, without being offered so much as a small stool, standing on icy marble. Meanwhile various dignitaries and obese eunuchs flitted in and out, apparently idly but busily, as did palace guards and extravagantly uniformed servants, but no one showed any concern for the old men, and no one spoke a word to them or even deigned to look at them, while from the walls the mosaic figures, ever emotionless and cold for all their colourfulness, stared down on them, and the columned dome above them rained down its golden opulence blended with the glare of the sun. But Benjamin and his companion from Pera waited quietly and patiently. Old men they were, too long inured to waiting to be troubled now by the passing of a mere hour or two. Only the restless young Joachim glanced inquisitively at every one that came or went, and in his impatience kept counting the little mosaic stones, to shorten the intolerably slow passing of each minute.

The sun had descended some distance from its zenith when at long last the Praepositus of the Sacred Chamber came to instruct them in the protocols demanded by Court convention of those who were to be graciously permitted to stand before the Emperor in person. Upon the opening of the door, he explained, they were to lower their heads and proceed to the extent of twenty steps, which would bring them to a line of white in the coloured marble floor slabs. There they must halt and go no further, lest their breath might be mixed with that of the Emperor. Before daring to raise their eyes towards the Autokratos they must prostrate themselves three times on the ground, arms and legs stretched wide. Only then would they be allowed to approach the porphyry steps leading up to the throne, there to kiss the overhanging purple train of the Basileus' robe.

'No!' protested Joachim under his breath. 'Before God alone may we bow down, never before man. I will not do this.'

'Be silent,' answered Benjamin sternly. 'Why should I not kiss the earth. Is she not herself God's creature? And even if it were wrong to bow before a human being, is it not permitted to do such a wrong to serve a sacred purpose?'

At this moment the ivory door to the audience room fell open. A Caucasian embassy stepped out, apparently having paid its due obeisance to the Emperor. Behind them the door closed again soundlessly. Perplexed, the strangers remained standing in their velvet attire and fur caps. There was considerable discomfort in their faces; clearly the great man had dealt with them imperiously and harshly for offering him merely an alliance in the name of their people, rather than complete submission. Joachim stared curiously at them and at their outlandish garb, but the Praepositus now intervened and bade him take up his veiled load again on his shoulders while warning the two elders to follow his instructions in every detail. He tapped on the ivory door gently with his golden baton. It responded with a thin, ringing tone and opened inwards, allowing the three to step in, an interpreter joining them at a given sign from the Praepositus. And now they had entered the Consistorium, the spacious throne room of the Emperor of Byzantium.

From the door to the middle of this giant hall, to right and left, stood soldiers in a double file through which the three had to make their way, a motionless line of men in red uniform, each with a sword at his side and a gilded helmet on his head, sporting an impressively large red horse tail. In one hand each held a long lance, and over all their shoulders hung the fearsome double-bladed Byzantine axes. As in a wall, stones of equal dimensions are laid alongside each other in neat unbroken lines, so these men stood in lines and stared impassively forward, while behind them were the equally lapidary commanders of the cohorts, holding banners in static stillness. Slowly the three advanced with the interpreter along this unmoving human wall, whose deadened eyes and bodies paid them no heed. And just as noiselessly did the party itself approach the far end of the room, where they surmised – for they were yet unable to raise their eyes – that the Emperor on his throne was awaiting them. But when the Praepositus, who preceded them, halted with his golden baton raised high, and they looked up to the throne as they had been instructed they could, there was no throne, nor any emperor, to greet them, but merely a silk hanging strung across the entire width of the hall so as to shield from sight everything that lay beyond it. Without moving, the three stood in astonishment before this colourfully forbidding barrier.

At this point the master of ceremonies once again raised his staff, and behold, whirring on invisible cords the said curtain opened wide to reveal a tableau: three porphyry steps rising to a bejewelled throne, on which was seated the Basileus under the shelter of a gold baldachin. He cut a rigid figure, more like a statue of himself than the great man in the flesh, an ample personage of powerful build, his forehead retreating beneath the dazzling aura of his crown, which shone resplendently above and behind his head like a saint's halo. Of equally stiff and sculpted appearance were the imperial guard who stood around him, one rank behind another, in white tunics and golden helmets, gold chains around their necks. Before these were stationed the senators, dignitaries of the court. The very breathing of all of these figures seemed stilled, and their eyes frozen; the studied rigidity of their posture was clearly aimed at inducing the same petrifying awe in any who stood for the first time before the Ruler of All the World.

And indeed the first elder and Joachim lowered their eyes in stunned reaction, as happens when one is suddenly caught unawares by the blinding glare of the sun. Only the ancient Benjamin was able to look, with unshaken vision, directly up at the Emperor. His long life had stretched over and beyond the reigns of ten emperors and rulers of Rome, and he knew that under their costly insignia and their crowns they were after all mere mortal beings, who ate and drank like all others, with just the same bodily functions and needs, and whose passing ultimately was the same as any. His soul remained steadfast and unperturbed. Calmly he raised his glance to see, and read, the eyes of him whom he had been sent to petition.

Hereupon he felt from behind him the urgent touch of the golden baton on his shoulders, and immediately remembered what was demanded by court custom. Notwithstanding the difficulty imposed on his decrepit limbs, he flung himself down on the cold marble floor slabs, fully stretching out his arms and legs, and three times he pressed his forehead to the marble, his tousled beard rustling incongruously as it swept against the unfeeling stone. Then he rose, supported by his helper Joachim, and with lowered head went forward to the porphyry steps and kissed the purple hem of the imperial robe.

The Basileus remained stock still. The pupils of his eyes peered fixedly like green stones, with not the slightest flicker of the eyelids or brows. He stared out coldly towards the old man, apparently indifferent to whatever was happening at his feet and whatever vermin might be crawling over the end of his robe.

At a sign from the master of ceremonies all three moved back again and stood in a line, with only the interpreter remaining one step in front as their effective voice. Again the Praepositus lifted his baton. And now came the interpreter's opening words. The man before him, he informed the Basileus, was a Jew who had travelled here on the instruction of his community in Rome, to bring thanks and felicitations to the Emperor on his having avenged Rome upon the robbers and having delivered the lands and seas from these evil pirates. All the Jews of the world, devoted subjects of the Emperor throughout all of his realms, had heard that in his wisdom he intended to build a new house of God dedicated to sanctified Wisdom herself, Hagia Sophia, a great temple that was to be more glorious and more costly than any hitherto seen on earth. In this knowledge it behoved them, despite their destitute state, to contribute some offering, albeit small, to the sanctification of this great building. Trifling was their gift when compared with the magnificence of the Emperor, but still it was the finest and holiest possession that had been passed down to them since ancient days. When their ancestors had been driven from Jerusalem, they had managed to rescue one stone from the great Temple of Solomon. This they had now brought, that it might be set among the foundation, and that thereby a fragment from Solomon's Temple might be an element, and a blessing, in the temple now to be Justinian's.

The Praepositus gave a sign, and Joachim brought forward the heavy stone and placed it alongside the gifts of furs and

Indian ivories and embroidered cashmeres that the Caucasian envoys had heaped up to the left of the throne. Justinian, though, forbore even to glance at either the interpreter or the gift itself. With a blank look of boredom he stared into the middle distance and his lips, barely moving for weariness, spoke irritably and disdainfully: 'Ask what they are after.'

The interpreter explained, with florid eloquence, that among the splendid spoils brought home by Belisarius was a paltry item that was, however, of particular importance to this people. For the seven-armed candelabrum, which the heathens of old had plundered and taken away from Rome, was earlier taken from Solomon's Temple, the Jews' House of God. They now earnestly implored the Emperor graciously to grant them the holy Menorah from out of the spoils, in return for which they would pay its weight, and double, nay ten times its weight, in gold. Not a single dwelling, however humble, would be found anywhere in the world where Jews would not daily record their thanks, uttering their prayers for the health of this most gracious of all emperors and for the long endurance of his reign.

Still the eye of the Basileus remained unmoved. Then he countered sourly:

'I have no need of prayers from any who are not Christians. But ask them, what is it to them, this candelabrum, and what do they propose to do with it.'

The interpreter looked at Benjamin while translating these words for him, and the old man felt a shudder in every limb at the coldness of the Emperor's eyes. He sensed opposition, and an ungovernable fear overcame him. Raising his hands in entreaty, he spoke:

'My Lord, consider, the lamp is the only thing remaining to our people, of all the sacred possessions they once had. Our city was sacked, our walls razed, our temple destroyed. All that was dear to us and belonged to us and was honoured by us, all is lost for all time. One thing alone, this lamp, has survived the ravages of time. It is a thousand years old, more ancient than anything on this earth. For centuries it has wandered homeless, and as long as it is condemned to wandering our people will find no rest. Sir, have pity on us. The lamp is our last possession; I beg you, let us have it once more. Consider how God has raised you on high from humble station and made you rich and mighty above all. He to whom is given, he should give in turn – so it is written. My Lord, what is this one object to you, this wandering lamp? Let its wanderings be at an end, and grant it peace and rest!'

The interpreter translated Benjamin's words with some courtly embellishment. The Emperor had listened at first unmoved, but on hearing Benjamin speak of his being raised by the Almighty from humble origins, his face darkened. It was no music to his imperial ears to be reminded that he, God's equal in majesty, had been born of peasant stock in a village in Thrace. His brow frowned sharply, and his lips were already parted to pronounce his refusal.

But anxiety had made Benjamin the more alert. Sensing the imminent denial on the Emperor's lips, and already hearing in his mind the dreaded and irrevocable 'No', his very fear gave him voice. As if prompted by a powerful inner force, and forgetting the prescription of court practice which forbade him to cross the white vein in the marble, he advanced, to the consternation of all present, to the very base of the throne, and without even knowing himself what he was doing raised his hands towards the Emperor in passionate entreaty:

'Sir, be mindful of your realm, your city! Beware of overreaching yourself! Do not attempt to keep a hold on that which none before you was able to keep. Babylon too was great, and Rome, and Carthage. Yet those temples have fallen that imprisoned the sacred lamp, the walls brought down that enclosed it. It alone remained unharmed, while all else fell in ruins around it. He who seeks to hold it will see his arm crippled in the deed, and any who rob it of its rest shall themselves fall victim to unrest. Woe to him who holds what is not his to hold! He shall know no peace from God till this holiest of objects returns to its holy place. Sir, be warned. Return to us the holy lamp!'

All were stunned. None had understood Benjamin's untamed words; this alone had awed the courtiers, that one had now dared what no one had ever done before, and had in the heat of emotion drawn close to the Emperor and abruptly silenced the speech of the mightiest ruler on earth. Shuddering in fear, they stared at this ancient figure of a man who stood before them shaken by overwhelming pain, the tears visible in his beard, his eyes glistening with anger. The elder of Pera, cowering, had retreated far behind him in the hall, and the interpreter too had drawn back. All alone now, Benjamin stood close to the Basileus, and the two faced each other eye to eye.

Justinian, now awakened from his rigidity, looked apprehensively at the enraged man before him, and then at the interpreter, impatient to hear what words he would convey. The interpreter translated with circumspect softening of the message. Might the Basileus in his goodness see fit to pardon the old man for his improper behaviour, seeing that nothing other than concern for the welfare of the empire had occasioned such turbulence on his part. He had been frank in warning His Majesty that God had laid a fearful curse upon the candelabrum; any who kept it under duress would surely suffer dire consequences, and any city that harboured it would fall to its enemies. Of this he had felt it his duty to warn the great Emperor, and to advise him to avert the curse by returning the sacred implement to its place of origin, to Jerusalem.

The tension showed in Justinian's countenance as he took in the words. Angered by the presumptuousness of this overweening old Jew who had dared raise his voice and his fist in his august presence, still he felt a distinct unease, for being of peasant stock he was no stranger to superstition, and like any child of fortune he nursed a dread of magic and omens. For some moments he was silent and sunk in thought. Then came a drily voiced command:

'Let it be. Let this thing be taken out of the spoils and sent to Jerusalem.'

The old man quaked as the interpreter translated the words. The joyful message shot through him and illumined his heart like a brilliant streak of lightning. All was now fulfilled. It was for this moment that he had lived. For this moment God had spared his life on earth, and unwittingly he raised his one uninjured hand and held it trembling high above him, as if in his gratitude he wished to reach out to his God.

But Justinian keenly observed the elder's face, radiant with joy, and was overcome by a vindictive desire. This audacious Jew should not be allowed to return and boast before his people that he had imposed his will on the Emperor and won him over. With a sharp, malicious smile he spoke:

'Save your rejoicing! It will not be to you Jews that the lamp belongs, and will not serve your false rites.'

He then turned to Euphemius, the Bishop, who stood at his right hand:

'When you leave at new moon to consecrate the new church in Jerusalem which Theodora has endowed, you are to take the candelabrum with you. But it is not to stand lighted upon the altar; it shall be placed below the altar, that it may be seen by all how our religion stands above theirs, and how truth vanquishes error. It shall be held in the true church, and not with them among whom the Saviour came and who knew him not.'

The old man was struck with fear, for though he had not understood the untranslated words, the malignity of the Emperor's smile showed clearly that some command was issued to counter his heartfelt wish. Should he again prostrate himself and attempt to change Justinian's mind? But the Emperor had already looked towards the Praepositus, who now raised his staff; there came the sound of the closing curtain, and Emperor and throne had vanished from view, the audience now ended.

Stunned, Benjamin stood before the drawn partition. The master of ceremonies touched him from behind on his shoulder; he was to leave now. The old man's eyes clouded over as, supported by Joachim, he walked out unsteadily. Yet again, he felt, God had rebuffed him just as the sacred Menorah was almost in his hands. Again, at the crucial moment, he had failed; again the sacred lamp was to be in the hands of despots.

Only a short distance from the palace they had just left, Benjamin, once more the sorely tested, again began to falter. The elder of Pera and Joachim had to muster all their strength to support him as he staggered a little further. They brought him to a nearby house, where he was put to bed. His face had lost all colour as he lay with closed eyes, and it seemed to them that death might claim him now; his arms hung limp and lifeless, and when the elder anxiously felt for any heartbeat, all he could sense was a feeble, hesitant ripple. It was as if in his vain appeal to the Emperor all strength had abandoned him, and now the old man lay for long hours wholly insensate. But then, as evening was already drawing in, to the two friends' astonishment, though he had been so close to death, his senses suddenly returned and he stared at them strangely, like one who might have come back to them from the world beyond. A moment later, on recognizing them, he again amazed them by requesting that they take him with all possible haste to the prayer house at Pera, as he wished to take his leave of the community. In vain the two begged him to rest a while longer to gather strength, and he obstinately insisted they obey his wish. They brought him in a litter to a ferry, and together they crossed the water to Pera. As if sleepwalking he let them lead him, his eyes vacant, saying not a word.

The Jews at Pera had long known of the Emperor's pronouncement. Their belief in an imminent miracle had been too certain for them to feel any rejoicing at news that the Menorah had been permitted to return home. Far too meagre was this limited fulfilment of their wildly immoderate hopes. Were the Menorah indeed now freed from further confinement in a heathen temple among strangers, could they then not themselves hope for freedom, for an end to their days of wandering and exile? Indeed, it was not so much the Menorah, but rather their own fate that concerned them. Like men crushed and defeated, they sat dejectedly nursing their secret resentment. How beguiling, they now saw, is the promise of success to one fool enough to believe it! As for miracles, so eloquently related in the scriptures, and so alluring to picture in a distant, however wondrous, world of make-believe, they shine down on us like fiery clouds from those times of old when God was near, those times never to reappear in these our mundane daily lives. God had forgotten his people; those that once he had chosen, now uncaringly He had left in suffering and affliction. No longer did He waken the words of prophets to speak in his name. Foolish indeed, to put one's faith in uncertain signs and then wait for wonders to follow! At Pera the Jews now prayed no more, and fasting had ceased. Dispirited, they crouched in the corners chewing onion bread, bitterness on their lips.

For now that their eyes and their foreheads no longer glowed in expectation of a miracle, they became the petty, rueful creatures they had been before, poor, downtrodden Jews; their thoughts, which so recently had soared proudly to divine heights, now returned to the crabbed and frugal concerns of their everyday lives. They griped and grumbled at each other: for what purpose had they made this long, costly journey to so little avail? They rued the extravagance of the clothing they had now worn thin along the way, not to mention the time they had lost, the neglect of their work and trading. With foreboding they knew what mocking reproaches they would face on returning home. Our hearts are ever disposed to turn with particular vehemence against those who have first raised, and then disappointed, our fondest hopes. Thus did these men heap all of their darkest rancour on their Roman brethren, and on none more than Benjamin Marnefesh, their false messenger. Now, if ever, was he Marnefesh, the bitterly tested one, whom God did not love, and indeed the bitterness issued forth from him. When he came back at night to the prayer house, they were not slow to show their anger. No longer did they draw close and stand before him in reverence; now there was no greeting, and deliberately they averted their eyes from him. What was he now to them, the old Jew from Rome, after all as weak and powerless as any of them? God, it seemed, had no more regard for him than for their own blighted fate.

Benjamin sensed at once the hostility in their silence, and sensed too the mire of resentment in which they turned from him. With sorrow he saw how they looked askance at him, their eyes avoiding his; their disappointment shook him, for in this he saw his own failing. He asked their leader to gather them, for he had one further word to say to them. And so it was done, and unwillingly, grudgingly, they raised heads from their meagre fare. What could he still have to say, this stranger, this bringer of false tidings? Yet even now a sense of pity came upon them when they saw this man of uncountable years laboriously raise himself from the seat on his stick. Hardly able to stand upright, still bent and stooping, he, the oldest of all present, faced the hush around him and every word strained him more:

'My brethren, I have come once more, to take my leave of you. But I have come also in all humility before you, for I have, though unwillingly, caused your hearts much grief. You know it was against my will that I went before the Emperor, but how could I refuse when this was what you yourselves enjoined? When I was still a child the elders took me with them, young though I was; they tore me from my sleep, and I knew nothing and was unwilling to go. And thereafter they never ceased to proclaim that therein lay the meaning in my life, to deliver our sacred lamp. I ask you to understand, brethren, that it is terrible to be one whom God is ever calling but whose prayers are never answered, one whom the Almighty, time and again, beckons with signs yet never fulfils them. How much better it would be for one such to remain in obscurity, to be seen by none, heard by none. And so I beg you to forgive me, to forget me, to dismiss me from your minds. Let not the name of that one pass your lips, who in his wrong did you such injury. I beg you also to await patiently the coming of that one who will show that the right is with him, who will redeem the Menorah and with it his people.'

Three times the old man bowed in humility before the congregation, like a penitent admitting his guilt. Three times he struck his breast with his now powerless left hand – the injured right arm hung limply down at his side. Then abruptly pulling himself up, he crossed the room and went to the door. No one moved, and no one said anything in answer. Joachim alone, mindful of his duty to support him, hurried after him to the threshold. But Benjamin resisted firmly:

'Return to Rome, and if they ask after me there, you are to say to them: 'Benjamin Marnefesh is no more, nor was he the rightly chosen one.' They are to forget my name and must never utter any prayer in remembrance of me. I wish for death even beyond my passing, to be wholly lost to our people's memory. For your part, go in peace and trouble yourself no more about me.'

Obediently, Joachim held back at the threshold, disquieted as his gaze followed Benjamin. Why, he wondered, was the old man, tottering with such difficulty and with only his stick to support him, now making his way along an unfamiliar narrow lane leading uphill? He dared not follow, but merely stared after him until the bent old figure had completely vanished in the darkness.

That night, in the eighty-eighth year of his life, Benjamin Marnefesh, hitherto a quiet and patient soul, for the first time berated God. In the turmoil of his hunted heart he knew no peace as he groped his way along the narrow, crooked lanes of Pera, ignorant of where they were taking him. All he desired was to flee, such was his burning shame at having lured his people into wildly excessive hopes. He wished to creep into some remote corner, where none would know him and his life could end like that of a dying animal. 'It was not my fault!' he murmured repeatedly to himself. 'Why did they burden me so with their hopes of a miracle? Why did they choose me, why pursue me so?' But he found no comfort in such inner thoughts and words, and fear drove him further and further away, the fear that someone might follow him. His feet had now for long been aching, his knees weary and trembling, and the sweat broke out on his deeply furrowed brow, the bitter saltiness running over his beard and his lips. His tortured heart beat fiercely and painfully in his breast, but on and on he went in his hunted, confused state, supported by his staff, higher and higher up the narrow path that now led out from the tangled cluster of houses and into open countryside beyond. To see no more of his fellow human beings, to be seen no more by them! Away now from dwellings and hearths, to be lost, forgotten and at last himself delivered from that everlasting delusion of another deliverance!

Staggering like a drunkard as he went along, Benjamin at last found himself high on the hilly ground overlooking the town. Here, out under the open sky, he leaned against the trunk of a protecting pine tree. Though he did not know it, the tree stood guard over a grave; here he paused a while, his heart now faltering, and breathed once more. There was a perfect autumnal clarity in that southern night; the sea was an expanse of shining silver scales resembling a giant fish, and close by lay the great serpentine curve of the Golden Horn. Beyond the stretch of water the gleaming domes and towers of Byzantium slept in white moonlight. Scarcely were any lights now to be seen heading over towards the city; midnight had come, and the bustle of human activity had ceased. But here among the hills the breeze wafted a gentle whisper through the vineyards, as here and there yellowing leaves flew from vine stems emptied of their fruit and fluttered slowly and silently to the ground. Somewhere nearby there must be wine-presses and storage sheds, for the breezes brought a scent, rich and tart, that reminded Benjamin of his past, and the old man's trembling senses breathed in the moist and musty vapour. Ah, to fade away, to become earth oneself, like those spinning vine leaves that sink and vanish in the soil, never to return! To be finally freed from the repeated stress and torment, delivered from the burden of existence!

As the very stillness of the place struck him more forcefully, and with it his awareness of being wholly alone, soon he was overpowered by an insuperable longing for eternal rest, and into the silence he raised his voice to God, half in protest and half in prayer: 'Lord, I long for death! To what end do I continue to live, of no use to myself, and to others a cause for grievance and scorn? Why do you spare me, though you know full well I wish it no more? Sons I have fathered, seven of them, each one of them vigorous and ardent for life, and into the grave of each of them I, their father, have cast the earth. You gave me a grandson, youthful and fair, but when still he knew neither desire for woman nor the sweetness of life itself, then did the heathens strike him down. He did not wish to die, assuredly he did not; for four days he wrestled, for all his wounds, against death.

Yet did you take him, him who wished for life. And me, who quakes with longing for death, you will not take unto yourself; no, you reject me, thrust me back. Lord, what is it that you want of me, who resists and wishes it not? When still a child I was torn from my sleep, and yet I went in obedience, but still I delude those who put their trust in me, and the signs were mere deceit. Lord, let there be an end! I have failed, so cast me forth! Eight and eighty years have I lived, and waited for some meaning in these years that you have prolonged, waited in hope that some deed of mine might prove worthy of my faith in you. But now I am wearied. Lord, there is no more in me. Lord, let it be enough, let me die!'

As he lifted his voice in such entreaty and prayer, Benjamin raised his eyes yearningly heavenwards, where the diffused light of the sparkling stars seemed to reflect his passionate outburst. There the old man stood, waiting. Would God now, finally, grant him an answer? Patiently he waited, and then slowly the hand that he had raised unconsciously began to fall, and weariness overcame him, a weariness beyond all measure. In his temples there was a sudden stupefying throbbing, while his feet and knees lost all power and he staggered and fell. Without his knowing or willing it, he sank down, enfeebled but relieved, a feeling both sweet and bitter, as if the blood were draining from his body, and his weakness tempered with pleasure. 'So this is death,' he thought gratefully. 'God has heard my cry.' Calmly, piously, he stretched his head on the earth, which gave off its odour of autumnal finality. 'I should have put on my prayer shawl,' he half reminded himself, but was by now too tired to take it, and instead half-consciously drew his cloak more tightly around him. Closing his eyes, he waited confidently for death to take him in answer to his prayer.

But death did not come that night upon Benjamin, the sorely tested. It was only sleep that held his wearied body fast in her more tender embrace, and filled his inner vision with the images of a dream.

And this is the dream which Benjamin dreamed in that night of his final testing. Once again, he was groping his way in flight along the dark and narrow lanes of Pera. Only the darkness was now darker than before, black clouds obscuring the sky above the hills and ridges. And terror had followed him into his dreaming and made his heart beat furiously when behind him he heard the sound of footsteps; then once again he was overcome with fear that he could be followed, and again he fled in panic. But still the footsteps sounded, now in front as well as behind, and now all around him in the gloom of that dark, forsaken place. He could not see who those were that walked to the right and left and after and ahead of him but knew they must be many, a great wandering multitude; he could make out the heavy tread of men and the brittle ring of women's lighter footwear, and the fainter scurrying patter of children. Here surely must be a whole people on the move through the metallic, moonless night, and this people could only be one grieving and oppressed. There came the constant dull groaning and murmuring and calling of voices from their unseen ranks, and it seemed to Benjamin that they must have been journeying thus since time immemorial, long since exhausted by their enforced wandering in ignorance of where they were going. 'Who can they be, this abandoned people?' he heard himself ask. 'Why does the sky hang so gloomily close above them? Why them? Why do they, and they alone, know no rest?' And though his questions received no answer in his dream, he was seized by brotherly compassion for them, their pitiful groans in the invisible darkness oppressing his senses more intensely than would any resounding clamour of complaint. And involuntarily he murmured: 'How can a people keep moving so unceasingly, always in the darkness and never knowing where they go? None can live thus, no home, no end in sight, ever wandering, ever surrounded by danger. A light must be lit for them, a way shown them, for otherwise they will lose all hope and wither away, this lost and hunted people. One must be found to guide them, to bring them home, to illumine their path. A light must be found; it is a light they need.'

His eyes burned with pain, so intense was his pity for these lost souls that made their way, amid plaintive and despairing cries, through the oppressive silence of night. But as in his own despair Benjamin surveyed the distance, a faint glimmer seemed to form, as far away as he could see. It was the tiniest trace of a light, a mere flicker, like a will-o'-the-wisp twinkling through the darkness. 'We must follow it,' he whispered, 'whatever it may be. The smallest spark may kindle the greatest of fires. Let us go to meet that light.' And in his dream Benjamin forgot the weakness of old age; like a child reborn, nimble once more and feather-light on winged sandals he ran to catch the light he saw, thrusting wildly forwards through the obscure, murmuring crowd that parted for him, though full of mistrustful resentment. 'Watch that light you see over there,' he called to them comfortingly. But still their heads were bowed, their hearts heavy as they dragged themselves slowly on and on. In their gloom they saw it not, the distant glimmer, for perhaps their eyes were blinded by tears, their spirits sapped by the all too heavy burden of daily adversity. To his own eyes, however, the light was becoming clearer by the moment, and now he could discern seven small sparks that seemed to be communing like seven sisters, and as he came closer to them, his heart hammering fiercely, he realized that somewhere here must be a lamp, seven-armed, that fed and held these little lights. But the lamp, which still he did not see, must itself be moving, wandering, just as this people wandered in darkness, mysteriously hunted and driven on by hostile winds. And surely for this reason the flames burned unsteadily, and emitted but a weakly glow. 'We must take hold of it, bring it to rest, this lamp,' thought Benjamin in the dream while the image of the dream ran on and on. 'How brightly it would burn, could we but give it peace and rest! And this people, how they might flourish and prosper, could they but find a home at last!' Blindly he hastened on after the lamp, and now that he drew closer and closer to it he could already see its golden stem and its towering branches, and in its seven golden cups the seven flames held down by the wind that savagely drove on the lamp, further and further over mountains and plains and seas. 'Stay! Pause a moment!' he groaned. 'The people waste away. They need the light to lighten their lives, for they cannot wander so for all time in darkness.' Still further and further the Menorah was borne away, its fugitive flames blinking in artful guile. Now the pursuer was seized by anger, and in one final burst he leaped forward, heart hammering within him, his hands ready to clasp the fleeing lamp. His powerful grip already felt the cool metal, already held fast the heavy stem, when a sudden bolt of thunder hurled him to the ground, shattering and splintering his arm in overwhelming pain. And his cry was answered by the people's own agonized wail, 'Lost! Lost for ever!'

But see now, the storm soon calmed, and the Menorah, halting in its flight and poised in upright grandeur, stood proudly still. There it hung in the air, stayed and straight and as if standing on a brazen plinth. Its seven flames, hitherto suppressed by the wind, now rose up in shapely golden brilliance and began to illumine all around them. Brighter and brighter they shone, till gradually all was golden light, dispelling all darkness even through the profoundest depths of all creation. Benjamin, just now struck down by the thunder, looked up in confusion at those who had followed and wandered through the night behind him, and it was no longer night on the pathless earth, and no longer was this a people wandering lost and forsaken. Here, fruitful and tranquil, was a southern land nestling beside the sea and shaded by mountains, palms and cedars swaying in a gentle breeze. And here were fruiting vines and golden crops, and flocks were grazing and gazelles gently gliding, nimble-footed, by. Men were working contentedly on land that was their own, drawing water from wells and ploughing the fields, milking, raking and sowing, bordering and adorning their dwellings with climbing plants and colourful shrubs. Here were happy children running and singing, while from the pastures came the sound of the shepherd's shawm, and at night the stars of peace kept watch over the sleeping houses.

'What land can this be?' asked his own voice in the dream, 'and is this that same people that just now walked in darkness? Have they found peace at last, at last come home?' But now higher still above him hung the great Menorah, brightening like the sun even the furthest extremities of the sky above the reposing land below. Mountains displayed their topmost crests in radiance, and on one of the hills shimmered the mighty battlements of a formidable city, and amidst them towered a colossal house of ashlar stone. In his sleep, Benjamin's heart leaped in wonder. 'This can only be Jerusalem and its Temple,' he gasped. But straight away the Menorah swung away further towards city and Temple, and the walls parted and vanished like water to let it pass within. Now within that sacred place it hung and shed its light, and the whole wondrous body of the Temple glowed with a brilliant sheen as if of alabaster. 'It has come home,' said the sleeping elder, and trembled within. 'Someone has done that which I always longed to do; someone has redeemed the wandering lamp. I must see it with my own eyes, I the witness! Just once more I will see before me the Menorah at rest in God's holiest sanctuary.' And see again, by his very wish he was borne thither like a cloud before the wind. There the gates opened to him, and he entered that holiest of chambers to behold the sacred candelabrum. And its light was bright beyond telling; like white fire the seven flames blazed as one, and the glare, dazzling and painful in its brilliance, caused him to cry out in his sleep. And then he was awake.

Benjamin had awoken from his dream. But still the searing glare pained his eyes, and he had to close the lids quickly to counter the intensity of the light; even then, the blood beneath them seemed to surge in a purple blaze. Only when he raised his hand to shade his vision did he realize that it was the sun that burned his face, and that he had lain in sleep, at that place where he had supposed he was dying, from night's end well into the morning, when the ascending sun's rays had pierced through the branches and woken him. Still confused, and raising himself with great effort by clinging to the trunk, he peered out into the world beyond, and there he beheld the infinite azure of the sea, just as he had seen it that first time as a small child, and over the water, glistening in all its stone and marble, was Byzantium. Here was the world revealed to him in all the colour and resplendence of a southern morning. God, he saw, had not willed that he should die. With awe the old man leaned forward, and lowered his head in prayer.

When Benjamin had ended his prayer to Him who gives and sustains life according to His inscrutable will, he felt a gentle touch on his back. It was Zacharias who stood behind him and, as Benjamin now sensed at once, had long waited wakefully as he slumbered. And before the old man could master his own astonishment – for how could this former companion have known the path he had taken, and how had he found this place where he slept? – Zacharias whispered to him:

'Since early morning I have been looking for you. When they

told me in Pera that you had wandered uphill in the night, I could not rest till I had found you. The others were deeply concerned for you, but I was not so troubled; I know that God still needs you here. But come now, come home with me. I have a message for you.'

'What message?' Benjamin was about to ask. 'I have done with messages.' The wilful words were almost on his lips. 'Too often has God tried me.' But still vibrant within him was the consoling of his dream; and of that glorious light, which had shone such blessing over the peaceful land he had envisioned, he now thought to perceive some mild reflection in the smiling countenance of his friend. And so he did not refuse, and the two walked down together. Crossing over from Pera in a boat, they came to the walls of the palace square. At the imperial gates stood the severe figures of the guards, but to Benjamin's renewed astonishment they willingly waved the two in. 'My workshop stands next to the treasury, where I ply my craft for the Emperor in secrecy and away from all danger. Please enter, and blessed be thy coming. Have no fear of others; we are, and remain, alone.'

The two men shuffled lightly through the workshop, which in the uncertain half-darkness glimmered here and there with finely crafted ornaments. Concealed in one place was a door, which the goldsmith opened to reveal a small flight of steps leading down into a chamber beyond, his dwelling and more private workplace. The windows were closed and barred, and here the walls disappeared in total darkness; only over the table a shaded work-lamp cast a small golden circle of light.

'Be seated, my friend,' said Zacharias to his guest. 'You must be hungry and tired.'

He cleared the table of his work, then brought bread and wine and a few beautifully beaten silver bowls containing fruits and dates and nuts, and raised the shade of the lamp a little higher, so that the light now covered the whole surface of the table, and with it the exhausted Benjamin's folded hands, gnarled and bony, those of a man wholly wearied by old age.

'Eat, dear friend,' exhorted Zacharias. To the ears of Benjamin, the sorely tested, it sounded gentle and intimate, this near-stranger's voice that came to him like a fragrant breeze from some distant land. Gladly he took some fruits and slowly broke the bread, and in small, silent mouthfuls drank the wine, which glowed purple beneath the light. It was comforting for him to sit in quietness and collect himself once more, and pleasing too that beyond the pool of light all was in darkness. Here also was this man, so recently a stranger, yet now a companion as trusted as if from childhood. From time to time, though diffidently and shyly, he sought his face opposite him in the shade, and as he did so he felt the emotion of tender concern.

Zacharias, as if sensing that Benjamin wished for greater closeness, removed the shade completely. The whole room was now bathed in light, and at last Benjamin was able to study more clearly the face of this friend that he had seen only fleetingly till now. It was sensitive and delicate, a wearied countenance and far from robust, furrows of anxiety lying deep and plentiful, a face showing private suffering and silent, patient endurance. Benjamin's own eyes were now open and looked more freely at him, and in those eyes there was a gleam of warmth. And Zacharias too smiled, a smile that gave the old man heart:

'How different you are from the others towards me. I have angered them all, for failing to work the miracle; and I myself had begged them not to expect any miracle from me. You alone, who opened my way to the Emperor's presence, you alone show no anger. And yet they are right to mock me. Why did I rouse their hopes? Why did I come here? Why should I live still, if only to see the Menorah again depart from us in its wandering?'

The smile was still on Zacharias's face, a smile at once strong and gentle, and with it came the consoling words:

'Do not be so headstrong, my friend. Perhaps it was still too soon, and ours was not the right way. What is the Menorah to us while the Temple lies in ruins and our people wander in exile among the nations? Perhaps it is God's will that the fate of the lamp remain secret, unrevealed to the people.'

Benjamin was comforted, and the words warmed his heart. He bowed his head and spoke, as if more to himself:

'I have been faint-hearted, and I ask forgiveness. My life has been narrow and confined of late, and death is all too near. Eight and eighty years I have seen; my heart has grown impatient. Ever since the child I was first longed to rescue the lamp, for one thing alone I lived, to see its return, its redemption. From year to year I waited patiently, true to that hope. Age then came upon me, and wherefore can an old man still hope, and still wait?'

'Your waiting will end. Before long now, all will be fulfilled.'

Benjamin looked up, and his heart beat more strongly.

Zacharias's smile was yet brighter now: 'Have you forgotten that I came to you with a message?'

'What message?'

'The message you long for.'

Benjamin's every limb trembled. His hands, just now resting tiredly on the table before him, shook like leaves in the wind.

'You mean . . . you mean, I may again go before the Emperor?'

'No, not that. Once he has spoken, he will never retract. He will never return the Menorah.'

'What, then, can I still live for? Why should I wait, and suffer, any longer, a burden to all others, and bid the holy symbol fare-well for ever?'

But Zacharias was still smiling, and brighter and brighter was the radiance his eyes expressed:

'It is not yet gone from us.'

'How can you know? What makes you say thus?'

'I do know it. You must trust me.'

'You have seen the Menorah?'

'I have seen the Menorah. Two hours ago it was still under lock and key in the treasury.'

'And now? They have taken it away.'

'No, not yet.'

'Then now, where is it now?'

Zacharias did not answer immediately. Twice his lips opened to speak, and trembled, but the words would not come. And at length he bent closer towards Benjamin across the table and spoke beneath his breath in a confidential whisper:

'Here, with me – with the two of us.'

Benjamin's heart leaped, and he shuddered. 'With you?'

'Yes, with me and in my dwelling.'

'Here, in your dwelling?'

'In this house. Here, in this room. That is why I came to find you.'

Benjamin trembled. Something in his companion's calmness confounded him. Without his knowing it, his hands had folded. He could hardly utter the words:

'Here, with you? But how can this be?'

'Strange though you may think it, there is no miracle in this. I have worked for thirty years in this palace as a goldsmith, and not one piece does the treasury hold that has not first been sent to my workshop to be inspected and weighed by me. This time too, I knew that everything Belisarius took as booty from the Vandals would be submitted to me for weighing and valuing. Among these spoils, the first I asked to see was the Menorah. Yesterday the treasurer's slaves delivered it to me. It is to be under my care for seven days.'

'And then?'

'And then the ship will take it thither.'

Benjamin paled once more. What, then, had Zacharias wanted with him, to bring him here? Was it merely to witness yet again how close the holy Menorah could be, before being torn away anew? But Zacharias smiled at him, and there was meaning in the smile:

'There is more. I am allowed to make a likeness of any, or all, of the precious holdings of the imperial treasury. Often, when an object here is the only one of its kind, unique among all the treasures, I am asked to make a copy, for they have faith in my art. It is a replica I made of Constantine's crown that Justinian now wears, and so also the diadem of Theodora I copied from that which Cleopatra wore long ago. Yes, now I have asked permission to craft a copy of the Menorah before it is sent to the new church over the sea. My work is to begin this very day. The crucibles are already fired as we speak, and I have the gold here at hand prepared and ready. In seven days a new candelabrum will have been made, so like ours that no one will be able to distinguish it from the other, because it will be exactly similar in weight and shape and adornment, and the granulation of the gold will be identical; they will differ only in that one will be sacred, the other the mere work of human hands. But which of the two is the sacred Menorah, and which the other, which of the two we shall hold in reverence and which we shall send on its way into the hands of strangers, this will be henceforth a secret known to two persons alone, to you and to me.

Benjamin no longer felt his lips trembling. The blood now suddenly flowed more warmly through his every limb, and he breathed more freely; his eyes brightened, and his wrinkled aged face beamed, reflecting the smile that came to him from Zacharias. He understood; what he had himself long ago sought to achieve, this man was now set to accomplish in full, recovering the Menorah from its captors, consigning to them a likeness identical in every detail of its weight and material, and retaining the true, sacred Menorah. To be sure, he did not envy Zacharias this task to which he had ascribed the very meaning of all his own long years on earth. In all humility he spoke:

'Praise be to God. I may now gladly die. You have found the way I sought in vain. I was merely called by God. You have been blessed by Him.'

But Zacharias countered: 'No, if anyone is to do so, it is you, and you alone, who will bring the Menorah to its home.'

'Not I. I am an old man. I might die on the way, and again it would fall into strangers' hands.'

Zacharias smiled as he answered: 'You will not die. You yourself now know that your life cannot end until its meaning is fulfilled.'

Benjamin recalled how just yesterday he had wished to die, and God had refused his wish. Perhaps in truth he did still have a mission, a purpose. And so he no longer resisted, and merely said, 'What is my will against the will of the Almighty. If He has indeed chosen me, how can I refuse? Let your work now begin.'

For seven days the workshop of Zacharias the goldsmith was barred to all entry. For seven days Zacharias did not set foot in the lane outside, nor was his door opened to any who knocked. Before him stood the eternal Menorah raised high on a stand, serene and grand, as it had been when once it stood before the Lord's altar. In the furnace, meanwhile, the flames danced silently as they melted the rings and clasps and coins for the gold that was soon to be beaten. In the course of these seven days Benjamin spoke not a word. He observed carefully how the molten substance seethed in the crucible, and how, when poured into the moulds he had prepared, it flowed smoothly, then cooled and hardened. And when, cautiously applying his knives and spatulas, he broke the shell of the mould, the shape of the new lamp was now well-nigh recognizable. The stem rose up, strong and august, from its supporting base, and from this grew forth in rounded elegance the seven curved branches, and on each of them was seen a shapely calyx, each destined to hold its lighted flame. The surfaces as yet were smooth, but here the craftsman's skilled and untiring hand hammered and incised ever more finely the exact same subtle embellishments of buds and floral patterns, just as they adorned the holy emblem itself. From day to day this newly crafted lamp came to resemble ever more closely the thousand-year-old Menorah, the replica mimicking its sacred forerunner. And on the final day, the seventh day of the goldsmith's labours, the two stood together and faced each other like twin brothers. And nothing was there to distinguish the one from the other, so complete was the likeness in colour and shape, in weight and in size. But still unceasingly, untiringly did Zacharias's practised eyes and hands compare the two, and with unremitting care continue to perfect in minute precision every detail, every refinement of notching and engraving and embossing that beautified this, the most cherished of all his works. Finally he drew back his hands from the task. Now there was no difference to be detected, and so exactly alike were the two that in order not to be himself deceived Zacharias took up his stylus one final time, and on the inner shaded surface of a petal in a blossom he scratched a tiny mark to indicate that this was the new lamp, the work of his own hands, and not the true Menorah of the Jewish people, that of Solomon's Temple.

This accomplished, he stepped back, removed his leathern apron and washed his hands. Then for the first time in the seven days since he had begun the work, he addressed Benjamin:

'My task is complete. Now yours begins. You are to take our lamp and do with it as you feel you must.'

But, to his surprise, Benjamin demurred.

'Seven days you have worked, and for seven days I have been

thinking, and I have questioned my heart. A fear has begun to trouble me: is it not simply fraud, what we are doing? For one of these was entrusted to you, and you are returning not that one but another to those who trusted you implicitly. No, it is not right for us to send back the false copy and keep the true one that we obtained by dishonest means and was not freely given to us. God has no love for force. When I was a child and attempted to seize the Menorah in my hands, He dashed and crippled my arm. But I know that the Almighty has no love either for deceit; for he who tricks and defrauds, his soul will be crushed by God.'

Zacharias thought for a moment. 'But if the Imperial Treasurer himself chooses the false one of the two?'

Benjamin looked up. 'The treasurer knows that one is old and one is new, and if he asks for the genuine one, the true Menorah, then that is the one we must give him. If God so wills that the treasurer ask no further question, because the two are the same in his eyes, equal in gold and weight, then, as I see it, we have done no wrong. If he freely makes his own decision and chooses your copy, then a sign will have been given us. But let not the decision be ours.'

Zacharias accordingly sent the treasury slave to the treasurer's quarters, and the latter soon came, a man of portly and cheerful bearing with small bulging eyes that peered out inquisitively from the red cheeks that cradled them. Even in the antechamber his connoisseur's fingers were already inspecting two beaten silver bowls on which the goldsmith had just recently finished working; he carefully tapped and tested them and examined the decorative chasing. The cut gems on the work table roused his curiosity, and he picked up one after another to look at them more closely under the light. So blithely and lovingly did he continue to inspect all of the pieces one by one, both the finished and the yet unfinished work of the goldsmith, that Zacharias had to remind him that it was the two great lamps that he had been called to view; these now stood, in their golden serenity, alongside each other on a display bench, the thousand-year-old and the newly fashioned, the original and the replica.

It was with some suspense that the treasurer approached the pair. Clearly it would appeal to his connoisseur's pride to detect some minute flaw, or some tiny inconspicuous difference between the new and the old. Carefully, diligently, he turned one and then the other this way and that, allowing the light to fall on them from every direction. He tested their weight and passed his fingernails over the gold, stood back and then went forward again, constantly scrutinizing, with mounting fascination, one against the other in their apparently faultless identity. Finally he bent forward and, with the help of a magnifying glass of ground crystal, passed his eye in close proximity over the fine details of the surfaces' contours and scorings. Yet still he could find nothing to distinguish the two. Exhausted by his unavailing efforts, he at last conceded defeat and clapped Zacharias on the shoulder:

'A master you are, Zacharias, yourself a veritable treasure to adorn our treasury! Never hereafter will anyone be able to tell the two apart, which is the old and which is the new, so sure is your hand and your art. Simply admirable, my dear friend!'

He had already turned away casually to look again at the cut gems, and to choose one for himself. Zacharias had to remind him once more:

'Which lamp, then, do you wish to keep?'

Indifferently, and hardly even turning back, the treasurer answered:

'Whichever you like. It is all the same to me.'

At this point Benjamin emerged from the shadows in which he had timidly, though in high agitation, concealed his presence:

'Sir, we ask you graciously to choose one of the two to be yours.'

The treasurer looked at the aged stranger in astonishment. Of what interest could it be to this curious figure, whose burning eyes looked so imploringly at him? But, good-natured as he was, and being too polite to stand in the way of an old man's wishes, he turned back again. Playfully he brought out a small coin and tossed it high in the air. It fell and rolled on the floor, turning three times before finally settling on his left. The treasurer smiled and pointed to the lamp on the left: 'This one, then.' Thereupon he turned to the slaves he had called, and they carried the lamp that he had chosen over to the treasury. Thankfully and courteously the goldsmith accompanied his patron to the door of the chamber.

Benjamin was left alone. His trembling hand touched the remaining lamp. It was the true Menorah, the sacred one; the treasurer had chosen the replica for the Emperor.

When Zacharias returned, Benjamin was still standing motionless before the Menorah, and as he contemplated it his gaze was so intense that he seemed to be absorbing it wholly into his own being. Finally the old man turned to face Zacharias. The reflection of the gold could be seen glowing in his eyes; that calm tranquillity had come upon the man sorely tested, as always it comes to the hearts of those who have made a firm and secure decision. Meekly, though, he made a request:

'May God give you thanks, my dear brother. And now I ask you to procure for me one thing: a casket.'

'A casket?'

'You must not be surprised. This too I have considered well and thoroughly in the course of these seven days and nights – how the great Menorah may be brought to rest. Like you, I too thought at first that if we were to rescue it, it must then belong to the Jewish people, whose most sacred pledge it would be to cherish it for ever. But our people, where are they, and where is their true abode? Hunted people we are over all the earth, and living only ever on sufferance; nowhere is any place assured where the Menorah may have due protection. If ever we have a house, soon we are driven out, and if we build a temple, they destroy it; as long as might and force prevail among the nations, the Menorah will never enjoy peace on earth. Only below the earth is peace to be found. There lie the departed, their feet now at rest from their wandering, and no gold that is there will lure the robber and rouse his greed. There the Menorah too will lie at rest, home at last from its thousand years of wandering.'

'For ever?' Zacharias was astonished. 'You mean to bury the Menorah beneath the earth?'

'Since when could we mortals even conceive of eternity? Who am I to set any limits of time, while I cannot even know my own span? My desire is to give the Menorah repose at last, but how long that rest may be, who can know save God? The deed can be mine, but it will not be for me to determine what comes of that deed, to know the mysteries of time and eternity. God shall decide, and he alone, the destiny of the Menorah. I shall bury it, for I know no other means to protect it, but who can say for how long it will remain beneath the ground? It may be that God will let it rest in darkness for all time, and our people will wander on and on, uncomforted, scattered like dust over the face of the earth. But perhaps – and my heart is filled with this hope – perhaps it may be His will that our people one day return to their home. And then – let us trust in this hope – then in his wisdom He may choose one who by chance will ply his spade and find the burial place of our Menorah, just as God has found me, that I may bring its restless wandering to an end. Do not be troubled about such a decision; we must leave it to God, and to time. Let it be thought that the lamp is lost for ever; we, who in ourselves represent God's mystery, we are not lost!

For neither will gold cease from existence in the bosom of the earth, as do our mortal remains, nor will our people fade away in the darkness of time. No, both will endure, the people and the Menorah. Let us therefore believe and trust that it will rise again from its burial and will burn once more for our people on their homecoming. Only as long as we keep our faith alive can we endure in this world.'

Both looked away from each other as their thoughts passed to the far-distant future. Then Benjamin spoke again:

'And now have the casket brought to me.'

The carpenter brought the casket. It was of the ordinary kind, for so was Benjamin's request, lest when he took it to the land of his fathers it should provoke any unwanted curiosity. Often enough did the pious bring their caskets with them on pilgrimage to Jerusalem, in order to lay parents or other kindred to rest in that sacred soil. There the lamp could be safely hidden in just such a simple spruce container, for the remains of the dead will be the last of all things to attract the covetousness of men.

Reverently the two placed the Menorah in the coffin. They carefully wrapped its seven golden arms in silken cloths and heavy brocade, as they would a Torah scroll, God's own child, and the surrounding space they filled with tow and wool to prevent the metal sounding against the wood and betraying the secret as they carried the casket. Their gentle hands trembled as thus they bedded the treasured emblem in this container, otherwise the cradle of the dead, and they shuddered at the thought that perhaps, if it did not please God to turn the fortunes of their people, they might be the last of all so to feast their eyes, and to feel under their touch the candelabrum of Moses, the holy lamp of Solomon's Temple. But before they closed the casket they took a sheet of strong parchment and wrote on it a statement testifying that the two of them, Benjamin Marnefesh, known as the sorely tested one, of Abtalion's line, and Zacharias of the line of Hillel, had, in Byzantium in the eighth year of Justinian's rule, with their own hands placed the Menorah in this casket, that any who, on digging, chanced upon it in the Holy Land might be assured hereby that this was the true Menorah of the Jewish people. The parchment roll they encased in a leaden sheath, which Zacharias used all his art and precision to seal against any incursion of damp or mould that could obscure the script of their testimony. With a gold chain he fixed this to the stem of the lamp in such a way that Menorah and statement would be found together. It remained only to close the casket with nails and clasps. Not another word passed between them until the slaves brought the casket to Benjamin on the ship bound for Joppa. Only then, as the sails were already flapping in the wind, did Zacharias kiss his friend and take leave of him:

'May God bless you and keep you. May He guide you on your way and bring you fulfilment. We two are the last and, to this hour, the only witnesses to the fortunes of the Menorah. Henceforth only you shall know its destiny.'

Benjamin bowed his head in pious respect:

'My own knowledge too, has little time remaining. And then only God will know where his Menorah lies at rest.'

Whenever a ship put in at Joppa there was a great crowd waiting in welcome at the quayside, full of curiosity about the newcomers. Among these local people were a few Jews. On noticing that this white-bearded old man was one of their own, and observing that he was followed by some deckhands carrying a coffin off the ship, they came together and followed the little procession in silent solidarity. It is a gentle, kindly custom for the Jews, and one that in their belief is pleasing to God, to accompany the dead, even when they are unknown to them, a little way along on their final journey to a place of burial; for thus they may show themselves both devout and helpful.

No Jew here, on learning that one of their number had brought a coffin across the sea, could fail to know his duty and act accordingly. From houses in every alley and lane they came in reverent silence, leaving aside all work and trade for the moment, and so with ever larger retinue the casket was carried to the roadside inn where Benjamin was to pass the night. Only there, when it had been set down next to his bed – for such was the old man's curious requirement – did they break their silence.

With the traditional blessing they bade him welcome, and asked him whence he had come and whither he was bound. Benjamin was brief in his answer, being much afraid that news might already have come to the ears of this pressing crowd from Byzantium, and one of them might then guess who he was. Worst of all would be to raise false hopes once again among his brethren. And yet, deceit and untruth must also be avoided, standing as he was in the very shadow of the Menorah. Might they permit him to save his words, he asked. He had been given the duty of delivering this casket and was charged to say no more. Studiously fending off any further inquisitiveness, he now resorted to questioning them instead. Where, he inquired, were holy sites to be found in this land, where the coffin could be laid in the earth? Smiling contentedly, proudly, the Jews of Joppa gave him their answer, that here in this holy land all earth was holy, and every place sacred. But then, naming each in turn, they told him of all the places where in their caves or open fields the graves of their ancestors were to be found, marked only by piles of stones, and those of the mothers of their tribes, not to mention the heroes and kings of their people; they extolled the mysterious power of these holy places, which no pious Jew would fail to visit for solace and comfort. Respectfully – for there was indeed something in this very old man's demeanour that commanded their reverence, even a presentiment of mystery – they offered to conduct him to such a place and, if he would allow, to join him in prayer at the interment of the deceased. But to safeguard his secret Benjamin politely declined their offer and thanked them as they left him. Then addressing the innkeeper, he asked him to find, in return for a fair wage, a man in good health and well acquainted with the terrain, to take him next day to dig a grave at a requisite place, and in addition he asked for a mule to carry the coffin. The innkeeper agreed: at dawn his own servant would be ready and would take him where he wished.

That night in the inn at Joppa was the final night of painful questioning and anguish of the soul in the life of Benjamin Marnefesh. Once again, certainty deserted him. Once again, his resolution wavered and weighed heavily and grievously upon him. Once again, he repeatedly asked himself: was he really doing right in keeping secret from his own brethren the redemption and homecoming of the Menorah, in failing to say what sacred treasure he was burying in an unknown grave? For if the bones and the graves of their fathers and forefathers could impart such powerful solace to those oppressed by grief, what blessing would it mean for this downtrodden, persecuted people driven and scattered far and wide, to catch even the slightest hint that the eternal Menorah, the most visible symbol of their unity, was after all not lost, was indeed rescued and now secure in a place beneath the earth of its homeland, awaiting the final day of homecoming?

'How can I deprive them of this hope?' he groaned as he lay unsleeping. 'And how keep this secret for myself alone, and take it with me to the grave, when to thousands it might have given hope and joy? I know how they thirst for comfort. Terrible is the fate of a people condemned to wait everlastingly for the "maybe" or "one day", to depend dumbly on the written word without ever receiving a sure sign. And yet I must remain silent, for only then will the Menorah be kept safe for my people. Lord, help me in my hour of need! How am I to do what is right for them, for my brethren? This servant promised me by the innkeeper – may

I send him back from the burial with the comforting message that a sacred pledge lies there in the grave? Or am I to keep silent, so that none of you shall know where the Menorah rests? Lord, decide for me! Once in the past you gave me a sign. Now give me another. Lord, take this burden of deciding from me.'

But the silence of night was unbroken, and sleep refused its mercy to the sorely tested Benjamin. He lay awake, his eyes burning, till dawn was about to appear. His questioning was without end, and with every question he asked he felt the strangling net of fear and grievance tightening more and more around him. Already the eastern sky was brightening, and still his mind was in turmoil, when the innkeeper came into his room, looking deeply troubled:

'Forgive me, but I can no longer send the man I promised you yesterday, who knows these parts so well. He has suddenly fallen ill in the night. His mouth was foaming, and he has a raging fever. I can only give you my other man. I must tell you honestly that he is a stranger to this land, and also that he is completely dumb. Since birth God has denied him the power of speech. But if you can make do with him, you may gladly have him.'

Benjamin did not look at his host but merely raised his eyes to heaven in thanks. God had answered his prayer after all. A mute servant had been sent to him, signalling silence. And the man was unacquainted with this land, so that the place of burial would remain for ever a secret. Benjamin's doubts were at an end, and with grateful relief he replied:

'Send me your mute servant. And do not be concerned; I shall know the way.'

From morning till evening, Benjamin made his way over the open country with his mute companion. Behind them the mule trotted calmly and patiently, the casket tied squarely across its back. Here and there they passed impoverished, dilapidated dwellings along the way, but Benjamin would not stop to take rest. If they met other wayfarers, he would exchange words of peace but avoid any further communication, driven as he was by the urgency to complete his task and see the Menorah laid in earth. The place itself he did not yet know, and a mysterious misgiving prevented him from choosing one himself. 'Twice now I have been given a sign,' he thought to himself trustingly, 'and I will await a third.' Thus they continued together through this deserted land as darkness gradually fell, and over the hills the black wings of night appeared. The sky was dimmed by heavy clouds, and behind them the moon, already risen to its highest quarter, would momentarily appear and then pass again from view, giving but a faint occasional glimmer. It might be an hour, or even two, to the next place of shelter for the night, but Benjamin strode on undaunted; beside him went his mute helper like a silent shadow, the spade on his shoulder, and still behind the two sounded the patient, even trot of the mule.

Suddenly the mule halted. The servant took hold of the bridle, trying to pull the animal forwards. But it stubbornly dug in its front hooves and threw the man back, fiercely baring its teeth and refusing to go any further. The servant countered angrily by bringing down the spade from his shoulder, ready to use the haft of it on the mule's flank, but Benjamin grasped his arm and told him to wait and leave the animal be. Maybe its stopping was the sign he had waited for.

Benjamin looked around. The darkened land here was hilly and empty, with no house or hut anywhere to be seen. They must have strayed off the Jerusalem road. But this, Benjamin thought to himself, was a suitable place, where the work could be done unobserved. He probed the ground with his stick; there were no stones, and the soil was rich and firm. Digging here would be easy and quick, and the surrounding hills would afford some protection from drifting sand that would remove the traces. All that was needed now was to find the precise spot.

He looked uncertainly to right and left, long pondering what might be the final choice. On the right, but three or four stones' throws from the path, he noticed a tree still casting shade in an otherwise deserted spot, curiously similar in shape and height to that under which he had lain on the hill at Pera and received word of the recovery of the lamp. He recalled that morning dream, and his heart was strengthened. At once he bade the servant untie the burden from the back of the mule; thereupon the mule immediately relaxed its tensed legs and came up to Benjamin, who felt the warm breath from its nostrils in his hand. His certainty grew apace: this was indeed the right place. He pointed to it, and his helper set to work. The spade rang softly as the fresh earth, itself mute as the digger, obediently yielded, and soon the depth was sufficient. The final task now was to commit the Menorah to its place of rest. Slowly, unsuspecting of what it contained, the servant lifted the burden in his broad arms and carefully lowered it; there at last the casket lay, to sleep eternally and shield in its wooden mantle this precious golden ward beneath the cover of the living, breathing, verdant, fertile earth.

With great reverence Benjamin bowed down: 'I am the witness, the last,' he said to himself, trembling again under the immense weight of this knowledge. 'No one on earth but I will know hereafter the secret of our Menorah. None but I can know its grave, or guess its hidden abode.' But suddenly at this moment the moon appeared and shone out from behind the clouds that had dimmed its rays ever since night had fallen but just now parted. Its light poured forth in a brilliant stream, and it was as if from the midst of the heavens a gigantic, dark-lidded eye had looked down – no human eye was this, shadowed between lashes, gentle and frail, but one that was perfectly round and hard as if formed of ice, everlasting and indestructible. Down into the depths of the open grave it cast its piercing radiance, revealing the four sharp corners of the pit, and the smooth pine surface of the coffin gleamed white like metal in the light. It was but one fleeting moment, one glance down from an immeasurable distance, and then once again the clouds veiled the wandering moon. But Benjamin knew that one other eye than his had observed the burial.

Benjamin gave another sign, and the servant started to shovel the soil back into the grave. As soon as he had finished, and the earth lay level again over the tomb, Benjamin ordered him on his way home, taking the mule with him. The mute servant gestured in despair at the thought of leaving this elderly man alone at night in a place he did not know, at the mercy of robbers and wild beasts. Could he not at least accompany the gentleman to the next place where he could safely spend the night? But Benjamin was resolute, and impatiently told the man to start back, and do exactly as he was instructed. When the latter still hesitated, Benjamin scolded him and firmly sent him away. He could hardly wait for man and mule to be out of sight, to be himself alone beneath the infinite stretch of open sky, enveloped by the great unfathomable night.

One last time he approached the grave, and with bowed head spoke the prayer for the dead: 'Exalted and hallowed is the name of the Eternal in this world and other worlds and in the days of the rising of the dead.' Though greatly desiring to observe the normal practice of piety in placing a stone or some token on the turned earth of the grave, he restrained himself, mindful of the necessary secrecy. Without turning again, he walked away into the emptiness of night, not asking himself where he was going. His mind freed of any aim or purpose now that he had brought the lamp to rest, all fear too had left him, and his soul was calm once more. He had done what was demanded of him; now it was in God's hands whether the Menorah was to remain hidden till the end of days and the Jewish people would be further scattered over all the earth, or at last He would bring them home and allow their Menorah to rise again from its unknown grave.

The old man walked on through the night as the clouds gathered and parted in the darkness to reveal the glimmer of the stars, and his joy grew stronger with every step. Magically the heavy burden of his life's long years fell from him, and from within he felt a lightness welling through all of his body, the like of which he had never known before. As if freed and loosened with soothing warm oil, his old and wearied limbs once more did his bidding. He might have been skimming the waters with wings on his feet. His head raised high, he floated, as if wafted by some intangible breeze. And his injured hand too he lifted, feeling – or was this merely a waking dream? – as though he could use it and fully master it once more for the first time since his childhood. All through him the blood ran warm and vigorous, rising like sap in the stem. A heartening ringing came to his ears and there was a pounding at his temples as he heard the sound of sublime song. He could not tell if it was the souls of the dead below the earth that sang in brotherly chorus to greet him on his homecoming, or was it rather from the stars, shining now ever more brightly above him, that this great music issued forth? But on and on he went, as if borne on wings, further and further into that sonorous night.

The next morning, tradesmen, making their way to the market of a nearby town, found an old man lying in a field not far off the road. He was dead. The unknown figure lay on his back, his head bare, his arms held open and outstretched, as of one seeking to clasp an infinity; the fingers were spread wide, the palms seemingly poised to receive a stupendous gift. His eyes were likewise open and bright, his face transfigured as he lay in blissful peace. And when one of the men bent down, as piety required, to close those eyes, he saw that they were full of light, and in their round pupils now at rest it was as if the totality of the heavens was reflected.

Only the lips were firmly closed beneath the old stranger's

beard: it was as if he held in them a secret, tightly guarded even beyond death itself.

Not many weeks later, the counterfeit lamp too was delivered to the Holy Land and brought, in accordance with Justinian's order, to the new church in Jerusalem, there to be displayed under the altar. But it was not to dwell there long. For soon the Persians burst in and broke it into pieces, with which to fashion precious clasps for their wives and a chain for their king. The work of human hands is prone to perish with the ravishing of time and man's destructive urge, and so this symbol too, the replica made by Zacharias the goldsmith, met its end, and every trace of it was lost for all time.

Secretly hidden, however, the eternal Menorah waits and watches to this day undetected, unharmed in the grave that is its home. Above it have swept the relentless forces of time, and from century to century one nation after another has disputed and fought and warred unceasingly over its land. But the Menorah itself no robber could seize, no greed destroy. Sometimes, to be sure, a hurried foot runs over the soil that protects it, and sometimes close to its place of slumber wayfarers may take their rest by the roadside in the searing heat of midday. But none have any inkling of its nearness, and no curiosity has caused any to dig down and disturb the ground in which it lies. As always with God's mysteries, so it rests in the darkness of passing ages, and none may know whether so it will rest eternally, hidden and lost to its people, who still wander, knowing no peace, from one strange land to another, or whether at last the Menorah will be found, on the day when its people find themselves once more a nation come home, a day when its light, once more at peace, will brighten the temple of peace itself.

Burning Secret

The Partner

The engine gave out a sharp whistle; the train had arrived at Semmering. For a minute the black carriages remained stationary in the silvery upland light, disgorging a small assortment of passengers and taking in a few others against a background of petulant vocal exchanges; then the engine moved forward again with a hoarse, rasping sound and dragged its rattling black chain of coaches off into the hollow of the tunnel. Once again, the wide expanse of landscape lay open and pure in its clarity, offering a background tableau swept clean by the wet wind. One of the arrivals, a young man of striking, indeed pleasing, appearance in his fine clothes and with a natural, relaxed manner of walking, quickly overtook the others and hailed a carriage to take him to his hotel. At a leisurely trot the horses made their way along the uphill road. Spring was in the air. Those restless white clouds that appear only in May and June were still bustling overhead, still youthful and playful as they flitted in their bright apparel across the blue expanse of sky, now hiding behind high mountains, now embracing each other and then parting again, now rumpling themselves like handkerchiefs or fraying into thin strips, and at last teasing the mountains by settling on their peaks like white headdresses. There was also a restlessness up there in the wind, which shook the slender, still rain-soaked tree trunks so wildly that the branches could be heard faintly creaking, and a thousand drops sprayed down from them and sparkled. Now and again the fragrance and coolness of the snow seemed to waft over from the mountains, and as it came there was something both sweet and sharp in the air one breathed. Movement was to be seen in everything in the air and on the earth, movement and seething impatience. Snorting gently, the horses made their way along the now descending road, their approach long heralded by the tinkling of their bells.

On arriving at the hotel, the young man made straight for the current register of guests. On skimming the list he was quickly disappointed. What was he doing here, he began to wonder uneasily. Staying up here alone in the mountains, no one to keep him company – this was even worse than the office! Clearly he must have arrived too early in the season, or too late. He never had any luck with his holidays! Not a single familiar name among all these people. If only there were just a few ladies, a chance of a little harmless flirting to get him through the week without complete dreariness.

The young man, a baron from a not conspicuously prominent titled family of Austrian civil servants, and himself employed in the administration, had taken this brief holiday without any real need for it; in truth he had done so simply because all of his colleagues had taken advantage of the week's spring leave, and he was not minded to gift his own leave to the state. He was, though far from lacking in inner resources, a thoroughly sociable type and known and liked as such, always a welcome addition to any company and fully aware of his inability to be alone. He was quite disinclined to spend time on his own; indeed, he did all he could to avoid such eventualities, since he had no desire whatsoever to get to know himself any better. He understood perfectly well his own need to strike the surface of other people like a match and allow all his talents, and all of his personal warmth and ebullience, to glow and dazzle; he knew that on his own he was inert as frost, of no use to himself, a match left in the box.

Downhearted, for a while he ambled up and down in the empty lobby, now and again leafing indifferently through the newspapers, or playing some notes of a waltz on the piano in the music room but without quite getting the rhythm under his fingers. In the end he sat down disconsolately by the window and watched the darkness gradually falling and the misty grey vapour issuing forth from the surrounding spruces. A nervous, fruitless hour was squandered in this way before he took refuge in the dining room.

There were so far only a few tables occupied, and these he surveyed hurriedly. No, again no luck. No acquaintances, only – he half-heartedly acknowledged a greeting – here was a trainer he knew from the racecourse, and over there was another face he recognized from the Ringstrasse, but otherwise no one. No feminine presence, no promise here of any even fleeting little adventure. The Baron was feeling increasingly ill-humoured, and increasingly frustrated. He was one of those young men whose good looks have brought them considerable success, and are ever ready to welcome a new encounter, a new experience. Such men will always be keenly anticipating any entry into new territory of this kind; having cannily assessed every aspect of a situation, they will never be taken by surprise and will never overlook an amorous opportunity, because their first glance at any woman is deep and probing, with no concern to distinguish whether this be the wife of their friend or the chambermaid who opens the lady's door to them.

There may be more than an element of glib disdain in calling such people 'woman-chasers', but those who do so fail to realize how apt is the image of the hunt; for in truth all the passionate instincts of the huntsman – the stalking, the excitement, the inherent callousness of it all – are clearly discernible in these men. Constantly ready for action, they are ever prepared, or rather determined, to follow the tracks of an adventure right to the edge of the abyss. They are at all times fully charged with passion, but not the nobler passion of the lover; rather, that of the gambler, cold, calculating and insidious. Some of these types are truly relentless in their pursuit: their whole lives, far beyond their youth, become an unending adventure driven by such expectation, and every day is resolved into a hundred little amorous events – a passing look, a momentary smile, a chance touching of the knee of one seated opposite – and then similarly the year becomes a hundred such days, in which the sensual experience becomes the ever-flowing, nourishing, vitalizing source of life itself.

Anyway, it was immediately apparent to our huntsman's eye that there was nobody here to share a game. And there is no greater irritation than that felt by the card-player who has the pack ready in his hands, well aware of his superiority as a player, and sits at the green-baize table waiting in vain for a partner. The Baron called for a newspaper. As his eyes peevishly scanned the lines of print, his thinking was dulled, and he followed the words only falteringly, like a drunkard. Then suddenly he sensed a dress rustling behind him, and a mildly irritable voice with an affected accent: '*Mais tais-toi donc, Edgar!*'

A silk garment audibly brushed his table in passing. At the same time a tall, voluptuous figure cast a brief shadow, and in its wake came a pale little lad in a black velvet suit. The child glanced at him curiously. The two sat down at the table reserved for them opposite the Baron, the boy making visible efforts to behave correctly, though the dark restlessness in his eyes suggested some conflict. The lady – and it was she alone who drew the Baron's attention – was decidedly *soignée*, being dressed with conspicuous elegance, and furthermore was of a type that greatly appealed to him, one of those quite sensuous Jewish women at an age just before becoming over-mature, evidently passionate too, but at the same time sufficiently experienced to mask her true temperament behind an air of refined melancholy. Unable at first to look directly into her eyes, he simply admired the finely drawn line of the brows; they traced a perfect curve over her delicate nose which, to be sure, betrayed her race but in its noble shapeliness made her profile markedly distinctive and interesting. Her hair, like everything else that was feminine about her shapely form, was of a striking luxuriance, and her beauty appeared to have acquired a self-assurance and vanity in its own awareness of the abundant admiration it inspired. She placed her order in a very discreet voice, chided the lad for playing with his fork and making a noise – all of this with apparent disregard for the cautiously suggestive looks given by the Baron, whom she appeared not to notice, whereas in truth it was nothing other than his acute alertness that necessitated her careful restraint.

The sombre face of the Baron now brightened at once; beneath its surface flowed an enlivening nervous stream, smoothing furrows and tightening muscles, so that his whole body now sat more upright and his eyes began to shine. He was himself not unlike those women who need some male presence to bring out all of their powers. Only the allure of sensuality could engage his full energy. The huntsman scented prey. A challenge – his glance sought to engage hers, and their eyes did meet at moments, but only in passing and with a twinkling indecisiveness, never quite offering any clear response. He also believed he sensed an incipient smile occasionally forming around her lips, but he could not be sure, and precisely this uncertainty thrilled him. The one thing that seemed promising was this constant looking past him, which indicated both resistance and disquiet on her part; and then the oddly fastidious way she conversed with the child, clearly designed for an observer.

There was something emphatic and forced in her show of composure, which, he sensed, showed that she was beginning to feel unsettled. He too was excited. The game had begun. He contrived to prolong his dinner, kept this woman almost constantly in his sights for all of half an hour, until his eyes had traced every line of her face and had invisibly touched every part of her sumptuous body. Outside, darkness was gloomily drawing in, the woods were sighing as if in childish fear of the massive rain clouds stretching out their grey hands towards them; darker and darker the shadows forced their way into the dining room, the guests appearing driven ever more closely together by the silence. The mother's conversation with her son, he noted, was growing steadily more forced and unnatural under this oppressive hush, and would soon have to end. This was when he decided on a stratagem. He rose first, and with his eyes staring straight past the woman he cast a long look out over the countryside and went slowly over to the door. At that point, however, he quickly gave a start, as if he had forgotten something, and turned his head. And he caught her glance keenly following him. This was enough to stir him.

He waited in the lobby. She came out soon after him, holding the child's hand, turned the pages of one or two newspapers as she passed and showed the boy a few pictures. But when the Baron approached the table as if he too just happened to be going that way to look for a paper himself – of course his real purpose was to delve more deeply behind the moist glistening of her eyes, perhaps even to start a conversation – the woman turned away and tapped her son gently on the shoulder: '*Viens, Edgar! Au lit!*' With these words, her dress rustling, she coolly brushed past the Baron. With some disappointment his eyes followed her out. He had really reckoned on becoming acquainted with her this same evening, and her abrupt manner was discouraging to him. Still, there was after all something enticing in this resistance, and the element of uncertainty itself kindled his desire. Come what may, he now had his partner. Yes, and the game could begin.

Quick Friendship

When next morning the Baron stepped into the lobby he saw the child of the beautiful unknown keenly conversing with the two lift boys, to whom he was showing pictures in a Karl May adventure story book. Mama was not in attendance and was probably still occupied with her dressing. It was only now that the Baron took a good look at the lad. He was a shy, still undeveloped and nervous young boy around twelve years old, awkward and jittery, with dark, restlessly searching eyes. He gave the impression, as children so often do at that age, of groundless timorousness, rather as if he had just been torn from his sleep and suddenly deposited in some strange, unfamiliar surroundings. His face was not unpleasing, but was still far from mature; the struggle between childhood and manhood seemed only just about to start, and everything about the face was still at the kneading stage, as yet unformed, not yet defined into clear lines but a mingling of pallor and insecurity. What was more, he was just at that unflattering stage of life when children's clothes never quite seem to fit, what with sleeves and trouser legs dangling droopily around skinny limbs, and vanity not yet having stepped in to advise on such external appearances.

The boy here made a rather woeful impression wandering aimlessly around the place. He really was getting in everyone's way. At one point the porter had to push him aside after being plagued with endless questions, and at another he was blocking the main entrance; clearly there was no friendly interaction or company for him. Wanting like most children companionship and a chat, he therefore attempted to fraternize with the hotel employees, who did answer his questions when they had time but instantly broke off the moment an adult came on the scene, or if there was something more pressing to be done. The Baron observed the unfortunate child with some interest. He smiled to see him looking around at all and sundry with great curiosity, despite the unfriendly disregard from all sides. He caught one of these inquisitive glances directed straight at him, but the child's dark eyes immediately retreated into themselves in alarm as soon as the Baron saw them looking out and went into hiding behind lowered lids. He was amused. The lad was beginning to interest him, and he wondered whether this little boy, whose shyness was obviously caused merely by youthful timidity, might not provide the quickest way to an approach. Anyway he would give it a try. At a distance he followed the child, who had just wandered out through the door and now, in his childish need for affection, was patting the pink nostrils of one of the carriage horses. But once again – luck really was not on his side – the coachman gruffly shooed him away. Feeling hurt and bored, he dawdled around a little longer with that vacant, rather forlorn look on his face. This was the Baron's moment to speak.

'So young man, how do you like it here?' he pitched straight in, taking care to maintain as jovial a tone as he could.

The child blushed a crimson red and stared up in fear. He managed somehow nevertheless to accept the handshake, dancing from foot to foot in embarrassment. This was the first time a gentleman he did not know had ever engaged him in conversation.

'Very much, thank you,' he was just able to stammer, the last words more by way of choking than speaking.

'Oh really? I'm a bit surprised,' said the Baron with a laugh. 'Isn't it actually a bit of a dead end, especially for a young chap like you? So how do you pass the time all day?'

The boy was still too confused to answer immediately. Was

this really happening, this elegant gentleman, a complete stranger, wanting to talk to him while nobody else paid him any attention at all? The thought made him shy, but proud at the same time. He pulled himself together, with some effort.

'I read, and then there are lots of walks we do. Sometimes we go for a ride in the carriage, Mama and I. I'm supposed to be getting better here; I was sick. That's why I've also got to sit in the sun a lot, the doctor said.'

The last words sounded a good deal more self-assured. Children always take some pride in an illness, knowing as they do that any danger they are in makes them twice as important within the family.

'Yes, sun's always good for young gentlemen like you. It'll give you a good tan. But you shouldn't spend the whole day just sitting around. A lad like you ought to be on his feet and running about, high spirits and all that, not to mention the odd bit of high jinks! Strikes me you're a mite too well-behaved, a bit of a stay-at-home, what with that big fat book under your arm. When I think of the kind of young rogue I was at your age, always coming back at the end of the day with trousers in tatters! Just make sure you're not too good!'

The boy could not help smiling, and the fear was now gone. He would happily have made some reply, but all he could think of saying seemed too cheeky and over-confident in front of this kindly stranger whose words and treatment of him were so friendly. He had never been a forward child, and was always quick to feel abashed, so that the combination of happiness and shame he now felt was acutely disconcerting. He would have so loved to continue the conversation, but no words occurred to him. By good luck just at that moment the huge tawny hotel St Bernard came padding up and sniffed at both of them, happily allowing them to pet him.

'Do you like dogs?' asked the Baron.

'Oh yes, I love them. My grandma has one at her villa in Baden, and all the time we're there he's with me all day long. But that's only in the summer, when we go to stay with her.'

'We have some at home on the estate, I'd say two dozen of them. If you're a good boy here you might get one as a present from me. A brown one with white ears. Do you like the idea?'

The boy's face shone red with happiness. 'Oh yes!' The words came bursting forth, full of warmth and eagerness. But then straight away he floundered in doubt, as if afraid. 'But Mama wouldn't allow it. She says she couldn't have a dog in the house. They're too much trouble.'

The Baron smiled. At last the subject had come round to Mama.

'Is Mama that strict?'

The boy thought for a moment, then looked up at him for a second, as if trying to decide whether one could really trust this stranger. The answer was still cautious.

'No, Mama isn't strict. Now I've been sick she lets me do anything. Perhaps she'll even let me have a dog.'

'Would you like me to ask her?'

'Oh yes, please ask her!' the boy cried jubilantly. 'She's bound to say yes if you do. And what does he look like? White ears, you said, didn't you? Does he fetch things?'

'Yes, you name it, he can do it.' The Baron had to smile again at the sparkling radiance he had so quickly brought to the child's eyes. In no time at all the boy was free of his initial diffidence, and all the passion previously restrained merely by shyness now bubbled out of him. With the speed of lightning he had been transformed from that timid, anxious little child into a genuinely high-spirited young lad. And the Baron could not but think: if only the mother too could be so transformed, so ardent behind that reserve of hers! But the boy was already assailing him with countless questions:

'What's the dog called?'

'Karo.'

'Karo,' boy repeated, overjoyed. Every word now somehow brought delight and laughter from him, so intoxicated was he by this unexpected turn, of someone actually befriending him. The Baron was himself taken by surprise at the speed of his own success; he must strike while the iron was hot. He invited the boy to take a little walk with him, and the poor lad, having been starved of genial company for weeks on end, was delighted by the suggestion. He prattled on unguardedly, delivering all the information his new-found friend teased out of him through seemingly random little questions, and in no time the Baron was very well informed about the family. For a start, Edgar was the only son of a Vienna lawyer evidently of the prosperous Jewish bourgeoisie. Subtle interrogation quickly informed him that the mother had shown herself distinctly unenthusiastic over their stay at Semmering, complaining about the lack of convivial company; indeed, he even thought he could deduce, from the guarded way Edgar answered the question of whether Mama was very fond of Papa, that here relations were not of the best. He felt almost ashamed how easy it was to coax all of these little family secrets out of the innocent child, for Edgar, proud as he was to find that anything he had to tell could be of any interest to a grown-up, was positively pressing his confidences on his new friend. His child's heart pounded with pride – as they walked the Baron had laid his arm on his shoulder – at being seen in public on such close terms with an adult, and by and by he even forgot that he was a child and chattered away freely and with such abandon as he might have done with a companion of the same age. It was obvious from the way he talked that Edgar was a very bright boy, somewhat ahead of his years, as are most poorly children who spend more time with their elders than their schoolmates, and also that he was an excessively sensitive type, in both his affections and his dislikes. There seemed nothing moderate in his relation to the world around him, and the way he spoke about anything or anybody showed either intense enthusiasm or a hostility so vehement that he would screw up his face in an unpleasant grimace that made him look almost ugly and malign. Something uncontrolled and capricious about him, perhaps arising from the illness from which he had so recently recovered, made his speech fiery and fanatical; it was as if his gaucheness was really a fear, hard to suppress, of his own strong emotions.

The Baron had no difficulty winning the boy's confidence; within a mere half-hour Edgar's ardent, restlessly beating heart was entirely in his hands. It is easy beyond words to deceive children, so guileless are they and so unused to having their affections courted. All the Baron needed to do was retreat into his own past for Edgar's childish chatter to become so natural and uninhibited that the two were as equals in the boy's mind, and any sense of distance was lost after a few brief minutes. What bliss, here in this out-of-the-way place, suddenly to have found a friend! And what a friend! Forgotten now were all of his playmates in Vienna, with their high-pitched little voices and juvenile talk; the very memory of them was entirely swept aside by this one hour of novelty. Every ounce of his unbounded fervour was now given over to this new friend, this great friend of his, and his heart swelled with pride when the Baron, before taking his leave, invited him back for another meeting next morning. And now Edgar's new companion was waving to him from a little way off, just like a brother. It may well have been the most wonderful moment in the boy's life. Yes, so easy is it to deceive a child.

Edgar charged off, and the Baron smiled. He now had his go-between. He could be certain the boy would be plaguing his mother to the point of exhaustion with stories, going over and over each and every word they had exchanged; at the same time he recalled with satisfaction how clever he had been in weaving in the odd words of praise specifically for her, never failing to refer to Edgar's 'beautiful Mama'. Forthcoming as he was, there was no doubt that the boy would not rest till he had brought the two of them together. Now he himself would hardly need to lift a finger in order to lessen the distance between him and the beautiful unknown; now he could happily dream away and contemplate the countryside, knowing that a child's warm hands were building him a bridge to her heart.

A Trio

The plan had succeeded splendidly in every detail, as became clearly evident within a few hours. The young Baron's entry into the dining room was artfully delayed, and when he did arrive Edgar leaped up from his chair and greeted him with an ecstatic smile. At the same time he pulled at his mother's sleeve and said something very fast and excitedly while pointing quite obviously towards the Baron. Reddening in embarrassment, she rebuked him for this unseemly show of enthusiasm, but she could hardly avoid glancing over just once, if only to do what the child wanted. This the Baron immediately took as his cue to offer a respectful bow in her direction. Acquaintance was achieved. She had to acknowledge the gesture, but from now on she kept her head lowered more deeply over her plate, and throughout the meal carefully avoided looking again. Edgar, by contrast, could not stop looking and at one point even tried to call over to the Baron, a breach of etiquette that brought an immediate sharp rebuke from Mama. After dinner it was made clear to Edgar that it was time for bed, prompting an energetic exchange of whispers between mother and child, the end result of which was the granting of his fervent wish, namely to go over to the other table and say hello to his friend. The Baron had a few warm words for him, once more bringing a sparkle to the boy's eyes, and chatted with him for a minute or two. But then suddenly, in a finely judged manoeuvre, he turned his head, rose to his feet, crossed over to the other table, complimented his somewhat bewildered neighbour on the bright little spark that was her son, referring with particular warmth to the morning they had spent together so enjoyably – Edgar positively blushed with pride and joy – and then came round to asking about the boy's health, inquiring with so many detailed questions that the mother was forced to reply. A more prolonged conversation naturally followed, to which the lad listened in delight and even a degree of awe. The Baron introduced himself and believed he could tell that his important-sounding name had to some extent appealed to the lady's vanity. At any rate she responded with impeccable good grace, albeit with due discretion, and indeed took her leave a little early – for the boy's sake, as she added by way of apology.

Edgar protested vehemently: he wasn't at all tired, and was more than ready to stay up all night. But by now his mother had offered the Baron her hand, which the latter kissed respectfully. That night the boy slept badly. His mind was a confusion of happiness and childish despair. The day had brought something quite new into his life. He had made his first entry into the adults' world; in his half-dreaming state he was forgetting he was a child and imagining that all of a sudden he was a grown-up. Up to now, having been brought up a lonely child and often in poor health, he had had few friends. To answer his need for affection there had been no one in his life apart from his parents, who paid him scant attention, and the household staff. And the strength of a love is never properly assessed if measured only in relation to what caused it rather than the mental strain that preceded it, that dark, empty realm of disappointment and loneliness that lies in wait before all great events in the life of the heart. An excessive, as yet unused, emotional faculty had been here biding its time, and now it hurtled with wide-open arms to overwhelm the first victim it could find to deserve it. Edgar lay in the dark, at once blissful and bewildered, wanting to laugh but forced to cry. For he loved this man in a way he had never loved any friend, had never loved his father and mother, or even God. All of the callow passion of the boy's early years now embraced the image of this person, without his even having known his name for more than two hours.

Nevertheless, he was clever enough not to be wholly confounded by the complete novelty and unexpectedness of this new friendship. What most disconcerted him was the sense of his own unworthiness, his insignificance. 'So can I really be anything to him, me just a boy of twelve still going to school and getting sent to bed before everybody else?' he tortured himself. 'What can he see in me? What have I got that I can give him?' It was this painful inability somehow to show his feelings that caused him such unhappiness. Up till now, whenever he had made friends with another boy, the first thing he did was to share with him the small number of treasures he kept in his desk, his stamps or stones, the things children like to collect, but all these things, which just yesterday had held such importance and exceptional glamour for him, now suddenly seemed worthless, silly, contemptible. How could he offer things like that to this new friend, whom he didn't even dare to address informally? How could he find some way to express his feelings? It was more and more painful, this sense of still being little, only half-grown, immature, a mere twelve years old; never before had he so thoroughly cursed being a child, or longed so earnestly to wake up as something different from this, someone big and strong, the man he dreamed of becoming, an adult like all the others.

In among these tormented thoughts were quickly woven the first colourful dreams of the new world of adulthood. Edgar did eventually fall asleep with a smile on his face, but his sleep was badly disturbed by the memory of the arrangement made for the next morning. He woke with a jolt at seven o'clock, terrified of arriving too late. Dressing hurriedly, he went to his mother's room and said good morning to her, much to her astonishment, as she usually had trouble getting him up in the morning, and then rushed off before she could question him any further. He hung around impatiently till nine without even remembering to take his breakfast; the one thought in his mind was the planned walk, and not to keep his friend waiting.

It was half past nine when the Baron eventually came along, strolling casually. Of course, he had long forgotten their appointment, but now that the young boy ran up to him so excitedly he had to smile at such enthusiasm and showed himself ready to honour his promise. Once again he took the boy under his arm. For a few minutes they walked up and down together, the child beaming all the while. Only gently, but clearly enough, the Baron resisted starting their walk together for the time being; he seemed to be waiting for something, or at any rate that was what his nervous glances towards the door suggested. Then suddenly he drew himself up straight; Edgar's mother had come in, and now she went up to the two of them with a friendly look, responding to the greeting she was given. She smiled appreciatively on hearing of the planned walk, which Edgar had kept from her as his precious secret, but was then quick to accept the Baron's invitation to come with them.

Edgar, at once put out, sullenly bit his lip. How annoying, that she had had to turn up just at this moment! The walk was supposed to be just for him; true, he had himself introduced his friend to Mama, but that was a favour he had done and didn't mean he was going to share him with her. There was already something like jealousy stirring within him as he noticed the Baron's friendly behaviour towards her.

The three set off together, and as they walked the child's

dangerous feeling of his own importance and sudden new significance was heightened by the striking interest the two adults showed in him. He was almost the only subject of their conversation, in which his mother spoke with somewhat affected concern about his pale complexion and nervous temperament while the Baron smiled and again played down these worries, making much of praising the nice manners of his 'friend', as he called him. It was Edgar's finest hour. Here he was, enjoying rights never previously granted him at any time in his childhood. He was now being allowed to take part in a conversation without being immediately silenced, and even to give voice to all kinds of impertinent wishes which in the past would always have fallen on disapproving ears. It was hardly surprising if his illusory feeling of being grown-up himself now burgeoned mightily. Now, in his bright dreams, his childhood lay as far behind him as some outgrown and discarded piece of clothing.

Come lunch, and the Baron was sitting with them at their table, having graciously accepted the invitation of Edgar's ever more affable mother. Hitherto sitting opposite each other, now they had drawn together; acquaintance had turned to friendship. The Trio was up and running, the three voices of woman, man and child now a harmonious ensemble.

Action

The huntsman was impatient; it was now time to stalk his prey. The easy harmony and familiarity so far observed did not please him. It was all very cosy chatting like this as a trio, but chatting was not quite what he had set his mind on. And he knew that this mix of sociability with the masquerade under which lay his true desire was a constant impediment to the amorous meeting of man and woman; this way his words would lack ardour, and there could be no fire to his attack. This kind of conversation should not allow her to forget his real intention, now that she had – of this he had no doubt – already understood what that was.

There was every likelihood that the effort he was making with this woman would not be in vain. Edgar's mother had reached that critical stage of life when women begin to regret having remained true to a husband they never really loved, when the twilight of their now waning beauty holds out one last urgent choice, whether to follow the maternal role or that of womanhood itself. The life that seemed to have settled such a choice long ago now, at this crucial moment, raises the question once again; for the last time the compass needle of the woman's will wavers between hope of experiencing true love and final resignation. Now she must face the dangerous decision: will she follow her own destiny or that of her children? To be a woman, or a mother? And the Baron, whose perceptions in such matters were of the sharpest, believed he could sense in her this perilous wavering: was it to be the fervour of life, or self-sacrifice? She repeatedly omitted to mention her husband in their conversations; it seemed obvious he was able to satisfy no more than her outer needs, and not the social conceits that her genteel way of life encouraged in her. It was evident, too, that deep down she knew precious little about her child. There was a tinge of ennui showing through a veil of melancholy in her almond eyes, darkening their sensuousness. The Baron decided to make his move quickly, but at the same time avoid any appearance of haste. On the contrary, like the angler who lures the fish by gently drawing in the bait, he would affect an outer indifference on his part to this new friendship and cause *her* to woo *him*, while in truth he himself was the suitor. He adopted a certain *hauteur*, more than hinting at the difference between them in social standing. It titillated him to think how he would win over the ample beauty and voluptuousness of that body simply by playing on his aloofness, his external appearance, the resonance of his aristocratic name and the very coolness of his manners.

Already the heat of the chase was beginning to arouse him, and he knew the importance of caution. That afternoon he remained in his room, pleasingly conscious of being sought, and missed. The absence, however, was noticed not so much by the mother, by whom it was meant to be felt; rather it was the cause of intolerable pain for her poor young son. For the whole afternoon Edgar felt utterly lost and helpless. With that stubborn loyalty characteristic of boys of his age, he waited hour after hour for his friend to appear. It would have seemed to him an offence against their friendship if he had just gone out, or done anything else, on his own. Thus at a loose end, he hung around in the corridors, and the later it became, the heavier and unhappier grew his heart. In his turbulent thoughts he was imagining some accident, or some unintentionally hurtful comment he might have made; he was very nearly in tears with impatience and anxiety.

When the Baron came in for dinner that evening he received the most rapturous welcome. Edgar sprang up, heedless of both his mother's reproof and the astonishment of the other guests, and ran straight over to fling his thin little arms around him. 'Where were you? Where have you been?' he cried uncontrollably. 'We were looking everywhere for you!' The mother went red in the face on hearing herself thus unwillingly included and said quite sternly: '*Sois sage, Edgar. Assieds toi!*' (It was always French she spoke to him, even though the language was hardly second nature to her, and any more detailed discourse soon landed her in difficulty.) Edgar obeyed but would not stop questioning the Baron. His mother again had to intervene: 'But please don't forget, the Baron can do as he pleases. Perhaps he's tired of our company.' This time it was 'our' company, and the Baron felt some pleasure at her fishing for compliments by way of rebuking the boy.

The Baron's inner hunter was awakened, acutely excited at
having scented the right trail, and at feeling his prey now a close
target. There was a glint in his eye, and the blood flowed
smoothly in his veins. His speech somehow bubbled out of him
quite spontaneously. His powers, much like those of any man
of pronounced erotic tendencies, and therewith the sense of his
own self, were doubled whenever he knew that he had won a
woman's approval; so it is that many an actor will discover his
true ardour only when he senses that his audience, that breathing mass of people out in front of him, are fully in thrall to him.
He had always been a good raconteur who could summon up
the liveliest of images with great skill, but today – in the course
of his performance he drank a few glasses of the champagne he
had ordered to toast the new friendship – he surpassed himself.
He told of Indian hunting expeditions that he had taken part in
as a guest of a noble-born English friend, cleverly choosing this
subject for its relative neutrality but at the same time sensing
the appeal to this woman of anything exotic and outside her
reach. But it was Edgar who was truly enchanted by these
accounts, and his eyes glowed with interest. He forgot all about
eating and drinking, and his fascinated gaze hung on the story-
teller's every word. He had never even dreamt of meeting face
to face a person who had actually had these extraordinary expe-
riences that he had read about, the hunting of big game, the
brown-skinned people, the Hindus and their Juggernaut that
crushed thousands beneath its awesome wheels. Until today
he had never seriously thought that such people existed, any
more than he believed in fairy-tale lands, and what he was now
hearing stirred powerful feelings in him for the very first time.
He couldn't take his eyes off his friend, and stared with bated
breath at these same hands that had killed a tiger. Hardly daring
to ask a question, when he did so his voice sounded feverish
with excitement. His quickly responsive imagination conjured

up vivid images to enliven what he heard; he saw his friend high on the back of a purple-caparisoned elephant, and brown-skinned men all around with costly turbans, and then suddenly he espied the tiger, baring its teeth as it leaped out of the jungle to sink its claws into the elephant's trunk. Now the Baron was moving on to an even more gripping subject, the crafty way you can trap elephants by getting old and tamed beasts to lure the young, wild, spirited ones into the enclosures; at this the child's eyes positively sparkled. And then, abruptly – it was as if a knife suddenly fell and sliced the air before those eyes – came the voice of Mama, glancing at the clock: 'Neuf heures! Au lit!'

Edgar went pale at the shock. For any child 'time for bed' is a very terrible announcement, signifying the most blatant possible humiliation in front of adults, an admission and stigma of being a child, of being small, and as such needing to sleep. But how much more terrible was such mortification at this most interesting moment of all, depriving him of hearing such extraordinary things.

'Just one more story, Mama, the one about the elephants – can't I just hear that one?'

He was on the point of begging, but quickly thought of his new-found dignity as a grown-up. He would give it just one try. But tonight his mother was remarkably strict: 'No, it's already late. Up you go! Sois sage, Edgar! I'll tell you all the Herr Baron's stories word for word afterwards.'

Edgar hung back. Normally his mother would go up with him, but he couldn't start pleading in front of his friend. His child's pride demanded at least a semblance of free will to mitigate this pitiful withdrawal.

'But really, Mama, you'll have to tell me everything, absolutely everything! The elephant story, and everything else!'

'Yes, darling.'

'Right away! Tonight!'

'Yes, yes, Edgar. Now, off with you this minute, to bed!'

The boy surprised himself by being able to shake hands with both the Baron and his mother without blushing, even though a sob was already rising to choke him. The Baron ruffled his hair cordially, bringing, or forcing, a smile to his tensed face, but then he had to make for the door quickly, otherwise they would have seen the thick tears running on his cheeks.

Elephants

The mother stayed down at the table with the Baron for a little while yet, but there was no longer any conversation about elephants and hunting. A mildly sultry element of self-consciousness appeared for a moment after the boy had left them. Presently they left the dining room and went into the lobby to sit in a corner together. The Baron was as dazzling as ever, the mother herself a touch enlivened by the glasses of champagne they had enjoyed, and the conversation quickly took on a more dangerous character. The Baron was not really what one would call handsome, but he was young, and there was a decidedly masculine, vigorous look in his tanned, boyish features and short hair; she was charmed by him and his uninhibited, almost unrefined movements. She now liked seeing him close up and was no longer unnerved by his glance. But, little by little, a certain audacity was creeping into his speech, which she found mildly disconcerting, somehow as if he might be reaching towards her physically, touching her and then withdrawing his hand; there was something unfathomably beguiling in it, which brought the blood warmly to her cheeks. But then once more there would be a gentle laugh, natural and boyish again, and all those little hints of lasciviousness would be easily seen as no more than innocent playfulness. Though at certain moments she felt that something he said deserved a frank rebuke, being one of nature's coquettes she was in fact merely charmed by such little licences, rather looking forward to some more. And, carried away by this risky sport, it was not long before she began to join in, imparting little flatteries by means of suggestive glances, even appearing to offer herself through words and gestures and raising scant objection to his drawing a little closer to speak to her in that voice whose breath she could feel warmly stroking her shoulders. Oblivious, like all gamblers, to the passing of time, they lost themselves so completely in the ardour of their conversation that they were startled back into reality only when midnight came and the lights were being put out in the lobby.

The woman leaped up sharply at the first sense of alarm, suddenly sensing how far she had allowed herself to go. Playing with fire was not entirely new to her, but this time her quickened instinct told her how near this game had brought her to something more serious. She shuddered at the realization that she was no longer feeling quite in control, and that something within her had begun to slide and was heading terrifyingly close to a precipice. In her head everything was a mêlée of fear, wine and unbridled talk; a dull, ill-defined anxiety took hold of her, a kind of fear that she had experienced more than once before in her life at such dangerous moments, but never as unsettling, as overpowering as now. 'Good night, good night, we'll meet in the morning,' she said hastily, intending to run off – to run off, that is, not so much from the Baron as from the peril of this precise moment, and a new and strange uncertainty in herself. Gently, yet firmly, the Baron held onto the hand she offered in taking her leave, and kissed it, not merely the once that decorum would require, but four or five times, his lips moving from her delicate finger tips up to the wrist, trembling as they went. And thereby a gentle shiver passed through her as she felt the roughness of his moustache tickling the back of her hand, from where a kind of warm, constricting sensation coursed with the flow of blood through her whole body; a dart of panic shot up and hammered threateningly at her temples. Her head burned as the fear, this futile fear, rocked her from head to foot; she quickly disengaged her hand.

'No, stay a little longer,' whispered the Baron. But she was already hurrying off with a degree of awkwardness in her haste that clearly betrayed her apprehension and dismay. This excited state she was in was exactly what he had intended, and she felt everything in her was in confusion. Hounded by a burning dread that the man might follow behind her and take hold of her, at the same time, in the very moment of escape, she felt a regret that he was not doing so. Just now, what for years she had unconsciously yearned for could finally have happened: the Adventure, which in her sensual longing hitherto she always loved to feel in the aura of its closeness, only to draw back from it at the last possible minute, the great and dangerous adventure, not merely some fleeting, wanton flirtation. But the Baron was too proud simply to exploit a momentary opportunity. Too certain of his conquest, he was not about to take this woman, seizing her like some predatory robber in a moment of weakness and insobriety; no, the sporting player likes a challenge, and a fully conscious submission on the part of his catch. There was no way she would escape him; the toxin was already in her veins.

She lingered a little at the top of the stairs, her hand pressed to her palpitating heart. She needed to rest for a second. Her nerves were failing her. A sigh broke from her breast, half of relief at having evaded a danger, half of regret; but the emotions were all in confusion, a lasting tumult in her blood that she felt only as a vague giddiness. Eyes half-closed, she groped her way tipsily to her room, breathing now more easily as she took hold of the cool door handle. Now, she felt, safe at last!

She opened the door quietly, and a second later started back in alarm. Something had stirred in the room, right over at the far end in the dark. Her frayed nerves rebelled violently; she was about to cry out for help, when quietly from within came the words, in a deeply sleepy voice:

'Is that you, Mama?'

'For heaven's sake, what are you doing in here?' She rushed over to the divan where Edgar lay curled up and was just now shaking off his sleep. Her first thought was that he must be ill or needing help.

But still only half-awake, and a little reproachfully, the voice continued: 'I waited so long for you, and then I fell asleep.'

'Why, though?'

'The elephants.'

'What elephants?'

Ah, that was it. Of course, she had promised to tell the child everything – and indeed tonight – all about the hunting and the Baron's other adventures. In his childish innocence the boy had crept into her room and, trusting to the last, had waited for her to come up and then soon dropped off to sleep. This was too much, and it angered her. Or more correctly, she felt angry at herself, at a little inner voice of guilt and shame which she had to shout down. 'Get off to bed this instance, you naughty child!' she bawled. Edgar stared back. What made her so angry with him? He hadn't done anything wrong, had he? But the look of surprise incensed her even more. 'Go to your room at once,' she shouted, her rage enflamed by knowing how unjust she was being to him. Edgar went without a word. He really was dreadfully tired, and only dimly conscious, amidst the enclosing mists of sleep, that his mother hadn't kept her promise and in some way or other he was being treated badly. But he did not rebel. His mind was too dulled by tiredness, and anyway he was very cross with himself for having gone to sleep instead of staying awake. 'Just like a little boy!' he upbraided himself, just before falling asleep again.

For since yesterday he really hated being a child.

Skirmish

The Baron had slept badly. Never a good idea this, going straight to bed when an adventure has been broken off before completion: a restless night of oppressive dreams, soon causing him regret at not having firmly seized his moment. When he came down in the morning, still sleepy and somewhat out of sorts, the boy ambushed him from a corner somewhere and rushed over to embrace him and pester him with a thousand questions. Overjoyed to have his grown-up friend back all to himself for a minute without having to share him with Mama, he demanded to be told the stories himself, not Mama any more, because despite her promise she hadn't told him any of those marvellous tales of his that she said she would. He bombarded the Baron, thus unpleasingly startled by his appearance and hardly managing to conceal his ill-temper, with a hundred childish importunities. And on top of this he punctuated all the questions with fervent affirmations of his affection, so happy was he to be alone again with his long-sought companion for whom he had been waiting since early morning.

The Baron's answers were curt. This constant lying in wait for him, the footling questions, and in all of it all this unsolicited emotion, were beginning to bore him. He was tired of swanning around day in, day out with a little shrimp of a twelve-year-old and talking twaddle with him. His sole concern now was to strike while the iron was hot and get the mother on her own, and this was becoming a problem, what with the child's constant unwanted presence. Now for the first time he was filled with discomfort at having incautiously occasioned such fondness, since he saw no immediate possibility of being rid of his all-too-devoted little friend.

But the attempt had to be made, come what may. Until ten o'clock, which was the time at which he had arranged for a walk with the mother, he allowed the boy's earnest chatter to wash over him without really listening, now and again interposing some little nugget to avoid offending him, but all the while casually scanning the newspaper. Finally, the moment the minute hand was perpendicular, he asked Edgar, as if suddenly remembering what he needed to do, to go over to the other hotel to inquire whether the Count Grundheim, his cousin, had yet arrived.

The unsuspecting child, overjoyed at being able at last to do something for his friend, and proud of his worthiness as messenger, ran off at once and hurtled along the road at such speed that the guests stared after him in disbelief; but nothing would prevent his showing how deftly he could discharge any duty entrusted to him. No, he was told at the other hotel, the Count had not yet arrived, in fact they had thus far had no word of his coming at all. Edgar rushed back with equal haste to deliver this news. But there was no sign of the Baron in the lobby. The boy went to his room and knocked on the door. No response. Puzzled, he ran round searching all the rooms, the piano room, the café, and then stormed off in great agitation to his mother to see if she knew anything. She too was out. The porter, to whom he now turned in utter despair, told him to his bafflement that they had gone out together just a few minutes earlier!

Edgar waited patiently. Guileless as he was, he suspected nothing amiss. They surely couldn't have gone for more than a short while; the Baron needed to know about his cousin. But one hour led to another, and then another, and despite himself he started to feel very uneasy. In any case, ever since this intriguing stranger had entered his innocent young life, the child had spent every hour of the day in a state of tension and confused anxiety. In such delicate organisms as those of young children, every emotion impresses its mark as if in soft wax. The nervous twitching of the eyelids now started up again, and he was already looking more pale. He waited and waited, patiently at first, then wildly agitated and finally close to tears. But still he was not feeling any suspicion. The blinkered trust he put in his wonderful friend suggested no more than some misunderstanding, and he nursed a painful hidden fear that perhaps he had not fully understood the Baron's instruction.

When, however, they did finally come back, how strange it was to see them still chatting away happily and showing no surprise whatsoever. It seemed that they had hardly missed him at all: 'We came back the same way you went, Edi,' said the Baron, not even asking for news of his cousin. 'We were hoping to meet you halfway.' And when Edgar, horrified to think they could have been searching for him in vain, started protesting that he had simply taken the most direct route and never left the main street and wanted to know which way they had chosen to come, his mother cut him off abruptly: 'All right, all right Edgar, enough now! Children shouldn't talk so much.'

Edgar turned red with vexation. That was the second time such a mean attempt had been made to put him down in front of his friend. Why did she always have to do this, constantly trying to make him look like a child, which he had now convinced himself he no longer was? Obviously she was jealous, that was it, jealous because of his new friend; she must be planning to get the Baron over to her side. And it was definitely also Mama who had deliberately taken the Baron the wrong way. Well, he wasn't going to allow her to treat him like this, she'd soon see. He'd stand up to her. And so Edgar resolved not to say a single word to her today at table, and talk only to the Baron.

But this wasn't so easy after all. Things turned out quite unexpectedly: his defiance passed unnoticed. They didn't even seem to see him – and just yesterday he had been the centre-piece of the trio! There they were, chatting away over his head, laughing and joking, and he might as well have disappeared under the table. The blood went to his cheeks, and there was a choking lump in his throat. It sent a shiver down him to realize how horribly powerless he was. So was that what he was sup-posed to do – sit here, looking on demurely while his mother robbed him of his friend, the one person he loved? And was there no way to defend himself, apart from keeping quiet? He felt he simply had to get up and suddenly hammer the tabletop with both fists. Just to be noticed! But he held back and merely put down his knife and fork without touching another morsel. Even this resolute abstinence went unremarked for some time; it was only when they came to change the plates that his mother noticed and asked whether he felt unwell. Sickening, he thought to himself, the way she can only ever think of one thing, whether I'm ill. She doesn't care about anything else. He answered curtly; he didn't want any more, and that seemed to satisfy her. Nothing, nothing at all could make them notice him. The Baron seemed to have forgotten him, at least he didn't address a word to him even once. His eyes smarted hotter and hotter, and he was forced to apply the child's trick of raising his napkin to his face to prevent anyone noticing the tears running on his cheeks and making his lips wet and salty. He breathed with relief when the meal came to an end.

During dinner his mother had suggested a joint carriage outing to the nearby shrine of Maria Schutz. Hearing this, Edgar had bitten his lip hard. So she wasn't going to allow him even a minute alone with his friend! But his hatred only truly flared up when she said to him, as they rose from the table, 'Edgar, you'll be forgetting all your schoolwork. You'd better stay at home for once, and do some studying.' Once again he clenched his little fist; same as ever, she was wanting to humiliate him in front of his friend, yet again announcing to everybody around that he was still just a little boy who had to go to school and enjoyed adult company only when allowed. But this time her intentions were just too transparent. He refused to answer, and instead abruptly turned his back on her.

'Ah, I've hurt his feelings again,' she laughed, and then said to the Baron: 'Would that really be so hard on him, spending an hour with his books for once?'

To which the Baron's answer came – and it chilled and froze the child's heart to hear it from the one who had called him his friend and had teased him for being a stay-at-home – 'Oh, an hour or two surely couldn't do any harm!'

Was there a pact between them then? Had they actually teamed up against him? There was a flash of anger in the boy's look. 'Papa forbade me to do any schoolwork here, Papa wants me to get well here.' He flung this out with all the pride he had in being ill, desperately clinging to his father's words and authority. The statement came out like a threat, and the most remarkable thing was that it did in fact appear to induce some discomfort in both of them. The mother looked away and thrummed her fingers nervously on the table. A painful, empty silence hung over them. Finally the Baron spoke, with a forced smile on his face. 'Quite right, Edi. Anyway, I'm not the one who has to take any exams, I failed all mine years ago!'

But Edgar, instead of smiling at the joke, gave him a searching, yearningly testing look, as if trying to reach into the man's soul. What was going on here? Something had changed between them, and he couldn't say what. Unsettled, his eyes wandered. In his heart there was a faint, rapid hammering: the first suspicion.

Burning Secret

'What's made them so different now?' the child pondered as he sat opposite them in the carriage on the way to Maria Schutz. 'Why aren't they treating me the way they did before? Why does Mama keep avoiding my eyes when I look at her? And he – why is he always trying to make jokes and fooling around in front of me? Neither of them is talking to me the same way as yesterday and the day before. It's almost as if they'd got new faces too; Mama's lips are so red today, she must have coloured them. I've never seen her do that. And he's always got that frown, as if something's got under his skin. Surely it wasn't me, something I said that annoyed them? No, it can't be me; they're even behaving differently with each other now, not like before. It's as if they've been up to something and won't dare come clean. They don't chat any more like yesterday, or laugh either. They're embarrassed, hiding something. There's some secret they're sharing, and they don't want to let me in on it. Yes, a secret, and I'm going to get to the bottom of it, whatever it costs. I bet it's the same thing as when I get shut out of the room, what people are always doing in books and in the opera, men and ladies opening their arms wide at each other while they sing, all that hugging and then pushing each other way. Must be something like that business with my French teacher when she behaved so badly with Papa and had to be sent away. It's all connected, I can feel it, but I just don't know how. If only I knew what it's all about, and I could find the key to all those doors, and I wasn't a child any more, with people hiding everything from me and covering up, and I wasn't being played along and told fibs all the time. It's now or never! I'm going to get it out of them, this terrible secret.' A deep furrow appeared in his brow, and the insubstantial little twelve-year-old looked almost old, brooding so seriously without once sparing a moment to look at the countryside that unfolded itself in a symphony of colours all around them, the mountains in the purified green of their pine forests and the valleys still in the gentle lustre of a now belated spring. He saw nothing but the two of them sitting opposite him in the back seat of the carriage, as if his fervidly searching looks could pluck out the secret, as an angler does a fish, from the glimmering depths of their eyes. Nothing hones the intelligence more than a burning suspicion, and nothing so deploys the capacities of an immature intellect as a trail leading away into the dark. Sometimes it is no more than a single flimsy door that separates children from the real world, as we call it, and a chance breeze is enough to fling it open for them.

Edgar suddenly felt himself closer than ever to the unknown, the great secret, almost able at long last to grasp it. He sensed it was just in front of him, even though it was still bolted shut and unsolved, but near, so near! The excitement was intense and gave him this sudden, solemn earnestness, for now he sensed, unconsciously, that he had come to the outermost edge of his childhood.

The couple sitting opposite were aware of a certain inert obstructiveness in the air, without realizing that its source was the boy. They felt hemmed in and inhibited, the three sitting together in the carriage. The pair of eyes peering at them with their dark, mercurial glimmer constrained them both, and they hardly dared to open their mouths, or even to look. There was no way back to the light-hearted tone of their earlier conversations; they were now far too entangled in the ardour of their confidences, and of those dangerous words in which prurient flatteries betoken the quivering of secret touches. Their talk was constantly broken off, faltering, now halting completely, now starting up again, yet stumbling repeatedly against the dogged silence of the child.

For the mother this persistent defiance was especially irksome. Venturing a sidelong glance at him, she was startled to observe for the first time, in the way the boy pursed his lips, a marked similarity with his father whenever he was irritated or angered. It was an uncomfortable sensation to be reminded of her husband just at this moment, now that she was toying, in a kind of hide-and-seek way, with an adventure of her own. Her son seemed like a ghost, a guardian of conscience, a doubly intolerable presence as they sat here cheek by jowl in the cramped confines of the carriage, he with those oscillating dark eyes and a hint of lurking in wait behind his pale forehead. Then suddenly Edgar looked up for a brief second. Both of them just as quickly lowered their eyes, each sensing their scrutinizing of each other for the first time. Until then they had trusted each other blindly, but now something had come between mother and child; something had suddenly changed. For the first time in their lives they began to watch each other, to separate their two destinies one from the other, and there was now a secret hostility between them, still too new for them to dare to acknowledge it, but there nonetheless.

All three breathed more easily when the horses came to a halt in front of the hotel. It had been an unhappy outing, all three felt, though none dared say so. Edgar was the first to jump out of the carriage. His mother excused herself with a headache and hurried off to her room. She was tired and wanted to be left alone. Edgar and the Baron remained. The Baron paid the coachman, looked at his watch and headed for the lobby without looking at the boy. He passed Edgar with that refined, slim back of his lightly and rhythmically swaying as he walked – a walk that had so enchanted the child, and which he had been trying to copy the day before. The Baron went straight past him, evidently quite forgetting the boy was there, and left him standing next to the coachman and the horses. There might as well have been no connection at all between them.

Something in Edgar was torn in two when he saw him walk past like this – this very person whom he still idolized despite everything. Despair broke from his heart as the Baron walked past without even touching him with his coat and not saying a word to him, while he himself was unaware of having done anything to deserve such a slight. His painfully preserved self-restraint collapsed, the weighty dignity with which he had burdened himself slid from his slender young shoulders, and he was once more the child, small and insignificant, that he had been the day before, and always up till then. It drove him on, even against his will, his trembling legs hurrying quickly after the Baron, and when they met, just as the latter had reached the stairs, Edgar ran ahead of him and accosted him in a strained voice, hardly holding back the tears:

'What have I done to you, so you don't even look at me any more? Why are you always being like that now? And Mama too? Why do you want me out of the way all the time? Am I bothering you, or have I done something wrong?'

The Baron started. There was something in the boy's voice that disturbed and moved him. Overcome by pity for the innocent child, he answered: 'Edi, how silly you are! I've just been a bit out of sorts today. And you're such a good lad, and I really like you.' As he spoke he gave his hair a good ruffling, but his face was half averted so as to avoid those large, moist, beseeching child's eyes. The little comedy he had been acting out was becoming painful for him, and he was really already feeling some shame at playing with this child's affections and using him so brazenly. The childish little voice, convulsed with suppressed sobbing, hurt him deeply. 'Upstairs with you now, Edi,' he said appeasingly, 'and tonight we'll be getting on as well as ever, you'll see.'

'But you're not going to let Mama send me straight off to bed, are you?'

'No, no Edi, of course not,' he smiled. 'Now, up you go. I have to get dressed for dinner.'

Edgar went, happiness restored for the moment. But soon the hammering in his heart started again. He had aged by years since yesterday; a stranger, mistrust, was now a lodger in his child's heart.

He waited. Now was to be the deciding test. They all sat together at table. Nine o'clock came, but his mother still didn't send him off to bed. He was becoming uneasy. Normally she was so particular, so why now, why today, was she letting him stay up so long? Had the Baron gone and told her what he wanted, and what they had said to each other? Suddenly he felt a sting of regret at having earlier run after his friend with such trust in his heart. At ten o'clock his mother promptly rose to her feet and said good night to the Baron. And, strangely enough, he too seemed wholly unsurprised at this early departure and made no attempt to keep her back as he always had done before. The hammer beat harder and harder in the child's breast.

Now for the real test. Edgar too pretended to suspect nothing and followed his mother without protest. And then with a sudden movement of his head he looked up and, sure enough, at that moment he caught a smile on her face, directed over his head towards the Baron, a look of connivance, of some kind of secret. The Baron had betrayed him after all. That was her reason for leaving early: today he was to be lulled into a sense of security so that tomorrow he would not get in their way any more.

'Skunk!' he murmured.

'What was that?' asked his mother.

'Nothing,' he hissed between gritted teeth. Now he had his

own secret, and its name was hatred, unbounded hatred for both of them.

Silence

Edgar's inner turmoil was over now. Finally he was enjoying a pure, lucid feeling: hatred, and open enmity. He had proved to himself that he was in their way; being together with them now became a cruelly intricate pleasure. He feasted on the prospect of disturbing them, of at last opposing them with all the concentrated power of his hostility. It was at the Baron that he first bared his teeth. When his former friend came down in the morning and greeted him in passing with a hearty 'G'day to you, Edi!', Edgar growled back a crusty 'Morning', without rising from his armchair or even looking up.

'Is Mama already down?'

'Don't know,' said Edgar, not lifting his eyes from the newspaper.

The Baron stopped short. What's this all about, all of a sudden?

'Slept badly, did we, Edi?' A joke always worked wonders. But Edgar simply threw out a contemptuous 'No' and buried himself in the paper again.

'Silly fellow,' muttered the Baron under his breath, and shrugged his shoulders and walked off. Open warfare now.

With his mother, too, Edgar was cool and formal. A maladroit attempt to dispatch him to the tennis courts was quietly dismissed. A smile curled his lips, betraying a slight tinge of bitterness, to indicate that he would no longer be fobbed off.

'I'd rather go for a walk with the two of you, Mama,' he said with feigned affection, looking her in the eye. The reply was visibly not to her liking. She hesitated, apparently at a loss. 'Wait for me here,' she finally told him, and went in to breakfast.

Edgar waited. But his distrust was fully alert; a keenly watchful instinct was now teasing out a secret, hostile intent in every word that passed between them. His suspiciousness made some of his deductions remarkably perceptive. Instead of waiting in the lobby as instructed, he decided to occupy a position in the street, from where he could survey not only the main entrance but every other door too. Something in him scented deception. But they were not going to give him the slip any more. Out in the street he hunkered down behind a wood pile, the way he'd learned the Red Indians did in his adventure books. And how gleefully he laughed when, sure enough, he saw his mother half an hour later leaving by a side door, a splendid bunch of roses in her hand, followed by the Baron, the traitor Baron!

They both seemed full of life. No doubt breathing easily again, having got away from him to enjoy their secret alone! Chatting and laughing happily, they started off down the road leading towards the woods.

The moment had come. Edgar ambled out casually from behind his woodpile as if he just happened to have been there by chance. Relaxed as could be, he approached them, and allowed himself time – and a good long time at that – to feast his eyes on their astonishment. Dumbfounded, the two of them exchanged a look of discomfort. Slowly Edgar went up to them, pretending this was the entirely natural course of events, and let his scornful gaze rest on them.

'Ah, there you are, Edi. We were looking for you inside,' the mother said finally. Barefaced liar, thought the child. But his lips remained tightly sealed, holding the secret of his hatred behind his teeth. Indecisively, the three stood watching one another. 'Well, let's go then,' said the woman, annoyed but resigned, and plucked out one of the beautiful roses. Again there was that slight trembling of her nostrils, a sure sign of anger. Edgar remained standing, as if this was their business and not his, stared up into the sky, waited for them to set off, then started walking after them. The Baron made one last attempt. 'Today's the tennis tournament. Have you ever been to one?' Edgar just looked back at him scornfully. He gave no answer and merely shaped his lips as if about to whistle. So much for his response; his hatred was baring its claws.

Edgar's uninvited presence was by now becoming a nightmare to both of them. This was the way convicts follow their guard, fists furtively clenched behind them. The child was in fact doing nothing at all, and yet was becoming more insufferable by the minute, as were the sly looks he gave, his eyes wet with tears grimly held back, and the crabby sullenness with which he snarled at any attempted approach. 'Go on ahead of us,' snapped his mother, suddenly showing her irritation and clearly unsettled by his constant eavesdropping on them. 'Stop this dancing around under my feet, it's making me nervous!'

Edgar complied, but after every few steps kept turning round and waiting for them if they had fallen behind, his gaze encircling them like Faust's Mephistopheles in the form of the black poodle, enmeshing them within this fiery net of hatred, in which they felt inescapably entangled. His baleful silence tore into their good humour like an acid, his staring vitiated their conversation. The Baron ventured no further words of courting; he sensed, to his chagrin, that the woman was slipping away from him again; the passion he had taken pains to foment in her was cooling, he now felt, through fear of this obnoxious child. Repeatedly they tried, and repeatedly failed, to pick up their conversation again, and in the end all three found themselves striding along in silence, and in their silence hearing only the leaves rustling in the trees and their own cheerless footsteps. The child had stifled their talking.

By now a peevish hostility had taken root in all three. It delighted the child, betrayed victim that he was, to sense how his mother's and the Baron's concentrated anger was helplessly aimed at his own neglected person. From time to time, his eyes twinkling in mockery, he would survey the Baron's morose expression and observe the curses being mouthed between grinding teeth, and he had to restrain himself from mouthing his own against the Baron, noticing at the same time, with equally devilish enjoyment, his mother's burgeoning wrath, and seeing that both were praying for a single reason to come down hard on him and send him packing, or render him harmless. But he gave them no such opportunity; his hatred had taken him long hours to cultivate, and was not going to allow any chinks to be exploited.

'Let's go back,' said the mother suddenly, feeling she couldn't take much more of this and must do something, anything, if only to scream out loud under this torture. 'What a shame,' said Edgar calmly, 'it's rather nice here!'

Both realized the child was laughing at them, but they didn't dare say anything; in two brief days this private little tyrant of theirs had mastered the art of self-control to perfection; there was no sign of movement in his face to betray his acute irony. Without a word, they retraced their steps on the long path back to the hotel. The mother's agitation was still surging when she and Edgar were alone together in her room, and she angrily tossed aside her gloves and parasol. Edgar could tell at once how her frayed nerves longed for some outlet, but as he wanted a real outburst he stayed with her on purpose to rile her even more. She paced up and down, sat down, drummed her fingers on the table, then sprang up again. 'What a mess you look, going about in such a filthy state! It's a disgrace, in front of all these people here. Aren't you ashamed of yourself, at your age?' Without saying anything to counter her, he went across the room to comb his hair. This silence, this obstinate cold silence, accompanied by the contemptuous curling of his lips, so enraged her that she was minded to strike him. 'Go to your room!' she shouted, unable to endure his presence a minute longer. Edgar smiled and left.

To think how they quaked in front of him! How frightened they were, both the Baron and Mama, of every hour they had to spend together, and of the merciless way he fixed his eyes on them! The more uncomfortable they felt, the brighter gleamed his satisfaction in staring at them, and the more challenging was the pleasure he showed. Edgar now tormented the two defenceless adults with all of that almost bestial cruelty often found in children. The Baron was still able to curb his anger, because he still hoped to wrong-foot the boy, and his thoughts were still focused on his final aim. With the mother it was different, now increasingly losing her composure. She found some relief in berating her son. 'Stop playing with that fork!' she scolded him at table. 'You are an ill-mannered little boy – you don't deserve at all to be sitting with adults.' The smile did not leave Edgar's face, his head tilted slightly to one side. He knew that her rebukes really meant desperation on her part and felt proud that he could make her betray herself in this way. He now assumed a quite placid expression, like that of a physician. Before this, he might have answered her insolently just to anger her, but hatred teaches much, and teaches quickly. Now he clammed up completely, saying nothing until the pressure of his silence was too much for her, and she began to scream at him.

She could bear it no longer. When they got up from the table and Edgar was about to follow her with that same apparently natural air of filial devotion, she suddenly erupted and, casting off all discretion, spat out the truth. Tortured by his insidious presence, she reared up like a horse beset by flies. 'Why are you hounding me the whole time like a child of three? I don't want you constantly hanging around me. Children shouldn't always be clinging to their parents, do you hear me? Can't you spend a single hour on your own? Go and read a book, or do anything you like, just leave me in peace! You're making me nervous with this endless creeping around after me and that dreadful sullen look on your face.'

At long last he had got it out of her, the admission! Edgar smiled, while his mother and the Baron now seemed embarrassed. She turned away from the boy and was about to leave, furious with herself for having revealed her discomfort to him. But Edgar merely answered coolly, 'Papa doesn't want me to be wandering around here on my own. Papa made me promise I wouldn't take any risks, and I would stay with you all the time.'

He stressed the word 'Papa', having previously noticed a certain paralysing effect it had on both of them. His father must also be mixed up in this mighty secret, he thought, and have some kind of hidden power over the two, a power he didn't himself know, because the very mention of his name appeared to induce anxiety and discomfort. This time, too, they failed to say anything in answer. They had laid down their arms. The mother went on ahead, the Baron with her. Behind them came Edgar, but he didn't come humbly like a servant; his was the grim, stern, implacable walk of a prison guard, shaking the invisible chains they jangled and could not loosen. Hatred had steeled his child's powers; ignorant he was of it, but stronger than the two whose hands were bound fast by the secret.

The Liars

But time was pressing. The Baron had but few days left now, and these needed to be used well. Any resistance to the cranky child's intractability was, they felt, fruitless, and so they resorted to the final, most ignominious solution, namely flight, simply to escape the boy's tyranny if only for an hour or two.

'Just take these letters down to the post office, please, and get them registered,' she said to Edgar. They were standing together in the lobby; the Baron was outside, speaking to a carriage driver.

Distrustfully, Edgar took the two letters. Earlier he had noticed one of the hotel staff giving some kind of message to his mother. Were they finally hatching some plot against him?

He hesitated. 'Where will you be waiting for me?'

'Here.'

'Definitely?'

'Yes.'

'Make sure you don't go away without me. So you'll wait for me here until I come back?' The boy spoke in full knowledge of the advantage he had over his mother, and his tone was high-handed. Much had changed since the day before yesterday.

He started off with the two letters. At the entrance he bumped into the Baron, and spoke to him for the first time in two days. 'I'm just going to post these letters. Mama will be waiting till I'm back. Please don't leave before that.'

The Baron pushed past him quickly. 'Don't worry, of course we'll wait.'

Edgar rushed off to the post office. There he had to wait. A gentleman before him had a dozen mundane questions. At length he was able to discharge his task, and he ran back at once with the receipts. And he arrived just in time to see his mother and the Baron setting off in the cab.

Rigid with anger, he was close to bending down, picking up a stone and hurling it after them. So they'd escaped him after all, and they'd used a common lie, and a despicable one at that! Of course, he had known since yesterday that his mother could lie, but the fact that she could do it so shamelessly as to violate an explicit promise, this finally shattered any remaining trust he felt. He no longer understood anything at all in life, now that he had seen how those words that he thought were backed up by reality were just so many coloured bubbles of air that sooner or later burst and vanished without trace. But what sort of terrible secret must this be, if it drove grown adults so far that they could deliberately deceive him, a child, and sneak away like criminals? In the books he had read, there were people who murdered and swindled each other to get money or power or kingdoms, but what could be the reason here, what was it that those two wanted, why were they hiding from him, what were they trying to cover up with such a mountain of lies? He racked his brains for an answer. He had a vague feeling that this secret was the bolt that he could slip to unlock the door out of childhood; opening it would mean finally having grown up, a man at last. Oh, to get to the answer! But he could no longer think clearly. The fire of rage at knowing they had got away from him burned in him, its heat and smoke clouding any clarity of vision.

Edgar ran out into the woods, where he just managed to take refuge in the darkness and be seen by no one; then he burst into floods of hot tears. 'Liars! Dogs! Cheats! Of all the . . . !' He had to shout the words out aloud, to avoid choking. The frenzy of anger and impatience, compounded by curiosity and helplessness and the betrayal he had suffered over these days, till now suppressed in his painful childish efforts to delude himself that he was an adult, now gushed forth from his breast in despairing tears. They were the last tears of his childhood, the last, wildest bout of weeping, in which he abandoned himself like a girl to the joyful relief of crying. He wept away everything in this hour of bewildered rage, all of his trust and love and faith and respect – his whole childhood.

The boy who then returned to the hotel was now quite a different one. This one was cool, and acted with forethought. He went straight to his room, washed his face and eyes so as not to grant his two antagonists the triumph of seeing the remains of his tears. Next, he prepared the reckoning. And waited patiently, without any residual unease.

The lobby was quite crowded when the cab arrived back outside with the two escapees. A few gentlemen were playing chess, and others were reading their newspapers while the ladies chatted with one another. Among them the child had been sitting quietly, a little pale, eyes restless as ever. Presently, when his mother and the Baron came through the door, slightly embarrassed to see him so immediately, and just about to stammer out their ready-prepared excuse, Edgar went up to them, calm and upright, and out came the challenge: 'Herr Baron, I have something to say to you.'

The Baron was clearly uncomfortable, feeling himself somehow caught out and cornered. 'Yes, yes, later, we'll see.'

Edgar now raised his voice and spoke with bell-like clarity so that nobody in the lobby could fail to hear, 'But I want to speak to you right now. You have behaved disgracefully. You lied to me. You knew that my Mama was waiting for me, and then you . . .'

'Edgar!' shouted his mother, rounding on him and aware of everyone's eyes now on her. But the child now screamed back, seeing that they were about to shout him down: 'I'll say it again in front of everyone!' he yelled. 'It was a horrible lie you told me, and that's mean, it was a beastly trick to play!'

The Baron turned pale, the people stared, some of them smiling.

The mother seized hold of Edgar, who was quivering wildly: 'Go up to your room this minute, or you'll get a smack right here in front of all these people,' she stammered hoarsely.

By now, though, Edgar had calmed down. Feeling some regret at having so violently lost his temper, he was unhappy with himself; what he had really intended was to challenge the Baron coolly, but his rage had been too much for his will. Calmly, taking his time, he turned towards the stairs.

'I must ask you to pardon his rudeness, Herr Baron. You know, of course, that he is rather highly strung.' She spoke falteringly, feeling flustered at the mildly gloating looks she was receiving from the onlookers all around them. Nothing in the world was more distasteful to her than scandal, and she knew she must maintain some dignity at this moment. Instead of withdrawing immediately, she went to the desk to ask for letters that might have arrived, made one or two other insignificant inquiries, then sailed away upstairs as if nothing had happened. In her wake, though, she left more than a hint of whispering and suppressed mirth.

While on the way up, she slowed her steps. In serious situations she was always at a loss, and was frankly fearful of having it out with the boy this time. That she was the guilty party was undeniable, and then again, she was actually afraid of the look in the child's eyes, this strange new expression, so remarkable, so stultifying and unsettling for her. Fearing the worst, she decided to broach matters gently. If it came to a real confrontation, she knew that the excitable child now had the upper hand.

She opened the door quietly. The lad was sitting there, calm and cool. His eyes, which he raised to her, showed no fear at all, or even any curiosity. He seemed quite self-assured.

'Edgar,' she started, trying to sound as motherly as possible, 'what on earth were you thinking? I was ashamed of you. How could you be so rude, a child speaking to an adult like that? You will go and apologize to the Herr Baron right now.'

Edgar looked out of the window. His 'No' was spoken as if addressing the trees. His firmness was beginning to disturb her.

'Edgar, what's the matter with you? You've become so different, I don't feel I know you any more. You were always such a clever, well-behaved boy in the past, nice for everyone to talk to, and now all of a sudden it's as if the devil had got into you.

What can you have against the Baron? You seemed to like him so much to begin with, and he's been so nice to you.'

'Yes, and that's because he wanted to get to know you.'

She became a little uneasy. 'Nonsense! How can you say things like that?'

The child now flared up.

'A liar, that's what he is, completely two-faced. Everything he does is worked out, and mean. He wanted to get to know you, that's why he made friends with me and promised me a dog. I don't know what he's promised to give you, and I don't know why he's so nice to you, but he definitely wants something from you, Mama, I know it. Otherwise why would he be so polite and friendly? He's a bad man. He tells real fibs. Just look at him properly for once, how fake he looks. I hate him, hate him, the horrible stinking liar . . .'

'But Edgar, how can you say such a thing?' In her perplexity she had no words to answer him. Deep down she had a feeling the boy might not be entirely wrong.

'Yes, Mama, he's a scoundrel, I'll never say anything different. You must see it, surely? Why do you suppose he's afraid of me? Why does he keep avoiding me? It's because he knows I can see through him, because I know him for what he is, that snake . . .'

'But, Edgar, you mustn't talk like that. How could anyone say such things?' Her thoughts seemed to have dried up, only her lips feebly stammering the same words again and again. Now she suddenly began to feel terribly frightened and could not tell whether it was the Baron she feared or her own child.

Edgar could see that his warning had made an impression. There was some attraction in the idea of winning her over to his side and gaining an ally in his enmity and hatred of the man. Tenderly, he went up to his mother and hugged her, and his voice became earnestly ingratiating.

'Mama, you must have noticed he doesn't mean any good. He's changed you for a start. You're the one who's different now, not me. He's turned you against me, just so he can have you for himself. He's definitely going to cheat you. I don't know what he's promised you. But I do know he won't stick to it. You should be careful of him. If someone lies to one person he'll lie to anyone. He's a bad man, Mama, and you mustn't trust him.'

The voice, soft now and almost tearful, seemed to her to speak from her own heart. Since yesterday a certain misgiving had awoken in her, which was giving her much the same warning, and more pressingly by the minute. Ashamed, however, to admit her own child was right after all, she saved herself, as so many do, from the discomfort of overwhelming embarrassment by resorting to acerbity. She straightened her posture.

'Children don't understand this kind of thing You shouldn't be interfering in such matters. You'd do best to behave yourself, and that's that.'

Edgar's face froze again. 'Have it your own way,' he said grimly. 'I've warned you.'

'So you're not going to say you're sorry?'

'No.'

They stood close, face to face. For her, it was her authority that counted now.

'Then you will eat up here on your own. And you won't be joining us downstairs until you have apologized. You'll learn some manners, and you won't be leaving your room until I say you can. Do you hear me?'

Edgar smiled. This spiteful smile seemed by now a natural feature of his lips. In his own mind he was angry with himself: how stupid of him to let his feelings run away with him yet again, and to want to warn her, liar that she was too.

She swept out, without looking at him again. Those eyes,

the incisive glance, disturbed her. The child had become an uncomfortable presence since she started sensing that he had his eyes open and was telling her precisely what she was reluctant to know or hear. It was deeply unnerving to have this inner voice, her own conscience, detached from herself and going around in the guise of a child, her own child, warning her and making a fool of her. Up till now this same child had been an inseparable part of her life, an adornment, a plaything, something cherished and familiar – yes, perhaps occasionally a burden, but something that always followed the flow of her life and kept in step with her. Today for the first time this same entity was rebelling and opposing her will. Something akin to aversion would, from now on, be mixed into her thoughts of her own child.

But for all that, as she now descended the stairs, a little wearied, the childish voice sounded from deep inside her: 'You should be careful of him!' The warning was insistent, not to be quelled. She came to a mirror which shone as she passed; looking into it searchingly, more and more intently, by and by she saw the reflected lips open in the hint of a smile and round themselves as if about to pronounce a dangerous word. Still that voice was there from within her; but then quickly throwing back her shoulders as if shaking off all of these hidden qualms, she gave the mirror a bright, open look, gathered her skirts and continued down the stairs with the resolute bearing of a gambler rolling that last gold coin noisily over the table.

Moonlit Trail

The waiter who had brought Edgar's meal to his room where he was under house arrest closed the door; the lock clicked behind him. The child erupted in anger. This was clearly his mother's orders, locking him in like a dangerous animal. He brooded gloomily.

'What's going on downstairs, while I'm all locked in up here? What are the two of them plotting now? Is the secret coming out now at last, and I have to miss everything? This secret, I feel it all around me the whole time when I'm with grown-ups. At night they shut the door so I won't hear anything and they start talking very quietly if I turn up when they weren't expecting me. This big secret, I know it's been really close to me for days now, almost within reach, and I still can't get to it! I can't think of anything I haven't done to get hold of it. There were those times I pinched Papa's books out of his desk and read them, and I found all those weird things in them, only I didn't understand them. There's got to be some seal or other that you have to break so you can get the answer. I wonder if it's inside me, or maybe in the other people. I asked the maid about it, asked her to tell me what those things in the books meant, but she just laughed at me. It's so awful being little, having things all around you that you want to know and can't ask anyone about, and always being made to look stupid in front of these bigger people, as if you're completely ignorant and useless. But I'm going to get to the bottom of it, I know it, quite soon now. I've already got part of it in my hands, and I won't give up till I've got all of it!'

He listened carefully to hear if anyone was coming. A gentle breeze was blowing in the trees outside, fragmenting the still reflection of the moonlight in the branches into a hundred shimmering splinters.

'It can't be anything good that they're planning, otherwise they wouldn't have made up such pathetic lies to get me out of the way. I bet they're having a good laugh at me now, damn them, having got rid of me at last, but I'm going to have the last laugh. What an idiot I was to get myself locked in here and give them a bit of freedom instead of sticking close to them so I could watch every movement they made. I know grown-ups are always being careless, so it won't be long before these two also give themselves away. They think we're still little and always fast asleep at night, and what they've forgotten is that you can look as if you're asleep but actually be listening carefully, and you can pretend to be stupid and really be very clever. It wasn't that long ago that my auntie had a baby, and they knew all about it long before it happened and only in front of me they made out as if it was a complete surprise to them and they'd never expected it. But I knew all the time, because I heard them talking weeks before that in the evening when they thought I was safely tucked up in bed. So I'm going to surprise them again, that rotten pair. I wish I could just peep through the doors and secretly spy on them while they think they're safe. I wonder if I shouldn't just ring now so the maid'll come and unlock the door and ask what I wanted. Or I could make a big racket, smash some crockery or something, and that'd make them open up. And when they do, I could slip out right there and then and go and listen to them. But no, I don't want to do that. I don't want anyone seeing how mean they've been to me. I've got some pride after all! I'll get even with them tomorrow.'

He heard a woman's voice laughing down below. Edgar started: that might be his mother. Of course, she could laugh, she could make fun of him as much as she liked, him the small, helpless one that they could lock in his room if they found he got in the way, and park him in the corner like a bag of wet laundry. Tentatively, he leaned out of the window. No, it wasn't his mother, it was only some high-spirited young girls he didn't know, teasing some young lad.

At that moment Edgar noticed how close to the ground his window in fact was. And he had hardly taken this in before the thought flashed into his mind: jump out, now, while they think they're safe, and go and listen to them. His mind glowed with delight at having made the decision. It was almost as if he held the great, glittering secret in his hands. 'Out, quick, out,' insisted a quivering inner voice. There was no danger. No people walking past at that moment. He jumped. A gentle crunch came from the gravel, but there was no one nearby to hear the noise.

Over these last two days, creeping about and crouching under cover had become his chief pleasures in life; hence at this moment he felt a great sense of joy, but also a slight trembling of anxiety, as he stole ever so softly round the hotel, carefully avoiding the strong glare of the lights. He first peered in at the dining room, pressing his cheek warily against the glass pane. Where they normally sat was empty. His spying eyes took him further, from window to window. He dared not enter the hotel itself for fear of suddenly running into them in one of the corridors. But they were nowhere to be seen. Edgar was about to despair of finding them when he caught sight of two shadows emerging from a door. He shrank back and hid in the darkness. Yes, coming out was his mother, with her now inseparable companion. So he had come at exactly the right time. What were they saying to each other? He couldn't make it out; they were talking softly, and the wind was making too much noise in the trees. But now a laugh came over to him quite distinctly. It was his mother's voice, but the laugh was one he had never heard before, a unusually sharp, nervously excitable laugh as if caused by tickling, and Edgar found it strange and disturbing. But all the same she was laughing, so it couldn't indicate any danger, anything really massive and daunting that they were hiding from him. He felt a little disappointed.

But why had they left the hotel? Where were they going, out on their own at night-time? Winds must be sweeping the clouds past high overhead on giant wings; the sky, just a little earlier clear in the moonlight, was now darkening. Black drapes cast out by invisible hands enveloped the moon from time to time, and the gloom of night became so impenetrable that hardly any of the path could be seen at all, and then suddenly it would reappear in all its previous brightness once the moon was free to shine again. A silvery sheen flowed coolly over the landscape. The vying of light and shade was mysterious, as evocative as a woman's play of unveiling and concealment. And just at this moment the landscape once more revealed its nakedness: Edgar saw the two moving silhouettes across the way, or rather it was more like one that he saw, for they were pressed close as if forced together by some shared inner fear. But where were they heading now, the two of them? The firs were groaning in the wind, and there was an eerie stirring all about, as if the woods were alive with the Wild Hunt. I'll follow them, he thought, they won't hear my footsteps with all this noise of wind in the trees. And as they continued along the broad path in the moonlight below him, he darted quietly, nimbly, from one tree to another, from shadow to shadow, in the wood above. Unrelentingly, doggedly he followed them, now blessing the wind for making his movement inaudible, now cursing it for constantly carrying away their words from him. Just one moment, if he could just once have caught their conversation, he was convinced he could have the secret in his grasp.

The two of them walked on below, suspecting nothing. They felt themselves blissfully alone in this mysterious vastness of night, lost in their mounting excitement. No presentiment warned them that up above, in the tangle of darkened undergrowth, every one of their steps was being followed, two eyes holding them fast in the full force of inquisitiveness and resentment.

Suddenly they stopped, and Edgar too stopped short immediately and pressed himself tight against a tree. A turbulent fear came over him. What if they now turned round and got back to the hotel before him, and he couldn't get safely into his room, and his mother found it empty? Then all would be lost; they would know that he had secretly stalked them, and he would have no hope of wresting the secret from them. But now he saw them linger hesitantly; there was apparently some difference of opinion between them. Fortunately there were no clouds blocking the light at this moment, and he could see everything clearly. The Baron was pointing to a dark narrow side path that led down into the valley, where, unlike here in the road, the moon did not cast a full wide stream of light over everything but filtered through the thickets in droplets and a few scattered beams. Why was he so keen to go down there? His mother appeared to be saying no, but the Baron was still talking to her, and Edgar could tell from his gestures how insistent his words were. The child was afraid: what did this man want with his mother? Why was the rogue trying to drag her off into the dark? From his books, which were the world as he knew it, there suddenly came back vivid memories of murders and abductions and all manner of devilish crimes. Yes, for sure, he was about to murder her, that was why he'd had him locked away and lured her out here on her own. Should he cry out for help? Murder! The word was almost out, but his lips were dry and couldn't utter any sound at all. Edgar's nerves were tense with excitement, and he could hardly remain on his feet; in his terror he reached out for some support, and a twig snapped under his hands.

Startled, the two turned and stared into the darkness. Edgar remained stock still, leaning against the tree with his arms clinging to it, his diminutive body sunk deeply into the shadows. There was a deathly hush all around. But still they seemed alarmed. 'Let's go back,' he heard his mother say. The voice sounded anxious. The Baron, evidently himself unsettled, assented. The couple slowly started back, huddled close together. Their inner awkwardness was Edgar's good fortune. Crawling low on all fours through the undergrowth, he made his way, scratching and grazing his hands till they bled, as far as the turn into the woods, and from there he hurried breathlessly back to the hotel as fast as his legs would carry him, finally running up the stairs several steps at a time. The key they had turned in the lock was luckily still in place on the outside of the door. He turned it, and rushed into the room and onto the bed. He had to rest for a few minutes, his heart beating violently in his breast like the clapper in a ringing church bell.

Then, finding the courage to get up, he went and leaned against the window and waited for them to return. They were long in coming; they must have been walking very slowly indeed. Edgar peered out cautiously through the shaded window frame, and presently they appeared, drifting calmly along, their clothing brightly reflecting the moonlight. They had a spectral appearance in this green glow, and once again Edgar was overcome with that titillating horror: might that really be a murderer down there, and what terrible event might he himself have prevented through his presence? He could see their chalk-white faces quite distinctly. In his mother's there was a look of rapture that he had never seen before, and the Baron's expression, by contrast, was hard and peevish. Obviously because he had failed in his plan.

And now they were close at hand. Only when they were almost in front of the hotel did their two forms separate. Would they now look up? No, neither of them looked towards his window. They'd forgotten all about him, thought Edgar with a sense of wild outrage, yet also with a secret feeling of triumph he reflected: 'But I haven't forgotten you! I know you think I'm fast asleep or I'm not worth thinking about, but you'll soon see how wrong you are. I'll be watching the two of you at every step until I've got the secret out of him, the blackguard, the terrible secret that's keeping me awake. I'm going to smash your plot to bits. I'm not asleep!'

Slowly the couple came through the front door, and as they entered the hotel, one after the other, the fading silhouettes united again for a brief moment, and the single black stripe of shadow they formed vanished behind the brightened doorway. After that, the square in front of the hotel again lay empty in the moonlight, like a wide snow-covered meadow.

Attack

Edgar drew back from the window, breathing heavily. The horror of all of it shook him: never before in his life had he been this close to something so mysterious. For him, the world of excitement and enthralling adventures, that world of murder and treachery that he knew from his books, had always been the same as that of fairy tales, closely connected with the world of dreams, a place unreal and unreachable. Now, all of a sudden, he seemed to have been transported straight into the middle of this scary realm, and his whole being was feverishly shaken by such a close encounter. Who was this person, this mysterious being who had suddenly intruded into their otherwise quiet life? Was he really a murderer always on the look-out for remote places where he could drag his mother off into the dark? Something terrible, Edgar sensed, was about to happen, and he had no idea what to do. Tomorrow he would definitely write to his father or send a telegram. But might it even happen before then, this very evening? His mother still wasn't safely back in her room, and she was still in the clutches of this hateful stranger.

Between the inner door and the outer one, a concealed jib-door easy to open and close, there was a small gap no bigger than the inside of a wardrobe. Edgar squeezed himself into this tiny, dark space so as to listen out for his mother's footsteps in the corridor; he had determined not to let her alone for a single moment. The passageway was now empty, it being midnight, and only dimly lit by a single light.

At last – he felt the minutes lengthening intolerably – he heard discreet footsteps coming up. He strained his ears: this was not the quick tread you would hear of someone just about to enter a room, but more the dragging, hesitating, lingering step of one making an interminably hard and steep ascent. And all the while he kept hearing alternating whispers and pauses. He trembled with excitement. Was this both of them after all, and he was still with her? The whispers were too far away. But the footsteps, though still hesitant, were drawing nearer and nearer. And now suddenly he caught the detested voice of the Baron saying something in a soft, husky tone, something he couldn't quite understand, immediately followed by his mother's quick rebuff: 'No, not tonight! No.'

Edgar shuddered. They were approaching, and soon he must surely hear every word. Every step closer, however soft it was, pained him deeply, and that voice! How ugly it sounded, that greedily imploring, repellent voice of his hated adversary! 'Don't be so cruel. You were so beautiful this evening.' And then the answer: 'No, I must not, I cannot, please let me go!'

There is such fear in his mother's voice that the boy is now quite terrified. What does he want from her? Why is she afraid? Nearer and nearer they've come, they must be right in front of the camouflaged outer door by now. Just the other side of it he crouches behind them, a few fingers' distance away, trembling and unseen, protected only by the thin cloth-covered panel of the door. The voices are now almost close enough for him to feel their breath.

'Come on, Mathilde, come on!' Again he hears his mother groan, more weakly now, in flagging resistance.

But what is this? They've moved on in the dark! Edgar's mother has not gone into her own room. Where is he dragging her? Why isn't she talking any more? Has he put a gag to her mouth? Is he throttling her?

The thoughts drive him wild. Hand quivering, he pushes the door open, far enough to see the two of them in the darkened corridor. The Baron has put his arm around his mother's waist and is leading her gently away; she appears to have given in to him. And now the Baron is stopping in front of his own room. 'He's going to drag her away!' says the terrified child to himself. 'And now he's going to do the ghastly deed!'

With a frantic lurch forward, the child slams the door of his room and rushes out at them. His mother screams out loud as something suddenly comes hurtling towards her from the darkness; she seems to have fallen in a faint, and the Baron can hold her up only with difficulty. But just at this moment the man feels a small, feeble fist in his face knocking his lip hard back against his teeth, and something crawling catlike all over his body. He lets go of the terrified woman, who hastily runs off, and strikes out blindly with his fist, before realizing who it is he is defending himself against.

The child knows that he is the weaker of the two but does not yield. Finally, finally the moment has come, the long-awaited moment for him to unburden all of his betrayed love and all his accumulated hatred. His little fists hammer away blindly as he bites his lips in a fever of mindless rage. Now the Baron has recognized his assailant, and he too is overcome with hatred for this secret spy who has poisoned these last few days for him and foiled him in the game he was playing; he strikes back fiercely wherever he can land his fists. Edgar lets out a groan but will not let go, will not cry for help. They wrestle with one another for a minute silently, furiously in the midnight corridor. Gradually the Baron comes to realize the absurdity of this fighting with a half-grown young boy and he grabs hold of him, ready to hurl him aside. The boy, however, feeling his muscles failing him and knowing that next minute he will be the defeated, the beaten one, snaps in frenzied anger at this powerful firm hand that tries to seize him around the neck. Involuntarily the man, bitten hard by the child, lets out a smothered cry and lets go of the child, giving him a brief moment in which to run to his room and hurriedly slide the bolt.

Only a minute has this midnight struggle lasted. No one to right or left of them has heard any of it. All is now still, all apparently sunk in sleep. The Baron wipes his bloody hand with his handkerchief and stares in bewilderment into the darkness. No one has been listening. Only above his head one last light flickers on and off, and he fancies there is mockery in the way it winks at him.

Tempest

Was it a dream? A horrible, danger-ridden dream? Edgar could not be certain when he woke next morning, hair all dishevelled, from a night of confusion and terror. His head ached with a dull throbbing, his limbs felt stiff and wooden, and when he looked down at himself he was shocked to see that he was still in his daytime clothes. He jumped up, ran unsteadily over to the mirror and recoiled at the sight of his own pallid, injured face and his forehead swollen in a reddish weal. Collecting his thoughts with some effort, he anxiously recalled everything, the midnight struggle outside in the corridor, his rushing back into his room, and how then, still fully clothed and ready to flee, he had flung himself down on his bed. He must have drifted off there and then, immediately sinking into this dulled, clouded sleep and its dreams that brought all the horror back, but in a different guise, even more terrible, along with a dank smell of fresh flowing blood.

Downstairs he could hear the crunching of feet on the gravel and voices flying up like invisible birds, and the sun was coming right into his room. It must be late morning already, he thought, but his watch, which he consulted anxiously, told him it was midnight; in all the excitement of yesterday he had forgotten to wind it. This uncertainty, this feeling of being loosely suspended somewhere in time, alarmed him, and worse still, he did not know what had really happened. He quickly made himself more presentable and went downstairs, ill at ease and nursing an intangible feeling of guilt in his heart.

In the breakfast room he found his mother sitting alone at the usual table. Relieved at not being confronted by his enemy and having to look at that hated face that just a few hours earlier he had pummelled with his fist, nevertheless he felt far from sure of himself as he approached the table.

'Good morning.'

There was no reply. Not even looking up, his mother continued to stare, with a peculiarly static gaze, into the distant countryside. She was very pale and had faint rings around her eyes; in her nostrils there was that nervous tremor he recognized, a sure sign of inner turmoil. Edgar bit his lips. Her silence confused him; he didn't know whether he had really badly hurt the Baron the night before, or for that matter whether she was aware at all of their night-time encounter. The uncertainty was torture for Edgar, but his mother's face remained so rigid that he did not even try to look at her for fear those lowered eyes might suddenly spring up from the languid lids and pounce on him. Edgar went quite still, not daring to make even the slightest sound. Very carefully, he would raise the cup to his lips, then put it down again, furtively glancing at his mother's fingers as they played nervously with her spoon, their contorted shapes seeming to betray her suppressed fury. And so he sat for a full quarter of an hour, in that oppressive sense of expectation, of waiting for something that never came. Not a word, not a single word to release him from this torture. And when she rose from the table, apparently still not having noticed his presence, he didn't know what he should do: stay here at the table, or follow her out? Finally he too got up and followed submissively behind her, though she steadfastly continued to ignore him, and he for his part felt all the while how absurd it was to be creeping along after her like this. He gradually shortened his steps so as to fall further and further behind, while she made her way to her room without paying him any attention. When Edgar finally caught up, he found himself before a firmly closed door.

So what had happened? It no longer made any sense to him. The certainty he had felt yesterday had left him. Had it been wrong of him after all to set upon the Baron like that? And were they preparing a punishment, or yet another humiliation, for him? Something was going to happen, he knew it, something awful, and very soon. Between him and his mother there was a sultry atmosphere of a brewing storm, the electrical charge between two opposite poles to be released any moment in a mighty flash. And for all of four hours Edgar carried the burden of this premonition around on his shoulders from room to room entirely on his own, until the invisible weight of it was too much for his young child's neck to bear, and he came to the lunch table with a new-found humility.

'Good day,' he greeted his mother once again. This silence of hers must be broken, this fearful, threatening taciturnity that hung over him like a black cloud.

Again there was no reply from his mother; again she looked straight past him. With renewed alarm Edgar felt he was confronting a well thought-out and fully fledged anger such as he had never seen in his life before. Thus far their quarrels had taken the form only of outbursts of pique, more of nerves than of genuine feelings, and they just as soon made up again with a placatory smile. This time was different: here was a wild emotion he had evoked from the innermost depths of her being, and he stood in dread of the force that he had so recklessly summoned up. He was hardly able to eat anything. A dryness blocked his throat, threatening to choke him. His mother appeared oblivious of all of this. Only when the time came to leave the table did she turn back calmly, with the words: 'Come up now, Edgar, I need to have a word with you.'

Her tone, though not threatening, was so icy that Edgar shuddered, as if an iron chain had suddenly been put around his neck. His defiance was quashed. Silently, like a dog after a beating, he followed his mother up to her room.

She prolonged his agony by also saying nothing for several minutes, minutes in which he heard the clock strike and a child's laughter outside, while he himself felt his heart hammering within him. But there must have been uncertainty in her too, for she avoided looking at him and had her back turned to him when she did begin to speak.

'I have no intention of saying any more about your behaviour yesterday. It was unconscionable, and I am ashamed even to think of it. You will face the consequences of your own actions. All I want to say for the moment is that this was the last time you will be allowed to be with adults on your own. I have just written to your father to say that you will be having a tutor or will be sent to a boarding-school, where you will learn some manners. I shall not be expending any more anger on you.'

Edgar stood with his head lowered. He sensed that this was merely a prologue, a threat, and waited uneasily for the main part of the message.

'You will now, this instant, make your apologies to the Baron.'

Edgar started at this, but she would not be deflected. 'The

Baron has left today, but you will write to him, and I shall dictate what you are to say.'

Again Edgar made a movement, but his mother remained firm.

'No buts now! Here is some paper and ink. Sit down.'

Edgar looked up. His mother's eyes had hardened in steely determination. He had never known his mother to be like this, so adamant and implacable. Overcome with fear, he sat down and took up the pen, but kept his head down low over the table.

'Date at the top. Have you done that? Before the "Dear Herr Baron" there's a space, that's right. Now, "Dear Herr Baron", now a comma. Now another line free. "I was very sorry to hear" – got that? – "to hear that you had already left Semmering" – Semmering with two *m*s – "and I must therefore write in a letter what I had intended to say to you in person, namely" – write faster, it doesn't have to be in calligraphy! – "namely, to ask your forgiveness for my behaviour yesterday. As my Mama will have told you, I am still recovering from a serious illness and tend to be excitable. In that state I often misunderstand what I see and the next moment come to be sorry . . ."'

The boy's back, hunched over the table, suddenly straightened. He turned round, defiant once again.

'I'm not going to write that, it's not true!'

'Edgar!'

The voice was threatening now.

'It's not true. I haven't done anything to be sorry about. I haven't done anything wrong, anything I'd have to apologize for. I only came to the rescue when you cried for help!'

Her lips were bloodless, and the nostrils tensed. 'I cried for help? What are you talking about?'

Edgar jumped up in an angry outburst: 'Yes you did! You cried for help, right out there in the corridor, last night, when he

caught hold of you. You were saying, "Let me go, let me go!"
And it was so loud I could hear it all the way from my room.'

'You're lying, Edgar. I was never in the corridor with the
Baron. He only came as far as the stairs with me . . .'

Edgar felt his heart stand still at such a brazen lie. Almost lost
for words, he stared at his mother with glazed eyes.

'You . . . weren't . . . in the corridor? And he . . . he didn't
catch hold of you . . . didn't throw his arm around you?'

She laughed. A cold, dry laugh. 'You've been dreaming.'

This was too much for the child. He knew well enough by
now that grown-ups lied, that they could always find their
cheeky little ways out of things and told fibs that could slip con-
veniently through the finest of nets, not to mention their crafty
ambiguities. But this latest outrageous, brazen lie, told straight
to his face, drove him wild.

'And this lump on my forehead – that's a dream too, is it?'

'God knows who you've been fighting with. But there's no
need for any argument now. You'll do as I say, and that's an end
to it. Now sit down and write!'

She had grown very pale and was doing her utmost to keep
her tension in check.

But something in Edgar was now somehow extinguished,
some last little flame of trust. That someone could so easily
stamp out the truth underfoot, like a burning matchstick, this
was quite beyond him. An iciness took hold within him, and
every word he now said became barbed, malicious, losing all
control.

'So I dreamed it all, did I? All that in the corridor, and these
bruises on my head? And you two going out last night for a walk
in the moonlight, and him trying to get you to go down that
path with him, that too? Do you really think I'd let you lock me
in my room like a tiny little boy? No, I'm not that stupid, I know
what I know!'

He looked impudently straight into her eyes, and that incensed her: to see her own child's face so close to her own, and twisted with hatred, brought out the full violence of her anger.

'Get on with it! Write, this instant! Or else . . .'

'Or else . . . ?' His voice was now not only defiant but challenging.

'Or else you'll get a smack, like a naughty little child!'

Edgar drew a step close, only sneering and laughing.

The hand shot out across his face. Edgar cried out. And lashing out blindly like a drunkard, with only a dull thumping in his ears and red flickering before his eyes, he raised his fists back at her. He felt himself strike something soft, now it was her face, heard a cry . . .

The sound brought him to his senses. Suddenly he saw himself clearly and realized the monstrousness of what he had done: he had struck his mother. A fear took hold of him, shame and horror, an overpowering need to be elsewhere, to sink into the ground, be anywhere but here to face those eyes. He rushed for the door, and then to the stairs, through the hotel and out onto the street, away, away, as if pursued by a frenzied pack of hounds.

First Inklings

Some way along the road he finally stopped. He had to lean up against a tree and support himself, his limbs trembling in fear and agitation, the panting breath breaking heavily from his overstrained lungs. Hard on his heels had followed the horror of his own deed, which now gripped his throat and shook him back and forward as if in a fever. What should he do now? Where could he run? Here in the middle of the wood, a mere fifteen minutes away from the hotel, he felt utterly abandoned. Everything seemed different and hateful, now that he was all alone and helpless. These trees, whose brotherly rustling had enveloped him just the day before, now suddenly loomed dark and threatening around him. How much more strange and unfamiliar must everything be that lay in wait for him! This loneliness in confronting the great outside world quite dizzied the child. No, he could not bear this, at least not on his own. But to whom could he go? His father? He was afraid of the man, who was unapproachable and quick to anger, and would undoubtedly send him straight back here. But he couldn't return to the hotel now; better to brave the dangers of the great unknown. He felt he would never be able to see his mother's face without thinking of the blow his fist had dealt it. His next thought was his grandmother, the kind, affectionate elderly lady who had always pampered and protected him if he ever faced any punishment or was threatened by some injustice at home. Yes, he would hide with her in Baden until the first wave of anger haul passed; there he would write a letter to his parents and say he was sorry. This quarter of an hour had so humbled him at the mere thought of his standing inexperienced and wholly alone in the world that he cursed his pride, this idiotic pride infused in him by no more than a stranger's lie. What could he want more now than to be the child he was before, obedient, patient, with none of that arrogance which he now saw had been absurdly excessive?

But how to get to Baden? How to make such a long journey? Hastily he reached into the little leather purse which he always had with him. Here, thank God, still glittered the new twenty-crown gold piece he had received as a birthday present. He had never been able to bring himself to spend it, but almost every day he had checked that it was still there, had feasted his eyes on it and felt like a rich man, then tenderly and thankfully put the coin back after wiping it clean with his handkerchief until it shone like a miniature sun. But – the sudden thought scared him – would this be enough? He had already travelled often enough by train without giving a moment's thought to the fact that you had to pay for the journey, let alone to how much was the fare, whether one crown or a hundred. For the first time he realized that life contained certain facts that had never occurred to him, that each of the many things that surrounded him, and those that he had held in his hands and played with, somehow possessed a value peculiar to it alone, a particular importance. He, the same boy who one hour earlier had fancied he knew everything, now appreciated that he had allowed thousands of secrets, thousands of questions, to pass him by; and he felt ashamed that his limited wisdom was stumbling at this very first true step on life's path. He grew more and more despondent, his uncertain steps becoming ever shorter on the way to the station. How often had he dreamed of such a flight, of making a first, stormy entry into life, becoming Emperor or King, a soldier or a poet; and now there before him was the gay little station building, and his only thought was whether twenty crowns would be sufficient to deliver him to his grandma. The rails glistened, stretching far away into the countryside; the station was quite empty. Shyly Edgar sidled into the ticket office and asked, in a whisper, so that no one else could overhear, how much a ticket to Baden cost. A surprised face looked out at him from behind the dark barrier, and two eyes smiled through spectacles at the diffident child:

'Full fare?'

'Yes,' Edgar stammered, but with no pride in his voice, more in fear that it might come to too much.

'That will be six crowns.'

'One ticket, please.'

Much relieved, he pushed the much-loved shiny gold piece through and the change came clinking back. Edgar felt once again fabulously wealthy. In his hand he held the little brown piece of card which promised him freedom, and in his pocket rang the faint music of rattling silver.

The train, the timetable said, was due in twenty minutes. Edgar huddled into a corner. A few people were standing on the platform, idle and without any suspicions of him. But in his own turbulent state of mind they all seemed to be looking at him, surprised that such a young child should be travelling on his own, as if his flight and his crime were pinned on his forehead. He breathed again when at last the train sounded its first whistle, followed by the roar as it pulled in. The train that was to take him into the world. Only as he boarded did he notice that his ticket was for the third class. He had only ever travelled first class before, and once again he felt something new here, that there were differences that had so far escaped him. His fellow passengers were quite unlike those he was used to. A few Italian labourers with rough hands and coarse voices sat right opposite him with spades and shovels in their hands, staring into space with desolate eyes. They must have been working hard on the road; some of them, exhausted, were sleeping in the rattling carriage, leaning back on the hard and dirty wood, mouths open. They had been working to earn money, Edgar supposed, but how much would that be? One thing, however, he did realize: money was not a thing everyone had, but had to be earned in some way. For the first time it dawned on him that he had been unquestioningly used to a life full of comforts, while all the time to right and left of him there were chasms sinking deep into the darkness, abysses his eyes had never looked into. All of a sudden he was realizing that there were trades and occupations, that people had their own different meanings in life, that innumerable secrets surrounded his own life, all within touching distance but never before noticed by him. Edgar learned much from this one hour on his own; he was beginning to see many things as he looked out of this narrow compartment's windows into the world outside. And gently something began to blossom even in the darkness of his anxieties, something that was not quite happiness at this point, but none the less a sense of awe at the great variety of life. He had fled, he was now able to tell himself, out of fear and cowardice, but still for the first time he had acted on his own, had experienced something of the reality that until then had passed him by. Perhaps also for the first time he had become as much a secret to his mother and father as the world had been to him until then. It was with new and changed eyes that he looked out; he now seemed to be seeing reality itself, as if a veil were removed that had masked everything, and now everything was revealed, all of its inner nature and purpose, the hidden source of all its activity. Houses flew by as if whirled past by the wind, and his thoughts went straight to those who dwelled in them: were they rich or poor, happy or unhappy, and did they yearn, as he did, to know everything, and were there perhaps children there too, who had up till now only played with things, as he had? The signalmen who stood along the railway tracks with their flags waving now seemed no longer mere inanimate toy figures, placed there only by random, indifferent chance; now he understood that such was their destiny, *their* struggle with life. The wheels turned ever faster; now serpentine curves carried the train down into the valley, and the mountains around grew more and more gentle, and further and further away. Soon their journey had reached the level plain. Just once Edgar looked back and saw the hills, now blue and in shadows, far distant and beyond reach, and it was as if there, where the uplands gradually merged with the misty sky, now lay his own childhood.

Perplexing Darkness

But there in Baden, when the train came to a halt and Edgar found himself alone on the platform, the station lighting already on and the signals showing green and red in the distance, all of this colourful prospect was unexpectedly clouded by a sudden fear of the impending night. During the day Edgar had felt safe, being surrounded by people, and it had been possible to rest, or sit down on a bench or stare in at shop windows. But how could he ever bear seeing all the people disappear into their homes, where they all had their beds and could enjoy a family conversation followed by a peaceful night's sleep, while he himself would have to wander round alone, plagued by guilt, in the loneliness of strange surroundings? Oh, just to have a roof over his head, and not to spend a minute longer on his own out in the open. This was the sole clear thought that came to him.

Quickly, without looking right or left, he made his way along the familiar street, until at last he came to the large house where his grandmother lived. The handsome building stood on a broad street, but was discreetly set back from direct view and hidden by the ivy and other climbers of a well-tended garden; it was a gleaming structure behind a cloud of green, a white villa, comfortable, built in the old style. Edgar peered through the grille like a stranger. There was no movement inside; the windows were closed; everyone must be round at the back with guests in the garden. He already had his hand on the cool metal latch when something odd happened: suddenly, what for the last two hours he assumed was so easy, so obvious, now seemed impossible. How did he suppose he could simply walk in, say hello to all of them and face all the questions that would follow, and how would he answer them? How to withstand the first searching look, when he would have to admit that he had secretly run away from his mother? And how to account for the monstrousness of what he had done, an act even he himself could no longer comprehend? Inside, he heard a door open. At once overcome by a thoughtless fear that someone might appear, he took to his heels, not knowing where he was going.

When he reached the spa gardens he stopped, seeing that it was dark there and guessing that there would be no one around.

Perhaps he would be able to sit down and finally, finally collect his thoughts, rest and consider more clearly what lay before him. Diffidently, he went in.

At the front of the park a few lighted lanterns gave the still young leaves an unearthly, watery glow of diaphanous green. Further in, though, where he had to go down the slope, everything lay like a single, black pulsating mass in that perplexing darkness of a premature spring night. Edgar crept timidly past the few people who sat chatting or reading under the light of the lanterns; he wanted to be alone. But even there in the shadowy gloom of the unlit footpaths he found no peace. Everything here was filled with a low, light-shunning rustling and whispering, frequently blended with the sound of breezes in the bending branches and foliage, the tread of distant footsteps in the gravel, the murmur of hushed voices; in all of this there was a hint of sensual sighing and anxious moaning that could have come all at the same time from people and from animals, and from nature herself, in an uneasy sleep. It was an ominous unease that breathed here, something veiled, furtive, unsettlingly enigmatic, some kind of subterranean scuffling in the woods, perhaps merely a symptom of early spring, but to the deeply troubled child none the less strangely frightening for that.

On a bench he curled himself up tightly into the profound darkness and tried to consider what story he might tell them back at the house. But the thoughts easily slid away before he could take hold of them, and instead he was forced against his will to listen, to keep listening, to the subdued murmuring, the bewitching voices of the dark. How terrible it was, this deep gloom, how perplexing and at the same time mysteriously beautiful! Was it animals he was hearing, or people, or only the ghostly hand of the wind that wove together all this rustling and creaking, this alluring whirr and humming? He listened. It was the wind, restlessly wafting through the trees, but – now he saw it clearly – there were also people there, couples arm in arm, coming up from the bright lights of the town and bringing the darkness to life with their puzzling presence. What did they want? He could not understand it; they were not speaking to each other, for he heard no voices but only their constant crunching tread on the gravel, and here and there he saw in clearer spaces their silhouetted forms floating quickly past like shadows but always huddled together in a single shape just as he had seen his mother and the Baron the day before. That secret! The great, glittering, fateful secret – it was here too, then! He heard footsteps coming closer and closer, and now also a muted laugh. He felt afraid: those people approaching might find him here. He sank further back into the dark. But the couple, now feeling their way carefully along the path through the impenetrable gloom, did not notice him. Entwined together they passed by, and Edgar breathed in relief, but then suddenly their steps halted immediately in front of his bench. There their faces touched and pressed each other. Edgar could not make out anything clearly, and only heard a soft moan from the woman while the man stammered heated, delirious words; a vague warm sensation infused his fear with a pleasurable shiver of emotion. They remained thus only for a minute before moving on, feet crunching the gravel again and soon falling silent in the dark.

Edgar shuddered. The blood rushed back into his veins, warmer, more impetuous than before, and suddenly he felt intolerably alone in this bewildering darkness; a primal instinct in him cried out for some affectionate voice, an embrace, a brightly lit room, the company of those he loved. It was as if all the baffling darkness of this tumultuous night had permeated his body and his breast might burst open.

He leaped to his feet. Home, he could think only of home, of being somewhere in the warmth, in a brightened room and back in human company once more. And what, anyway, was the worst that could happen to him? He might get a hiding and a scolding, but nothing scared him any more now, not after feeling this darkness and the terror of loneliness.

Thus driven forward without his even realizing it, in no time he was standing once more in front of his grandmother's house, his hand again on the latch. He could see the light from the windows shining through the mass of green, and in his mind's eye also the room he knew so well, and the people in it, behind each of the brightened glass panes. Even this very closeness was enough to make him happy once more, this first comforting feeling that he was near to people he knew loved him. And if he still hesitated, it was only to savour more deeply this joyful presentiment.

A loud voice pealed out behind him in amazement:

'Edgar, he's here!'

His grandmother's maid had spotted him and rushed out and taken him by the hand. The inner door was thrown open, and a dog jumped up, barking, to greet him; then they all came out of the house with lanterns, and he heard voices calling in a blend of jubilation and alarm, a joyous tumult of shouts and footsteps running towards him, human shapes he now recognized: first of all his grandmother with arms outstretched, and behind her – was he dreaming? – his mother! With tears in his eyes, trembling and sheepish, there he stood in the middle of this cheering, effusive outburst of emotion, uncertain how to react or what to say, indeed not even quite knowing what he was feeling himself. Was this fear, or joy?

The Final Dream

They had been looking for him here in Baden, waiting for him for a long time as it turned out. His mother, despite her anger, had been appalled by her child's sudden desperate disappearance and had had him searched for all over Semmering. Then, amidst the most fearful general alarm and all manner of terrifying conjectures, a gentleman had brought news that he had seen the child at the railway ticket-office counter a little before three o'clock. It was quickly revealed that Edgar had bought himself a ticket to Baden. The mother had lost no time in going after him, her arrival there preceded by telegrams to Baden and to his father in Vienna, serving to spread the alarm, and for the last two hours no efforts had been spared to track the fugitive down.

Now they had him safely with them, but no force was needed. In an atmosphere of discreet triumph they led him into the house. But how strange it was for him that he hardly noticed their reproaches and strong words, because what he saw in their eyes was only happiness and love. And even the act they put on, the feigned anger, lasted only a moment before Edgar's grandmother hugged him again, her tears running, and no one spoke any more of his wickedness, so that he felt himself in the tender embrace of a wonderful attentive care. The maid took off his jacket and brought him a warmer one. His grandmother asked him if he was hungry or wanted anything else, and they all questioned him and pressed on him their affectionate concern, but when they saw how embarrassed he was they stopped pestering him. It was pleasant, this feeling that he had disdained and yet also missed, of being the child through and through, and he felt ashamed of his presumptuous behaviour of these last few days, in which he had wanted to leave his childhood behind him and exchange it for the sham enjoyment of his own solitariness.

The telephone rang in the next room. He heard his mother's voice, and caught the occasional word: 'Edgar . . . back again . . . came here . . . last train.' He was surprised that she hadn't flown at him in anger and instead had just embraced him with so curiously restrained a look in her eyes. His remorse grew more and more overpowering, and he would dearly have liked to slip away from all his grandmother's and aunt's fussing and attentiveness, to have gone to that next room and begged his mother to forgive him, to confess to her in all humility, speaking for himself alone, that he wanted to be a child again, to be obedient. But when he quietly rose to his feet, his grandmother said, in some alarm: 'Where are you off to?'

He stood there, ashamed. They were even afraid of any slight movement he made. He had scared them all, and they now feared he would run off again. How were they to understand that he, more than anyone, regretted his running away?

The table was laid, and a quickly prepared supper was brought to him. His grandmother sat beside him and kept her loving eyes on him throughout. She and his aunt and the maid enfolded him in a little circle of calm, and he felt wondrously soothed by the warmth of it. His only worry was that his mother did not come back into the room. If only she could have guessed how humbled he was, she would certainly have come!

At this point the clatter of a carriage was heard arriving outside the house. It gave the others such a jolt that Edgar too became uneasy. His grandmother went out, voices flew back and forth in the dark, and it was at once clear that his father had come. With some misgiving Edgar noticed that he was now on his own again in the room, and this brief moment was disconcerting. His father was stern, and was the only person he really feared. Edgar listened to what was happening outside. His father sounded agitated, speaking loudly and angrily. At the same time there were the more conciliatory voices of his mother and aunt, obviously wanting to appease him. But his father's words remained hard, as were the footsteps that now came nearer and nearer; there they were now, in the next room, now finally just by the door, which was instantly flung open.

His father was a towering figure, and Edgar felt excruciatingly dwarfed before him as he entered the room, irritated and genuinely angry, or so it seemed.

'What got into you, young man, running away like that? How could you do such a thing to your mother?'

His voice was irate, and his hands were gesturing wildly. Behind him, Edgar's mother came in quietly, her face in shadow.

Edgar did not answer. He felt he had to explain himself, but then again, how could he tell his father how he had been deceived and beaten. Was he likely to understand?

'Well, what's the matter, have you lost your tongue? What was going on? You can tell me! Did something happen? You don't just run off without some good reason! Did somebody hurt you in some way?' Edgar hesitated. The memory made him angry again, and he was minded to bring his charge. Then he saw – and his heart stood still at the sight – he saw his mother make a strange sign behind his father's back, a movement he did not understand at first. But now she was looking at him with a pleading look in her eyes and gently, very gently, she raised her finger to her lips to signal silence.

In that moment the boy felt it: something warm, a powerful, overwhelming joy that coursed through his whole body. He understood that she, his mother, was entrusting the secret to him to keep, that on his small child's lips rested someone's entire fate. Edgar was filled with a wild, triumphant pride at the thought that she trusted him; all at once a sense of self-sacrifice possessed him, a readiness even to magnify his own guilt so as to show how much the man he now was. He pulled himself together:

'No, no . . . there was no reason. Mama was very nice to me, but I was rude, I behaved very badly . . . and then . . . well, I ran away because I got scared.'

His father looked at him in bemusement. This was the last thing he had expected, this confession. His anger was quite disarmed.

'Oh, I see, well if you're really sorry, I suppose that's all right. Then we won't dwell on it for today. I'm sure you'll think before you act another time. Just make sure nothing like that happens again.' He stood there a little longer and looked at his son. His voice was now gentler.

'How pale you look! But I do believe you've grown again. I hope you won't be getting up to any more of these childish tricks; you're no longer a little boy now, and quite able to behave sensibly!'

All the while Edgar was looking over at his mother. He fancied he saw a sparkle in her eyes. Or was this just the reflection of the light? No, there really was a moist, bright gleam there, as well as a smile appearing around her mouth, a smile that said 'thank you'. Now they sent him off to bed, but he didn't feel sad that they left him alone; after all, he had so many rich and colourful thoughts to occupy him. All of the pain of the last few days was gone, as he lost himself in the powerful sense of his first true experience in life, and he felt a happy instinct, deep down within him, for more things to come. Outside, night had fallen, and trees rustled in the darkness, but he was not afraid now. He had lost all his impatience with life now that he knew the riches it had to offer, as if now for the first time he had seen it in its true light, no longer veiled behind the thousand lies of childhood but revealed in all its sensuous, precarious beauty. It had never occurred to him that days could be so tightly filled with constant alternations of pain and joy; it delighted him to think that many more such days lay in store for him, that a whole life was waiting to unveil its secret to him. Here was a first inkling of the manifold richness of life; for the first time he believed he had understood something of people's true nature, that they needed one another even when they appeared to be at odds, and he had come to know the sweetness of feeling loved by them. Unable to think of anything, or any person, with hatred, he regretted nothing; even for the Baron, the abductor, his bitterest enemy, he now discovered a new sense of gratitude for having opened to him the door to this world of first true emotions.

All of this was indeed sweet and gratifying to be pondering in the dark, with images from dreams subtly mixed in, and sleep was almost upon him when he became vaguely aware of the door opening, and a new presence quietly coming into the room. He could not be certain, since he was already too sleepy to open his eyes. Then he felt a face breathing above him, soft, warm and gentle, stroking his own face, and he knew that it was his mother now kissing him and running her hand over his hair. He felt the kisses, felt the tears and gently responded to her caresses, which he took to be nothing more than her thanking him for his silence. Only later, many years later, did he come to recognize that in those silent tears was a vow, that of a woman now facing her middle years, a vow that from this day on she would exist for her child alone; it was a final rejection of adventure, a farewell to all her own desires. How could he know that she was in that moment thanking him for more than his silence, for he had rescued her from a profitless adventure? And how could he know, either, that in her embrace she was committing to him, as a legacy, the bitter-sweet burden of her love for his future life? Of all of this the child that he was then understood nothing, and yet he felt somehow blessed to be so loved; for through this love he now surely shared something of the world's great secret.

When she withdrew her hand, when her lips left his, and her gentle form, and the rustling dress, moved away, still a certain warmth remained, a breath he felt on his lips. And a beguiling sense of longing came over him, to feel such soft kisses again and again, and to be embraced so tenderly, but this intuitive sense of the secret he had yearned to know was already clouded by the shadow of sleep. Once again all the impressions of these last hours flew vividly through his thoughts; once again the book of his youth alluringly opened its pages. Then the child fell asleep, and the deeper dream began – the dream of his own life.

ONE-WAY STREET AND OTHER WRITINGS

Walter Benjamin

Walter Benjamin – philosopher, essayist, literary and cultural theorist – was one of the most original writers and thinkers of the twentieth century. This new selection brings together Benjamin's major works, including 'One-Way Street', his dreamlike, aphoristic observations of urban life in Weimar Germany; 'Unpacking My Library', a delightful meditation on book-collecting; the confessional 'Hashish in Marseille'; and 'The Work of Art in the Age of Mechanical Reproduction', his seminal essay on how technology changes the way we appreciate art. Also including writings on subjects ranging from Proust to Kafka, violence to surrealism, this is the essential volume on one of the most prescient critical voices of the modern age.

'There has been no more original, no more serious, critic and reader in our time' George Steiner

METAMORPHOSIS AND OTHER STORIES

Franz Kafka

'When Gregor Samsa awoke one morning from troubled dreams,
he found himself changed into a monstrous cockroach in his bed'

Kafka's masterpiece of unease and black humour, *Metamorphosis*,
the story of an ordinary man transformed into an insect, is brought
together in this collection with the rest of his works that he thought
worthy of publication. It includes *Meditation*, a collection of his
earlier studies; *The Judgement*, written in a single night of frenzied
creativity; 'The Stoker', the first chapter of a novel set in America; and
a fascinating occasional piece, 'The Aeroplanes at Brescia', Kafka's
eyewitness account of an air display in 1909. Together, these stories
reveal the breadth of his literary vision and the extraordinary
imaginative depth of his thought.

'What Dante and Shakespeare were for the ages, Kafka is for ours'
George Steiner

KING, QUEEN, KNAVE

Vladimir Nabokov

Franz, a bespectacled young man from a small German town, has been sent to Berlin to work in the department store of his well-to-do relative Dreyer. When he meets Dreyer's wife, the ripe-lipped Martha, he is enchanted and they begin a secret affair. As the relationship deepens, her considerable passion grows, but Franz finds himself increasingly manipulated, losing his own will, moral judgement and ultimately his humanity. And when Martha hatches a plan to destroy her tiresome husband, events take a turn that no one could have predicted.

'Vladimir Nabokov was a literary genius' David Lodge